Praise for *The Wishing Game*

"Meg Shaffer's beautiful novel is part Willy Wonka, part magical realism, and wholly moving. It broke my heart and patched it over and reminded me that even as an adult, if you look hard enough, you can find the child still inside you."

    —Jodi Picoult, *New York Times* bestselling co-author of *Mad Honey*

"Shaffer blends tragedy and triumph in a whimsical and gratifying debut about what makes a family. This is wish fulfillment in the best way."

    —*Publishers Weekly* (starred review)

"A tender spin on *Charlie and the Chocolate Factory* that balances darkness with humor, hopefulness, plot twists, and a hint of romance."

    —*BookPage*

"[A] whimsical, wistful first novel."

    —*Shelf Awareness*

"Magical, emotional, and charming."

    —*Booklist*

"A meditation on the power of hope when all else seems lost."

    —*Kirkus Reviews*

"A heartwarming, page-turning story of found family, love triumphing over indifference, and the world-changing power of a good book."

    —Melissa Albert, *New York Times* bestselling author of *The Hazel Wood*

"A dreamy, inventive novel about how books can not only change lives but save them, too . . . Full of the power of imagination, it's one of my favorite books of the year."

    —Sarah Addison Allen, *New York Times* bestselling author of *Other Birds*

"A magical ode to storytelling, imagination, and the mystery of the creative life . . . Wildly imaginative, clever, and inspiring, *The Wishing Game* is for anyone who has found light in a story just when they need it."

    —Patti Callahan Henry, *New York Times* bestselling author of *The Secret Book of Flora Lea*

"Meg Shaffer's debut establishes her as one of the best. *The Wishing Game* sees the secret child hidden inside all of us, and it takes us on the thrilling, magical journey we all long for—where we might end up with everything we want but only if we risk it all."

    —Gwenda Bond, *New York Times* bestselling author of *Mr. and Mrs. Witch*

The Wishing Game

A NOVEL

MEG SHAFFER

BALLANTINE BOOKS

NEW YORK

The Wishing Game is a work of fiction. Names, characters, places, and incidents are the products of the author's imagination or are used fictitiously. Any resemblance to actual events, locales, or persons, living or dead, is entirely coincidental.

2024 Ballantine Books Trade Paperback Edition

Copyright © 2023 by 8th Circle LLC
Book club guide copyright © 2024 by Penguin Random House LLC
Excerpt from *The Lost Story* by Meg Shaffer copyright © 2024 by Meg Shaffer

All rights reserved.

Published in the United States by Ballantine Books, an imprint of Random House, a division of Penguin Random House LLC, New York.

BALLANTINE BOOKS and colophon are registered trademarks of Penguin Random House LLC.

Random House Book Club and colophon are trademarks of Penguin Random House LLC.

Originally published in hardcover in the United States by Ballantine Books, an imprint of Random House, a division of Penguin Random House LLC, in 2023.

This book contains an excerpt from the forthcoming book *The Lost Story* by Meg Shaffer. This excerpt has been set for this edition only and may not reflect the final content of the forthcoming edition.

Library of Congress Cataloging-in-Publication Data
Names: Shaffer, Meg, author.
Title: The wishing game: a novel / Meg Shaffer.
Description: First edition. | New York: Ballantine Group, [2023]
Identifiers: LCCN 2022038749 (print) | LCCN 2022038750 (ebook) |
ISBN 9780593598856 (trade paperback) | ISBN 9780593598849 (ebook) |
ISBN 9780593724101 (international edition)
Subjects: LCGFT: Novels.
Classification: LCC PS3618.E5726 W57 2023 (print) | LCC PS3618.E5726 (ebook) |
DDC 813/.6—dc23/eng/20220830
LC record available at https://lccn.loc.gov/2022038749
LC ebook record available at https://lccn.loc.gov/2022038750

Printed in the United States of America on acid-free paper

randomhousebooks.com
randomhousebookclub.com

2 4 6 8 9 7 5 3 1

Book design by Ralph Fowler
Map by Olivia Walker
Compass and numerals licensed by Shutterstock
Clock illustrations by red_spruce / Adobe Stock

This book is dedicated to Charlie

and to all of us who are still looking
for our golden tickets.

THE CITY OF SECOND HAND

THE HOUSE

CLOCK ISLAND

I - One O'Clock Picnic Spot
II - Tide Pool at Two
III - Puffin Rock at Three O'Clock
IV - Welcome Ashore at Four
V - Five O'Clock Beach
VI - Southernmost Six
VII - Seventh Heaven Guest Cottage
VIII - At Eight O'Clock We Wish You Well
IX - Nine O'Clock Dock
X and XI - Forest and Fen at Eleven and Ten
XII - Noon and Midnight Lighthouse

The Wishing Game

PROLOGUE

May

EVERY NIGHT, HUGO WENT for a walk on the Five O'Clock Beach, but tonight was the first time in five years his wandering feet spelled out an SOS in the sand.

He traced the letters carefully, drawing them large enough that they could be seen from space. Not that it mattered. The tide would wash the Five clean by dawn.

It had been a bit of whimsy on Jack's part naming it the Five O'Clock Beach. Destiny, Jack said of finding this little patch of Atlantic forest twenty-odd years ago. These ninety acres right off the coast of southern Maine formed a near-perfect circle. Jack Masterson, who'd created Clock Island on paper and in imaginations, could now build it in real life. In his living room, Jack kept a clock with the numbers marked by pictures of places on the island—the lighthouse at the twelve, the beach at the five, the guesthouse at the seven, the wishing well at the eight—which led to conversations like . . .

Where are you going?
Five O'Clock.
When will you be back?
By the lighthouse.

Places were times. Times were places. Confusing at first. Then charming.

Hugo found it neither confusing nor charming anymore. One could go mad living in a house like that. Maybe that's what happened to Jack.

Or maybe that's what happened to Hugo.

SOS.

Save Our Sanity.

The sand was so cold on his naked feet it felt wet. What day was it? May 14? May 15? He couldn't say for sure, but he knew summer would be here soon. His fifth summer on Clock Island. Maybe, he thought, one summer too many. Or was it five summers too many?

Hugo reminded himself he was just thirty-four years old, which meant—if he was doing his maths correctly (unlikely as painters weren't known for their maths skills)—he'd spent almost 15 percent of his life on an island playing bloody nanny to a grown man.

Could he leave? He'd been dreaming of leaving for years, but only the way a teenager dreams of running away from home. It was different now. Now he was making plans or at least making plans to make plans. Where would he even go? Back to London? His mum was there, but she was finally starting over—new husband, new stepdaughters, new happiness or something like it. He didn't want to be in the way.

All right, Amsterdam? No, he'd never get any work done there. Rome? Same story. Manhattan, then? Brooklyn? Or five miles away in Portland so he could keep an eye on Jack from a close but healthy distance?

Could Hugo do it? Could he abandon his old friend here with no one left to help him tell one hour from the next, the lighthouse from the guesthouse?

If only the old man would start writing again. Pick up a pen, a pencil, a typewriter, a stick to write in the sand . . . anything. Hugo would even take dictation if Jack asked him to—and he had offered.

"Please, for the love of God, Charles Dickens, and Ray Bradbury," he'd said to Jack as recently as yesterday, "write something. Anything. Wasting talent like yours is like burning a pile of money in front of a poorhouse. It's cruel and it stinks."

They were the very words Jack had thrown into his face years ago back when Hugo was the one drinking his talent to death. They were just as sharp and true now as they were then. Millions of children out there, and former children, too, would weep with joy if Jack Masterson ever published a new book about Clock Island and the mysterious Master Mastermind who lived in the shadows and granted wishes to brave children. Jack's publisher regularly sent boxes of fan mail to the house, thousands of children urging Jack to write again.

SOS, those letters begged.

Save Our Stories.

But Jack had done nothing for five years but futz around in his garden, read a few pages of a book, take a long nap, drink too much wine at dinner, and fall into his nightmares by the time the little hand was on the Nine O'Clock Dock.

Something had to change. Soon. At dinner tonight, Jack hadn't made it to the bottom of his wine bottle as usual. He'd been quieter, which was either a good sign or a very bad one. And no bitter riddles either, not even Jack's favorite . . .

Two men on an island and both blame the water
for the loss of a wife and the death of a daughter
but neither ever married, and neither's a father.
What is the secret of the girls and the water?

Too much to hope that Jack was coming out of it? Finally?

Hugo strode across the sand to the edge of the tide. He let the waves creep up close to his toes but no further. He and the ocean weren't on speaking terms anymore. Was this eccentric? Yes. But that was fine. He was a painter. He was supposed to be eccentric. Once, he'd loved the ocean, loved seeing it every morning, every night, seeing all its facets, all its faces. Not many people knew what the sea looked like in all seasons under all phases of the moon, but he did. Now he knew the ocean was as dangerous as a sleeping volcano. At peace, it was magnificent, but when it wanted to, it could bring down kingdoms. Five years ago, it had brought low the small, strange kingdom of Clock Island.

Jack might believe in wishing—or he had once upon a time—but

Hugo didn't. Hard work and dumb luck got him to where he was. Nothing else.

But tonight, Hugo wished and wished hard that something would shake Jack from his apathy, break the spell, give him a reason to write again. Any reason. Love? Money? Spite? Something to do besides slowly drowning himself in overpriced Cabernet?

Hugo turned his back on the water. He found his shoes and dusted the sand from them.

When he came to Clock Island, he'd sworn to himself he'd stay one or two months. Then he said he'd stay until Jack was back on his feet. Five years later and here he still was.

No. No more. Time's up. Time to go. By this time next spring, he'd be gone. He couldn't sit and watch his old friend fade like ink on old paper until no one could read the writing anymore.

His decision made, Hugo started for the path. Just then, he saw a light come on in a window.

The window of Jack's writing factory.

The writing factory that only the housekeeper had set foot inside for years . . . and today was her day off.

The light in that window was low and golden. Jack's desk lamp. Jack was sitting at his desk for the first time in years. Was the Mastermind putting pen to paper again?

Hugo waited for the light to go out, proof it was a mistake, a whim, Jack looking for a lost letter or misplaced book.

The light stayed on.

It was too much to hope for, and yet Hugo hoped for it with all his heart and wished for it on every star in the night sky. He wished and hoped and prayed for it.

Prayed for the oldest miracle in the book—a dead man coming back to life.

"All right, old man," Hugo said to the light in the window of the house on Clock Island. "It's about bloody time."

PART ONE

Make a Wish

Astrid woke from a deep and dreamless sleep. What had woken her? Her cat jumping on the bed? No, Vince Purraldi was sound asleep curled up in his basket on the rug. Sometimes the wind woke Astrid up when it rattled the roof of their old house, but the tree branches were quiet outside her window. No wind tonight. Although she was scared, she got out of bed and went to the window. Maybe a bird had tapped on the glass?

Astrid gasped as the room was flooded with white light, like a car's headlights but a thousand times stronger and brighter.

Then it was gone. Is that what had woken her? That blast of light in her room?

Where had it come from? she wondered.

Astrid grabbed her binoculars hanging off her bedpost. She knelt at the window, binoculars pressed to her eyes, and gazed across the water to where a lonesome island lay like a sleeping turtle in the cold ocean.

The light flashed again.

It had come from the lighthouse. The lighthouse on the island.

"But," Astrid whispered to the window, "that lighthouse has been dark forever."

What did it mean?

The answer came as suddenly to her as the light in her window.

Quietly as she could, she left her bedroom and slipped into the room across the hall. Max, her nine-year-old brother, was sleeping so hard he was drooling on his pillow. Ugh. Gross. Boys. Astrid poked Max in the shoulder, then did it again. It took twelve shoulder pokes to get him to wake up.

"What. What? Whaaat?" He opened his eyes, wiping away the drool with his pajama sleeve.

"Max, it's the Mastermind."

That got his attention. He sat straight up in bed. "What about him?"

She smiled in the dark.

"He's come back to Clock Island."

—From *The House on Clock Island*, Clock Island
　　Book One, by Jack Masterson, 1990

CHAPTER ONE

One Year Later

THE SCHOOL BELL RANG at two-thirty, and the usual stampede of little feet followed. Lucy took backpack duty and lunch box duty while Ms. Theresa, the class's teacher, called out her usual warnings.

"Backpacks and lunch boxes and papers! If you forget anything, I'm not bringing it home to you and neither is Miss Lucy!" Some of the children listened. Some ignored her. Thankfully, this was kindergarten, so the stakes were pretty low.

Several of the kids hugged her on their way out the door. Lucy always relished these quick squishes, as they called them. They made the long draining days of being a teacher's aide—refereeing playground fights, cleaning up after potty accidents, tying and retying a thousand shoelaces, and drying a thousand tears—worth the endless work.

When the classroom finally emptied, Lucy slumped in her chair. Luckily, she was off bus duty today, so she had a few minutes to recover.

Theresa surveyed the damage with a garbage bag in hand. All the round tables were covered in bits of construction paper, glue bottles left open and leaking. Fat pencils and fuzzy pipe cleaners were littered all over the floor.

"It's like the Rapture," Theresa said with a wave of her hands. "Poof. They're gone."

"And we're left behind again," Lucy said. "What did we do wrong?"

Something, obviously, because she was, at that very moment, prying a wad of gum off the bottom of the table for the second time that week. "Here, give me the garbage bag. That's my job." Lucy took the bag and dropped the gum into it.

"You sure you don't mind cleaning up alone?" Theresa asked.

Lucy waved her hand to shoo her away. Theresa looked as exhausted as Lucy felt, and the poor woman still had a school committee meeting today. Anyone who thought teaching was easy had obviously never tried it.

"Don't worry about it," Lucy said. "Christopher likes to help."

"I love when the kids are still young enough that you can trick them into doing chores because they think they're playing." Theresa dug her purse out of the bottom desk drawer. "I told Rosa she couldn't mop the kitchen because that was for grown-ups, and she literally pouted until I let her do it."

"Is that what being a mother is?" Lucy asked. "Pulling a long con on your kids?"

"Pretty much," Theresa said. "I'll see you in the morning. Tell Christopher hello."

Theresa left, and Lucy glanced around at the classroom. It looked as if it had been hit by a rainbow-colored tornado. Lucy walked around every table with the trash bag in hand, scooping up sticky paper apples and sticky paper oranges, sticky paper grapes, and sticky paper lemons.

When she finished the cleanup, she had glue all over her hands, a paper strawberry stuck to her khaki slacks, and a crick in her neck from bending over the short tables for half an hour. She needed a long ten-thousand-degree shower and a glass of white wine.

"Lucy, why do you have a banana in your hair?"

She turned around and saw a slight wide-eyed black-haired boy standing in the doorway staring at her. She reached up and felt paper. Good thing she'd been practicing self-control for a couple of years as a teacher's aide, or she would have let loose a string of creative expletives.

Instead, and with as much dignity as she had remaining, she peeled the paper banana out of her hair.

"The question is, Christopher, why don't *you* have a banana in your hair?" She tried not to think about how long the banana had been stuck there. "All the cool kids are doing it."

"Oh," he said, rolling his hazel eyes. "I guess I'm not cool."

She stuck the banana gently onto the top of his head. His dark hair had just enough of a wave that it always looked as if he'd been hanging upside down for a few hours. "*Voilà*, now you're cool."

He shook off the banana and slapped it onto his worn blue backpack. He ran his hands through his hair, not to settle it down but to refluff it. She loved this weird kid of hers. Sort of hers. Someday hers.

"See? I'm not cool," he said.

Lucy pulled out one of the tiny chairs and sat down, then pulled out a second one for Christopher. He sat with a tired groan.

"Are too. I think you're cool. Sock hunt." She grabbed his ankles and put his feet on her knees for her daily archaeological excavation into his shoes to dig out his socks. Did he have weirdly skinny ankles or unusually slippery socks?

"You don't count," Christopher said. "Teachers have to think all kids are cool."

"Yes, but I'm the coolest teacher's aide, so I know these things." She gave each sock one final tug up his leg.

"You aren't." Christopher dropped his feet onto the floor and clutched his blue backpack to his stomach like a pillow.

"I'm not? Who beat me? I'll fight her in the parking lot."

"Mrs. McKeen. She throws pizza parties every month. But they say you're the prettiest."

"That's exciting," she said, though she didn't flatter herself. She was the youngest teacher's aide, and that's about all she had going for her. She was, at best, average in every other way—shoulder-length brown hair, wide brown eyes that always got her carded, and a wardrobe that hadn't been updated in years. New clothes required money. "I'd better get a certificate that says that on Award Day. You have any homework?"

Lucy stood up and started cleaning again, wiping down the tables and chairs with Lysol. She hoped the answer was no. He didn't get much attention from his busy foster parents, and she tried to make up for what he didn't get at home.

"Not a lot." He threw his backpack onto the table. Poor thing, he looked so tired. He had dark circles under his eyes, and his shoulders drooped with exhaustion. A seven-year-old child shouldn't have eyes like a world-weary detective working a particularly grisly murder case.

She stood in front of him, cleaning bottle dangling from a finger, arms crossed. "You okay, kiddo? You sleep any last night?"

He shrugged. "Bad dreams."

Lucy sat back down next to him. He laid his head on the table.

She laid her head on the table and met his eyes. They were pink around the edges like he'd been trying not to cry all day.

"You want to tell me what you dreamed about?" she asked. She kept her voice soft and low and gentle. Kids with hard lives deserved gentle words.

Some people like to talk about how resilient kids are, but these were people who'd forgotten how hard everything hit you when you were a kid. Lucy still had bruises on her own heart from the knocks she'd gotten in childhood.

Christopher rested his chin on his chest. "Same thing."

Same thing meant the ringing phone, the hallway, the door open, his parents on the bed seemingly sound asleep but with their eyes wide open. If Lucy could have taken his bad dreams into her own brain, she would have done it to give him a good night's sleep.

She put her hand on his small back and patted it. His shoulders were thin and delicate as moth wings.

"I still have bad dreams, too, sometimes," she said. "I know how you feel. Did you tell Mrs. Bailey?"

"She told me not to wake her up unless it's an emergency," he said. "You know, with the babies."

"I see," Lucy said. She didn't like that. She appreciated that Christopher's foster mother was taking care of two sick babies. Still, somebody had to take care of him too. "You know I meant it when I said you can call me if you can't sleep. I'll read to you over the phone."

"I wanted to call you," he said. "But you know . . ."

"I know," she said. Christopher was terrified of phones, and she didn't really blame him. "That's okay. Maybe I can find an old tape recorder and record myself reading you a story, and you can play it next time you have trouble sleeping."

He smiled. It was a small smile, but the best things came in the smallest packages.

"You want to take a nap?" she asked. "I'll put down a mat for you."

"Nah."

"You want to read?"

He shrugged again.

"You want to . . ." She paused, tried to think of anything that would distract him from his dreams. ". . . help me wrap a present?"

That got his attention. He sat straight up and grinned. "Did you sell a scarf?"

"Thirty dollars," she said. "Yarn cost me six. Do the math."

"Um . . . twenty-two? Four! Twenty-four."

"Good job!"

"Can I see it?" he asked.

"Let me get it out, and we'll wrap it and write a letter."

Lucy went to the desk where she and Theresa locked up their purses and keys every day. Inside a plastic grocery bag was Lucy's latest creation—a spiderweb weave scarf knitted in a soft, silky pink and cream yarn. She carried the bag over to the table and pulled it out, modeling it for Christopher like a feather boa wrapped around her shoulders.

"Like it?"

"It's girly," he said, shaking his head side to side as if weighing its merit.

"A girl made it, and a girl bought it," Lucy said. "And I'll have you know, back in the nineteenth century, pink was considered a boy's color, and blue was considered a girl's color."

"That's weird."

Lucy pointed at him. "You're weird."

"*You're* weird," he countered.

Lucy lightly tapped him over the top of the head with the end of the scarf, and he laughed.

"Go get our letterhead," she said. "We have to write our thank-you note."

Christopher ran for the supply closet. He loved the supply closet. That's where all the fun stuff was hidden: the new packages of construction paper, the bags of pipe cleaners, the glitter, the markers, the pens and colored pencils, the Halloween decorations. There was also some nice stationery, donated by the mother of one of last year's kids who owned a local office supply store. Lucy had claimed the sky blue paper with white clouds for their "company."

"Can I write it while you wrap it?" Christopher asked, running back to the table with the paper in hand.

"You want to write the letter?" she asked as she carefully ran the lint brush over the scarf. She sold about one or two scarves a week on Etsy. To most people, the extra thirty or forty dollars a week wasn't worth the time it took to knit a four-needle scarf. But for Lucy, every penny of that money mattered.

"I've been practicing letters," Christopher said. "I wrote a whole page last night."

"Who did you write a letter to?" she asked as she folded the scarf neatly into quarters and wrapped it in a sheet of white tissue paper.

"Nobody," he said.

"Who's Nobody?" she asked. "New friend?"

"I just wrote nobody," he said.

"Okay." Lucy didn't push him. Especially because she had a very good idea who he'd written his letter to. More than once she'd caught him writing notes to his parents.

I miss you momy. I wish you wer at my school piknic today.
lots of moms came today.

Dad today I got a star on my homwork.

Little letters. Heartbreaking notes. She'd tried to talk to him about it, but he never wanted to admit to writing to his parents. It embarrassed him. He understood they were dead and probably thought other kids would laugh at him if they knew he still talked to them sometimes.

Christopher squared the cloud paper in front of him on the table and got out his pencil.

"What's the scarf lady's name?" he asked. The kid was smart enough to already know how to change the subject.

"Carrie Washburn. She lives in Detroit, Michigan."

"Where's that?"

Lucy went over to the map of the United States on the wall. A blue star marked where they were—Redwood Elementary School in Redwood Valley, California. She pointed her finger at the blue star and then ran it halfway across the map and stopped near Lake Erie.

"Wow. That's far," Christopher said.

"I wouldn't want to walk there," she said. "Detroit gets very cold in winter. Good to have a lot of scarves."

"I know where the Mastermind lives."

"Who?" she asked. The non sequiturs of small children never ceased to amaze her.

"The Mastermind from our books."

"Oh," she said. "You mean, Jack Masterson? The author of our books?"

"No, the Mastermind. He lives on Clock Island."

Lucy wasn't sure how to reply. Christopher was only seven, so she wasn't in any hurry to tell him that the characters he loved in books and movies weren't real. He didn't have a lot to believe in right now, so why not let him think that the Mastermind from their Clock Island books was a real guy out there granting real kids' wishes.

"How do you know where the Mastermind lives?"

"My teacher showed me. Want to see?"

"Go for it, Magellan."

"What?"

"Magellan. Famous navigator. Had a rough time in the Philippines. Probably deserved it. But that's beside the point. Show me Clock Island."

He hopped up and pointed at the tip-top far right corner of the map.

"There," he said, and Lucy was surprised to see he'd gotten it exactly right. His fingertip touched a patch of water right off the coast of Portland, Maine.

"Good job," she said.

"Is it really Clock Island?" he asked, scrunching his face at the map. "Is there a train and unicorns there?"

"You mean like in the books?" Lucy asked. "Well, it's pretty amazing there, I hear. Did you know some people think the Mastermind and Jack Masterson are the same person?"

"But you said you met him."

"I did meet Jack Masterson. A long time ago. He, um, signed a book for me."

"He wasn't the Mastermind, right?"

Damn. He had her there. The Mastermind always hid in shadows, shadows that cloaked him in darkness and followed him wherever he went.

"No, he didn't look like the Mastermind when I met him."

"See?" Christopher was triumphant. Nothing made a kid happier than proving a grown-up wrong.

"I stand corrected."

Christopher traced a line from Clock Island back to their city— Redwood, California. "That's really, *really* far."

His face was scrunched up tight. Maine was about as far as you could get from California and still be in the same country, which was precisely why she'd moved to California from Maine.

"Pretty far, yeah," she said. "You'd want to fly there."

"Can kids go?"

Lucy smiled. "To Clock Island? They can, but they probably shouldn't without an invitation. The island is private, and the Mastermind owns all of it, like it's all his house. It would be kind of rude to show up without being invited."

"Kids do it in books all the time."

"True, but still, let's wait for an invitation." She gave him a wink.

Lucy knew better than anyone about the kids who showed up uninvited on Clock Island. Not that she was going to tell Christopher about that, not until he was older anyway.

He dropped his hands from the map and looked at her. "Why aren't there any more books?"

"I wish I knew," Lucy said as she went back to wrapping the scarf with tissue paper and twine. "When I was your age, they were coming out four or five times a year. And I read every one of them the day they came out. And about ten times the week after."

"Lucky . . ." Christopher said wistfully. The Clock Island books weren't very long, 150 pages or less, and there were only 65 of them. Christopher would have read them all in six months if she hadn't doled them out to him one week at a time. Even so, they'd finished the whole series and started over from Book One a few weeks ago.

"Don't forget the letter to our customer." Lucy winked at him.

"Oh yeah. How do you spell Carrie?" he asked, putting his pencil on the paper.

"Sound it out," she said.

"*K-A*—"

"It's a *C*," Lucy said.

"Carrie starts with a *C*? *C-* is a *K* sound," he said.

"But so is *C*, sometimes. Like the *C* in *Ca-hristopher*." She booped his nose.

Christopher glared at her. He disapproved of booping. "There's a Kari in my class," he explained as if Lucy wasn't as bright as she looked. "It starts with a *K*."

"You can spell names a lot of ways. This Carrie is with a *C*, two *Rs*, and an *I-E*."

"Two *Rs*?"

"Two *Rs*."

"Why?" Christopher asked.

"Why does it have two *Rs*? I don't know. Probably being greedy."

In his child's hand, Christopher carefully blocked out the words *Dear Carrie* and made sure to put both *Rs* in the name.

"Your spelling and handwriting are getting a lot better."

He smiled. "I've been practicing."

"I can tell."

Lucy included a thank-you note for buying a hand-knitted scarf from the Hart & Lamb Knitting Company in every package. Not a real company, just her Etsy store, but Christopher got a big kick out of being "co-president."

"What do I write now?" he asked.

"Something nice," Lucy said. "Maybe . . . *Thank you for buying a scarf. I hope you like it.*"

"I hope it keeps your neck warm?" Christopher asked.

"That's good. Write that down."

"Even if it's a supergirly scarf."

"Don't write that."

Christopher laughed and started writing again. Making him smile or laugh was better than winning the lottery, although she'd have a lot more time to make him laugh if she did win the lottery. She glanced over his shoulder as he wrote. His writing was getting really good. Even a few months ago he was misspelling about every other word he wrote. Now it was just every fourth or fifth word. His reading and math skills were improving too. That hadn't been the case last year when he'd been shuffled between half a dozen foster homes. This year he had a steady living arrangement, great therapists, and Lucy tutoring him every weekday after school. His grades had been stellar ever since. If she could only do something about those bad dreams and his terror of ringing phones.

She knew what he needed, and it was the same thing she wanted for him—a mother. Not a foster mom with two sick babies who demanded every minute of her day. He needed a forever mom, and Lucy wanted to be that mom.

"Lucy, how much money do you have in your wish fund?" he asked while printing his name carefully at the bottom of his letter.

"Two thousand two hundred dollars," she said. "Two-two-zero-zero."

"Whoa . . ." He stared at her with wide eyes. "All scarf money?"

"Almost all of it." Scarf money and any babysitting job she could get. Every day she thought about going back to waitressing, but that would mean never getting to see Christopher, and he needed her more than she needed money.

"How long did that take to make?"

"Two years," she said.

"How much do you need?"

"Um . . . a little bit more."

"How much?"

Lucy hesitated before answering.

"Maybe two thousand," she said. "Maybe a little more."

Christopher's face fell. The kid was just too good at math.

"That'll take you another two years," he said. "I'll be nine years old."

"Maybe less? Who knows?"

Christopher dropped his head onto the letter he was writing to Carrie in Detroit. Lucy went over to him, lifted him out of his chair, and held him on her lap. He wrapped his arms around her neck.

"Squish," she whispered, hugging him tightly. It would be two years until she was his mother the way things were going. At least two years.

"We're gonna get there," she said softly, rocking him. "One of these days, we're gonna get there. You and me. I'm working on it every single day. And when we get there, it'll be you and me forever. And you're going to have your own room with boats painted on the wall."

"And sharks?"

"Sharks all over the place. Sharks on the pillows. Sharks on the blankets. Sharks driving the boats. Maybe a shark shower curtain. And we'll have pancakes for breakfast every morning. Not cold cereal."

"And waffles?"

"Waffles with butter and syrup and whipped cream and bananas. Real bananas. Not paper bananas. Sound good?"

"Sounds good."

"What else are we going to wish for while we're wishing?" This was Lucy and Christopher's favorite game—the wishing game. They wished for money so Lucy could buy a car. They wished for a two-bedroom apartment where they both had their own rooms.

"A new Clock Island book," he said.

"Oh, that's a good one," she said. "I'm pretty sure Mr. Masterson is retired, but you never know. Maybe he'll surprise us one of these days."

"You'll read to me every night when I get to live with you?"

"Every night," she said. "You won't even be able to stop me. You can put your hands over your ears and scream, '*LA LA LA CAN'T HEAR YOU, LUCY,*' and I'll keep on reading."

"That's nuts."

"I know it. But I'm nuts. What else do you want to wish for?" she asked.

"Does it matter?"

"What? Our wishes? Of course they matter." She pulled him back a little so she could meet his eyes. "Our wishes do matter."

"They never come true," he said.

"You remember what Mr. Masterson always says in the books. '*The only wishes ever granted—*'"

"'*—are the wishes of brave children who keep on wishing even when it seems no one's listening because someone somewhere always is,*'" Christopher finished the quote.

"Right," she said, nodding. It amazed her how well he remembered the things he read. He had a little sponge for a brain, which is why she tried to pour so much good stuff into it—stories and riddles and ships and sharks and love. "We just have to be brave enough to keep wishing and not give up."

"I'm not brave, though. I'm still scared of phones, Lucy." He gave her that look, that terrible disappointed-in-himself look. She hated that look.

"Don't worry about that," she said, rocking him again. "You'll get over that soon. And trust me, a lot of grown-ups are scared of their phones when they ring too."

He rested his head against her shoulder again, and she held him close and tight.

"Go on," she said. "One more wish, and then we'll do homework."

"Um . . . I wish for it to be cold," Christopher said.

"You want it to be cold? Why?"

"So you can sell a lot of scarves."

CHAPTER TWO

IT HAD BEEN A long time since Hugo strolled the streets of Greenwich Village. How long? Four years? Five since his last art show? It looked just the same. A few new restaurants. A few new shops. But the neighborhood's essential character was the same as he remembered—bohemian, bustling, wildly overpriced.

When he was a kid, he'd romanticized the idea of living in the Village, the stomping grounds of Jackson Pollock and Andy Warhol and so many other of his idols. What he wouldn't have given to pile into one of the old prewar brownstones with a dozen other aspiring painters and eat, drink, and breathe art day and night. Pity the poor young artists who'd hung on to that fantasy. They couldn't even afford to sleep in a box in the bottom of someone's closet in the Village. Now that Hugo could afford it, he found he didn't want it anymore. Or Park Slope or Chelsea or Williamsburg . . .

Nothing like success to kill the fire that used to burn in his belly. Every flat, every condo, every brownstone he'd looked at that morning had seemed like a stranger's home, and if he moved in, he'd be living a stranger's life. Maybe he'd simply outgrown that old dream and hadn't found a new dream to replace it yet.

Hugo abandoned his plan to apartment-hunt all day. Instead, he headed down to his favorite gallery in the city, the 12th Street Art Station, which managed to stay open despite the rent increases. He told himself he just wanted to see what was new, maybe grab a cup of coffee. He was always impressed by his ability to believe the lies he told himself.

Cool air slapped him in the face as he pushed through the glass doors and into the main gallery, all primary colors and funky faux cowhide rugs. He took off his sunglasses, slipped them into the case, and put on his other eyeglasses—a recent necessity he did not love.

The gallery had a new exhibit, classic movie monsters—Dracula, Frankenstein, the Blob—depicted as ancestral portraits with antique gilt frames. The show was called *Great-Grandpa Was a Monster*, and the artist was a twenty-three-year-old Puerto Rican woman from Queens.

Hugo liked her style and was impressed with her early success. Twenty-three? He hadn't gotten his first solo show until twenty-nine.

Somewhere in the gallery, Hugo had a few paintings on display. He went from the main gallery to the Brick Room, where the art hung in black frames against exposed brick walls. There they were—a trio of paintings at prices so exorbitant he doubted they'd ever leave these walls. Which was fine by him. He was happy to see them in public. They were some of his best work, though not nearly as popular as his more recent paintings of Clock Island.

"I'll have you know, Hugo Reese, it's all your fault I can't bring my daughter here."

Hugo turned his head and saw a woman standing a few feet behind him. Black hair in a bob, brown eyes in a glare, and red lips in a tight line because she wanted to smile but didn't want him to know it.

"Piper," he said. "I didn't know you still worked here." A bald-faced lie.

"Part-time," she said with an elegant shrug. "Something to do now that Cora's started preschool. Her teacher asked if we could make a class field trip to the gallery. Because of you, I had to say no."

She raised her eyebrow, but Hugo could tell she wasn't angry. They were long past that.

"They're very tasteful nudes." He pointed at the trio of paintings he'd made of Piper over a long winter years ago. The poses were classical, a beautiful woman naked and lounging in bed. What made them Hugo Reese paintings were the bizarre scenes painted outside the large window—a circus of demon-faced clowns, a castle in flames melting like a candle, a single great white shark floating across the sky like a Zeppelin.

"It's not the nudity that's the problem. Cora's scared to death of clowns."

"They are a bit mad," he admitted, giving his demonic circus a sidelong glance. "What was I going through back then?"

"Me," she said, then laughed. Piper took a step forward and kissed him on the cheek. "Good to see you."

"You too. You look lovely."

"You're not so bad yourself. Cleaned up, I see. No more hipster beard." She patted his cheek. His breakup misery beard was long gone. He'd even dressed up, which for him meant a clean pair of jeans, a T-shirt with no holes in it, and a tailored black blazer. And he'd cut his hair and started running again, so he looked like a human being, which was quite a step up from how he used to look, like self-loathing brought to life.

"The beard had to go," Hugo said. "I found a spider in it one day."

"The glasses are new, aren't they? Very chic. Bifocals?"

"Don't even joke about that."

Smiling, she took his glasses off and put them on herself. The black frames looked much better on her than him, in his opinion.

"If Monet had these," she said, looking at herself in her phone camera, "we never would have had impressionism." She slipped the glasses off and returned them to him.

"Bad eyesight has made the career of many a painter. Myself included." He slipped his glasses back on, and Piper came beautifully into focus again. "Tell us, how's Bob the Knob?"

"*Rob*. Not Bob. Not a knob. My husband. And he's wonderful."

"Still pet sitting?"

"He's a veterinary surgeon, as you know, and yes, he is. How's Jack? Any better? Or should I not ask?"

He hesitated before answering. "Possibly? I hear the typewriter sometimes at night. Loud enough to wake the dead. And he's cut back on his drinking."

"Does that mean you're moving out? Finally?"

"Apparently so."

She gave him a look that seemed to say, *I'll believe it when I see it.* But she was nice enough to keep that comment to herself.

"Is that why you're here?" Her tone was lightly amused but suspicious. Any woman would be when her ex-lover showed up at her workplace. "Moving to the Village?"

"Considering it. You'd have to hate yourself to pay these rents around here, so I should fit right in."

"Oh, Hugo. I swear, the more successful you are, the more miserable you are." She was annoyed with him now. He'd missed annoying her.

"No, no." He waved his finger at her. "The more miserable I am, the more successful I am. Got to suffer for the art, yeah? Why do you think I did my best work after you chucked me out on my arse?"

Piper gave him a wave goodbye and turned on her heel. "Not listening to this anymore."

She started to walk away, and Hugo jogged a few steps to catch up with her.

"I don't blame you," he said. "I would have chucked me out too."

"Nobody chucked you out. You chose to continue hiding on that island with Jack over moving back to the real world and starting a life with me."

"The real world's overpriced. And you can't deny I did some damn good work after you left." This was true. After Piper broke up with him, he started painting Clock Island landscapes—the herd of piebald deer, the moon reflecting off the ocean, the lighthouse, the abandoned park . . . all in shades of watercolor gray, the colors of heartbreak. Those abstract landscapes attracted the attention of the wider art world for the first time in his life. People over the age of eighteen finally knew his name. So why was he hoping against hope that Jack was writing again? Did he really miss painting pirate ships and castles and kids climbing a secret staircase to the moon?

Maybe a little.

"I have two things to tell you. Number one—you're full of shit—and number two—"

"Full of shit should be number two if you think about it." He tapped his temple.

She ignored that. "And number two—tell yourself whatever you want, but I know this—I was a fabulous girlfriend, and you really wanted to marry me."

"Not arguing with any of that."

"And you still picked that island and Jack over me. Don't pretend you hate it there. You love it there. You love it and you love Jack, and you don't want to leave."

Hugo wasn't buying it. "You know how hard it is to find a date on a private island, population two men, twenty deer, and a raven who thinks he's a writer?"

"If you want my advice—"

He glanced around as if looking for help. None to be found. "Not sure I do."

Piper poked him in the chest. "Find a woman who loves Jack as much as you do."

"All right . . . you see the problem with that?" He wasn't smiling now. Neither was she.

Here was the problem—not that Hugo would admit it out loud—but nobody loved Jack as much as he did.

"Fact is, Pipes—" She hated when he called her Pipes as much as he hated it when she said Hugo was short for Huge Ego. "—I do love it on that bloody little island."

The forest, the fen, the harbor seals sunning themselves on the shore outside his cottage, the cries of gulls in the morning. Gulls in the morning? In London, growing up, he'd wake up to the sound of the couple in the flat below fighting World War III. And now . . . seals and gulls and ocean air and sunrises even God woke up early to watch.

"Knew it," she said.

"I hate that I love it, but I don't . . . I don't deserve to be there."

"Why not?"

"Because Davey would have sold his perfect golden soul to have taken one step onto Clock Island, and my useless worthless hide lives there rent-free."

Piper shook her head. "Hugo, Hugo, Hugo."

"Pipes, Pipes, Pipes."

"A first-year psychology student could diagnose you with survivor's guilt from a mile away."

Hugo raised his hand as if to bat her words away. "No. Not—"

"Yes." She poked his chest again. "Yes."

A family of four in matching "I ♥ New York" T-shirts strolled through the gallery. Piper smiled politely at them. Hugo tried to smile. Quickly they moved on to another gallery.

"It's not survivor's guilt," he said when they were gone. Piper raised her eyebrow in disbelief. "I don't feel guilty about being alive. Being alive is . . . well, not my first choice, but because I'm here, might as well stick around. What I have is *thriver's* guilt. It's not just that I'm alive. I'm alive and . . . God, look at my life—my career, my house, my . . . everything. Every day I wake up and ask myself, Why am I here on this island and Davey's in the ground? Why did everything good happen to me and everything crap happen to him? Thank God you dumped me so I don't hate myself more than I already do."

"Hugo—"

"No, the end." He cut her off with a wave of his hand. "No more armchair diagnosing the mental illnesses of modern artists. I know it's your favorite sport, but I don't want to play anymore."

"I'm sorry," she said. "I didn't mean to touch a nerve."

"Davey isn't a nerve. Davey is my entire nervous system."

"You can be angry at me if you want but believe it or not, I actually want you to be happy."

As much as he didn't want to believe her, he did.

With a long exhalation, he leaned back against the wall between *Frankenstein's Monster*, a gentleman's portrait in top hat and frock coat, and *The Bride of Frankenstein*, her hair tucked under a black-and-white parasol.

"Jack's writing again," Hugo said. "I am happy. Well, happier. Now I can leave Clock Island with a clean conscience. I can be miserable in Manhattan or bitter in Brooklyn."

She raised her eyebrow at him, but it didn't last. She smiled and sighed.

"Truce?" She held out her hand, and he shook it. When he tried to take his hand back, she held on to it. "Not so fast. While I have you—"

"Ah, dammit."

"I want paintings, and I want them now."

Like a wolf caught in a trap, he pretended to gnaw his own hand off at the wrist.

"You said you owe your career renaissance to me," she said, squeezing his fingers. "If you meant that, then the least you can do is bring me a Clock Island cover painting or two or fifty, please."

"Cover paintings are not for sale. Jack's publisher will send the fiction police after me."

"For a show then only." She squeezed harder.

"Release me, wench. I won't be press-ganged." This was not how artists usually did business with galleries. Usually there were managers and agents and emails, not arm wrestling.

She released his hand. "As you were."

"Counteroffer," he said. "I want a full solo show. I'll bring five original Clock Island cover paintings and ten to twenty of my more recent pieces—which you *can* sell. Plus, an opening-night party with the good caterer this time."

"Hmm . . ." She pretended to stroke a nonexistent beard. "This could work. A Hugo Reese retrospective. I like it. Deal."

"Buy me a coffee, and we'll pick a date," he said. "I should have a few old cover paintings in my secret stash under the floorboards where I store the bodies."

She crooked her finger at him—which had meant something very different when they were together—and led him to the gallery's coffee bar.

A young woman in a red apron stood at the counter pouring steaming hot water over some sort of contraption balanced on top of a coffee cup.

"What's she doing?" Hugo whispered. "Chemistry experiment?"

"It's a pour-over, Hugo. It's the best way to make coffee."

"I'll stick to my Mr. Coffee. Although I've always wondered . . . is there a Mrs. Coffee?"

"Ashley," Piper said as they reached the counter. "Could I get a cup of coffee for my guest?"

"No, thank you," Hugo said as he looked at the prices on the menu. "Thirteen dollars for one cup? Is it brewed with diamonds and the blood of endangered species?"

"The gallery is buying," Piper said.

"Trust me," Ashley, the barista, said. "It's worth the thirteen bucks." She pulled out a large white mug and another funnel contraption.

"Ashley, this is one of our artists, Hugo Reese. He used to illustrate Jack Masterson's Clock Island books."

"Oh my God." Ashley slapped her hands onto the counter. Her eyes were huge and her voice reverent. "Are you serious?"

It never got old. There was a specific age range of people who reacted to the name Clock Island and Jack Masterson the way teenaged girls once reacted to the Beatles.

"Serious," Hugo said. "Unfortunately."

Piper whacked his arm.

"What's he like?" Ashley whispered as if Jack were standing behind them.

"Oh, he's Albus Dumbledore, Willy Wonka, and Jesus Christ all rolled into one." If Dumbledore, Wonka, and Christ had depression and drank too much.

"That's so awesome," she said. Hugo was English, and he noticed Americans had trouble differentiating between his accent and his sarcasm.

"You know, you seem way too young to have worked on them," she said.

Flattery would get her everywhere.

"I wasn't the original illustrator. After forty books, they wanted to repackage and re-release the series with new artwork. I got the job when I was twenty-one." Fourteen years ago. Felt like a million years ago. Felt like yesterday.

"Yours were definitely the best covers," Piper said. "The old illustrator wasn't bad, but the art was derivative, too much like the Hardy Boys series. Yours were like . . . I don't know, if Dali did children's art."

"For the sake of the children, let's be glad he didn't," Hugo said.

"Can I ask you something?" Ashley put her hand on her hip and cocked her head to the side flirtatiously.

Here it came. The autograph request. Or the selfie request. He didn't get the star treatment often, and he planned on enjoying it.

"Go ahead," he said.

"Why is a raven like a writing desk?" she asked.

"They both can—Wait." Hugo narrowed his eyes. "Why do you ask?"

A sleek black phone sat on the counter. She tapped the screen a few times and held it up to display a web page. "It's on Jack Masterson's website today. It's all over Facebook too."

"What?"

"Let me see," Piper said. She took the phone from Ashley's hand. Hugo peered over her shoulder and read aloud:

> *My Dear Readers,*
>
> *I have written a new book—A Wish for Clock Island. There is but one copy in existence, and I plan to give it away to someone very brave, very clever, and who knows how to make wishes.*

Hugo's heart started racing so fast his mind couldn't keep up with it. Jack was doing *what*?

"Gotta run," he said.

"Already? What's going on?" Piper looked worried.

"No clue." He kissed her cheek and bolted for the street, leaving behind his thirteen-dollar diamond-studded cup of coffee. He waved a hand at a passing taxi. It pulled over, and he got inside.

"Penn Station, quickly, please." Hugo grabbed his phone from his back pocket. He'd put it on airplane mode while he'd been touring flats. Now he flicked it on, and suddenly a torrent of emails, text messages, and missed calls hit his phone in a cacophony of beeps, bells, and buzzes.

Eighty-seven missed calls and approximately two hundred new emails, all from media outlets and friends he suspiciously hadn't heard from in years.

"Oh God," Hugo groaned.

He called the house. Jack answered.

Hugo didn't let him get a word out.

"What the hell are you up to?" Hugo demanded. "The *Today* show left me five voice-mail messages."

"It's a foot," Jack said, "but it's not part of the body."

"I hate your stupid riddles. Could you tell me in short, simple sentences exactly why a girl at a coffee shop just asked me why a raven is like a writing desk?"

"It's a foot," Jack said again, more slowly this time, as if he were talking to a child. "But it's not part of the body."

Then he hung up.

Hugo growled at the phone and considered tossing it out the window. But he probably shouldn't do that as CBS News was apparently calling him. He sent the call to voice mail.

"You okay, man?" the cabdriver asked.

"What's a foot but isn't part of your body?" Hugo asked. "Any ideas? It's a riddle, so the answer will be stupidly, annoyingly, and infuriatingly obvious once you figure it out."

The driver chuckled. "You don't know *Sherlock?* You should. You kinda talk like him."

"What do you mean by—" And then Hugo got it.

What's a foot but not part of the body?

Afoot, not a foot.

As Sherlock Holmes once said, "The game is afoot."

Jack Masterson was playing a game. Now. Out of nowhere. Had he lost his mind? Jack had barely left the house in years and now he was playing a game? With the world? With the entire bloody world?

Hugo swore so violently it was a good thing the cabdriver didn't know who he was, or he'd never get another job in children's publishing again.

He called Jack back.

"When I told you," Hugo said, biting off the end of each word, "to start plotting again, I meant *in your books.*"

And there came that laugh again, *the-devil's-at-the-back-door-and-nobody-remembered-to-lock-it* laugh.

"You know what they say, my boy . . . be careful what you wish for."

CHAPTER THREE

LUCY STOOD IN FRONT of her bathroom mirror, trying to make herself look responsible, adult, and mature. The pigtails had to go, that was for sure. She loved wearing her hair in pigtails because it made the kids at school laugh, especially when she tied big bows around them. But she'd taken a half day off from work for a meeting, and it was too important to show up looking like an overgrown Powerpuff Girl.

She straightened her hair and changed into clean and pressed khakis and a classy white blouse she'd found at Goodwill for a few dollars. Instead of a reject from an anime convention, now she wouldn't look out of place at church or a business meeting.

Reluctantly, Lucy went into the living room. Chloe's girlfriend called their living room The Pit of Despair, and it was a pretty accurate name for it. The ancient mismatched furniture was fine. She was no snob. But there were pizza boxes and vodka bottles everywhere. There were dirty socks on the floor and the gray Berber carpet was starting to take on a distinctly pale brown hue from her roommates' refusal to take their shoes off in the house. There were only three spotlessly clean rooms in the entire three-story house—Lucy's bedroom, Lucy's bathroom, and the kitchen, which she cleaned because no one else would.

She hated the place and wanted to move, desperately, and not just for Christopher's sake. But it was cheap, and it let her save money, so she stuck it out. It hadn't been bad two years ago when all her roommates were college seniors and fairly tidy. But they'd graduated and freedom-drunk freshmen took their places.

Right now, Beckett, her youngest roommate, was lying on the beer-stained plaid sofa in the living room watching something on his phone. Knowing him, it was either porn or funny cat videos. The boy had range.

"Beck, buddy, you awake? You said you'd let me borrow your car."

He slowly blinked himself back to awareness. "What?"

"Beckett. Wake up and focus," she said and snapped her fingers.

He blinked. "Uh, L. What are you wearing? Are you, like, a nun now? You look way hotter with the pigtails."

Lucy took a deep breath. Her roommates would test the patience of a Zen master.

"I'm not going to take fashion criticism from a man in a pot leaf shirt who hasn't showered in six days."

"Five. And overshowering is bad for your skin. It's called self-care."

"It's also called hygiene," Lucy said. "I suggest you try it sometime. Also, keys, please?"

"I'm tired. My head hurts."

Lucy turned on her heel, went into the kitchen, and returned carrying a bottle from the fridge. "Try it. I dare you."

He opened the bottle, took a sip. His eyes widened. "Oh my God, what is this?"

"It's called . . . *water*."

"Wow."

"Feel better?"

"Amazing," Beck said. "You're so wise, like a sexy wizard."

"Can the sexy wizard have your keys now?"

"Fine." He dug his car keys out of his jeans pocket. Lucy took them with a smile.

"Thank you. Now please take a shower."

OUTSIDE THE GLASS DOUBLE doors of the Children's Service Center, Lucy rechecked her outfit, took a deep breath, and willed herself to be calm and in control. The woman she was meeting was Mrs. Costa, the social worker in charge of Christopher's foster placement and care. There had to be something Lucy could do to speed up the process. The look on his face when he'd done the math and realized he'd be nine years old before they'd be together haunted her.

In the waiting room outside Mrs. Costa's office, Lucy stared at her phone. She hated being here. It reminded her too much of a hospital waiting room—institutional tile, garish paint, brightly colored laminated signs—FIRST AID, CHILDREN'S AID, FINANCIAL AID. Financial aid for adoptive families and foster families, for kids with parents in prison, for kids with parents on drugs. But nothing for a broke twenty-six-year-old single woman trying to be one little boy's mother.

The largest poster on the wall said in big black letters, YOU DON'T HAVE TO BE PERFECT TO BE A FOSTER PARENT. Great. Fabulous news considering how not perfect she was.

Of course the family pictured on the poster looked happy, smiling, and absolutely perfect.

There were no picture-perfect families here in the waiting area. Women with crying babies. Women with screaming toddlers. Women—and a few men—sitting next to quiet, distant teenagers who had likely experienced the sort of horrors most people only read about in books and newspapers. Would Christopher be one of these traumatized teenagers someday? She felt like the window of opportunity to save him from that fate was closing fast.

On the table next to her were information packets and brochures. Lucy found one titled *Foster Facts*. The first fact said that the average time a child spends in foster care is twenty months, just shy of two years. Christopher was in his twentieth month already. Another foster fact, far more troubling—children in foster care are twice as likely as veterans to develop post-traumatic stress disorder.

"Lucy Hart?" Mrs. Costa stood in her office doorway. She smiled but not broadly. A polite smile. Lucy already felt like she was wasting the woman's time.

Lucy went in and sat down in the chair opposite Mrs. Costa's cluttered desk. Files teetered on the edge, ready to drop at any minute.

"So, Lucy," Mrs. Costa said with obviously feigned enthusiasm. "What can I do for you?"

"I wanted to talk to you again about fostering to adopt Christopher. No relatives have come forward?"

Mrs. Costa looked at her. She was an older woman, sun-weathered face, gray-brown hair, eyes that had seen things no one should ever have to see.

"Obviously, family reunification is always the best-case scenario," Mrs. Costa said, "but no, no family at all except a great-uncle in prison and another in a nursing home. So yes, he qualifies for foster-to-adopt. It would be a long process, but Lucy—"

"To Christopher, I'm his new mother in everything but paperwork."

"I know he wants to live with you. I know you want to be his mother—"

Lucy didn't let her finish. "Christopher's getting older. He's asking more questions. He can tell his foster mother isn't crazy about dealing with him and the twin babies she's also fostering."

"Catherine Bailey and her husband are one of our best families. He's lucky to have them."

"I would be better for him. He has a strong attachment to me," she said. Childhood attachment was important. She knew that. Mrs. Costa knew that.

"They feed him, clothe him, put a roof over his head, keep him safe, make sure he does his schoolwork, and Mrs. Bailey shows up prepared to every court hearing, every team meeting . . . What more do you want?"

"I want him to be loved. They don't love him. Not like I do."

Mrs. Costa exhaled heavily. "That isn't a crime."

Lucy interrupted. Her voice was so sharp even she was surprised by her vehemence. "It should be."

"Listen to me," Mrs. Costa said. There was a gentleness to her voice that forced Lucy to meet her eyes. "I would give that boy to you this minute if I could. If love were enough, you'd be the perfect person to adopt him."

Lucy waited. Her stomach knotted up. She knew what was coming because she'd heard it all before. "But—"

"Right. *But.* You will never pass the home study. Not with things as they are right now. You're in a lot of credit-card debt, Lucy. You don't have access to reliable transportation. You live with three roommates in a house that's one grease fire away from going up in smoke. Oh, and one of those roommates has a recent DUI conviction. Even if we got you enrolled in all the public assistance available to you, you still wouldn't be able to afford appropriate housing *and* a car. I mean, Lucy, think about it—if I sent Christopher home with you today, where would he sleep? On the floor of your bedroom?"

"I'd sleep on the floor. He can have the bed."

"Lucy—"

"We get money, right? Foster parents get a stipend from the state. I'd use it to get us better housing."

"You need to have appropriate housing before you foster a child."

"Look," Lucy said and pulled out the *Foster Facts* brochure. "It says right here that kids in foster care are seven times more likely to suffer from depression and five times more likely to have anxiety than other kids. And four times more likely to go to jail. You want me to keep going?" She waved the brochure. "Isn't living in my crappy house for a couple of months a small price to pay for saving him? He needs a real mom. He's better off with me than with someone just going through the motions."

"The motions are pretty darn important too. I know you think kids need nothing but love, but a strong dose of stability doesn't hurt either. I hate to say it, but your life is currently not stable enough for a child. He has school. He has therapy sessions twice a week. And what happens when he wakes up sick and needs medicine in the middle of the night, and the only pharmacy open is ten miles away? Wait two hours for a bus? Wake up one of your roommates and ask them to drive you? Ride your bike at four A.M. on a highway?"

"I can borrow one of their cars. I can—"

Mrs. Costa waved her hand, cutting her off. "You need a new job."

Lucy tried explaining that she'd planned on teaching but couldn't afford the classes she needed, the license and certification fees.

"A second job then?" Mrs. Costa said.

"If I got a second job, I'd never see Christopher. He doesn't use phones, totally terrified of them. You would be, too, right? You're asking me to abandon him."

"I'm asking you to make some hard choices."

"Right, because all the choices I've been making lately have been so easy."

"Lucy, Lucy, Lucy . . ." Mrs. Costa shook her head. "I know you've heard it takes a village to raise a child. Where's your village? Where's your support system?"

"I don't have one, okay? My parents only cared about my sister. Still do. I lived with my grandparents, and they're gone. I don't have anybody anymore."

"What about your sister?"

Lucy snorted a laugh. "Didn't you hear me? She was my parents' favorite. We haven't talked in years either."

"Well . . . she might regret that? Ever think about that? Maybe give her a call, see about getting some support in your life."

"I would sell my bodily organs on the black market before I'd call my sister begging for money."

Mrs. Costa crossed her arms, sat back. "Then I'm afraid I don't know how to help you if you won't help yourself."

Lucy blinked away tears. "You should have seen the look on his face when I told him it might be another two years or more until I had enough money saved up for a car and an apartment. You would have thought I'd said twenty years. Or forever." Lucy held out her hands, her empty hands. "Poor people should be allowed to have children. Shouldn't they?"

"Yes, yes, yes, of course they should," Mrs. Costa said. "Although I also believe poor children shouldn't have to be poor. But they didn't put me in charge of that."

"There has to be a way," Lucy said, leaning forward, her eyes imploring. "Isn't there anything?"

"If I believed in miracles, I'd say hope for one, but . . . I haven't seen any miracles lately." Mrs. Costa had the same hollow look in her eyes as some of the teenagers out in the waiting room. "It might be time to tell Christopher it's not going to happen."

Lucy shook her head. "What? I can't. I just . . . I can't do that."

What had her ex said to her? *People like us shouldn't have kids, Goose. We're too fucked-up. Fucked-up people fuck up their kids. You'd be as bad a mother as I'd be a father . . .*

She forced the words from her head. Tears ran down her face. With a graceful gesture that surely came from years of practice, Mrs. Costa reached behind her without even looking and pulled a few tissues out of the tissue box and offered them to Lucy.

"The last time I spoke with Christopher," Mrs. Costa continued, "he said you and he play a wishing game. You both make all kinds of wild wishes. You know it doesn't work like that, right? You know wishes don't come true just because you want them to badly enough?"

"I know that." Lucy's voice was hard to her own ears, hard and bitter. "But I wanted Christopher to have . . . I don't know. Hope?"

"Did you give him hope?" Mrs. Costa asked. "Or did you just get his hopes up?"

Outside the office door was a waiting room full of people in need, people much worse off than Lucy, and kids who were even worse off than Christopher.

"I can tell him if you want," Mrs. Costa offered. "I'll go to the Baileys' house and have a little heart-to-heart with him. I'll tell him I made the decision, and it's not your fault."

It was a kind offer to do a terrible thing. Lucy almost wanted to take her up on it, but she knew that was the coward's way out.

"I'll . . ." Lucy wiped her face. "I'll think of something to tell him. It should come from me." She swallowed the lump in her throat.

"He'll understand it, eventually. But it's safe to say it'll be harder for both of you the longer you wait. The time will come when a family wants to adopt him. It'll be easier for him to accept a new family if he's not waiting on you."

Lucy couldn't even wrap her mind around Christopher being adopted by someone other than her. Mrs. Costa gave her another tissue.

"Believe it or not, you'll probably feel a little relieved in a few days. It'll be a weight off your shoulders."

Lucy met her eyes. She replied slowly and deliberately, "If Christopher were my son, it would not be a weight on my shoulders. If he were my son, my feet wouldn't even touch the ground."

Mrs. Costa's face was a blank page. "Is there anything else I can do to help you?"

Lucy was being dismissed. And why not? There was nothing left to discuss.

"No, thank you," Lucy said. "You've helped enough."

CHAPTER FOUR

LUCY RETURNED THE CAR to Beckett. She would walk back to school. She needed to move, to breathe, to compose herself before going back to work.

A relief? A weight off her shoulders? Did Mrs. Costa think Christopher was some sort of project for Lucy? Some charity work that kept her from having a life? She'd had a life. She'd done everything she was supposed to do in college. She'd gone to parties, hooked up with sexy jerks, gone to Panama City on spring break, six girls to one crappy hotel room. She'd even gone above and beyond the call of duty in college and dated one of her former professors, who also happened to be one of the most famous writers in the country. A renowned award-winning writer who took her to cocktail parties on New York rooftops and dinners at mansions in the Hamptons and on tours through Europe. She'd lived her life. She'd been wild. She'd been young. She'd had fun.

And she would have traded every wild party, every fancy dinner, every famous face she'd met, and every night in a five-star hotel for one week as Christopher's mother. Or one day. One single day.

But according to Mrs. Costa, none of that mattered.

Lucy kept her head down, hoping no one would see her red eyes and think she was wandering the streets drunk or stoned. It was a Friday afternoon. After school she could tell Christopher that she'd seen Mrs.

Costa again, and the state had decided Lucy couldn't be his foster mother. Maybe she would take him to the movies this weekend to cheer him up. She had more than two thousand dollars saved. Why not start spending it now on little things to make Christopher happy? Maybe if she spent the whole weekend spoiling him, by Monday he'd be okay with it all. Nothing would have changed, really. Lucy would always be his friend. She just wouldn't ever get to be his mother.

Not so bad, right?

Then why did it feel so very, very bad?

While cutting through a parking lot, Lucy passed a boutique toy store, doubled back, and went inside. A parent was volunteering in the classroom today, so Theresa didn't need Lucy in class just yet.

The moment she set foot inside The Purple Turtle, Lucy realized immediately she'd made a mistake. Nearly everything was insanely expensive. What would it be like to be one of those mothers who had enough money to buy imported wooden blocks from Germany and hand-painted dolls from England?

"Can I help you?" a young woman asked from behind the counter. Lucy turned and saw her staring at her phone, her brow furrowed.

"Do you have anything for a boy who likes sharks or boats? He's seven." She wanted to get Christopher something to soften the blow. Something that would remind him she would always love him and want to be in his life. "Something small?"

Something not expensive.

"There's a LEGO pirate boat over there, but it's pretty huge." The girl pointed at the set, and Lucy saw that the price was almost two hundred dollars. That would wipe out nearly 10 percent of her savings.

"Anything else? Something smaller?"

"We also have the Schleich animals," the girl said, "if you want something tiny. A couple of sharks, I think."

Lucy followed the direction of the girl's pointing finger. She went to a large wooden case full of animals of every genus and species—lions, birds, and wolves, of course, but also dinosaurs and unicorns and, yes, even sharks.

They were seven dollars each but three for fifteen. Lucy spent almost ten whole minutes debating whether she should buy three of them—the tiger shark, the great white, and the hammerhead—or only one. Finally, she picked up all three and carried them to the counter. What the hell, right? It was fifteen dollars, and deep down she knew she could blow all two thousand dollars out of her wish fund, and it still wouldn't heal his broken heart or hers. Not like she was going apartment hunting or car shopping anytime soon.

No, she couldn't justify a two-hundred-dollar LEGO set, but she could let herself buy him all three sharks.

"Do you have free gift wrap?" she asked.

The girl raised an eyebrow. "You want me to gift wrap three little sharks?"

"If you don't mind. Please?"

"Sure thing," the girl said. "These for your son?"

Lucy swallowed the knot in her throat again.

"It's for a little boy in my school," Lucy said. "He's going through a hard time, and he doesn't get a lot of presents."

"You a teacher?" she asked as she put the sharks into a cardboard box. Lucy pointed at the blue dinosaur paper. Christopher would like that better than the paper with rainbows on it.

"Teacher's aide at Redwood."

"Do you know riddles and stuff?"

"Riddles? I guess," Lucy said, confused by the question. "We do a unit on jokes, puns, and riddles with the kids every April."

"Do you know this riddle—*Why is a raven like a writing desk?*" The girl wrapped the paper around the box.

"Yeah, of course," Lucy said. "It's from either *Alice's Adventures in Wonderland* or *Through the Looking-Glass*. I can't remember which one."

"You know the answer?"

Did she know the answer? Once, long ago, someone had asked her the same riddle as the setup to a joke. There wasn't a solution, at least not according to Lewis Carroll.

"There isn't a real answer," Lucy said. "It's a Wonderland riddle. Everyone's mad in Wonderland."

"Hmm," the girl said. "Bummer."

"Why do you ask?"

"People were talking about it online," the girl said. "I've been trying to figure it out all day."

"Good luck."

The girl put the wrapped box into a brown bag with a handle and a purple turtle printed on the front. It was a nice gift for fifteen dollars plus sales tax.

But the pirate ship, she thought as she left the store, *would have been a lot nicer.*

BY THE TIME LUCY made it to school, they were singing the final songs—"*De Colores*" followed by "The Farmer in the Dell" in English and Spanish. When *el queso* was finally standing alone, the first bell rang, and it was the Rapture all over again. In seconds the classroom was empty but for Lucy and Theresa.

"How'd it go?" Theresa asked Lucy as they both started on cleanup duty.

"Don't ask," Lucy said, trying not to cry.

Theresa gave her a quick hug. "I was afraid of that." She was a woman wise enough not to turn it into a long hug, or Lucy really would start crying again.

Lucy took a shuddering breath and tried to pull herself together for the third or fourth time that day.

"It's okay. You'll get there. Just keep saving your pennies."

She shook her head. "Pennies aren't going to be enough."

"Welcome to America," Theresa said. "They tell us taking care of children is the most important job you can do, and then they pay us like it's the least important. You know I'd give you the money if I had it to give."

"It's okay. Don't worry about it. I'll just kill myself later."

"Oh no. You keep that nasty talk out of your mouth."

"Sorry. Bad day."

Lucy stepped away from her, picked up the cleaning spray and the rag for the marker boards.

"Lucy?" Theresa stood by her and stared at her. Lucy couldn't meet her eyes. "Come on, talk to me."

"It's not going to happen."

Theresa gasped softly. "Baby girl, no . . ."

"I tried everything. The social worker flat out told me today it's just not possible for me to foster Christopher, and that it was time to tell him."

"What does she know? She doesn't know you like I know you."

"She's right. He deserves better."

"Better? What's better than the best? And you are the best for him. *You* are." Theresa poked her gently in the shoulder.

Lucy took a deep breath and forced herself to focus on the marker boards. She wiped them down until they were gleaming white. "What do I know about being a mother? I had terrible parents. I date shitty guys—"

"Sean? Is this about Sean? Because if it is, I don't care if you're twenty-six years old, I'll turn you over my knee right here."

Lucy laughed softly, miserably, tiredly. "It's not about Sean. Although he was a dick."

"World-class dick," Theresa said. "Broke all the dick records."

"It's about reality. And the reality is, it's never going to happen."

Theresa exhaled heavily. "I hate reality."

"I know. I know," Lucy said, "but for Christopher's sake—"

"For his sake, do not give up on him." Theresa took her by the shoulders and gently shook her. "I've been a teacher almost twenty years. I've met all the bad parents you'd ever want to meet. Parents who buy themselves new clothes and let their kids go to school in shoes three sizes too small. Parents who spank a five-year-old for dropping his glass of milk. Parents who don't give their kids baths for weeks or wash their clothes. Parents who drive drunk to school with their kids in the front seat with no seat belt on. And those aren't even the worst ones, Lucy, and you know it."

"I know, I do. Some of them make my parents look like saints. Well, not really but it could have been worse." She sat on one of the small round tables. "Mrs. Costa pretty much patted me on the head, told me that it takes a village to raise a child, and said I should call my sister to ask for help."

"She's not wrong about needing a village. Why not call her?"

"What?" Lucy boggled at her.

Theresa waved her hand. "I hated my sister growing up too. We could've made wigs out of the hair we pulled out of each other's heads. We'd kill for each other now. I wouldn't let her borrow my favorite jacket, but I'd shiv anyone who roughed her up. I'd call her if it was me in your shoes. Baby girl, the worse she can do is hang up on you."

"No." Lucy said it emphatically. Then for good measure said it again. "No."

"Fine, fine." Theresa raised her arms and surrendered. "But at least don't tell Christopher today. Take a little time. Think it over. Okay?"

Lucy blinked back tears. "Nothing's going to change in a week."

Theresa stood up straight and pointed her finger at Lucy's chest. "No? Let me tell you, my cousin JoJo—he is the biggest man-whore on the planet, so help me God if I'm lying—was two days from losing his house to the bank when his girlfriend set his bed on fire for cheating on her with her sister. Whole place burned to the ground in an hour," she said with relish. "*Huge* insurance settlement. Now he's living in Miami in a condo with two girls half his age."

Lucy met her eyes. "Very inspiring and uplifting story. Thank you. You should give TED Talks."

"One week. Even one day, okay? Just not today. Don't ever break a heart on a Friday. Ruins the whole weekend."

"I got him some toy sharks to soften the blow."

"Save the sharks. And don't tell him yet."

Laughing for the first time all day, Lucy said, "Yes, ma'am."

Theresa left for a planning committee meeting. Alone in the empty room, Lucy got out her phone and pulled up Google. Just out of curiosity, she typed in "Angela Victoria Hart," then "Angela Hart," and "Angie Hart Portland Maine."

Didn't take Lucy long to find her. Angie Hart of Portland, Maine, age thirty-one, was a top-tier agent at Weatherby's International Realty. Lucy clicked on her photo and saw her sister all grown up. Pretty, not beautiful. But she had perfect white teeth and flawless makeup, and she wore a gray skirt suit and jacket that probably cost more than Lucy's rent. According to the company's website, Angie had just sold a two-million-dollar property. Just to twist the knife, Lucy googled standard commission for real estate agents—3 percent. Three percent of two million was sixty thousand dollars.

Right under Angie's smiling face was all her contact information. Phone number and email.

Sixty thousand dollars? For one single sale?

Lucy's finger hovered over the phone number. Wouldn't kill her to try a text message?

Her heart raced at the thought of it. She began to sweat. What would she even say? *Thanks for telling me Mom and Dad never wanted me? Thanks for reminding me I was unloved and unlovable? Thanks for making me a stranger in my own home? Oh, by the way, can I borrow some money?*

No, she would say nothing, because there was nothing to say.

Lucy tossed her phone back in her bag. The battery was nearly dead anyway.

BY THE TIME CHRISTOPHER made it to the classroom, Lucy was calm enough to pretend everything was okay.

"Hey, sweetheart," Lucy said brightly as he came to her for a hug. He leaned into her wearily, but she could tell this was playground tired, not worn-down-by-sadness tired.

"Rough day?" she asked. He looked a little better than yesterday. No more raccoon eyes.

"So . . . much . . . math," he said with a groan. He threw his backpack on a table and sank down into a chair with an exaggerated flop of his skinny arms.

"Do you have a lot of math homework?" she asked as she did her daily dive into his shoes to find his socks. She was going to have to start duct-taping his socks around his ankles.

"Nah, got that done." He pulled his fingers through his hair until his sweaty locks stuck out like Einstein's. "But my brain is fried."

"I did see the smoke coming out of your ears. Wait until you start multiplication tables." Lucy sat in the tiny chair across from him. "What other homework do you have?"

"Reading. Ms. Malik wants me to read a story in a book and answer ten questions about it. Complete sentences," he said, then added, "Ugh."

"A story and ten questions? That sounds like a lot," Lucy said. That was more like fourth-grade-level homework than second. "The whole class had to do this? Or just the Eagles?"

Christopher was in the Eagles reading group. The Eagles were the best readers in the class, the students reading above grade level. Below the Eagles were the Hawks, and below the Hawks were the Owls. Even with such innocuous animal names, the kids picked up immediately that being an Eagle made you special and being an Owl made you an object of pity and scorn. She'd never been more relieved in her life than when she found out Christopher qualified for the Eagles group. Kids picked on him enough already for being in foster care.

"Um . . . just me," he said as he stuck his fingers in his hair and shook it for no reason.

"Just you? Did you get in trouble or something?"

He put his fingers on his lower eyelids and pulled them down so he looked like a zombie. He was clearly very excited about something. Lucy extracted his hands from his face before his eyes dropped out of his sockets.

"What?" she said, holding his wrists.

"Ms. Malik said I'm reading even too good for the Eagles. She thought I might want to go higher."

She stared at him, wide-eyed. "Are you serious?"

He nodded rapidly, which he did in moments of high emotion.

Lucy grabbed his hands and did a little dance with him. Where was the ticker-tape parade when you needed it? Where were the balloons? How did parents not pass right out when kids came home from school with news like this? No, she definitely couldn't tell him the bad news today, not when he was happier than she'd seen him in a long time.

"You are amazing," she said. "You're higher than an eagle. What flies higher than an eagle? Swans maybe? Geese? Wanna be a goose?"

"I do *not* want to be a goose," he said.

She snapped her fingers twice when she got it. "A condor. You, Christopher Lamb," she said, pointing at him, "are a condor. We're changing your name. Christopher Condor. Good job, Mr. Condor."

They high-fived.

"Okay, so what's this story? And what are the questions?" she asked as he got out his book.

"The first story—'A Day at the Beach.' I'm supposed to learn the difference between . . . something articles."

"Something articles? Let me see here." Lucy opened to the page and found the story. It wasn't a very exciting tale, but that was okay. He wasn't ready for Chekhov yet. The instructions said Christopher was supposed to pay attention to when *a* and *an* were used as opposed to *the*.

"Oh, definite and indefinite articles," Lucy said. "That's easy. You'll get those in no time. Ready?"

She pulled her chair closer to Christopher's, but before they could start on the story, Theresa returned from her trip to the front office. She was reading something so intently on her phone that she bumped into one of the tables on the way back to her desk.

"Theresa?" Lucy said, trying to get her attention.

"Why is a raven like a writing desk?" Theresa said. She sat behind her desk and scrolled through something on her phone.

"You are the second person to ask me that today. What the heck is going on?" Lucy asked.

"A raven is a bird, right?" Christopher asked.

"It's like a crow," Lucy said, "but bigger. Is this some kind of meme going around online?"

Theresa finally looked up from her screen. "You all read those Clock Island books, right?"

Lucy's heart jumped. She was suddenly terrified Jack Masterson had died. A long illness could explain why he'd quit writing the books. "What's going on?"

"He's doing some contest thing for his new book."

Lucy looked at Christopher, who was staring back at her with astonished eyes.

"Lucy . . ." he whispered. "We wished for a new book."

"Somebody heard our wish," Lucy said, grinning.

She grabbed Christopher by the hand, and they ran over to Theresa.

"What's the contest?" Lucy asked.

"You can't enter it," Theresa said. "So don't get excited. It's by invitation only, apparently."

Lucy sat down on the floor, cross-legged, and pulled Christopher into her lap so he could see what she saw. The web page was a simple sky blue, and the riddle was written across the screen in an ornate black font. *Why is a raven like a writing desk?*

She scrolled down and read aloud to Christopher.

> *My Dear Readers,*
>
> *I have written a new book—A Wish for Clock Island. There is but one copy in existence, and I plan to give it away to someone very brave, clever, and who knows how to make wishes. Some of my most courageous readers from long ago will be receiving a very special invitation today. You know who you are if you know my answer to this riddle: Why is a raven like a writing desk? Check your mailbox.*
>
> *With Love from Clock Island,*
> *The Mastermind*

Lucy inhaled sharply.

"What's wrong?" Christopher asked.

She didn't answer at first. She was too shocked to speak.

You know who you are if you know my answer to this riddle.

"Lucy?" Christopher slid out of her lap and turned around. Theresa was oblivious.

"Christopher," Lucy whispered. A smile spread across her face so wide it made her ears wiggle.

"What?" he whispered back.

"I know the answer."

CHAPTER FIVE

"COME ON," LUCY SAID. She grabbed Christopher by the hand, and they ran through the halls.

"Where are we going?"

"Computer lab," Lucy said. "My phone's almost dead, and we need to research."

They found the lab empty but for the presence of Mr. Gross, their poor technology teacher. Gross was not a surname anyone who worked with small children wanted or needed.

"We're going to borrow a computer for a couple of minutes," Lucy said to him as they rushed to the computer in the back corner of the room.

"All yours." He was trying to set up a new color printer, and judging from the kid-friendly curses he uttered, he wasn't having much luck with it.

As soon as Lucy sat down, she popped Christopher onto her knee again. That lasted all of one second before he jumped off and pulled a chair next to her. Sitting on her lap was fine in private, but not when grown men were around. She was too distracted to take it personally.

Quickly, Lucy typed in her staff credentials and password. She went straight to the Clock Island Facebook fan page, but there was nothing there she hadn't seen on Theresa's phone. Just Jack Masterson's announcement and thousands upon thousands of comments from readers wanting to know more.

Lucy checked her messages inbox. College friends had inundated her with questions.

Did you see the Jack Masterson thing? That was from Jessie Conners, her senior year roommate. *Didn't you meet him once?*

A former co-worker from the restaurant where Lucy used to wait tables wrote, *Hey, you know Jack Masterson, right? Do you know why a raven's like a writing desk?*

Lucy didn't bother replying to any of them. She went to Google and typed in "Jack Masterson contest wish Clock Island." Christopher looked over her shoulder while she clicked on a Twitter link. She knew she probably shouldn't be doing this with him watching. Grown-up social media was not for little eyes, but she was too excited to stop herself.

The tweet was from a popular CNN reporter who wrote, *I want to play the game! Where's my Hogwarts letter, Jack?* A link to a news article announcing Jack Masterson's sudden return to the literary world followed.

"Hogwarts letter?" Christopher asked.

"People must be getting actual paper invitations to Clock Island or something. I wonder . . ."

"What?"

"Can you keep a secret?" she said.

"Yeah."

"I mean it. This is a big one. You can't tell anyone else."

Lucy hated asking a child to keep a secret. It was too much pressure, and she knew it. Yet she truly did not want this story to get out. Parents would be out for her hide.

"I won't tell anybody, I swear." Christopher was exasperated with her already.

"Okay," she said. "Here's the thing . . . I've been to Clock Island."

Christopher's reaction was everything she could have hoped for. His eyes widened. His jaw dropped. "You've been there?"

"I've been there."

Christopher screamed.

"Shh!" she said, batting her hand against the air. This really was the best part about working with kids. She became a child herself again for a few hours a day. Instead of a tired adult, scared about money and work and bills, she was just a kid, scared of getting in trouble for being too loud.

"Everything okay?" Mr. Gross asked.

"Fine," Lucy said. "When you gotta scream, you gotta scream."

"I'm about to start myself," Mr. Gross said and punched the printer.

"Shh! Calm down," she told Christopher. "You're scaring Mr. Gross."

Christopher didn't seem to hear her.

"You went to Clock Island! You went to Clock Island!" He was panting, shaking his hands. Lucy grabbed him gently by the wrists before he knocked a computer off the table.

"Yes, all that is true," she said. "I know because I just told you."

"You lied!" Christopher said. Damn kid was too smart for his own good. "You told me you met him, and he signed your book."

"I didn't lie. No. Never. I wouldn't—well, yes, I would lie. I have absolutely lied. But in this case, I just didn't tell you the whole story. I told you I met Jack Masterson, and he signed my book. All true. I just didn't tell you I met him on Clock Island."

Christopher glared at her. "You lied."

Lucy stared him down. "You told me Superman was your neighbor."

"I thought he was! I swear! He looked just like him!" Christopher scrunched up his face. "Sorta."

"Do you want to hear the story, or do you want to send me to jail for slightly misrepresenting past events?"

"Lying."

"Fine. I lied."

"What was it like? Did you meet the Mastermind? Did you see the train?" Christopher asked a thousand questions.

"It was amazing. I didn't see any men hiding in shadows," she said, "or trains, but I was in the house."

"How did you get there?"

And this is where the secret part of the story came in.

"When I was thirteen," she said, "I ran away from home."

Christopher's mouth fell open. To a child, running away from home was the ultimate kid caper, the pinnacle of kid crime. Every child dreamed of it, talked about it, threatened it, and almost no child ever did it, and the ones who did rarely returned to tell the tale.

He looked at her with new respect, almost awe.

"Why?" he breathed.

"Because," she said, "my parents didn't love me as much as they loved my sister. I wanted to get their attention."

"But you're so nice," he said, sounding heartbreakingly confused. "Why?"

"Are you sure you want to hear this story? It's a little sad," she said.

"It's okay," Christopher said. "I'm used to being sad."

Lucy looked at him, her heart breaking for the second time that day. It was true, though. Christopher wasn't lying. He was used to being sad. Well, so was she.

"Okay," she said. "Here's the story. It is sad. But don't worry. It has a happy ending."

CHRISTOPHER LISTENED INTENTLY WHILE Lucy told him the story she'd never told him before—the story of Angie, her sister.

Angie was sick all the time. They called her a PIDD kid, which basically meant Angie didn't have much of an immune system. Lucy's parents threw themselves into doing everything they could do for Angie. Lucy, their younger daughter, was healthy and didn't need their attention, so she didn't get any of it. And she didn't get much of their love either.

"That's sad," Christopher interjected.

"I told you so." Lucy kissed his forehead. He let her. She kept talking.

Young Lucy might have been destroyed by the lack of caring and tenderness she experienced in her family if it hadn't been for Jack Masterson and his Clock Island books.

"I won't tell you the whole long story about how I found the books," Lucy said. "But let's just say, they found me at the right time. Eight was a tough year for me. When I started reading those books, it got a lot better."

Lucy had been in the waiting room at the children's hospital, stuck there while her parents spent hours with her sister. She'd wanted to go back and see Angie, but she was too young. A sign on the ward said, NO CHILDREN UNDER THE AGE OF 12 ARE ALLOWED TO VISIT THE PEDIATRICS WARD. Lucy wasn't even looking for a book to read. She'd been digging through a basket of used-up coloring books when she'd found it.

A thin paperback. On the back it listed the age range as nine to twelve. This wasn't a book for babies. There weren't pictures on every single page, just on some of them. And it didn't look like a book just for boys either. No fire-breathing robots or pirates with swords. This book cover had a boy, but he was standing next to a girl. The boy and the girl looked about her age or a little older, maybe nine, maybe ten, and they both carried flashlights. They appeared to be creeping down a long shadowy hallway in a strange, spooky old house. The title of the book was *The House on Clock Island*. Lucy liked it immediately because the girl on the cover was leading with determination, and the boy was behind her, looking terrified. In other books, it was usually the opposite.

Curious, Lucy opened the book to a random page and read:

> *Astrid didn't like the rules. When her parents told her she had to wait an hour after eating to swim, she always jumped in after twenty minutes. And when she saw a sign that said* NO KIDS ALLOWED! THAT MEANS YOU, KID!, *she walked right past it.*

Lucy was hooked. A girl who broke the rules? A girl with a cool name like Astrid instead of a dumb old lady name like Lucy? If Astrid had been at the hospital, she would have found a way to sneak in and see her sister.

She wished Astrid was her real sister . . .

In Lucy's mind, she erased little Max from the cover of the book and replaced him with herself. Now it was Lucy and Astrid on Clock Island together.

Hours after her parents left her alone, Lucy's grandparents came and picked her up. She took the book with her.

"You stole it?" Christopher sounded more impressed than horrified.

"It seemed like something Astrid would do," Lucy said. Christopher accepted that.

After that, nothing could get in the way of Lucy and her Clock Island books. She checked out everything the school library had. When her birthday came, she asked for nothing but money. When her grandmother took her to their local bookstore, Lucy bought every book there was in stock, even the ones she'd already read from the library. She even dressed up like Astrid for Halloween, wearing white clamdiggers, a nautical blue-and-white-striped shirt, and a white sailor hat. Nobody knew who she was, but she didn't care. And when her fifth-grade teacher assigned them all the task of writing a letter to their favorite author, Lucy already had her writer picked out.

Jack Masterson. Easy enough. If you wanted to write him—or Master Mastermind—then all you had to do was write—

"I know," Christopher said. "You write 'Clock Island,' and the letter will go right there."

"How did you know that?" Lucy asked.

He looked at her as if she were possibly the stupidest person alive.

"It's in the back of the books," he said.

"Oh yeah," she said. "Forgot."

Lucy spent a whole week working on her letter to Mr. Masterson before working up the courage to give it to her teacher to put in the mail. The assignment said they were to tell the authors why they first read their books, why they liked the books so much, and then ask the authors one question. They were graded on their letter-writing abilities and not on the author's response, thank goodness.

Mr. Masterson never wrote her back.

When she didn't receive a reply after several months, Mrs. Lee told her not to be discouraged. Mr. Masterson was one of the biggest-selling authors in the world. His kids' books sold more copies than those of many famous adult writers.

Lucy had been hurt but not heartbroken. She was used to love being a one-sided sort of thing. And really, at that age, she couldn't quite conceive of Jack Masterson as a real person. He was a name on the cover of the books, and that was it. The thought of him living in a house and sleeping in a bed and eating cake or going to the bathroom seemed as crazy as Jesus doing all those things. Or Britney Spears.

"Who's Britney Spears?" Christopher asked her.

"You don't know the Great Britney?" Lucy asked.

Christopher shrugged.

"I have failed you, child," Lucy said. "But we'll get to her later. Back to Mr. Masterson."

Although Jack Masterson hadn't written her back after her first letter, Lucy decided to keep writing him. Every couple of months she sent him a letter. Without her teacher reading the letters first, Lucy could write more honestly than what she'd written before. She wrote about how her parents didn't love her the way they loved her sister, how she lived with her grandparents because nobody wanted her around.

In fact, she told him about how she'd gotten to go home for spring break that year. And how for that one week, Lucy had counted the words her parents said to her. From Monday morning to Sunday night, she kept a running total.

The final tally?

> *Mom: 27 words.*
> *Dad: 10 words.*

She counted the minutes they spent in the same room together.

> *Mom: 11 minutes.*
> *Dad: 4 minutes.*

When she counted how many times they said they loved her that week, it looked like this:

> *Mom: 0*
> *Dad: 0*

Maybe that was what had done it.

That was the letter Jack Masterson answered.

CHAPTER SIX

CHRISTOPHER LEANED IN CLOSE as if she were about to reveal nuclear codes to him.

"I remember that day like it was yesterday," Lucy whispered. She was having too much fun telling him this story.

One autumn day she came home from school, and there on her grandparents' kitchen table lay a pale blue envelope with her name on it. She'd only just turned thirteen, but she knew it wasn't a birthday card. Nobody sent her birthday cards. She found a kitchen knife and with a *zzzt*, she opened the envelope.

"What did the letter say?" he asked.

Lucy told him word for word. She'd read it so often she had the letter memorized.

Dear Lucy,

Here is a secret—I have a monster in my house. He stands behind my chair in my writing factory and doesn't let me leave until I've finished all my work. This monster is called an editor, and he's green and covered in fur, and his teeth are long and full of the bones of other writers he's eaten for not making their deadlines. At the moment, he's tied up in the corner of my writing room, gagged and blindfolded.

He'll get out soon enough, but while he's chained up, I finally have a chance to write you back.

It's a terrible thing your parents have done to you. Oh, I guess you could make excuses for them. Your sister is chronically ill, and while being a parent is a full-time job, being a parent to a chronically ill child makes you a prisoner to the illness. Nobody wants to be a prisoner. No one asks for that. I wish that hadn't happened to your sister or anyone's sister or brother or mother or dad.

That being said, it's a terrible thing your parents have done to you. It's so awful I wrote it twice. I may even write it a third time.

It's a terrible thing your parents have done to you.

If you were my daughter, the numbers would look very different.

Words spoken to you in a week?

100,000 (mostly about what a rotten monster I have to deal with daily).

Minutes spent together in a week?

Somewhere between 840 and 1,000. That averages out to three to four hours a day. It would be that many minutes because I would give you a harpoon and a flamethrower, and you and I would fight side by side every day to keep the editor monster out of my house. It's thirsty work, I'm telling you. I go through pots of tea every day. I could use a sidekick. My current one is not pulling his weight, and you can tell him I said that.

I'm afraid the monster in the corner has almost chewed through the ropes. I wish I could do more for you than tell you how sorry I am for what a terrible thing your parents have done to you. You are clearly a brave child and intelligent, and even if they don't see that, I do. And my opinion counts more than theirs does, as I am rich and very famous. That's a little joke there. Well, not really. I am rich and famous, but that's not why my opinion counts for more. The real reason is that I know things other people do not know. Mystic secrets and hidden knowledge, the sort of stuff men in fedoras kill and die for. And the runes and tarot cards and the raven that lives in my writing room all tell me the same thing about you: Lucy Hart, you are going to be fine. You are going to be even better than fine. You are going to be loved like you deserve to be loved. And you are going to have a very magical life (if you want it; feel free to say no, as magic always comes with a price).

Don't give up, Lucy. Always remember that the only wishes ever granted are the wishes of brave children who keep on wishing even when it seems no one is listening because someone always is. Someone like me.

Keep wishing.

I'm listening.

Your Friend,
Jack Masterson

P.S. Oh God, he's loose again. SOMEONE BRING ME THE HOLY WATER AND THE CRUCIFIX!

"That's a joke," Lucy told Christopher. "He was joking that his monster editor was a vampire. You have to use holy water and crucifixes to keep vampires away."

She thought Christopher would ask her about the monster or say something about how funny and weird Mr. Masterson's letter to her was. Instead, he put his arms around her neck and rested his chin on her shoulder.

"I'm sorry your parents didn't want you," he said.

Lucy smiled. She wasn't about to cry, not over them. They didn't deserve it.

"I'm not," she said, returning his hug with a squish.

"You aren't?"

"If they'd wanted me, I wouldn't be here with you," she said. "Maybe I'd still be living in Maine. And . . . if they wanted me, I would never have run away. And because I did run away, I know the answer to the riddle."

"What is it?" Christopher whispered.

"I'm getting there."

After Lucy had read that letter from Mr. Masterson a few hundred times, she decided she liked his numbers better than hers. And didn't he say he needed a new sidekick?

In her technology class at school, she'd learned how to use the internet to find places and how to get there. So Lucy packed her clothes and all the money she'd saved from babysitting and doing chores for her grandmother—$379. She would take a bus to Portland's ferry terminal. Then she'd ask an adult which ferry went to Clock Island. Someone would probably tell her just to show off that they knew where a famous person lived and how to get there. In the Clock Island books, adults were constantly underestimating kids. Maybe someone would tell her.

And the funniest thing is . . . they did.

"They told you?" Christopher asked.

"I asked the ticket lady. She just told me," Lucy said. "She said I couldn't get off at Clock Island. It only stopped there for mail delivery, but I could take pictures. But when the ferry got to the dock, and the mailman got off, as soon as his back was turned, I got off too. Just like that."

For all her planning and plotting and thinking of everything that could happen, everything that could go wrong, it was actually pretty easy to get to Clock Island. It was like Jack Masterson was just a regular person. You wanted to know where a normal person lived, you asked someone who knew. And if you wanted to go to their house, you just went there. Lucy puzzled over how easy it was as she walked up from the beach to a stone path sloping upward toward what felt like the peak of a hill. Where were the electric fences? Where were the bodyguards? Did people not know how famous and important Jack Masterson was?

And then there it was—the house on Clock Island. No doubt in her mind. It was enormous, spooky, white with black shutters, ivy climbing the sides . . . Yes, this was *The House*.

She knew nothing about houses as a kid except there were rich people houses and normal people houses. And this was undoubtedly a rich person's house.

As an adult, she'd figured out that the house was a grand Victorian, the house of someone too rich and a little bit wacky. Turrets and towers and stained-glass windows, oh my.

She was scared as she approached the house. Her heart pounded as if it would break out of her chest and run away back home to her grandparents. The reality of what she'd done sank in when she stood behind the trunk of a pine tree, staring at the most beautiful house she'd ever seen. What had she done? And how would she get back home? What was she doing here?

Then she remembered . . . She remembered how, in every Clock Island book, the kids were always terrified to go up to the house, to ring the bell, to ask Master Mastermind for help. And he was scary, but that didn't make him bad. Storms were scary. Wolves were scary. But Lucy loved storms and wolves.

Before she knew it, Lucy was at the front door. She rang the bell.

She waited.

A man opened the door.

She knew it was him immediately. Jack Masterson—an older white man, gray-brown hair gone a bit wild, brown eyes, and a permanently furrowed brow. Navy cardigan. Rumpled khakis. Rumpled face. That was him all right. She couldn't believe he'd answered his own door. Didn't he have a million servants?

"Mr. Masterson," Lucy began before he could get a word out. "I'm Lucy Hart. You wrote me back. You said you needed a sidekick. So . . . here I am."

He must have been the wisest man in the world. Any other man, any other writer, who had a fan with a backpack show up on their doorstep asking to be their sidekick would likely call the police, a psychiatric hospital, and the fire department just for backup. And if that had happened, Lucy would have been a broken girl. Broken so badly she would have never gotten unbroken, no matter how many Christophers she'd meet.

Instead of doing that, the sane thing, Mr. Masterson did the Jack Masterson thing. He said, "Ah, Lucy, I've been expecting you. Come in. There's tea brewing up in my writing factory. Do you take it American or English style?"

It wasn't a yes or no question, but she answered, "Um . . . no?" She was pretty sure she'd never had hot tea before.

"'Then I'll make it the way I like it—ninety percent sugar. Let's go up and talk.'"

She followed him inside and up the main staircase. She barely remembered what the interior looked like, she'd been so overwhelmed. But she did recall seeing weird paintings on the dark green walls. Weird but wonderful.

They walked down a long hall to his writing factory, where there was a teapot on a hot plate and bags hanging out of the lid and over the side.

Jack Masterson sat her in a big brown leather chair and gave her a cup of steaming hot tea full of sugar like he'd promised. And it was good. (To this day, she drank black tea with sugar, no milk.) She looked around the office in wonder and amazement. All the bookshelves. All the books. Masks. Model rockets. A glowing glass jack-o'-lantern in place of a desk lamp. Moths with eyes on their wings in glass boxes. A globe of the moon. A black bird on a driftwood perch by the open window looking out on the ocean.

A living bird.

"That's a crow," she said in shock when the bird moved.

Mr. Masterson raised his hand to his lips and shushed her.

"*Raven,*" he said softly. "Thurl is very sensitive. But he's only a baby, so he'll grow out of that. Come here, Thurl."

He whistled and the raven flapped his wings, flew across the room to land on Jack's wrist.

"Wow," Lucy said. "What's his name? Thurl?"

"Yes, Thurl Ravenscroft. No relation."

"Relation to who?"

"Thurl Ravenscroft."

She stared at him. He was weirder than she'd expected. She never *ever* wanted to leave.

"You have a pet raven?"

"'*Hope is the thing with feathers,*' the lovely Miss Emily Dickinson once wrote. Well, if that's the case, then a wish is a thing with *black* feathers." He smiled as he stroked Thurl Ravenscroft's glossy black chest. "Black feathers, a sharp beak, and talons. Dangerous things, wishes. Sometimes they come to you when you call. Sometimes they fly away after biting you." He put his finger up to Thurl's beak, but the raven didn't bite him. Jack whistled again and Thurl returned to his perch, a piece of carved driftwood.

"Wish carefully is all I'm saying."

"I just wish I could stay here," she said. "I want that more than anything."

Mr. Masterson turned to her, put his hand to his chin, and eyed her like he was taking the measure of her. She must have passed some sort of test because he said then, "Lucy, would you like to see something I've been working on?"

"Sure," Lucy breathed. "What is it?"

"There was a very strange man named Charles Dodgson—you probably know him as Lewis Carroll, yes?"

"Yes, I know him," Lucy said eagerly.

"Personally?" Mr. Masterson asked.

"We've never met," Lucy said. That made him smile.

"He asked a riddle in a book once. *'Why is a raven like a writing desk?'* I could never figure it out," he said. "Nothing worse than hearing a riddle and not knowing the answer to it. Maddening, which was certainly his point. Because I was on deadlines, I didn't have time to go mad. I made up an answer of my own."

"You made up an answer?"

Jack Masterson grinned at her. According to his entry in the online encyclopedia, he was fifty-four years old, but at that moment, he looked like a little boy.

"Watch this," he said and went to his window where Thurl was perched. Mr. Masterson opened the window wide. Then he picked up a little wooden lap desk, not much bigger than a cafeteria tray. With a flourish, he tossed it out the window. Lucy gasped. Was Mr. Masterson crazy? She ran to the window, looked out, expecting to see the writing desk on the ground below.

But the most amazing thing happened, Lucy told Christopher. The desk didn't fall to the ground. It hovered in the air. Mr. Masterson held some kind of remote control in his hand.

"I put toy helicopter rotors under the bottom of the desk," he explained as he pushed buttons on the controller. "Flies just like those little hovering thingos you see in the shopping malls."

The writing desk fluttered and hovered and rose and fell and eventually came back to the window, where he snatched it out of the air.

Lucy knew at that very moment that Jack Masterson was the most incredible man who had ever lived and would ever live, and she had to be his sidekick, or she'd never be truly happy as long as she lived.

Jack Masterson asked her, "Now you know . . . why is a raven like a writing desk?"

NOW, THIRTEEN YEARS LATER, Christopher answered the riddle.

His voice was soft and full of wonder as he said, "They both can fly."

"Exactly," Lucy said with a smile. "Turns out . . . with a little help, they both can fly."

Christopher stared at her in wide-eyed amazement.

"Anyway," Lucy went on—she'd promised Christopher that the story had a happy ending, so she better give him one—"I had to leave, of course. You can't just show up on your favorite writer's doorstep and actually move in with him when you're thirteen years old. But he was supernice, and he did sign a book for me. And he said when I was older, I could come back and visit him again. So maybe I'll get to do that someday."

"Can I come with you?" he asked.

She was about to say yes, of course she'd take him anywhere, when she remembered what Mrs. Costa had said, that she was never going to be Christopher's mother, not unless a miracle happened.

She needed to say something, though. Christopher was looking at her, waiting for an answer. Maybe now was the right time to tell him, to at least start breaking it to him that things weren't going to work out the way they'd wished.

"You know, sweetheart. I wanted to talk to you about—" she began, but suddenly Theresa appeared in the doorway of the computer room.

"There you are," Theresa said. Lucy saw she was holding a blue envelope in her hand. "This was just delivered for you. By courier. Hope you're not getting sued, baby girl."

She looked at the blue envelope. She looked at Christopher. Christopher looked at the blue envelope. Christopher looked at her.

He screamed. She screamed.

When you gotta scream, you gotta scream.

PART TWO

Tick-Tock.
Welcome to the Clock.

In the middle of the deep green wood stood a house half-hidden by towering maple trees. Astrid had never seen a house so strange or so dark. Although the house was tall and wide and made of red brick, so much green ivy grew over it that she could only tell where the windows were by the way the moonlight glinted on the glass.

"Is that it?" Max whispered behind her. "Is that his house?"

"I think so," Astrid whispered back. "Let's go in."

"It's dark. No one's inside. We should go home."

"Not when we just got here." Astrid wanted to go home too. Nothing would be easier than to go home. But they wouldn't get their wish if they gave up now.

A light appeared in the window. Someone was inside.

Astrid gasped softly. Max gasped loudly.

They looked at each other. Slowly they approached the house on a path made of slick mossy stones. Max followed close behind her.

When they reached the door, it was so dark Astrid had to turn on her flashlight to find the bell. She pushed the button and waited to hear a ring.

She didn't hear a ring but a voice, a weird mechanical voice.

"What can't be touched, tasted, or held but can be broken?"

Astrid jumped back, which made Max jump. They were both panting with fear.

"What was that?" Max asked, eyes wide.

"I think it was the doorbell." Her hand was shaking, but she pressed it again.

The voice spoke again, and it was like listening to a clock talk, and every syllable was a tick.

"What. Can't. Be. Touched. Or. Taste. Ed. Or. Held. But. Can. Be. Broke. En?"

"It's a riddle," Astrid said. "We can't get in unless we answer the riddle. What can't be touched or tasted or held but can be broken? Think, Max!"

But Max wasn't thinking. He was shaking. "Astrid, I want to go home. You promised if it was scary, we could go home."

Then it hit her. She knew the answer.

Astrid called out to the door, "A promise!"

After a long pause, the mechanical voice said, "Tick. Tock. Wel. Come. To. The. Clock."

The door creaked open.

—From *The House on Clock Island*, Clock Island
Book One, by Jack Masterson, 1990

CHAPTER SEVEN

HUGO WAS IN EXILE. His own fault. Three stories up in the air, he stood at the railing of the widow's walk and watched as the boats and ferries came and went, bringing boxes and grocery bags, even temporary household staff to handle the cooking and cleaning. A small army of staff had been temporarily enlisted by Jack to put on this insane contest of his. So far only one priceless marble bust made by a dead artistic genius had been broken. Jack had laughed and said, "That's why we have insurance." Hugo's head had nearly exploded, which was when Jack sent him to the widow's walk to "supervise the boats."

Hugo protested. "Supervise the boats? Someone has to make sure nothing else gets broken down here."

"Hugo," Jack said with a large and rather terrifying grin on his face, "your bad mood is scaring the children."

Hugo waved his arms around the room. "There are no children here."

"Weren't we all children once?" Jack said.

Point taken. Hugo retreated to the roof.

But even up here, he couldn't find peace and quiet. His pocket began to vibrate. Yet another phone call from yet another unknown number, no doubt. Who was it this time? TMZ? The *New York Post*? *National Enquirer*? Out of pure spite, he answered the call.

"Yes?"

"Hugo Reese? This is Thomas Larrabee with *Shelf Talker*."

"Never heard of it."

"We're a renowned literary blog."

"What's a blog?" Hugo asked with pure unadulterated spite.

"It's a, well, it's a—"

"Never mind. What do you want?"

"We were hoping you'd answer a few questions—"

"I have a one-question limit."

"Oh, well, all right," he said. Hugo heard pages flipping in a notebook. "What's the real Jack Masterson like?"

"Good question," Hugo said.

"Thank you."

"If I ever meet the real Jack Masterson, I'll tell you."

Hugo hung up. How were these people getting his phone number? Because he was on the roof, he could get just enough cell phone reception to google *Shelf Talker*. No surprise, this renowned literary blog had all of seventeen followers, most of which looked like Russian bot accounts.

It wasn't a bad question, though. *What's the real Jack Masterson like?* Hugo wished he knew.

Suddenly last year, out of nowhere, without warning, and with no explanation, Jack got out of bed one day and started writing again. And then, again with no explanation, without warning, out of nowhere, and all of a sudden, he decided to throw a contest in his own house on the island?

The old man loved routine, loved his privacy, loved peace and quiet. Social butterflies did not live on private islands. No, Jack was whatever you called the opposite of a social butterfly—an introverted moth, maybe. Yet for a whole week, the house would be overrun with strangers. Why?

When Hugo tried asking him that, Jack simply said, "Why not?"

Maddening. Absolutely maddening. But that was Jack for you—a living, breathing riddle. Had Hugo ever met the real Jack? Maybe once. Maybe a long time ago.

After Hugo won the contest to be the new illustrator, Jack Masterson himself had rung him and invited him to spend a few months on Clock

Island, staying in one of the many guest rooms or even taking over the guesthouse if he preferred. At twenty-one, Hugo had never even left the UK much less crossed the ocean. How could Hugo have said no? Davey would never have forgiven him.

The first time he flew in an airplane was the day he left London's Heathrow for New York's JFK. A black Caddy had picked him up at the airport, driven him to Lion House Books in Manhattan to meet Jack's editor and the art team. One night at the Ritz—Jack's treat—and the next day another plane to Portland's Jetport. Another car service. Then a ferry. Then he was standing on the dock of Clock Island, a place until the week before he would have sworn existed only on the pages of the books he read to his brother every night.

He'd expected a servant, a butler in livery maybe, to greet him, but no. No servants. No entourage. Just Jack Masterson himself waiting for him all alone. If he'd imagined Jack as some sort of posh wanker, he was surprised to find a normal-looking bloke about fifty in a navy-blue cardigan, and a light blue button-down shirt with ink stains on it, as if he'd gone ten rounds with a fountain pen and lost.

"Nice to meet the man in person," Jack said to him, acting as if Hugo were the famous one, not him. "Welcome to the Clock."

Hugo didn't even remember what he said in reply. *Nice place?* Or *Thanks?* A classic *You all right?* which seemed to massively confuse Americans when you said it to them. Maybe he didn't say a thing, overwhelmed as he was, except for a surly *Hey.*

After that, he remembered Jack offering him something to eat and Hugo being too proud to admit he was famished. He told Jack they should probably get straight to work if they really wanted forty new covers in six months' time.

Young idiot he was, pretending to be all business. Meanwhile, Jack walked him around the clock that was Clock Island. The Five O'Clock Beach, and the Southernmost Six, a great place for a cookout, Jack said. Hugo would be staying in the Seventh Heaven Guest Cottage, but he could work in the main house if he preferred. Plenty of empty rooms and cake in the kitchen.

Jack showed him the white Alpine strawberries he was growing in his greenhouse (*"Try one, Hugo. They taste like pineapple!"*), the tide pools (*"If you see a starfish, detain it. I have some questions I'd like to ask it."*), the widow's walk where you could stand and see a 360-degree view of the island (*"You could sleep out here if you like to stargaze and don't mind bats shitting on your face."*). Weren't they supposed to be working on some massive project?

Finally, poor old Jack gave up on trying to get Hugo to lighten up. When Jack asked him if he wanted to get some rest before getting to work, Hugo waved him off.

"Rather get started now," Hugo had said. Fourteen years later, he wanted to reach back in time and shake some sense into his younger self, tell him to stop pretending to be a serious artist—all black clothes and black looks and bad attitude. It had taken a few years until he'd figured it out—there was no such thing as a *serious artist*. It was an oxymoron, and it was Jack who'd tried to teach him that the day they met.

During the quick tour of Jack's house, Hugo pretended he wasn't gob-smacked by every room. The priceless first editions in the library. The dining table for twelve. The kitchen as massive as his mum's whole flat. The paintings of dead people Jack wasn't related to. The bat skeletons in shadow box frames. The secret panel that led to a secret hallway that led to a secret exit into the not-so-secret garden. And everywhere clocks and hourglasses and sundials. Even a pendulum. The whole place was like a mad Victorian scientist's summer home. And Hugo loved it. Not that he told Jack that.

"Welcome to my writing factory," Jack said as they entered the last room. More bookshelves. A desk as big as a boat, and—according to Jack—made from a boat.

"Writing factory?" Hugo said.

"Willy Wonka had his chocolate factory where he tortured and re-warded children. I have my writing factory where I torture and reward children. Only on paper, of course."

He gestured toward a collection of typewriters—a half dozen or more manual and electric typewriters. A red Olivetti. A black Smith Corona. A pale blue Royal. A neon pink Olympia. All of them looked older than Hugo by at least a decade or two.

"Typewriters?" Hugo asked as Jack sat behind his desk, an orange typewriter in front of him with "Hermes Rocket" stamped on the top in metal. "Bit old school there, yeah? Don't use a computer?"

"Too quiet," Jack said. "I need something loud enough to cover the sound of my characters screaming for help."

Hugo was starting to think Jack might be a little touched in the head.

"More fun too," Jack said. "Even Thurl likes to help me write. Come here, Thurl."

If Hugo had noticed Jack's pet raven, he'd have thought it was a statue or something and ignored it. Couldn't ignore him now, flying from a perch by the south window to land on Jack's desk by the east window. A raven. A real live black raven with a wingspan the length of Hugo's leg.

"That's a raven." Hugo pointed at the bird. "Where'd that come from?"

"The sky," Jack said, stroking Thurl's glossy wings.

"A big beast, innit?" The shock must have shown in Hugo's face.

"Oh, he's just a baby. Well, a big baby. Thought you had ravens in London?"

"Got the Tower Ravens, but they don't let us take 'em home. Always wanted to," he admitted. "Couldn't figure out how to hide a raven under my coat."

"You can pet him. He'll let you."

Hugo had to pet the raven if only to tell Davey he'd done it.

Slowly he approached the bird, who seemed more than content to sit on Jack's typewriter and peck at the keys. It looked up when Hugo approached, ebony eyes gleaming.

"All right, mate," Hugo said as he slowly stroked the back of the bird's sleek head once, then twice, and after that Hugo's courage ran out. That beak looked sinister. But once he stopped, he wanted to do it again. He gave the wing a stroke and Thurl allowed it, didn't even seem to mind. Maybe old Jack was mad, but he had good taste in strange pets.

"Found him half-dead in the woods after a windstorm. No mother in sight. Hand-reared him, so now he's too tame to go back out into the big blue yonder."

"He's brilliant," Hugo said, daring to stroke the bird's glossy head again.

"Glad you like him. You two can be friends."

Hugo was smiling and Jack had caught him. He didn't like anyone to catch him smiling. Serious artists didn't smile. They scowled.

He snatched his hand back, shoved it in his pocket.

"So how do we do this?" Hugo asked, getting down to business.

"You've read my books, yes?" Jack asked as he slid a fresh sheet of paper into his typewriter and started hammering away at the keys.

"Yeah. To my brother, Davey." He had to raise his voice over the typewriter.

"And my editor or someone at Lion House explained the process yesterday?"

"The brass told me what to do and how to do it." The art department at Lion House had given him a long lecture on the cover-making process. The Clock Island books were special, he was told, in that the covers were still painted as opposed to being computer designed. Jack's preference (though the way they said "preference" made Hugo think it was more like a "demand"). The paintings would be displayed at book events and school visits, donated to children's hospitals and family shelters. Then they gave him a list of requirements—medium, paint, dimensions. He might have walked out except they also told him how much he'd be paid per cover, which got him to sit down and pay attention. Peanuts compared to what Jack made per book, but it was more money than he or his mum had seen in a lifetime. So now here he was, in Maine talking to a madman with a raven for a co-writer.

"Then go on. Paint. Have fun."

"I need a bit more help than 'Have fun.'"

Jack kept typing and as he typed, he recited:

> *We are the music makers,*
> *And we are the dreamers of dreams,*
> *Wandering by lone sea-breakers,*
> *And sitting by desolate streams;—*
> *World-losers and world-forsakers,*
> *On whom the pale moon gleams:*
> *Yet we are the movers and shakers*
> *Of the world for ever, it seems.*

Jack paused long enough to say, "First stanza. *Ode* by Arthur O'Shaughnessy. Always cite your sources."

Then he returned to madly typing.

"Poetry doesn't solve my problems," Hugo said, almost shouting over the clacking of the keys.

Finally, Jack dropped his hands from the keys. The silence was heaven.

"Why would anyone have problems poetry couldn't solve?" Jack demanded.

Did this man not understand the pressure Hugo was under? Jack's publisher had said that each Clock Island book sold ten million or more copies, and there were forty of them so far. Ten million forty times over was a calculation even an artist could do in his head.

"You're rich," Hugo said. "I'm not about to say you should say you're sorry about it," though Hugo thought he probably should. "But that bag over there"—he pointed at his black duffel—"is about everything I own in this world. I can't mess this up. You have to give me more to go on than 'Have fun.'"

"Kid, this"—Jack pointed at the page in his typewriter—"is my art. That"—he pointed at a painting of Clock Island, tempera on paper, the one Hugo had entered into the contest—"is your art. You don't tell me how to do my art. I don't tell you how to do your art."

"Jack?"

"Yes, Hugo?"

"Tell me how to do my art."

Jack sat back in his industrial green swivel chair. The ancient wheels squeaked, sending Thurl flapping back to his perch.

"What's the best gift anyone ever gave you?" Jack asked. "And don't tell me something you think I want to hear like a teacher encouraged you and that was the best gift. I mean toys. Drum set. Bow and arrow. Something Santa brought or a maiden aunt with money and a grudge against your mother."

"Batmobile," Hugo said. He almost blushed to admit it, but he'd loved that thing too much to deny it. "Mum somehow scraped up the cash to buy me a radio-controlled Batmobile. It was used, I think. Maybe Mum found it in a charity shop, but it was still in the box, and it worked like a dream."

"Did you play with it?"

"Course. I, uh . . . God . . ." Hugo chuckled at the memory of his younger self. "I played with it until the engine burned up and the wheels came off."

"How do you think your mother would have felt if you'd never taken it out of the box? Just set it on a shelf and admired it from afar?"

Hugo remembered his mother laughing until she wheezed as the little black car careened off the table, around their flat, around her ankles, even while they were eating breakfast. She pretended to be cross about it, but her eyes were always laughing. He'd even heard her bragging about it to their neighbor Carol, how she'd found a toy for Hugo, and he hadn't stopped playing with it for weeks.

"Would've broken her heart."

"There," Jack said as if he'd proven his point. What point?

"What's there?"

"God—or whoever is in charge of this planet—got drunk on the job one day and decided to give me the gift of writing. The way I see it, I have two choices. I can set that gift on a high shelf so it won't get dinged up and nobody can make fun of me for playing with it." He smiled until the crinkles at the corners of his eyes were deep enough to hide state secrets. "Or I can have fun with it and play with the gift I was given until the engine burns out and the wheels come off. I decided to play. I suggest you do the same, young man. Go paint or draw or collage or whatever you want to do. Come back when there's smoke coming off the canvas. And for God's sake, go have some fun. Please?"

Then Jack waved his hand, dismissing Hugo. And what was he going to do? He went out and he had fun, if only to prove Jack wrong. Except he didn't prove Jack wrong. Three days later he'd painted a cover for *The Ghost Machine*, Clock Island Book Eleven. There weren't any owl pirates, but there was a crescent moon grinning, two stars for eyes, and a boy about ten years old climbing an impossible Escher-esque staircase toward the night sky, and behind him on the steps was a smoke-colored ghost in the shape of the boy it followed. A shadow in the window of the house on Clock Island revealed the silhouette of the Mastermind, watching the boy and his ghost race each other to the moon.

It was weird and it was good, and Hugo had fun painting it.

He remembered showing it to Jack, feeling shy and scared and proud and stupid all at once. Like a kid waiting for a pat on the back.

Jack stared and studied, looked closely, stood back, came forward again, and hovered a fingertip over the strange painted staircase that went everywhere and nowhere.

Then softly he mumbled, "*Yesterday, upon the stair, I met a man who wasn't there. He wasn't there again today. I wish, I wish he'd go away . . .*'" Then softly Jack said, "Hughes Mearns."

Right, right. Always cite your sources.

Was that the moment Hugo had seen the real Jack Masterson? When he witnessed the smile fade and the veil slip? But which one was the real Jack? The watching moon? The haunted boy running toward the light?

Or the lonely Mastermind, trapped behind the glass, unable to intervene in a world where even children were haunted?

"You like it?" Hugo finally asked. He couldn't bear to wait another second for Jack's answer.

"It's perfect," Jack said, not smiling but somehow exuding a deeper sort of joy. He lightly elbowed Hugo in the side. "One down. Thirty-nine to go."

By the end of the second week, Hugo had learned to paint with a raven sitting on his easel. By the end of the month, he'd finished five covers, and they were better than anything he ever thought he could have done. And by Christmas, Hugo had finished the job and was hired for Clock Island Book Forty-One through infinity.

On Christmas morning, two days before Hugo would fly back to London, back to Davey, he opened a wrapped box to find a vintage, mint condition radio-controlled Batmobile toy. Hugo gave it to Davey, who played with it until the wheels came off.

Now he saw the last boat of the day chugging away from the dock. Probably safe for Hugo to return downstairs. But first, he turned around, taking another good long look at the island. Hard to believe he'd be leaving here soon, moving away, getting on with his life like he should have years ago whether he wanted to or not.

With the sun gone, Hugo went down into the house. Everything was in place, more or less. Tomorrow the first contestants would arrive. Hugo planned to stay until the contest was over to make sure nothing else got broken. Including Jack.

Especially Jack.

CHAPTER EIGHT

*H*OPE FOR A MIRACLE.

So said Mrs. Costa. So said Theresa. Lucy hadn't believed them then. Now . . . maybe she was starting to believe.

Today was Monday. The day Lucy was leaving for Clock Island.

At four in the morning, she woke up and made herself eat some cereal. After a shower, makeup, hair, and getting dressed, she checked her bags, making certain she hadn't forgotten anything.

After college, she'd sworn she'd never go back to Maine, and she went about forgetting how much she missed the cold and wild Atlantic Ocean, missed the whipping winds, the loons and the puffins, the blueberries and the lobster rolls and the popovers—those insanely delicious pastries she cursed herself for never learning how to make. And she pretended she didn't miss sweater weather nine months out of the year either. Even when she was honest with herself about missing home, she still had no regrets about coming to California. It had saved her life, the long sunny days pulling her out from the deep, dark place she'd been afraid she'd never escape. And meeting Christopher had made it all worth it.

Thank God she hadn't told Christopher she would never be his mother. After two years of scrimping and saving and sacrificing and getting almost nowhere anyway, *finally* she had a chance to make it happen. The game rules said that she could do anything with the book if she won it, including selling it to any publisher. That was her plan. Win it. Read it. Sell it. A new Clock Island book would probably go for a lot. At the very least, she'd have money for a car and an apartment. She had to win. For Christopher. For her. She wasn't going to get a second chance like this ever again.

A car horn gave a little *honk-honk*.

Time to go.

She stood up, took a deep breath, and hefted her bag over her shoulder. Outside, Theresa was waiting for her. She'd volunteered to drive her to the airport. Lucy laughed when she came out of the house and saw Theresa's old beige Camry decorated with a sign that read, CLOCK ISLAND OR BUST!

"You're nuts," Lucy said as Theresa took her suitcase and put it in the trunk. She had to move some blue and gold streamers out of the way to get it in.

"My kids wanted to do it for you. Don't blame me," Theresa said.

Lucy got in the passenger side.

"Did you get any sleep last night?" Theresa said, pulling away from the curb.

"Two hours maybe."

"Excited or scared?"

"Excited for me. Scared for Christopher."

"He'll be fine," Theresa said. "I'll keep an eye on him. He'll miss you like crazy, but he's out of his mind with excitement. He knows you'll win the book."

Lucy shook her head. "I don't even know what we'll be doing on the island. They didn't tell me anything about the game. All I know is that a car will pick me up at the Portland Jetport, and a boat will take me to the island. They said to pack for five days, and that's it."

"Very mysterious. You sure this isn't a cult thing?" Theresa winked at her.

"I promise I won't join any cults or buy any time-shares."

"Will you have time to see friends in town?"

"Not really. I think I'll just be on Clock Island until the game's over. Then straight back here."

"Good."

Lucy gave Theresa a look. "I wasn't going to see Sean anyway. You couldn't pay me enough to see him."

"Just checking. I know you left all your stuff at his place when you moved out. If you were thinking it might be worth it—"

"It's not worth it, I know." More than once, Lucy had contemplated calling Sean, asking him to ship her stuff to her. She could have used the Jimmy Choo heels he'd bought her. She would have pawned them.

"Good girl. Nobody needs money that bad. And if you do, ask Jack Masterson for it. This crazy contest sent his books back onto the bestseller lists. That was probably the plan."

"Maybe," Lucy said, although the Jack Masterson she'd met didn't seem all that interested in money or bestseller lists. If he was, why hadn't he published a single book for the past six years?

Lucy looked around. They should have been on the highway to the airport already.

"Are you sure this is the way to the airport?"

"One quick stop first."

They had time, so Lucy wasn't worried. She stared out the window, trying to calm her nerves. Eyes on the prize. She needed to focus. Winning wouldn't be easy. Three days ago she'd been a guest—via satellite—on the *Today* show. They'd interviewed all the contestants, asking them to tell the story of how they'd run away to the island and why.

Andre Watkins had told the story of being the target of racist bullying at his New England prep school. He ran away during a school field trip. Jack called Andre's parents, he said, and told them there was no point sending him to a fancy school if it destroyed his love of learning. He got to go home to a school where he felt safe, and Jack wrote the letter of recommendation that helped Andre get into Harvard. Now he was a successful lawyer.

Melanie Evans, the other woman playing the game, talked about moving to a new town, new school, not having any friends. Jack had sent copies of his books to all her classmates with a note in them that they were gifts from him and his dear friend Melanie. She'd been the most popular girl in the school after that, and now she owned her own children's bookstore.

Dr. Dustin Gardner had revealed he'd been scared to come out to his parents. Jack had encouraged him to be honest with them but promised that if they didn't take it well, they'd be answering to him. Having his favorite writer in the world on his side had given him the courage to be his real self. And Jack had been right. His parents had struggled at first but eventually they'd come around and were his biggest supporters. When the talk show hosts asked him what he'd do if he won the book, he said he'd sell it to pay off his student loans. Then he asked if there were any bidders. That got a big laugh.

When it was her turn, Lucy fudged the truth a little. She said she'd only wanted to be Jack Masterson's sidekick. He'd joked in a letter about how he'd needed one, and she planned to apply for the job. The part about her parents neglecting her and her sister's medical issues seemed too depressing to talk about on morning television.

"You're too quiet, baby girl. You okay?" Theresa asked, interrupting her daydreaming.

"Fine, fine. Just nervous. Thanks, by the way."

Theresa waved her hand dismissively. "It's just a ride to the airport."

"No, I mean, thank you for talking me out of telling Christopher."

Theresa reached out and squeezed Lucy's hand. "You're going to win, and you're going to be his mother. I refuse to believe anything else."

"It's way more likely I'll lose."

"Fine, then steal some of Masterson's silverware while you're there. We'll sell it on eBay when you get back. Call it plan B."

"Great idea."

"Seriously, though, while you're back in Maine," Theresa said, wagging her finger at Lucy, "I want you to think about a real plan B, okay? I don't care if it's a new job or guilt-tripping your sister into writing you a check, but it's time to make it happen. All right? For Christopher?"

A new job meant she wouldn't be able to tutor Christopher after school. And she couldn't even text her sister without wanting to vomit, much less ask her for money. Not a chance.

"Okay. I'll think of something."

"I know you will." Theresa pulled into the driveway of a small bunga-low with overgrown shrubs in the front yard. Where on earth were they?

The house's front door opened, and Christopher burst out in a run toward the car.

Lucy looked at Theresa.

"You're welcome," she said.

Lucy got out and grabbed him in a hug, spinning him.

"Lucy, I get to go with you to the airport. Mrs. Bailey said so. I even get to be late to school!"

"That's amazing. Let's go!" She got into the back seat of the car with Christopher and made sure he was buckled in correctly as Theresa pulled out of the driveway.

"Great surprise." Lucy squeezed Theresa's shoulder.

"Thought you needed the moral support."

"I'm your morals support, Lucy," Christopher said.

"My morals need a lot of supporting."

The entire way to the airport, Christopher and Theresa talked about all his favorite Clock Island books—*The Ghost Machine, Skulls & Skullduggery,* and especially *The Secret of Clock Island.*

"Why is that one so good?" Theresa asked.

"That's the one where the Mastermind adopted a girl who came to the island. She gets to live there with him forever."

Christopher glanced shyly at Lucy.

It was Lucy who introduced Christopher to the Clock Island books. When the social worker picked him up from the hospital after his parents were declared DOA, she asked him if there were any grown-ups he wanted to stay with for a little while since they couldn't locate any relatives.

He told her, "Miss Lucy."

That was how, for one week, Lucy got to be Christopher's mother. It was summer when she received the call during an evening shift at the bar where she worked while school was out. A co-worker drove her to the police station and then drove them to Lucy's house. Christopher, still in shock, said nothing in the car.

The bar manager was nice enough to give her paid time off while she stayed with the frightened and traumatized little boy around the clock. She'd put down a sleeping bag on the floor by her bed, and given him every extra blanket she could borrow from her roommates—who, for once in their lives, kept the noise down in the house. Desperate to get Christopher talking, she pulled a box from under her bed. When she left Maine for California, she had taken an airplane. She had two suitcases with her. One full of clothes. One full of books. The Clock Island books were the only ones that made the cut. She told him to pick a book, and she would read it to him. He chose *The Moonlight Carnival*, Clock Island Book Thirty-Eight. Why? Probably because the cover caught his eye—the floating Ferris wheel, the winged roller coaster, and the little boy dressed like a circus ringmaster. It was one of her favorite covers too. She tucked Christopher into bed with her, and he rested his head on her arm while she read page after page of the book, waiting for him to say something. When they got to the middle, it was bedtime. When he asked if she would read one more chapter to him, those were the first words he'd said since she'd brought him to her house. And it was the moment she knew she'd do anything for him, anything to make him happy, to keep him safe, to give him a life full of love.

The day the social worker came to collect him to take him to his first foster home, Christopher didn't want to let her go. He clung to her neck and sobbed. That day she promised him she would get him back someday. As soon as she could, they would be a family.

As they pulled up to airport departures, she wanted to tuck him into her carry-on bag and take him with her.

Theresa got out of the car and pulled Lucy's suitcase from the trunk.

"I got you something," Lucy told Christopher.

"What?"

She took the bag from The Purple Turtle out of her carry-on and gave it to him. He opened the wrapped box with wide eyes and found not one, not two, but three sharks.

"Oh, cool . . ." He looked at them in amazement. "I can keep them all?"

"All of them. Which one is your favorite?"

"This one." He cradled the hammerhead shark the way other kids might cradle a kitten.

"Smile!" Lucy took a picture of him holding up his shark like it was flying. Then he threw his arms around her neck and clung to her tightly.

She hugged him back, just as hard. He smelled like No More Tears baby shampoo, her favorite scent in the world.

"I gotta go," she whispered.

Christopher pulled away and smiled bravely. "Good luck."

"I'll need it." She held his face in her hands, met his eyes. "I'll text Mrs. Bailey when I can, and she can give you messages from me. Okay?"

"Okay." He nodded. Then he said softly, "I'll try to answer if you call me."

"You will? You don't have to do that. I can send messages. And I'll definitely bring you Mr. Masterson's autograph."

"And the book?"

Now it was her turn to smile bravely. "You know, there's a chance I may not win it. Four people are competing."

"I wished for you to win it."

"That should do it then." She gave him a last hug, told him she loved him, and then as if ripping off a Band-Aid fast, she got out of the car, hugged Theresa, and took her suitcase.

"Knock 'em dead," Theresa said. "Don't let anyone intimidate you. You're a kindergarten TA. You can handle that? You can handle *anything*."

Lucy blew Christopher one last kiss. He waved out the window the entire time the car was in view.

She took a deep breath and headed into the airport. It had been several years since she'd taken a trip by plane, or any trips at all. She was *really* going back to Clock Island. She still couldn't quite believe it.

By the time she got through security and reached her gate, it was nearly time to start boarding. She anxiously paced, trying to get her nervous energy out before she had to sit for six straight hours. At first, she didn't feel her phone vibrating in the back pocket of her jeans. It stopped and then started again. She pulled it out and saw someone was calling from Maine, an unknown number.

This past week she'd answered every call she'd gotten from an unknown number in case it was Jack Masterson's people calling.

Trying to sound adult, detached, and professional, she said, "This is Lucy Hart."

There was a brief pause before the person on the other end spoke.

"Hey, Goose."

Lucy knew that voice. She knew that voice and hated that voice. Her blood went cold.

"Sean? What . . . Why are you calling me?"

"Heard a rumor you were coming back to Portland for a few days. Congrats, by the way. On this contest thing, I mean. What's that all about anyway?"

She took a deep breath. "You can google it," she said.

Her ex-boyfriend was the last person on the planet she wanted to talk to right now. Actually, no. He was the second-to-last person in the world she wanted to talk to. Her sister, Angie, would be first, but Sean was a close second.

"Why don't you tell me? Sounds fun." Once upon a time, she thought this man hung the moon in the sky just for her. Now she knew he hung the moon in the sky because he wanted her to see how handsome he looked in the moonlight.

"I'm about to board. What do you want, Sean? Seriously."

"Come on, Goose. Don't be like that. I know things ended badly between us. Mostly my fault, but we're both grown-ups. Let's act like it and let it go."

Mostly his fault? *Mostly?*

There was no point getting angry at him. Anger was a form of attention, and he fed off attention like plants on sunlight.

"What can I do for you, Sean?" she said as calmly as she could, though her eyes kept darting to the gate agent, praying they would start boarding soon.

"Let's get coffee when you're in town."

"I can't. I'll be on the island the whole time."

"Island. Nice. Playing in the big leagues again," he said, and she pictured a smug grin on his face. "Good for you."

She didn't say anything to that. She knew better.

"So hey, congrats again. I know you loved those little Clock books. Never understood them myself, but I never really read children's fiction, even as a child. Too simplistic, you know?"

"I'm simplistic," Lucy said.

"Nah. I wouldn't have fallen for you if you'd been simplistic. You're a lot smarter and more interesting than you think you are."

She didn't trust his compliments. By flattering her, he flattered himself because that meant he had good taste. "What happened to 'Stop being so stupid, Lucy'?"

"Hey. As I said, we both behaved badly there. I admit it. Can't you?"

The gate agent at the desk picked up the microphone and announced they would now begin preboarding. Lucy could have kissed the woman.

"I have to go. I'm boarding now. First class," she said because she couldn't help herself. "Bye, Sean."

"Don't hang up," he said. He wasn't begging. This was an order. "I have the right to know what happened with the kid."

She took a deep breath, closed her eyes. She was not going to cry before boarding her plane. She was going to remain calm.

"You're right. You deserve to know," she said. "But why wait until now to call? You never even texted. Not once. In three years."

Was Sean capable of feeling shame? Probably not, but at least she'd finally asked a question he didn't have a slick answer for. She knew why he was calling her now. The contest was all over the news. Sean had heard her name and remembered she existed. Even better—Lucy was getting her fifteen minutes of fame. Why not call and bask a little in that fame? Why not call and make her big adventure about him? Everything in the world was about him anyway.

"I'm asking now, Lucy."

"There was no kid," she said. "Congratulations. You're not a father. Happy? You can admit it."

His cold laugh made the hair on her arms stand up. "I should have known you were lying. Sorry your little game didn't work on me."

"Of course you'd assume I'm as awful a person as you are."

"I don't think I—"

"I don't care what you think. Goodbye, Sean. Never call me again."

"Whatever you—"

Lucy ended the call. She stood up and gathered her bags. It was a relief to rush onto the plane, to settle into the big wide soft chair, to turn her face to the window and hide her eyes. She took slow breaths to calm her racing heart. She hoped whoever sat next to her would think she was shaking because she was afraid of flying, not because her ex-boyfriend still had the power to rattle her like this. She hated that he could ruin her day with one phone call. No, she wasn't going to let him do this to her again. She wasn't a kid anymore. She wasn't his little doll anymore. She wasn't under his thumb anymore. She would not give him the satisfaction.

No, she decided then and there she would win this contest. She would win the book. She would read it to Christopher to celebrate, and the very next day she would sell it to a publisher for as much money as she could get.

Then she would walk into The Purple Turtle with Christopher at her side, and when the shopgirl asked if she could help them, Lucy would say, "Yes. We'll take everything. And gift wrap it, please."

CHAPTER NINE

LUCY ARRIVED AT THE Portland Jetport shortly after six that evening. She was tired, frazzled, hungry for real food, and excited out of her mind. She had enough mental capacity left after the cross-country flight to send Theresa a quick text message saying that she'd made it safely to her first destination. She wasn't sure they'd have cell reception on Clock Island. Jack Masterson was notoriously private and reclusive these days, but then again, so were most Mainers. Still, she worried Jack's people would confiscate their phones. Since she had cell service now, she also sent a text message to Mrs. Bailey, asking her to tell Christopher she loved him, and she was safe, in that order.

She'd been told a driver would meet her at the Jetport's baggage claim and that she should look for a man holding a sign with her name on it. Her flight had landed a little early, so she wasn't surprised when she didn't see her driver in the arrivals area. Lucy found a quiet spot to watch the sliding doors. Part of her hoped she might look up and see her parents or sister coming through the doors or waiting by the baggage carousel for her. Stupid, useless hope. Her family had never gone out of their way for her in her entire life. Her grandparents had loved her dearly, but they'd never truly understood how much being discarded hurt her. To them it made sense that the sick child received the lion's share of attention. Lucy was the lucky one, she was told over and over again. Would she rather have attention, they asked her, or would she rather have her health? If it meant her parents loving her, coming to get her, then she might have cut off an arm for five minutes of their time.

They weren't waiting for her, obviously. Even if they had known what time her flight landed, they still wouldn't have come. This was just an old fantasy of hers that refused to die.

Would she ever stop waiting for her family to show up and take her home?

All around her, she watched families reuniting. Parents hugged college kids who didn't want to be hugged—or at least were pretending they didn't want to be hugged. Husbands kissed wives. Grandkids swarmed grandparents. A little girl about five years old raced to greet her mother as she came down the escalator. At the bottom, the woman swept the girl off her feet. Lucy smiled as the woman held her daughter to her shoulder and patted her back. As they walked past Lucy, she heard the woman cooing in her daughter's hair, "Mama loves you. Mama missed you so much."

See, Mom, Lucy thought. *That's all you had to do. All I wanted was for you to come to my school and let me run into your arms and have you pick me up and carry me away and say, "Mama loves you. Mama missed you so much."*

"Lucy?" She turned and saw an incredibly tall, broad-shouldered man in a black chauffeur's uniform holding a marker board that read, LUCY HART.

She picked up her bags. "That's me."

"Pleasure to meet you, Lucy." He took her suitcase from her. "The car's waiting this way."

He was in his midfifties with a Bronx accent and a big grin. He led her to the curb to wait for him. Five minutes later, he returned in the largest car she'd ever seen in her life.

"Yikes," Lucy said as he got out of the car to open the door for her. "This is a monster truck."

"Stretch Caddy Escalade. Mr. Jack wants the best for his guests. Says he owes it to you kids because you had to hitchhike on boats the last time."

He opened the door for her, and Lucy peered inside. The back seat was cavernous. She'd been in cars like this before with Sean. They always made her carsick. Or maybe that had just been the company?

"Can I sit in front with you instead?" she asked.

The driver raised his eyebrow and said, "Be my guest." He shut the back door and opened the front. Lucy got in, and he went around to the driver's side.

Once he got in, Lucy said, "What's your name? I forgot to ask."

He gave her a look like he was trying not to smile. "Mike. Mikey, if you likey," he said with a wink. Clearly, this was a joke he made a few thousand times a day.

"Thanks for the lift, Mikey."

She pulled her sweater tight around her and stared out the window at the passing streetlights. A few things looked familiar, but most of it passed by in a blur. She took a shuddering breath. She was back. She swore she'd never come home, but here she was.

"You okay, kid? Don't be scared. Jack's a good guy."

She didn't want to unload onto her poor driver her love-hate relationship with her home state. She loved Maine. Everything else—her parents, her sister, her ex-boyfriend, all here in town—she could do without for all eternity.

"Just nervous about the game," she said.

"Sit back. I got the heated seats turned on. And don't you worry. I been sizing up your competition. You'll be all right."

It took about twenty minutes from the airport to the ferry terminal, where a boat would be waiting to take her out to Clock Island. Lucy nervously lobbed questions at Mikey for the entire drive. She learned that she was the last one to arrive, the one and only West Coaster playing the game.

"I'm not very good at games," Lucy said.

"I don't think Jack's gonna make you kids play football or nothing like that. It'll be fun. Don't freak yourself out."

"Too late. I'm freaking out."

Mikey chuckled, then waved his hand. "Don't freak out, kid. It'll be fine. The other contestants are nice. Jack's nice. Hugo's even nice when you get past his, you know, personality."

"Wait, you mean Hugo Reese? The illustrator?"

Hugo Reese wasn't just the illustrator of the Clock Island books, he was her favorite living artist. And she'd met him before. He had been at the house when she'd run away.

"He lives on the island too," Mikey said. "Somebody has to keep an eye on Jack. He's a nice guy. A grouch, but don't buy the act."

"Oh, I remember. Except I bought the act." She laughed.

"You know our Hugo?"

"Know him? No. But he, ah . . . kept me occupied while Mr. Masterson called the cops on me."

She hadn't told Christopher that part, but, of course, that's what happened. You don't get to show up at the front door of a world-famous author without getting the cops called on you. Yeah, Jack Masterson gave her tea and cookies and let her pet his raven, but he couldn't keep her. Some wishes came true, and some wishes didn't, and the *I want to live on a magical island with my favorite author and be his sidekick* was one of the wishes that never came true.

After showing her the flying writing desk, Jack had excused himself, promising her a nice surprise. He returned with a young man in tow.

Lucy still remembered what he looked like. Impossible to forget those electric blue eyes scowling, the messy rock star hair, and, of course, his tattoos.

He had a full sleeve of tattoos on each arm. Colorful swirls of red and black and green and gold and blue. Not rainbows. Not stripes. Just colors. Like his body was a palette. He was more paint than man.

"Lucy Hart, meet Hugo Reese," Jack had said. "Hugo Reese, this is Lucy Hart. Hugo's a painter. He's going to be the new illustrator for my books. And Lucy's come to be my new sidekick. Would you mind showing her how to draw the Mastermind's house? She'll need to know that."

Did she believe that? Did she fall for it? Did she genuinely believe that Jack Masterson was going to let her stay in his house? Be his sidekick? His daughter? His friend? She'd wanted to believe it, so she held out her shaking hand to Hugo Reese.

Hugo only looked at her hand, then at Jack Masterson. "Have you gone soft in the head, old man?" His accent was British. Not fancy British like a prince, more like punk rock British.

Jack Masterson tapped the top of his head. "Hard as a rock."

Hugo rolled his eyes so dramatically that Lucy imagined he could see inside his own skull.

"Take your time," Jack said. "I'll be right back."

They were alone then, she and Hugo Reese. He made her incredibly nervous and not because he was scowling, not because he was the new illustrator of the Clock Island books, but because he was the best-looking guy she'd ever met. Usually she didn't pay too much attention to boys, but she couldn't take her eyes off him.

"Lucy Hart, eh?" he said.

She was suddenly very very *very* nervous. There were cute boys at her school. But Hugo wasn't a boy. He was a man. A really really *really* handsome man.

"You ran away from home? To here? Do you know how incredibly stupid that is? You could have been killed. Did your parents drop you on your head?"

Lucy was taken aback by his anger. She'd expected him to be as nice as Jack.

"Maybe," she said, on the verge of tears. "They don't care about me, so I wouldn't be surprised."

Hugo looked away. "Sorry. My brother's about your age. I'd have kittens if he ran away from home."

Have kittens? She liked that expression. "But Jack said—"

"I don't care what Jack said. You nearly gave him a heart attack showing up at his front door."

Lucy giggled. Hugo glared.

"Sorry, sorry. Just . . . my last name's Hart. I thought you were making a pun. Hart attack." Lucy looked at the floor, then back at him again. "I'm sorry."

His eyes softened. The storm of his anger had passed. She wasn't used to getting chewed out by, well, anyone, much less sexy punk artist guys. It was actually kind of nice that he seemed to care about her safety so much.

"All right, sit down," he said. "And pay attention. Drawing is a skill like driving or roller-skating. You aren't born knowing how to do it. You have to learn it, and if you want to learn it, you can learn it. But if you don't want to learn, don't waste my time."

Nobody ever told her that before, that things like art could be learned. She assumed she didn't draw because she couldn't draw, and here was an actual artist saying she could learn? Wild. Lucy sat down, paid attention, and did everything Hugo Reese told her to do. She screwed up. She started over. She tried and tried again. And thirty minutes later, she had a passable drawing of a spooky-looking house covered in ivy and weird windows like watching eyes.

Not just any house . . . the house on Clock Island.

When she was done with her drawing, Hugo Reese took a long look at it and said, "Not bad, Hart Attack. Keep it up."

She hadn't kept it up, but she never forgot that drawing lesson he gave her or how much she liked being called Hart Attack in that funny way by the best-looking guy she'd ever seen.

Safe to say, she was a little in love with him by the time the lesson was over. And it was over way too soon. Thirty minutes or so later, the office door opened again. She'd looked up, smiling, expecting to see Jack Masterson. Instead, it was a police officer in uniform followed by a woman who said she was a social worker. They were there to take her home.

"Here we go, toots. Boat's waiting."

Mikey's voice dragged her out of the past and into the present.

He carried her bags over to the boat, where the skipper took them and helped Lucy aboard. He settled her in a chair with some hot coffee. She was the lone passenger on the small blue-and-white ferry.

While she still had a few minutes, she checked her phone. Theresa had replied to her text with lots of love, hugs, and well-wishes. Mrs. Bailey replied with a text that Christopher was glad she'd made it safely. That was it.

She put her phone away before she did something pointless like trying to call Christopher and telling him the news about Hugo Reese. All those wild, strange, mesmerizing paintings of the fictional animals that lived on Clock Island or the ghosts that haunted it or the train that stopped on it—though how a train could make it out to an island, the Mastermind could never fully explain . . . Hugo made those. Christopher loved the pictures almost as much as he loved the stories.

Lucy knew she ought to stay inside the cabin with her hot coffee. She couldn't sit still, though. Careful of her land legs, she got out of her seat and went to the door. She pushed it open and went to the railing, clinging tightly to it as the ferry bobbed in the water and sputtered and churned its way to the island.

Breathing deeply, she brought the ocean breeze into her lungs. She couldn't believe how much she missed cold spring nights and the sweet salt air of the Atlantic Ocean. If it were a perfume, she'd buy a bottle and wear it every day. If only Christopher was with her. He dreamed of living by the ocean and swimming with sharks, and they were out here in the water, right under her nose. Sand tiger sharks. Blue sharks. No hammerheads, sadly, but there were great whites, which would certainly impress him. Oh, she'd have to warn him not to feed the seagulls and never pet the seals, but he would love it here. This would be his heaven.

She felt thirteen again, scared to death but excited beyond words. Was she excited about meeting Jack Masterson again? Of course. He was one of her idols. Maybe the one idol who had yet to disappoint her. But more than anything, this was her chance, her one chance, to make something happen for her and Christopher. If she won.

There was the catch. *If.*

The dark sky lightened. The engine changed pitch. The boat slowed.

Up ahead, not too far away, was a house—a big beautiful Victorian house covered in climbing ivy with strange towers that looked down over the beach and the dock and the water.

Her heart pounded like the beat of a drum.

There it was. Clock Island.

In her head, she heard a mechanical voice speaking.

Tick-tock. Welcome to the Clock.

She was back.

PART THREE

Riddles and Games and Other Strange Things

He was there, but Astrid couldn't see him. All she saw was the outline of a face in the shadows by the fire. The Mastermind.

"Sir? Mister, um," Astrid began, and Max coughed. "I mean, Master Mastermind. My brother and I were hoping we could maybe get a wish?"

"A wish?" said the voice from the shadows. "Do I look like a genie to you?"

"Maybe?" Astrid said. "I don't know what a genie looks like, so maybe a genie looks like you."

He said nothing to that, but she saw the shadow that was his face almost smile.

"Master Mastermind?" Max said. His voice was shaking. "Our dad had to move away, far away, for a job. We really miss him. If he could get a job in town, he could come back. We sort of wish for that—"

"Tell me what flies but has no wings," said the man in the shadows. "And you'll have your answer."

Max looked up at Astrid, but she didn't know the answer. Wildly, she looked around the room, trying to get her brain to work, to see if the solution was hiding somewhere. The room was so quiet she could hear the beating of her heart. It sounded like a clock ticking.

A clock ticking?

"Time," she said. "Time flies and has no wings."

"In time, if you're patient, your father will come back to your home."

Max tugged Astrid's sleeve. "Come on. I knew this wouldn't work. Let's go home."

He turned to leave, but Astrid stayed standing where she was.

"I don't want to wait. We miss Dad now. Haven't you ever missed anybody? When they're gone, a day feels like a million years."

Again, the Mastermind was quiet for a long, long time. In fact, he was quiet for so long that time could have grown wings and learned to fly while she waited for him to speak again.

"Will you be brave?" he asked. "Only brave children get their wishes."

Astrid was scared, terrified even. But she lifted her chin and said, "Yes. I'll be brave."

And Max took her hand and said, "I will too. If I have to."

The Mastermind laughed a laugh that was scarier than any scream.

"Oh, you'll have to."

—From *The House on Clock Island*, Clock Island
Book One, by Jack Masterson, 1990

CHAPTER TEN

THE BOAT SLOWED DOWN even more as it neared the long wooden dock. The headlights of the ferry lit up the pier. A man stood at the end. Lucy couldn't make out his face, but it wasn't Jack Masterson. This guy looked too young and too tall. He stood with his hands in the pockets of a dark-colored peacoat facing the night wind as if the cold couldn't touch him. And when the ferry skipper tossed the rope to him, he caught it quickly and tied the boat to the dock with hands that knew what they were doing.

She moved to the front of the ferry, arms tight around herself to fend off the cool evening air. The man on the dock offered his hand to help her out of the boat. She concentrated on not falling as she took the big step up and off.

"Bags?" the man on the dock said. The skipper handed them over and told Lucy a quick good-night.

The man looked her up and down. "Typical Californian. No coat?"

English accent. Sounded familiar. Could it be? But where was the rock star hair?

"No coat," she said, feeling sheepish. She'd talked herself out of buying a winter coat, telling herself she probably wouldn't need it for such a short trip. Turned out she did. "I'm okay. I have a sweater in my bag."

"Here. Put this on." He handed her a man's flannel-lined winter jacket that he'd brought with him as if expecting her to be stupid about her clothes. She did as she was told, grateful for the warmth as she wrapped the oversized coat around her. It smelled, she noticed, like the ocean.

"Thank you," she said. "I don't have a lot of winter clothes these days."

"Of course not," he said. "I'm sure you're not used to being somewhere that isn't actively on fire."

"Offensive," Lucy said, tongue in cheek. "Not inaccurate, but still offensive."

He almost smiled. Maybe. But he didn't.

"This way," the man said and started down the pier toward the house, her suitcase wheels making a *dut-dut-dut* sound as they rolled over the planks. She had to half jog to keep up with his long strides.

"You're Hugo Reese, right?"

He stopped abruptly and looked at her with thinly concealed annoyance. "Unfortunately. Come on. Jack's waiting."

Same Hugo she remembered, even if he didn't look quite so punk anymore. Midthirties, strong jaw, intelligent and intense blue eyes behind a pair of black-framed glasses. He wore a navy-blue peacoat, the collar open to show his very nice-looking neck. She'd thought he was gorgeous when she was thirteen. Now she'd say he was handsome, very handsome, despite the ferocious scowl. Almost distinguished. More professor than rock star these days. She decided she liked the upgrade.

She followed him, wondering how much he remembered from her last visit here. Probably nothing. He was a young man but certainly an adult back then while she'd been thirteen, the most impressionable of ages. She remembered every single word he spoke to her.

She'd been standing in the entryway to the house, the social worker's hand on her shoulder as she told Mr. Masterson goodbye. Jack Masterson gently told her that she would have to go back home, that he hated to make her go, but it was against the law for him to keep the kids who showed up on his doorstep. He wished he could, truly and with all his heart. She could be Thurl Ravenscroft's butler. Maybe when she was older, he said.

Hugo had been sitting on the stairs behind him. As the social worker escorted her out of the house, she heard him say to Jack, "Stop making promises you can't keep. You're going to get somebody killed one of these days, old man."

That made her furious back then. Now that she was twenty-six, she had to admit Hugo had a point. Lucy could have gotten herself killed running away from home because a world-famous author made an off-hand joke in a letter about needing a sidekick.

But she never forgot what Jack Masterson said in reply. "Hugo, always be quiet when a heart is breaking."

Hugo had scoffed. "Yours or hers?" he'd asked.

That was the last time she'd seen Hugo Reese.

"Something wrong?" Hugo asked her. Had she been staring at him? Oops. Lucy was glad the cold crisp air had already turned her face red.

"We met before," she said. "I was just wondering if you remembered."

"I remember." He didn't sound happy about it. Okay, so not a good memory but still better than being forgotten.

"You look different."

"It's called aging. Thank you for pointing it out." Then he turned away from her and said, "Come on. Everyone's waiting."

They reached the cobblestone walkway and followed it to the front door, the same cobblestone walkway Lucy had taken years ago.

She stopped in her tracks and looked up at the house. Every light in every window glowed like Christmas. A metal clock hung over the grand arched double doors, just like she remembered. Already Lucy felt welcome, warm, like this was where she belonged, though she knew she didn't.

"Coming?" Hugo asked.

"Yes, sorry." They headed forward. "I *am* sorry, you know."

His brow furrowed in that fierce scowl she remembered so well. "For what?"

"I don't know if you remember, but you yelled at me for putting myself in danger by running away. Back then, it never occurred to me how much trouble I could have gotten Jack Masterson into by showing up on his doorstep. It was stupid and dangerous and could have hurt his career if it had gotten out that he was, I don't know, *luring* girls to his house."

"He's the one who should be apologizing to you." He glared at the house as if his worst enemy lived inside. "Bloody fool, thinking he can play God to a messed-up kid and get away with it scot-free."

"I wasn't that messed up," she said, trying to make him smile. Didn't work.

"I wasn't talking about you. Let's go."

Without another word, Lucy followed Hugo to the house on Clock Island.

CHAPTER ELEVEN

FINALLY, THE LAST OF the contestants had arrived. Now this bloody game could begin. Hugo was already counting the minutes until it was over and the house was quiet again. Then he could sit down with Jack and let him know it was time for Hugo to get on with his life. With everyone safely here, he relaxed a little. They weren't the obnoxious invaders he'd been dreading. Andre was cordial and curious. Melanie, the Canadian, was endlessly polite. Dustin, the doctor, seemed a live wire of nervous energy. And Lucy Hart? As young and slight as she looked, he might have written her off, but she was the only one of the four who'd had the decency to apologize for putting Jack's entire career at risk by running away to his house. He didn't realize people still apologized. God knew Hugo certainly tried to avoid it whenever possible.

"This way," he said, carrying her bag up the cobblestone walkway to the front double doors. He opened the door for her and let her inside.

She shrugged off the coat he'd given her and held it out to him. "Is this yours?"

"Keep it. I have loads of coats. Unless you have a parka in your suitcase, you might need it. Give it back to me later."

She held it to her chest. "Thanks again." She looked up, then around, turned a circle under the old stained-glass chandelier that hung in the entryway, and smiled. He looked at her, trying to see the scrawny thirteen-year-old he vaguely recalled. What he remembered most about that bizarre afternoon was his absolute fury at Jack for being so stupid as to encourage a troubled kid to think she had a real connection with him just because she read his books. Didn't he realize that every kid on the planet thought they were special, that they'd be princes or queens or wizards if the universe hadn't betrayed them by dropping them into the wrong family, into the wrong house in the wrong city in the wrong world? The last thing those kids needed was to think that some rich and famous writer could and would magically change their lives if they just wished for it hard enough. Poor Lucy Hart had bought into that dream. He hoped she'd woken from it.

Hugo had wanted to be an artist as a kid. He'd sketched and painted ten hours a day, every day, for his entire life before he finally made one single half-decent painting. Wishing hadn't delivered his dream to him; he'd had to work to make it come true.

"The others are in the library," he told Lucy. "We'll get started soon."

She started to pick up her suitcase, but he held out his hand. "I'll take it up. This way."

Lucy followed him into the sitting room. God, she'd really grown up since he'd seen her all those years ago. Pretty girl, he begrudgingly admitted to himself. Brown hair fell to her shoulders in soft waves, slightly damp from the ocean air. Bright brown eyes. Big smile, soft pink lips, and pink cheeks from the cold night air. Jack said she was a kindergarten teacher or something. Did he ever have primary school teachers this young and pretty? Not likely. He would have remembered.

The oak doors to the library were closed. When they reached them, Lucy stopped.

"What is it?" Hugo asked her.

She smiled. "I'm on Clock Island again. This is crazy."

"Every morning I say the same thing. I don't smile when I say it, though." He was joking, but she didn't laugh. She didn't seem to be paying any attention to him. Instead, Lucy Hart was in a trance. Or, more accurately, was entranced. Her purse, which was just a canvas tote bag with the words REDWOOD ELEMENTARY and a redwood tree on the front, slipped down her shoulder and landed with a soft thud at her feet as she turned and gazed around the room.

"We have time. Look around if you want."

"I want."

Jack's house could dazzle anyone. It had dazzled him all those years ago. The room, the whole place really, was something out of a Victorian fever dream. Deep purple wallpaper patterned with silver chains and skulls . . . a ceiling painted the palest sky blue . . . a large bay window that looked down the hill that led to the ocean, not that they could see it now in the dark . . . Lucy paused at the massive marble fireplace, a low fire murmuring inside, and picked up a long piece of rusted metal off the mantel.

"What's this?" Lucy asked. "Railroad spike?"

"Coffin nail," Hugo said.

She looked at him, eyes wide. "From a real coffin?"

"A hundred years ago, this island belonged to a wealthy industrialist's family who buried their dead in their own private graveyard. The pine boxes rot, but the nails don't. Sometimes they work their way up to the surface."

"And onto the fireplace mantel?"

Hugo took off his coat, tossed it over the back of the sofa. "Jack's an eccentric, if you hadn't figured that out yet."

"'Jack's an eccentric,' said the artist who literally painted himself?" Her tone was teasing. She looked pointedly at his forearms.

He'd rolled his sleeves to the elbows. Both arms, from wrist to shoulder, were covered in full-sleeve tattoos, abstract swirls of paint colors so that his arms looked more like a paint palette than a person.

"He's an eccentric and I'm a hypocrite," he said, rather pleased she'd noticed his tattoos. He looked at both forearms, seeing his ink again through her eyes. "Overkill, you think? I blame youth and sambuca."

"No, I like them," she said. "Makes you look like you're made of paint. Paint and pain."

"I'm made of poor decisions," he said, though he was impressed she'd intuited the meaning of his ink. Because what was the life of an artist but paint and pain?

Lucy carefully touched the eye socket of the cyclops skull hanging on the wall by the fireplace, a prop from the Disney Channel film version of *Skulls & Skullduggery*.

"This house is amazing," she said. "I was so nervous the first time, I don't remember much of the house." She studied the wall clock that served as a map of Clock Island, her finger hovering over the times and the little pictures of wishing wells and tide pools . . .

> *The Noon & Midnight Lighthouse*
> *The One O'Clock Picnic Spot*
> *The Tide Pool at Two*
> *Puffin Rock at Three O'Clock*
> *Welcome Ashore at Four*
> *The Five O'Clock Beach*
> *Southernmost Six*
> *Seventh Heaven Guest Cottage*
> *At Eight O'Clock We Wish You Well*
> *The Nine O'Clock Dock*
> *The Forest and Fen at Eleven and Ten*

"How is this place real?" Lucy said.

Hugo shrugged. "Sometimes I'm not sure it is."

She looked up, eyeing the chandelier curiously. "Antlers?"

"Loads of deer on the island. Even some piebald ones."

"Piebald?"

"White with spots. They're rare in the wild, but we have quite a few on the island. Small gene pool. An artist friend of mine in New York uses their antlers to make chandeliers and *extremely* uncomfortable chairs."

She stopped again at a painting hanging over the back of the green velvet sofa. "I don't remember that either."

At a glance, it looked like an ordinary painting of the house they were standing in—the famous house on Clock Island—but if you looked twice, you saw that the windows were painted like eyes, and the grand double front doors resembled a weird laughing mouth.

"You don't remember it because I hadn't painted it yet."

"You tried to teach me how to draw the house."

"I did?"

"Probably not how you wanted to spend your afternoon, teaching a snot-nosed runaway how to draw while waiting on the cops to drag her away."

"I happen to like teaching kids to draw."

"Really?" She raised her eyebrows. He didn't blame her for being skeptical. When he'd started working with Jack on the books, he'd been dragged all over the country on school visits. No one was more surprised than Hugo himself when he realized he enjoyed that part of the job.

"Really."

"You live on the island too?" she asked.

"For the moment," he said.

"I have never been so jealous of anyone in my life. Jack really should have let me be his sidekick."

"It's not all it's cracked up to be. You know how hard it is to get good Chinese takeaway on a private island?"

"Fair point, but I think I could trade takeout for piebald deer on my lawn, pet ravens, and flying writing desks." She raised her hand in his direction. "Plus, this place has its own personal world-famous artist in residence."

"I'm famous only to children under twelve." This wasn't true, but it sounded good.

Lucy looked out the dark bay window, though there was nothing to see but the lights on the dock. "What's going to happen?" she asked.

"I honestly don't know," Hugo said. "He didn't consult me."

Something in his tone must have betrayed something he didn't want to betray. "You're worried about him."

"He's getting older, slowing down," Hugo said. "Of course I'm worried about him." When talking to the children—and the former children—who read his books, Jack's number one rule was *Don't break the spell.* Lucy was under the spell of Jack Masterson and Clock Island. Hugo wasn't about to tell her that it wasn't as wonderful as it looked, that the mysterious, mystical, magical Mastermind from the stories who could solve everyone's problems and grant every child's wish had been drinking himself into an early grave for the past six years.

She looked to the library. Voices murmured behind the closed doors.

"It's safe to go in. It's just a game," Hugo said softly.

She shook her head. "Not to me."

Hugo hesitated before speaking again. "I won one of his games, you know. It can be done, even by a fool like me."

"You did? How?" She sat on the edge of the sofa. Hugo crossed his arms and leaned against the bookcase across from her. A bookcase haphazardly stuffed with rare first editions of legendary children's books—*Alice's Adventures in Wonderland, The Wind in the Willows, The Hobbit, Peter Pan in Kensington Gardens* . . . Books worth a few million dollars displayed as casually as the magazines in a doctor's waiting room.

"Jack never liked his old illustrator. The publisher hired him, not Jack. When his publisher decided to re-release the books with new covers, Jack held a fan art contest. Davey, my younger brother—he loved Jack's books more than life. I'd draw him pictures from the stories all the time—the Storm Seller, the Black & White Hat Hotel, all those. Davey saw a story about the contest and demanded I send in my drawings. Never thought anything of it except I wanted to make him happy. Lo and behold—"

"You won."

He raised his hands to say, guess so. "I won. The prize was supposedly five hundred dollars. That wasn't the real prize. I won the chance to be the new illustrator."

Lucy grinned. "I bet Davey reminds you that you owe him big-time every single day."

"He did, yeah," Hugo said. "He died a few years ago."

She looked at him, her eyes full of tender sympathy. "Mr. Reese, I'm so—"

"Call me Hugo."

"Hugo," she said. "You can call me Lucy. Or Hart Attack, I guess. That's what you called me back then."

"Sounds like me. Classic ass back then."

"Only back then?" she said with a grin.

"Offensive," he said. "But not inaccurate."

"Hey, that's my line."

Hugo wanted to say something, to keep chatting her up, but they were out of time. Every clock in the entire sitting room and library began to toll the hour.

"We should go in," he said when the clocks were silent again. "Jack will show his face soon, I hope."

"Once more into the breach." She reached for the doorknob.

Before he could stop himself, he put his hand on the door, preventing her from opening it.

"Do you remember the name of the man who drove you here?" he asked and immediately regretted it.

"Mike. Mikey if you likey. Why?"

"Never mind. Go on."

She put on a brave face and opened the door.

"Lucy," he said, and she looked back at him. "Good luck."

CHAPTER TWELVE

LUCY'S HAND SHOOK WITH nerves as she pushed open the library door. When she stepped inside the library, three pairs of eyes turned her way, scrutinizing her, sizing her up. Her competition.

She smiled shyly as she made her way into the room. "Evening, fellow runaways," she said, giving them a little wave. "I'm Lucy."

"Hi, Lucy. I'm Melanie. It's nice not to be the only girl here." An Asian woman in her late thirties with a Canadian accent approached her and held out her hand to shake. She was tall and thin with long dark hair pulled into one of those perfectly sleek ponytails that Lucy had never been able to master. She wore a soft cream-colored sweater, cashmere from the look of it, slim dark jeans, and brown leather boots.

Lucy shook her hand. "Nice to meet you."

Melanie waved her hand at a handsome Black man standing by the sideboard in a dark blue suit. "This is Andre Watkins. Attorney from Atlanta."

"How you doing, Lucy?" Andre took a step forward and shook her hand vigorously, like a politician. "You were great on TV. A real pro."

"So were you," Lucy said. "You nearly made Hoda fall out of her chair."

"It's what I do," Andre said. Lucy could picture him running for governor of Georgia in a few years.

"Dustin," said the other man in the room. "Welcome to the party."

Lucy said her hellos. Dustin, she recalled, was the ER doctor. He looked like someone who hadn't seen the sun for a long time. He was wearing jeans and a blazer, a crisp white button-down underneath. Everyone was better dressed than she was. Better dressed and older, and they seemed much more comfortable. She felt as if she'd shown up a day late at summer camp, and everyone had already made friends. It didn't help that the library was so grand and imposing—dark wood and a massive fireplace, dark green wallpaper, and even one of those rolling library ladders.

"Sorry if I held things up. Long flight from California." Lucy found the coffee on a sideboard, poured a cup for herself. Her stomach growled. She hadn't eaten real food since breakfast.

"Thought you were from around here," Dustin said, head cocked to the side as if he were weighing her in his mind.

She hadn't expected these people to know her life story, but if they saw her as the competition, she guessed it made sense. She'd watched them on TV and googled *their* life stories. They'd been watching and googling her too.

"I was, yeah," she said. "Then I moved out to California. Tired of being cold all the time." That was her stock answer, and it usually warded off follow-up questions.

Dustin started to say something else when the door opened again. Jack?

But no, it was Hugo. He walked into the library and stood in front of the fireplace.

"Against my will and my better judgment . . . hello," Hugo said.

He looked simultaneously miserable and handsome. Lucy laughed at him behind her coffee cup.

He might have looked different to her eyes than he had years ago, but Hugo Reese was exactly as she remembered him—crotchety as an old man yelling at kids to get off his lawn. They were the kids, and Clock Island was his lawn.

The contestants all responded with a wary hello.

"I have a message from Jack. My apologies in advance. The message is, 'The game will begin at six o'clock.'"

"Wait, at six?" Melanie said. "It's already almost eight. Six in the morning, then?"

Hugo sighed as if in physical pain. "Name? Hugo Thomas Reese. Rank? Underemployed artist. Serial number . . . I don't know what that means. And Jack's message is, 'The game will begin at six o'clock.' That's what he said, and it's all I can say."

Andre snapped his fingers so loudly that Melanie jumped a little.

"Game begins at six o'clock?" Andre said to Hugo. "That's the message?"

"That's the message."

Andre pumped his fist, then pointed at Hugo. "I got you. Come on. We're going." He waved his hands, indicating everyone needed to stand up.

"Wait. What's happening?" Melanie said as she picked up her purse.

"We're on Clock Island," Andre said. "It's not six o'clock, the time. It's Six O'Clock, the place. Right? I'm right, right?"

Hugo gave a golf clap.

"Knew it. I remember Dad teaching me to drive, saying, 'Hands at ten and two, always ten and two.'"

Lucy was annoyed at herself for not guessing that immediately. She'd seen the clock in the sitting room with her own eyes but couldn't remember what was at the six. Time to stop acting like a fangirl and focus.

"Follow the smell of smoke," Hugo said. "And don't trip and break your legs in the dark."

Andre, clearly ecstatic over his first victory, ushered everyone out of the library with the brisk efficiency of a school principal. He led them out of the house to the front porch. "Let me get my bearings," he said, glancing around.

Lucy smelled the smoke first. Delicious smoke. A bonfire.

"This way," she said and started down a path. Her stomach rumbled and she caught herself hoping there would be hot dogs and s'mores waiting for them.

There was little conversation as the four of them made their careful way on the worn wooden planks toward the scent of smoke. Small solar lights in the ground illuminated their way, but it was still eerie walking under the bright and wild stars. It had been a long time since Lucy had lived anywhere without light pollution. Out here on Clock Island, the stars seemed so close she could imagine lifting her hand to the sky and running her fingertips through them like a slow-flowing river.

The path led them to a sandy patch of beach. Benches and seats made from a tree trunk ringed a firepit. A woman in a white apron pointed them toward a picnic table laden with food and drinks. There were, in fact, s'mores. S'mores galore. And hot dogs and chips. And bottled water and Gatorade. No beer or wine, Lucy noticed, as if they were all still children in Jack's mind.

The night was cool, but the wind had died down at last, and the fire was bright and warm inside the ring of benches. Ten minutes passed. Fifteen. Everyone was comfortably chatting with one another. Melanie was telling Lucy about her children's bookstore in New Brunswick. Dustin seemed to be trying to shock Andre with horror stories from the ER.

The woman in the apron snuck away down the path as if following a secret summons. Just the four of them now. The four of them and a shadow. A shadow of a man outside the ring of benches where the light from the fire couldn't quite reach.

Lucy gasped and covered her mouth with her hands.

"Lucy?" Melanie said. "What's wrong?"

Lucy pointed at the figure in the darkness.

"He's here," she whispered.

The four of them went silent and turned and waited . . .

From the darkness, a voice—solemn yet laughing, stern yet playful, old but young—spoke and said:

"What has hands but cannot hold? What has a face but cannot smile?"

And Lucy answered, "A clock!"

Out of the shadows stepped Jack Masterson.

TO LUCY, JACK MASTERSON looked now just as he had back then—he smiled benevolently, like a kindly king. An old and courteous king in a brown cable-knit sweater and corduroy trousers. Lucy had last seen him in person thirteen years ago when his hair had still been mostly brown. Now it was all white, his beard too.

"Tick-tock," he said. "Welcome to the Clock. Or should I say, Welcome *back* to the Clock?"

They were all silent, all of them, as the man who'd changed their lives spoke.

"I'm not the Mastermind, just his creator," Jack Masterson began, "but I do share one of his powers—I can read minds. I know you are all asking yourselves this one question: Why have I brought you all here?" He went on, "I'll tell you why you're here. Once upon a time, I wrote a book called *The House on Clock Island*. And once upon a time, you read a book called *The House on Clock Island*. Writing that book changed my life. Reading it changed yours. And all of us, I think, are hoping one of my books will change our lives again. The stories write us, you see. We read something that moves us, touches us, speaks to us and it . . . it changes us."

He waved his hand, gesturing at each of them. "You kids are proof of that. Four kids came here because they read a book that inspired them to be brave enough to ask for help. There is nothing braver than a child asking for help. And bravery like that deserves rewarding."

One by one he looked them in their eyes.

He pointed at Andre. "I remember Andre, who wanted to be like my character Daniel, who came to Clock Island to prove his school bullies wrong. I remember Melanie"—he waved his hand at smiling Melanie—"who adored Rowan, the girl who came to Clock Island hoping to stop her parents' divorce. And Dustin, dear boy, wanted to be just like young Will, who ran away to Clock Island, fleeing a cruel father. And Lucy . . ." He grinned at her and Lucy smiled back. "She wanted to be my Astrid, my original heroine. Wanted to be her so much she dressed like her for Halloween. Did you know, Lucy, Astrid lives here? And Rowan? And Will? And Daniel? They're all here if you look hard enough. I'm looking. I can see them now."

With his hand over his heart, Jack said with a voice full of genuine tenderness, "It's good to have my kids back."

"Dammit, Jack," Andre said with real emotion in his voice. "It's good to be back."

Melanie was the first to go to him, almost running. He gave her a quick but tender hug and patted her back like an embarrassed but proud father. Andre went next. Jack beamed at him, told him how proud he was of the pro bono legal work he was doing for children in Atlanta. Dustin was next, and he hugged Jack as if he were reuniting with his long-lost grandfather. Lucy remembered Dustin saying the Clock Island books helped save his life, giving him an escape during a childhood filled with hiding and fear.

Then it was Lucy's turn.

"There's my last sidekick," he said as he gently took her hand in both his hands. He did look older, tired, careworn. As a child, she'd dreamed of having Jack Masterson for a father. Now he looked like he could be her grandfather.

"Lucy, Lucy." He shook his head as if he couldn't believe she'd grown up so much. He smiled, and it seemed he wished to say something but wouldn't let himself. "How was your flight?" he asked instead.

"It landed, so I can't complain." She was beyond flustered. The most famous living author of children's fiction was holding her hand.

"And your drive? Who brought you in?"

"Mikey. Nice guy. Gave me some good gossip."

"Yes, a good man, our Mikey, even if he can't shut up to save his life." He smiled intently, searching her face. "And how are you doing, Lucy Hart?" He had this way of looking at her, as if seeing her as no one else did. Or maybe she imagined that because the Mastermind character in his books did that sort of thing. He could look into your eyes and see the deepest wish in your heart.

"Better," she said. "Much better than the last time we met."

"I knew it would come out all right for you." He squeezed her hands and released them. He turned to face them all. "I knew you'd all be all right. And I see you are. My brave kids. Now brave adults. Ah, I wish we had nothing but time together, but alas"—Lucy decided Jack Masterson was the only man who could get away with using the word *alas* in conversation—"the clock is, as always, ticking."

Lucy returned to her bench and wrapped her—well, Hugo's—jacket tight around her. The night was growing colder, but Jack seemed unmoved by it.

"Perhaps you think you know why you're here—to win my new book. But it's more than that, of course. The first time you came here, you carried in your hearts a wish. A wish to be like the children in my books. Well, now you're going to get it. While you are here this week, you will become, as you once wished, like a character in one of my books. Sadly, I'm not nearly as impressive or shadowy as the Mastermind, but he's authorized me to speak on his behalf. And he has one message for you all. But I don't need to say it. If you've read my books, you already know what he wants to tell you. Anyone?"

Andre furrowed his brow. Dustin stared blankly. Melanie shrugged.

But Lucy remembered. Even Christopher could have told them.

"Um . . . so, if the Mastermind is going to tell us what he tells the kids in the books," Lucy said, "his message will be, 'Good luck. You're going to need it.'"

CHAPTER THIRTEEN

AFTER THEY FINISHED EATING and catching up, Jack led them back to the house. Hugo had stayed behind in the library with his sketchbook, working on something. Maybe the new book's cover? Lucy wanted to peek, but Jack asked them to take their seats. Lucy folded herself into a large armchair patterned in book print. It was a relief to be inside again, warm and cozy. But that relief was short-lived.

"Now," Jack said with a heavy sigh, "I'm afraid that as much as I would have liked to keep this game between us . . . the powers that be had other ideas. Hugo?"

"I'll fetch the brass," Hugo said as he closed his sketchbook and got up and left the room.

"What's the brass?" Andre asked.

Lucy left her chair to pour a cup of tea for herself.

"I am." A woman stood in the library's doorway, wearing an expensive-looking pantsuit. Jack began humming the theme from *Jaws*. Ah, Lucy got the joke. She was a shark—a lawyer.

"My name is Susan Hyde, attorney for Lion House Books, publisher for the Clock Island books. You all will be playing for the only extant copy of—"

"Extant," Jack said, nodding. "Good word."

Ms. Hyde continued, unamused by Jack's interruption. "All contests, riddles, and games have been submitted in advance and approved by us to ensure fairness. In the event of cheating in any form or fashion, including but not limited to using your landlines, smartphones, computers, or any other internet-connected device, you will be immediately disqualified. Colluding with other contestants and/or attempts at bribery—"

"Are always welcome," Jack said. "I accept tens and twenties and chocolate truffles."

Everyone laughed. Everyone but the lawyer.

"First things first," Ms. Hyde said. "Paperwork. Critical paperwork that should have been signed the minute you entered the house."

Jack looked up at the ceiling and said, "Lord, save me from lawyers."

"Hey now," Andre said, half joking.

"Yes, forgive me, son," Jack said. "Would you mind signing some satanic piece of paper that says you won't sue me, my agent, or my publisher if you don't win the game?"

"It's also a release," Ms. Hyde continued. "You won't press charges if you, say, go for a swim and drown."

"I promise if I drown," Melanie said as she got up for tea, "I won't press charges against anyone."

"It's not a joke," Hugo said from the doorway. "The water out here can kill you in a heartbeat."

"It's fine, Hugo," Jack said. "None of them are going to get hurt. Yes?"

Everyone agreed they'd behave.

The lawyer simply said, "Good."

She pulled four clipboards out of her briefcase and passed them around.

"Nobody signs anything yet," Andre said, holding up his hand. "Let me look at it first."

The room fell silent as Andre paced the floor while he read through the agreement. Hugo stoked the fire in the fireplace. Dustin's leg bounced so hard it shook the floor. Melanie sipped her tea. Meanwhile, Jack blithely whistled the theme song to *Jeopardy!*.

Twice.

"Looks good," Andre said. "Nothing out-of-bounds."

He was the first to sign. Lucy took the clipboard and signed her name on the line. If it hadn't felt real before, it did now.

Lucy handed the clipboard back.

"Also," Ms. Hyde continued, "in the likely event that none of you win the book, publication rights will default to Lion House Books."

"In other words," Jack said, "they threatened to sue me if I didn't let them run the show. Don't worry. I think at least two or three of you have a real fighting chance."

The four runaways all looked at one another.

Lucy was strangely delighted by the cryptic remark. It was something the Mastermind would say. He always played fair, but that didn't mean he always played nice.

"Which two or three?" Andre was brave enough to ask.

"Only Lucy and Melanie bothered to ask the name of the driver who picked them up from the airport. Well done, ladies. If that had been a game, you each would have a point already."

"Wait, what the hell?" Dustin said. "You're going to just randomly test us without telling us it's a game?"

Jack grinned fiendishly and said, "Very likely."

He'd meant it as a joke, maybe, but the friendly convivial atmosphere was gone. The tension in the room was thick as fog.

The brass, Ms. Hyde, passed them another sheet of paper with the rules.

There would be games every day, Lucy read. To win the book, a contestant must score ten points. Most games were worth two points to win and one point for second place. Except for the last game. The final game was worth five points.

"Five points for the last game?" Andre asked.

Jack grinned. "I always bet on the underdog."

"And if no one scores the requisite ten points," Ms. Hyde reminded them, "the book will go—immediately—to Lion House."

"Requisite," Jack said, nodding. "Also a good word."

"If one of you does win the book," the lawyer continued, still ignoring Jack, "Lion House has authorized me to purchase the manuscript from you for a very generous six-figure sum."

Six figures. Lucy's breath quickened. One hundred thousand dollars—or maybe more? With that amount of money Lucy could easily afford an apartment and a car and take care of Christopher. It wouldn't last long in California, but it would be a great start.

Jack waved his hand dismissively. "Take it to auction."

"What if two people score ten points?" Dustin asked.

"No one will," Jack said. "It will be very impressive if even one of you does."

Jack didn't seem old now, not when he met her eyes and held her gaze without smiling. She didn't feel like she was in the presence of Jack Masterson, beloved children's author, anymore. Here was the Mastermind, the king of Clock Island, the wizard of riddles, the shadow-wearing secret keeper who gave children their wishes but only if they earned them.

The room turned quiet, hushed, as if secrets were about to be revealed. The only sound came from the ocean breeze rushing past the house and the occasional crackle of the fire.

"Oh, fair warning, there will also be"—Jack paused as if searching for the right word—"*challenges* presented. They will not be worth any points, but if you refuse to meet the challenge, you will be disqualified and sent home. Do we all understand?"

Andre shook his head. "Not really, Jack."

"I can hardly blame you," Jack said, still playing the enigmatic Mastermind. "But let's begin, shall we?"

Outside, the wind blew harder. Lucy took a deep breath.

Let the games begin.

AS THE WIND PICKED up, it rattled the shutters and sent the fire in the fireplace flickering.

Jack waited. The wind died as if he'd asked it to, and it politely obliged. He began to speak:

> *On the moon is a room*
> *With a green glass door.*
> *I can't go in.*

You can't go in.
What is it for?
Kittens go in.
Puppies too.
But no cats and no dogs.
A drill but not a screw.
A queen but not a king.
A rabbi but not a priest.
Kisses allowed but no hugs.
Not in the least.
You can roll there but not rock
And you won't find a clock
In the room on the moon
With the green glass door.
Jill can go in.
Jack can't go in.
So what is it for?

CHAPTER FOURTEEN

A LONG SILENCE FOLLOWED. JACK said, "Two points for the first to correctly guess the secret. One point for the runner-up. Do not reveal the secret if and when you do finally guess it. Just play along . . ."

"O . . . kay," Dustin said. "Got a hint?" He laughed nervously.

"Of course," Jack said. "I'll give you many, many hints."

Lucy took a deep breath.

Jack turned and chose a book off a shelf. "A book can pass through the door," he said. He opened the book and held up a page. "But not a single page can pass."

"What?" Andre asked. He looked around wildly as if searching for clues.

Jack put the book back on the shelf. He started a slow walk around the room. "Coffee can pass through the green glass door," he said as he poured the coffee into a cup and held the cup high as if making a toast. "But not in a mug. Coffee can pass, but not tea."

Melanie said, "Okay, anyone else confused?"

Jack walked over, clapped a hand onto Hugo's shoulder. "Hugo can't pass through the door, but Mr. Reese can."

"Oh, Lord." Hugo groaned so loudly Lucy giggled.

Jack pointed at her. "You can giggle through the door, but you can't laugh."

"Okay, what the hell are you talking about?" Andre demanded. "I don't even know what he's talking about. Anybody?"

"You have to figure it out yourself," Hugo said. "Welcome to my world."

Jack gave a soft, rather wicked little laugh. Lucy could tell he was enjoying himself. Good thing he was enjoying himself. No one else seemed to be having fun.

He walked back to the fireplace and pointed at the painting above it. "A Picasso," Jack said. "It can pass through the green glass door. But not any old painting."

"It's not a Picasso," Hugo said, glaring. "I did that one."

"It's very nice," Lucy said. The painting was eye-catching, bright with wild colors, trees and sand and a house made of squares and triangles.

"You can't pass a compliment through the door either," Jack said. "But you can send through a bit of flattery."

"Useless," Dustin said, collapsing back onto the sofa.

Melanie buried her face in her hands. "What are you talking about?" When she lifted her head, she didn't look quite so perfectly put together as before.

"Shall I give you all another hint?" Jack asked.

They all loudly said, "Yes!"

Jack pointed his finger and scanned the room with it. It landed on Andre. "Andre—what was the last movie you watched?"

"Ah ..." He thought about it a second. "Probably *Star Wars*, with my son."

"Excellent." Jack rubbed his hands together. "I've actually heard of that one. Let's see ..." He snapped his fingers. "Here we go. You can pass Harrison Ford through the door. And also Mark Hamill. You may send in Carrie Fisher, may she rest in peace. And also Princess Leia. But Han Solo isn't allowed, and neither is Luke Skywalker. Billy Dee Williams can pass through the green glass door three times. But certainly, never Darth Vader. He shall not pass."

"Heroes can go through? Not villains?"

"Picasso was not a hero," Hugo said. "Ask any of his mistresses."

"True," Jack said. "But his mistresses are also welcome through the door. As are villains."

Melanie placed her fingertips on her temples and rubbed them as if a massive headache were brewing. "I'm going to scream," she mumbled.

"It has to be one thing," Dustin said, looking up at Jack. "One thing they all have in common, yes?"

"Yes," Jack said. "It's one thing they all have in common."

Jack said nothing as if waiting for them to absorb this hint.

Lucy took a breath. Okay, okay . . . something they all have in common. One thing all those objects and people and concepts had in common . . . Carrie Fisher. Princess Leia. A book. A Picasso. Flattery? What on earth was he talking about?

She closed her eyes, thought long and deep. Jack wrote kids' books. This was probably a riddle a kid could solve.

Something rang a bell . . . the tiniest of bells when Jack said Carrie Fisher. Oh, she remembered. She'd been teaching Christopher how to spell *Carrie*. He had a girl named Kari in his class, so it was eye-opening for him to learn that some words could sound exactly alike but have different spellings. *Kari. Carrie.*

Words. Some words are spelled one way . . .

Lucy felt a little spark fire in her brain.

What they all had in common was that they were all words. Of course *painting, artwork, page,* and *Hugo* were all words too. So it couldn't be that. Still, something about the words themselves, not the meaning . . .

Mr. Reese.

Picasso.

Book.

Harrison Ford.

Princess Leia.

Carrie Fisher.

Billy Dee Williams. Three times.

Three names. Three times. Three names. Three words.

Green.

Glass.

Door.

Thirteen.

She pictured Christopher painstakingly spelling out the name *Carrie* in their thank-you note. She could see his tongue out, and his brow furrowed in adorable concentration as he slowly carved the two Rs into the paper.

C-A-R-R-I-E.

Carrie Fisher.

Princess Leia.

Harrison Ford.

Picasso.

Book.

Green.

Glass.

Door.

Thirteen. Harrison. Carrie. Billy Dee.

Carrie written on their company letterhead. *Carrie*, not *Kari*. *Carrie*, not *Kari*. *Carrie* . . . *Carrie* with two Rs.

Lucy's heart leaped in her chest. Her eyes flew open. She raised her head.

"Sheep can go through the door," Lucy said. "But not their lambs. And a tree can go through the door, but not its limbs."

Jack slowly opened his arms wide, a smile spread across his face. Then he pointed at her.

"She's got it."

SHE'S GOT IT. THOSE were the three best words Lucy had heard in her life.

She beamed in triumph. Jack applauded, but no one else did.

"What?" Andre stood up as if he couldn't sit still anymore. "What the—What the hell do Picasso and some sheep have to do with *Star Wars?*"

"What is it, Lucy?" Dustin asked. "It's killing me."

"No, no, no." Jack wagged his finger again. Dustin looked at Jack as if he were about to bite that finger off. "Lucy, you may be excused. And don't give any hints on the way out. The others can play for one point for second place. Hugo, would you take Lucy to her room, get her some dinner if she wants something more substantial than a s'more."

"I'd be thrilled beyond all comprehension to get out of here," Hugo said as he stood up.

"A thrill can pass through the glass door," Jack said. "But not excitement."

As Lucy followed Hugo from the library, she heard someone moaning in abject frustration.

"Let's go," Hugo said as soon as they left the library. "Before things get violent."

It sounded like he wasn't joking.

She followed him quickly to the entryway, and then he led her up the main staircase. Once they hit the landing, Hugo looked back at her over his shoulder.

"How did you figure it out?" he asked.

Lucy winced. "I wish I could say I was a genius, but I just taught a seven-year-old boy how to spell the name *Carrie*. He thought it had one R, but it has two. Two *R*s in *Carrie*. Two *R*s in *Harrison*. Two *S*s in *Picasso*. Two *E*s in *Reese*."

"Two *O*s in *book*, two *F*s and two *E*s in *coffee*," Hugo said. "Good job."

"It wasn't that hard."

Someone—it sounded like Dustin—yelled out a certain four-letter word that had never appeared in any of Jack's books. She laughed.

"Told you so," Hugo said. "And most people don't figure it out. They get furious, and then they give up and demand the answer. Jack writes for children. His riddles are on that level usually. Kids figure it out quicker than adults because kids are more literal."

"I guess I'm just a big kid then."

She remembered this hallway from her first visit. Turning left, they'd reach Jack's office with his pet raven. They turned right instead. Hugo pushed open a set of oak double doors.

"Over here." Hugo took a set of keys from his pocket and unlocked the door. "Jack gave you the Ocean Room."

He opened the door and switched on the light. Lucy's eyes widened in shock and delight. She thought maybe the Ocean Room would just have an ocean view, but it was so much more than that. The room was painted the palest silvery blue, like the ocean on a winter morning. The brick fireplace had a white mantel, and on the mantel sat a ship in a bottle. The bed was a massive four-poster, big enough for three people.

Hugo showed her the bathroom, the closet where lanterns and emergency supplies were stored, the schedule for the week on the mantel. She ignored the schedule. The painting hanging over the fireplace had caught her attention. A shark swimming not through the ocean but the sky, chasing a flock of birds.

"Nice. One of yours?" Lucy asked.

"One of mine," Hugo said. "It's called *Fly-Fishing*."

"It's wonderful. I know a little boy who'd love it too."

"Son?"

She paused, wanting to say yes. *Yes, he's my son. My son, Christopher. Christopher, my son . . .* But she shook her head no.

"A boy I tutor. Christopher. He loves sharks." She pulled out her phone and before she knew it, she was showing Hugo the picture of Christopher holding the toy hammerhead she'd given him.

"Cute kid. Hair like a mad scientist."

"Tell me about it," Lucy said. "And magical disappearing socks. Would it be too weird to buy sock garters for a seven-year-old? They keep ending up in the toes of his shoes."

"You know how to fix that?"

"Gorilla Glue?"

"Sandals," he said. "I see he's going through the shark-obsessed phase. Dinosaurs are next."

"Dinosaurs were last year," she said. "I'm guessing either outer space or ancient Egypt next."

"Or the *Titanic*," Hugo said. "My brother, Davey, was obsessed with the *Titanic*." He pulled out his own phone and showed her a photo of his brother in front of a poster for a *Titanic* museum exhibit.

"That's Davey?" she asked, smiling at the picture of a boy about ten years old, grinning hugely. He had the slightly tilted eyes and the button nose of a child with Down syndrome.

"Yeah, when he was nine or ten, I took him to the *Titanic* exhibit in London. It was either that or show him the movie, and no chance I'd let him see that movie until he was at least thirty."

"I'm sorry he's—"

"Yeah, me too." Hugo shoved his phone back into his pocket. "Anyway," he said, all business again. "Hungry at all?"

"A little."

"I'll have dinner sent up to you."

"Thank you," she said. He started to leave. "Hey, Hugo? Can I take a picture of that painting for Christopher?"

He gave a look, slightly confused, but then waved his hand. "Be my guest."

After he left, Lucy walked around the room. She couldn't believe it was hers for the entire week. A thick plush comforter covered the bed. The sheets were nautical, white with blue stripes. And when she went to the window, she could see the dark outline of the ocean racing up the sandy beach before quietly retreating, only to race up again, inching closer.

She could have stared at that view all night, but she knew she ought to unpack and settle in. She set her suitcase on the luggage rack and started unpacking. She took out a photograph of her and Christopher that Theresa took of them on the playground and framed for her. Lucy set it on the fireplace mantel.

Now it felt like home.

"Dinner is served."

Hugo stood in her doorway with a covered tray.

"You know you're a really famous artist, right?" Lucy asked him.

"The most famous artist is still less famous than the least famous reality TV star. Where do you want it?"

"Um . . ." She looked around, saw a little vanity with a chair. "There?"

He set the tray on the table. Lucy was starving, so she went straight over and lifted the lid.

"Oh . . . is that lobster bisque?"

"They said you're a Mainer."

"Ayuh," she said.

"Yes, a Mainer, God help us."

Lucy sat down and started in on her lobster bisque. Either she'd been gone from Maine for too long, or this was the best lobster bisque she'd ever eaten in her life. A moan of pure delight escaped her throat, so loud she blushed.

"Sorry," she said. "That was a little pornographic."

"Pleased you like it that much." He wanted to laugh at her, she could tell.

The next bite, she managed to taste without moaning. Hugo, for some reason, was still standing in her doorway.

Another roar came from downstairs, another very impressive display of expletives.

Hugo glanced over his shoulder toward the sound.

"Someone's got their knickers in a twist," he said. "Suppose I ought to go down and make sure no one is about to bludgeon Jack with the fire poker."

"Good luck."

He took a melodramatically deep breath and started to turn.

"Hugo?"

He looked back at her.

"Why did you give me a hint?"

He furrowed his brow. "I didn't."

"You asked me if I remembered the name of the man who drove me here."

"I asked. I didn't tell you the answer." He shrugged. "Just curious if you were a contender or not. Turns out you are." Someone suddenly yelled out, "Shit!" from downstairs. Hugo glanced over his shoulder. "Right. That's my cue to save Jack's life. Night, Lucy."

"Hey, just a sec."

She got up and opened her bag. From it, she pulled out a scarlet red scarf she'd finished knitting on the airplane. "Here," she said, offering it to him.

He took it and looked at it. "Pretty. But—"

"I make and sell scarves on Etsy. You lent me your coat. You can keep the scarf as collateral until I leave."

"Thank you." He wrapped it around his neck and suddenly looked very sexy wearing something she'd made. Lucy felt a blush beginning and sat down to eat again before he noticed.

"Anyway, good luck down there," she said. "Please don't let them kill Jack."

"No promises." He paused in the doorway. "Keep your door locked tonight. As of now, you're in the lead. Don't let them put you in cement shoes."

"I'll sleep with the harpoon just in case."

An actual, if small, antique harpoon hung on the wall over the door. "Good thinking."

With that, Hugo left. Lucy got up and shut the door, locking it as ordered.

Then she finished her lobster bisque, took a long shower in the *en suite* bathroom, put on her pajamas, and crawled blissfully into bed. The sheets were luxurious, soft, and scented with lavender.

Ten o'clock in Maine was only seven P.M. in Redwood. She didn't know if Mrs. Bailey would pass on the message, but she couldn't help herself—she sent a text message.

Can you please tell Christopher this message? I'm winning so far.

Lucy waited. She'd almost given up when her phone vibrated in her hand.

He's screaming.

So was Lucy, on the inside. Lucy wrote back, *When you gotta scream, you gotta scream.*

There was no reply after that. Now seven-thirty. Christopher would probably be getting his bath and into bed soon. But that was fine. Lucy needed to sleep anyway. And she would sleep well tonight. She'd not only won the first game, she'd won it easily. The others were still downstairs racking their brains.

A lawyer.

A doctor.

A successful businesswoman.

And Lucy Hart, kindergarten teacher's aide, ten grand in credit-card debt, three roommates, no car . . . she had wiped the floor with them.

What if she could actually pull it off? As long as she didn't screw up, didn't make stupid mistakes, didn't let anything distract her or throw her off track, then maybe, just maybe, she could win this thing. And she could do it all on her own. She didn't need a plan B, didn't need to give up the two precious hours she spent every day with Christopher, wouldn't need to go begging to her parents or sister, guilt-tripping them for help or money. Mrs. Costa said it took a village to raise a child. Maybe for some people, but maybe Lucy didn't need a village. Maybe she could do it on her own.

Lucy decided to try success on for size. She imagined the moment she would call and tell Christopher the news. Sure, he was scared to talk on phones right now, but this was a dream, so why not dream big?

She imagined calling him, the sound of the phone ringing, and hearing his tentative "Hello?" at the end of the line.

She wouldn't say "Hello" back. She wouldn't say, "Hi, how are you?" Lucy already knew what she would say to him.

"Christopher . . . I win."

CHAPTER FIFTEEN

IN THE SITTING ROOM, Hugo waited for the game to end. As he sketched ideas for the new book cover, he eavesdropped. He could hear everything through the closed doors of the library—the wild guesses, the groans of frustration, loads of begging for more and more and more hints.

It was nearly one in the morning when Jack asked Andre, Melanie, and Dustin if they were ready to give up. If they all agreed to forfeit the single point for coming in second, Jack would tell them the answer.

They jumped at the chance to give up. When Jack told them the secret of the green glass door, the house echoed with screams. Hugo chuckled. Oh, he hated riddles when he was on the receiving end, but he didn't mind them so much when Jack inflicted them on unwanted houseguests.

All three bleary-eyed contestants shuffled out of the library, mostly silent but for Melanie who muttered to herself, "Billy Dee Williams? How did I not see it?"

"I didn't see it either," Hugo told her. "Hope that helps."

"No, it doesn't help," she said. "At all. In the least."

Hugo bade them all good night with a jaunty, "Better luck tomorrow." When Jack didn't follow them out, Hugo closed his sketchbook and went into the library. He found Jack with an antique carriage clock in his hands, winding it with a tiny key.

"You're up late," Jack said as he turned the clock to face him, checking the time against his wristwatch.

"Am I? Didn't bother to check the time."

"In this room, that's an act of aggression," Jack said, nodding sagely toward the wall of clocks, nearly fifty of them in total. "Come to scold me again?"

Hugo stood with his back to the fireplace. The fire had died down, but ambient heat still radiated from the embers.

"I won't scold you. Just curious how you're enjoying having company?"

He nodded, looking pleased. "It's been better than I hoped. They're wonderful kids."

"They're all middle-aged and miserable like the rest of us."

"I wouldn't call Lucy Hart middle-aged." Jack picked up a second clock, an old-fashioned alarm clock, and wound it back to life. "Glad to see her win the first game. She seemed a little out of her depth around the older kids."

"It's such an unbearably stupid game."

"It's just a silly old game we played at summer camp," Jack said.

"Was your camp counselor named Lucifer by any chance?" Hugo sat on the hearth, his sketchbook on his lap.

"Can't recall his name, but he had a nose a proboscis monkey would envy. When he breathed in, we had to cling to a sturdy tree to keep from being sucked up into his sinuses." Jack looked at Hugo's sketchbook on his lap. "I always envied people who could draw. Takes me fifty words and ten metaphors to say a character has a gigantic schnoz. You can do it with one pencil stroke."

"I always envied writers who sold six hundred million books."

"Ah, touché." Jack chuckled softly.

Sometimes Jack was in the mood to talk at night. Sometimes Hugo could ask a thousand questions and get zero answers. What would it be tonight? Hugo decided to spin the wheel and take his chances.

"I've been attempting to work up a cover for this book of yours, but

I'm not having much luck, as I have no clue what it's about." Hugo spun his pencil between his fingers, then pointed it at Jack. "Why is that?"

Jack waved a hand, dismissing Hugo's concern. "You wouldn't be the first cover artist to create a cover without reading the book."

"True, but could I at least get a hint?"

"Do something like, oh . . . *The Keeper of Clock Island*. That was always my favorite of your covers." Jack gave him a wink for seemingly no reason, though surely there was one.

"This new book does exist, yes? This isn't like my fan art contest, where I was supposed to win five hundred dollars? I'm still waiting on that check."

Jack was setting the time on an *Alice in Wonderland* clock that ran backward. "Would you rather have had the five hundred bucks or the job of illustrating my books?"

"Wouldn't say no to both."

Jack chuckled. "The book exists. And there is only one copy of it in the world. I typed it up and hid it away."

"And you're seriously going to entrust it to some stranger?"

"No, but I shall whimsically entrust it to some stranger."

"The sharks are already circling. Rare books collectors, billionaires, social media influencers . . ." He shuddered dramatically in mock horror at the word *influencer*. But it was true. Collectors had even called him, told him to name his price if he could get his hands on Jack's new book.

"So be it," Jack said. "I trust the kids will make the right choice."

"Don't know about the others, but Lucy Hart seems decent enough," Hugo said. "She's the only one who apologized for jeopardizing your career by showing up at your front door."

"Is that a new scarf?" Jack asked. "Doesn't Lucy knit scarves like that? Do you always wear scarves indoors, or is this a new fashion statement?"

Hugo glared at him. "You are deliberately trying to change the subject."

"What is the subject?"

"The book. This miraculous out-of-nowhere book. You aren't dying, are you?" Hugo asked. "Just tell me you aren't dying."

"Hmm . . . *The Nowhere Book* might be a good title."

"Jack."

Smiling, Jack plucked a singing bird clock off the wall. With his sleeve, he dusted the face of it.

"I am not dying," Jack said. "I've simply come to the realization that the amount of sand in the top of my hourglass is far less than the sand in the bottom. I want to keep my promises before it runs out entirely. Especially my promise to you."

Jack glanced at him out of the corner of his eyes, then returned to his clocks. "What promise to me?"

"The promise I made when I told you I would be all right if and when you finally left the island and moved on with your life."

Hugo tensed. "You know?"

"I know. I know you've had one foot out the door for years. And I know," he said as he placed the clock back on its nail, "the only reason you stayed."

"Care to enlighten me?"

"Because I'm like a father to you. You know how I know that?" He straightened the clock on its hook.

"Because I've said it?"

"Because you resent me. Just like a son would."

Hugo felt his heart deflate like a popped balloon. "I don't—"

The song sparrow began to sing. "That's our cue," Jack said. "You should get some sleep, son. I'll see you at the crack of the Eastern bluebird for breakfast. The red-winged blackbird at the very latest."

Jack started for the library door. He paused and turned back.

"You don't have to worry about me. I know exactly what I'm doing and why I'm doing it."

Hugo wanted to believe that. Like a clock with invisible gears, Hugo could see the work of Jack's hands, but he never figured out quite what made the old man tick.

"At least one of us does," Hugo muttered as Jack turned to go. "Jack?"

He looked back at Hugo, who stood up to face him.

"I don't resent you. It's the bloody world I resent. Look at you. You create stories children love and donate wads of cash to hospitals and children's charities and commit no crimes but the crime of caring too much sometimes, trying too hard . . . and when I leave, you'll end up alone in an empty house with only a bottle of wine and an elderly raven for company."

Jack scowled at him. "Let's hope Thurl didn't hear you call him elderly. You know he's very sensitive." Then his face softened. "I don't want to see you alone either. And I do like that new scarf," Jack said, laughing quietly to himself as he walked away.

LUCY WOKE WITH A start. Heart racing, she listened for something, anything, to explain what had jolted her out of a deep sleep. She glanced at her phone for the time—almost one in the morning.

"Hello?"

Someone knocked softly on her door.

"Who is it?" Lucy's voice shook. Why would someone be knocking on her door this late?

No one answered. She flipped on the bedside lamp and got out of bed to check the door. A white envelope lay on the rug. Someone had slipped it under the door?

Lucy picked it up, then unlocked the door.

The hallway was empty and dark.

She shut the door, locked it again, then sat on the bed. She pulled a card from the envelope and read it.

Meet me at the City of Second Hand if you want to win a prize.

What was this? She knew the City of Second Hand from the books, a tiny town that seemed to disappear and reappear at the whim of the Mastermind. Whoever left the note had drawn a map for her. Apparently the City of Second Hand sat in the very middle of the island.

Was this a game? One of Jack's mysterious challenges he'd warned them about? She couldn't think of what else it could be, though it seemed strange to be playing in the middle of the night. Maybe they thought she'd still be awake? One A.M. in Maine was only ten P.M. in California.

Lucy decided to go just in case. She wasn't about to let a little cowardice and jet lag keep her from winning.

Lucy threw on her clothes—jeans, a long-sleeved T-shirt, socks, shoes, and then, finally, the coat Hugo had lent her. When she wrapped it around herself, she smelled the salt of the ocean, the salt of sweat, and a more subtle scent like pine or cedar, like an evergreen forest. It must have been from his soap or his shaving cream.

She took the lantern from the closet. Quietly, she slipped out of her room and into the hallway, then down the stairs. She smiled at the ancestral paintings in their gilt frames on the wall. She remembered those from last time. A plaque on one painting read, I HAVE NO IDEA WHO THIS MAN IS.

Nice to know Jack Masterson was as strange and whimsical as his fictional alter ego, Master Mastermind.

The bottom step creaked loudly. Wincing, she froze and waited, but no one appeared to send her back to bed. She went to the front door, opened it carefully, and slipped out into the night feeling like that brave and wild child who'd run away from home to seek her fortune here on Clock Island. Now she was doing it again. Maybe this time, she'd find it.

With a push of a button, her lantern came on. Warm yellow light cast a fairy circle around her feet. She followed the cobblestone walk to where it wound around the house, then past the garden gate.

Back when she'd lived with Sean, she'd spent a little time among the rich and famous. She'd visited her fair share of country estates and mansions and seen their overly manicured lawns with their infinity pools, fake Roman statues, and massive fountains. Nothing like that here. No infinity pools. No Roman fountains. No weird shrubs trimmed to look like no trees in nature should ever look.

There was nothing there but a forest, a real forest, deep and dark.

She was shivering, but Lucy followed the path into the trees toward the center of the island. She felt like Astrid with her flashlight, sneaking around Clock Island. At thirteen she would have killed to be here. She wished she could go back in time and tell her younger self to just wait, she would get her chance someday.

On her left, sudden movement . . . A small herd of deer dashed through the woods. The lantern light revealed that a few were spotted white all over. The piebald deer Hugo had mentioned. It was like seeing a fairy in the forest.

She stepped back to give them room to run and nearly tripped when her foot hit something hard. Lucy lowered her lamp to see what she'd stumbled over. She expected to see a rock or tree branch.

Iron. An iron rail. And connected to it was a wooden plank. A cross-tie.

Train tracks? Was there a train on Clock Island? She thought that was just in the books. Who installed a train on a ninety-acre island? The rails were narrow, however. These weren't for Amtrak, that was for sure. Lucy followed the tracks for about a hundred yards or more until she came upon a wooden sign staked into the ground. Painted on it were the words WELCOME TO THE CITY OF SECOND HAND. POPULATION: YOU.

Lucy smiled. She'd found it. She passed the sign and stepped onto a cobblestone road. The trees were sparse, so the stars and the moon illuminated the town as she walked deeper into it, waiting for someone to come out and ask her a riddle or give her a challenge to complete. But it seemed she was alone in the little city.

On her left, she found the little red post office where you could send a letter anywhere in the world. The stamps were all clocks. One of the books even came with a sheet of clock stamps. But the window was dark and the red door locked. On her right stood a narrow three-story building, which tilted a little to the left. THE BLACK & WHITE HAT HOTEL, said the sign on the awning. Oh yes, she remembered this place. Sometimes the kids in the stories would have to go there to meet someone who could help them on their quest. The one rule of the Black & White Hat Hotel was that you had to wear a black-and-white hat at all times. According to the books, they served delicious gossip and even better chocolate-vanilla-swirl ice cream.

But it, too, was dark and locked up tight. And so was Redd Rover's Treasure Hunt Supply Store (free shovel with purchase of one bucket) and the Clock Island branch of the Library of Almost Everything. Kids could go into the library and check out anything they might need for their adventure, including but not limited to Ms. Story, Clock Island's seemingly immortal librarian. She was always happy to help if she wasn't too busy feeding Darles Chickens, the library's resident rooster.

Lucy peered into the windows of the library. She saw books turning to dust on the shelves, but sadly, no Ms. Story behind the counter. No rooster perched on a stack of overdue books.

The whole place was a ghost town. Could a town be a ghost town if no one had ever lived in it? The paint was peeling. The windows were clouded. Why had Jack given up on this place?

As she went deeper into the ghost town, she finally saw the train station. The building looked like the picture on the book cover, a pale green rectangle with THE SECOND HAND DEPOT painted on the side in large block letters. The train was parked at the station—a black-and-yellow miniature locomotive with a couple of passenger cars hooked to the engine. It reminded her of those trains at children's parks, only big enough for a dozen kids and their parents. The poor train was covered in bird droppings. A destination sign pointed down the tracks. SAMHAIN STATION. In the stories, a child might board the *Clock Island Express* for Samhain Station, where the Lord and Lady of October reigned and it was Halloween every day.

But the train didn't look like it was going anywhere anytime soon. In fact, it appeared the track had never been finished. The whole place had the feel of a lost cause about it.

It reminded her of the night her grandparents had taken her to live with them. She'd been at the hospital for hours by the time they finally arrived. Since she'd had no extra clothes with her, they'd had to run back to her house to pack her bags. In her attic bedroom, a puzzle lay unfinished on the floor—two kittens in bow ties. One of Angie's cast-off toys. Lucy could have put the pieces into the box and taken it with her, but she didn't. Her sister was going to be in the hospital for a long time, and Lucy had to go live with her grandparents. Kittens in bow ties suddenly seemed so stupid and childish.

That's what this place reminded her of, that puzzle left behind, never finished. Lucy knew something bad had happened here. Jack Masterson hadn't retired from writing because he was so rich he never had to work again. No, for some reason, he'd lost heart.

She wanted to leave, to go back to the house. But who had left that note? Lucy was about to give up when she spotted lights on in a quirky-looking cottage, painted white and gray with a circular front door like a hobbit house. The painted sign by the front door read, THE STORM SELLER.

Even though she knew it would be locked up like the other buildings, she turned the doorknob anyway. Surprisingly, the door opened. Ten thousand tiny fairy lights illuminated the shop like ten thousand winking stars.

Walking through the Storm Seller made her feel like she was stepping into the temple of her childhood dreams. She'd always wanted to come to this strange little store where a peculiar little man sold storms inside jars, bottles, and boxes. Just like in the books, here was a crystal triangle in a glass vial claiming to be *The Tip of the Iceberg*. A white ceramic jug on the shelf next to it held *A Rain to Hide Your Tears*.

Someone had gone to a lot of trouble to get the Storm Seller just right. It was like being in a medieval apothecary's shop. Jars, bottles, and carved wooden boxes sat here, there, and everywhere on shelves and tables and racks. Handwritten paper labels revealed what was inside. Lucy picked up one jar and read, *The Storm Seller at Clock Island—Snow Day in a Jar.*

The blue glass jar was eerily cloudy as if there were a real snowstorm trapped inside, and if she were to open the lid, snow would cover the island, and no one would have to go to school tomorrow. She looked at the other jars on the shelves, so lovingly re-created from the stories.

The Wind in Your Sails.

Stolen Thunder.

A shimmery gray ribbon in a glass box proclaimed itself *A Cloud's Silver Lining.*

A Wind in Which to Throw Your Caution.

A clear glass sculpture of a human head held a *Brainstorm*.

She was tempted to steal the *Tempest in a Teapot* since it came in an actual pale blue teapot. She held it in her hands for a long time before she put it back on the shelf.

"Take it, kid. Nobody'll miss it."

Lucy spun around. A man in a gray overcoat was standing at the back of the shop. He looked about fifty with steel-gray hair and steely eyes.

"Who's winning?" the man asked.

"I am. Two points. Who are you?" Lucy asked.

"My card," he said with an unctuous smile. He stepped out of the shadows and passed her a business card. *Richard Markham, Attorney.*

"You're a lawyer?"

"I have a client," he said, "who is very interested in buying Jack Masterson's new book."

"Do they want to publish it?"

"He's a collector of rare books. The only copy of what may be the last book in the bestselling children's series in history is about as rare as it gets, Lucy. He's willing to go as high as eight figures. Eight figures. Not low six, which is what you'd get from Lion House. Cheapskates. Six figures will last you six months in California."

"Does he just want the original manuscript? I mean, can we make a copy—"

"No copy. You walk off this fantasy island with the book, you hand it to me, I hand you the check. The end."

That meant not even Christopher would get to read it.

"I can't do that. Kids all over the world want to read that book." She tried to give the card back to him. He held up his hand, leaned in close, so close she stepped back, hitting the shelves. The glass bottles rattled.

"Can I ask you a personal question?" Markham said. Without waiting for her answer, he asked, "Why would a sweet girl like you date an asshole like Sean Parrish?"

"What about Sean?"

He shrugged. "Sean Parrish. Big-time author. Not as big as Jack Masterson, but who is, right? You met him in a writing class you took at school. Six months later, you start shacking up with the man. For the money, right? God knows it wasn't love. But me? I don't judge. I love gold diggers. Married one." He laughed like he'd made the funniest joke in the world.

"How do you know all this?"

"I know a lot of stuff. About you, about Andre Watkins, Melanie Evans . . . I know your parents sent you to live with your grandparents. I know you have no relationship with your family anymore." He gave her a thumbs-up. "I like that about you, Lucy. I'm a big believer in cutting my losses. Except now, here you are," he continued, "twenty-six years old. The kids you went to school with are getting married and having babies. Meanwhile, you're so poor you can't pay attention."

"You think because I'm broke I'm going to sell the book to a collector who will lock it up forever?"

"Why not, sweetheart? I would. Wouldn't it be fun for your sister to show up on your doorstep one of these days begging for a second chance just because you're rich as God? Success is the best revenge, Lucy. And eight figures can buy a whole lot of revenge."

"I don't want revenge," she said.

"*Sure* you don't. But you want something. We all want something, don't we?" He reached into the breast pocket of his jacket. She expected him to pull out a handkerchief or another business card. Instead, she saw he had Christopher's school photo tucked inside. He flashed it at her before tucking it back into his coat pocket. "Everybody wants something."

"You should leave. Now."

"Fine, but uh, hold on to that." Gently he folded her hand over the card, then softly said, "*Carpe per diem*, Lucy. Seize the money."

With those words, he left her alone among the storms.

CHAPTER SIXTEEN

HUGO DEPARTED JACK'S HOUSE through the back door, which took him through the garden and down a path to his cottage. He was dead on his feet when he spotted Lucy walking alone toward the abandoned Clock Island park.

Not a good idea in the middle of the night. There were railroad tracks to trip over, and the stupid buildings in the park were probably about to implode. He told himself she was allowed to walk around the island if she wanted to, and she did have her lantern. But halfway back to his cottage, he turned around and headed into the woods to find her and make sure she was all right.

He jogged past the library, the post office, and the hotel until he saw the lights were on in the Storm Seller. As he reached the door, it opened and Lucy stepped out. She searched the surrounding darkness with the light of her lantern, her eyes frantic.

"Lucy?"

"Hugo," she said breathlessly, "did you see him?"

"Who?"

She turned in a circle, ran a few steps toward the woods.

"What's wrong?" Hugo demanded.

"There was a man here," she said. "Now he's gone. He was just here."

"What man? Lucy?" He took her gently by the arm.

She exhaled. In the cold night air, it looked like she was breathing clouds. She handed him a business card, then told him a wild story about someone knocking on her door, a card inviting her to the park, a man who claimed to be a lawyer but talked like a television Mafia hit man.

"I thought it might be part of the game," she said. "Some challenge or something."

Hugo read the business card by the light of Lucy's lantern.

"I know this name," Hugo said. "Offered you a ton of money for Jack's book, right?"

"Yeah, he did. Eight figures."

"Bastard. He only offered me seven."

He was joking, hoping to make her feel better. Must have been terrifying for her, being lured out of her bed in the middle of the night, not knowing why.

"I'll have to tell Jack, get some extra security on the island maybe. I'd bet he has a boat waiting for him at the Nine."

"The Nine? Wait. The Nine O'Clock Dock?"

He nodded, impressed with her memory. No wonder she was winning. As smart as she was pretty.

"Is he really a lawyer?" Lucy asked. She kept turning her head, looking around as if afraid he'd come back. "He was creepy."

"Real lawyer. Works for that Silicon Valley billionaire who wants to program AI to write novels. He ought to be flogged and forced into a three-year MFA program."

"Brutal," Lucy said with a little laugh. She took another deep breath, blew out another cloud. "All right. Note to self—don't trust every single piece of paper someone slips under my door."

"Good plan. Come on. Let's get you back to the house."

They found the path and started down it. Lucy wrapped herself up tighter in the coat he'd lent her. Hugo wondered if it would smell like her when she returned it to him. Wait, why was he wondering what her skin smelled like?

"I had planned on exploring the island," she said, "but not at two in the morning. What is this place anyway?"

"Supposed to be a park for the patients at the children's hospital in Portland. Jack wanted families to visit, to let the kids forget they were sick for a day or two."

"Oh, I'm very *very* familiar with the children's hospital." Her voice sounded world-weary.

"Were you sick as a child?"

She shook her head. "My sister. She was a PIDD kid. That's a catchall term for children with compromised immune systems. She was sick all the time. I couldn't even . . . I wasn't even allowed to live at home with her."

His heart tightened. Davey had never been very healthy either, but he couldn't imagine being separated from him. That would have been torture.

"That's terrible. For you and her."

Lucy shrugged as if it had been no big deal, but the look in her eyes gave away the pain.

"My sister's probably the main reason I ran away. She made it pretty clear that she liked not having me around. I guess I thought that if I could get here and live with Jack . . ." She paused, exhaled. "I don't know what I was thinking. Cry for attention, I guess."

"You wanted to go home," Hugo said. She looked at him as if he'd hit a tender spot. But then she smiled.

"That's it exactly. I had it in my head that this was my real home. Kids do that. We all think we're aliens, and we can't believe our parents are really our actual parents. I'm sure I'm one of a million kids who wanted Jack to be their father."

"One of a billion," Hugo said. She smiled again.

"Well, that didn't work out, but if I had to do it all over, I still would. Especially because I'm here now."

He pointed to the tracks ahead. Lucy stepped lithely over them, and they continued down the path.

"What happened to the project?" she asked. "Why didn't it get finished?"

"Same reason Jack quit writing."

"Why did Jack quit writing?"

Hugo didn't answer at first. He remembered Jack's number one rule—*Don't break the spell.*

"Let's just say he went through a rough patch," he finally said. "A rough patch that's now been going on"—he checked his watch—"six and a half years."

Lucy looked at him, eyebrow arched. "That's more than a patch. That's a rough cross-country highway." He couldn't argue with that. "Is he finally over the rough patch?"

"Damned if I know," he said. "Hope so. Don't know if he is or if he's faking it."

"He seemed happy tonight."

"Happy? Jack's forgotten the meaning of *happy*." Hugo stuffed his hands into his coat pockets, kicked a stone off the path into the woods. "Beautiful private island, three-hundred-sixty-degree ocean view, house anyone would kill to live in . . . and for years he's been the most miserable man on Earth. Jack is living proof that money does not buy happiness."

"Maybe not for him, but it would for a lot of people," Lucy said, her tone gently chiding. He didn't buy it.

Hugo shook his head. "I've met those supposedly happy people with money. They're miserable, just like everyone else. I speak from experience, having both money and misery."

"Money would buy my happiness."

He rolled his eyes. He couldn't help himself. She was living in a dreamworld. "Are you already spending the money you'll get when you sell Jack's book to Markham or some other bottom-feeder?"

She turned and glared at him. "What? Like you've never imagined what you would do if you won the lottery?"

"The lottery isn't the only copy of a children's novel in existence. And yes, I have imagined it, but unlike you, I've been the guest at many castles in the air. Too draughty for my taste but keep wishing and hoping for one if you want. Maybe you'll get one someday."

She gave a cold, resentful little laugh, surprisingly bitter. "I've visited my fair share of castles, and I have no interest in buying one of my own. All I want is a house and a car for Christopher and me."

She stopped at a gas lamppost and faced him. The warm light illuminated her cheeks, flushed pink from the cold. He found himself staring at her lips. Pale pink lips, soft, made for smiling, though she wasn't smiling now.

"Christopher?"

"The boy I tutor."

"You're buying him a house? A bit above and beyond the call of duty," he said.

"He's not just a child I tutor, okay? He was in my class two years ago. Great little kid. Right away, though, I could tell he was struggling at home. His father was a construction worker before he was injured on the job. He got hooked on painkillers. His mother did too. It happens all the time. His parents loved him, but I could tell he was struggling at home. He was withdrawn some days, clingy other days, cried to go home half the time, didn't want to go home the other half . . . but smart. God, *so* smart. Reading was his strong suit, so whenever he was having a bad day, I'd get a little group together, and we'd just read. But there's only so much you can do for a kid in your class when you have twenty other kids to teach. Summer came, and then school was out. One day I got a call from a social worker. She told me Christopher Lamb's parents had died from an overdose. A bad batch of something got around. Sixteen people in the city overdosed that day, and eleven died."

"Damn," Hugo said.

She didn't look at him, just kept talking. "Christopher stayed with me for a week until they found a foster home for him. I would have sold a kidney to keep him. But I can't even afford to foster him, much less adopt him. I have three roommates and no car, credit-card debt, and a job that pays minimum wage. Oh, and I have a hole in my favorite shoes."

She held out her foot to display a small hole where the canvas of her trainer had come away from the rubber sole.

"So maybe I *will* sell the book to the highest bidder." Her tone was sharp as a knife. Every word cut him. "You live on a private island. Easy for you to say money doesn't buy happiness when you have money. It would buy a lot of happiness for Christopher and me. And forget happiness." She waved her hand as if she were erasing him and every stupid thing he'd just said. "For once in my life, I would love to spend fifteen dollars on a toy for Christopher without getting sick to my stomach. Sorry you disapprove of me daydreaming about the money a little bit, but that's all Christopher and I have right now—wishes and dreams. But it's better than having nothing."

"Lucy, I'm—"

"You know what teachers call kids like you when we're all gossiping in the teachers' lounge?" She slapped her hand against his chest. "Spoiled brats."

He looked at her, his jaw clenching. "Now that's unfair."

"Wake me up when the world is fair. Good night, Hugo. I can find my way back alone."

She walked off. Hugo just stood there. What could he do but watch her go?

A flutter of white caught his eye. Paper. He picked it up off the ground. She hadn't slapped his chest in anger. She'd given him Markham's business card.

CHAPTER SEVENTEEN

AT NINE THE FOLLOWING day, Lucy dragged herself into the dining room and found the other players already there. They all looked up from their plates as she shuffled through the oak double doors.

"Sorry," she said. "Jet lag."

"Of course," Andre said. "Help yourself to the spread."

She got coffee with milk and filled her plate. There wasn't much conversation. Everyone looked as exhausted as she felt. She'd had trouble getting back to sleep after her run-in with Markham and her fight with Hugo. Luckily the coffee had cooled just enough that she could gulp it down.

"That's coffee, Lucy," Dustin said. "Not beer. You're not supposed to chug it."

"Long night," she said over the top of her mug.

"Was it?" Melanie asked. "You got out early. We were up past midnight."

"Who came in second?" she asked.

An awkward silence followed. Andre cleared his throat. "We all gave up finally."

"Oh," Lucy said because she didn't know what to say that wouldn't make them want to throw butter knives at her.

Dustin got up to refill his coffee off the sideboard. "Anybody else see any strange characters on the island? Men in suits?"

"I may have," Andre said. "You?"

Melanie moved a half-eaten sausage around her plate. "Maybe."

"Markham," Lucy said. "I met him too. He tried to make me an offer I couldn't refuse."

"Same, same," Andre said, nodding. "What did you do?"

"Refused him," she said. "I mean, the book has to be published, right?"

"Definitely," Melanie said. Andre agreed. Dustin just shrugged.

Suddenly the doors opened again, and Jack walked in wearing a wide smile. "Good morning, kids."

They all greeted Jack with as much enthusiasm as they could muster, which wasn't much.

"I know, I know. Harder nights for us all. Lucy, you'll be pleased to know we've secured the docks. No more late-night shark attacks."

"Shark attacks?" Melanie asked.

"The lawyer guy came to my room in the middle of the night," Lucy explained. "Thanks, Jack."

"My pleasure. The only sharks I like are the ones in the ocean. That is why I tend to throw my lawyers off the pier. Anyway, let's talk about our next game."

Everyone sat up a little straighter, eyes bright and ready.

"Look for the king of Clock Island. Under his crown, you will find the instructions for our next game."

"Say that again, please?" Andre asked. He had out a notebook and pencil and wrote down every word Jack said.

Look for the king of Clock Island. Under his crown, you will find the instructions for our next game.

"There are no points," Jack said, "so feel free to work together or separately. But until you find the instructions, the next game can't begin. Good luck."

Jack smiled benevolently at them all, then left the dining room.

Andre exhaled heavily. "Maybe my mom was right. Maybe running away to Clock Island was the dumbest thing I've ever done."

The four decided to work together since no points were at stake. They all left the house to explore the island, looking for this mysterious king.

They started at the WELCOME ASHORE AT FOUR sign and worked counterclockwise past Puffin Rock at Three O'Clock, the One O'Clock Picnic Spot . . .

They tossed out idea after idea.

The king of Clock Island?

Was Jack the king of Clock Island? He didn't wear a crown. What were they going to do? Cut the crown of his head off?

"I could do that," Dustin said, grinning. "Done it before."

"Let's maybe not cut Jack's head off quite yet," Andre said. "Keep your eyes out for a statue or sculpture or something."

Suddenly Melanie stopped in the center of the path and snapped her fingers. "*The King of Clock Island?* It's one of the book titles."

"No," Lucy said. "The full title is *The Lost King of Clock Island*. But . . ."

She remembered reading that book to Christopher the last night he stayed with her. He'd picked it out because he liked the cover. A boy king rode a black horse through a cursed forest of evil grinning trees. He wore a golden crown on his head of black hair. Black hair just like his, which was probably why he'd chosen it.

"Hugo's paintings are all over the house," Lucy said. "Maybe one of the cover paintings? Does anybody remember seeing a painting of a boy on a horse riding in a forest?"

Andre snapped his fingers. "End of the hall by my room. Let's go."

They made their way back to the house, walking faster than when they'd left. The morning was warming. Lucy was grateful. She'd felt guilty after calling Hugo a "spoiled brat" last night, so guilty she couldn't bring herself to put on the coat he'd lent her.

But it seemed she couldn't escape him. They got back to the house and climbed the stairs. Down one hall, then up another short set of stairs. They reached the painting hanging over an antique butler table with an ancient black Royal typewriter atop it. A piece of paper was rolled into the typewriter. The words *Found me!* were typed at the top.

Melanie carefully unspooled the paper from the typewriter.

On the back, it said, *The next game will begin at one at two.*

Andre shook his head and looked up at the ceiling. "I miss the real world."

"One O'Clock is the picnic spot," Lucy said. "I guess we'll meet there at two this afternoon?"

Jack stuck his head out of a door at the opposite end of the hallway. He whispered, "Yeeesssss," in a spooky voice before disappearing again.

Well, they had their orders. Melanie, Andre, and Dustin left the hallway and went back downstairs.

"When I was a kid," Melanie said as she walked away, "I never understood why Dorothy wanted to leave Oz and go home to Kansas. Now I get it."

They all laughed. All of them but Lucy. She stayed behind, studying the painting, the boy on the horse fleeing the dark forest. A beautiful painting, one of Hugo's best. No, she would have happily stayed in Oz forever. And on Clock Island too. If only she could.

ON CLOCK ISLAND, a girl with soft brown hair and a long wooden spoon fed freshly caught stars to the Man in the Moon.

These were the things that got Hugo out of bed in the morning. He liked where this painting was going—the strangeness of it, the wistfulness. Was this the cover for Jack's new book? No way to tell, but Hugo was enjoying watching the image in his mind come to life on his canvas. It had the feel of a Remedios Varo painting. In Hugo's opinion, it was never too soon for children to learn their *ABC*s and their female Spanish-Mexican surrealists.

Hugo had been up and painting for hours. At five o'clock that morning, he'd woken from a night of a thousand dreams about Davey, all demanding Hugo paint them.

In one dream, they were kids again. Hugo was sitting in a chair by Davey's bed, reading him stories while sharks swam past the window and birds perched on the footboard. Somewhere in the dream, Lucy Hart came into the room, smiled, and said it was her turn to read to him.

And the book she read Davey had this image on the cover—the Man in the Moon, the spoon, the stars, and the girl who looked a little like a young Lucy Hart.

Hugo never tried to analyze the strange images his brain threw at him. He left the symbology and theorizing to the art critics. He dreamed. He imagined. He painted. Don't ask him what anything meant. None of his business. All that mattered was that his dream had been a good one, one he wanted to stay in when he woke up. Davey was alive again for a night, and the book that Lucy read to his lost brother was a book Hugo wanted to hold in his hands.

Davey . . . God, he missed that kid. Even now, so many years later, Hugo caught himself whispering into the silence, "Where are you, Davey? Where did you go?"

Back then, when Davey was alive, Hugo had been bored stiff reading those bloody kids' books to his baby brother. Now he'd kill to read him one more story. For a long time, *Mr. Popper's Penguins* was Davey's favorite, and Hugo had to read a chapter every night for weeks and weeks, and when the book was over, he had to re-read it.

Desperate to find a new book his brother might like, Hugo had gone to a jumble sale in a local church to see if he could pick up any old children's books for cheap. One table had a stack of Clock Island books. Hugo had never heard of them, but at only four for a pound, why not try them?

His whole life began that day for the bargain price of a quid.

Hugo piled moonlight-colored paint onto his fan brush. It had been a long, long time since he'd had a dream about Davey. Why last night? Because of Lucy, he thought, because he mentioned Davey to her. She hadn't even asked. He just told her. And then, stupidly, he followed her into Second Hand City, telling himself he was worried she might hurt herself. Instead, he had hurt her.

With more force than necessary, Hugo cleaned his brush again. He needed coffee and a good strong punch in the face. Piper had told him more than once he should stick to talking about art and leave the important stuff to the grown-ups. He should have listened to her. As he was leaving the studio, he glanced out the window. Lucy Hart was strolling along the rocky spit of beach outside his guesthouse as seagulls swooped and soared over the water.

Hugo wanted to go to her and apologize for crapping all over her dreams last night, but he didn't trust his motives. Did he want her forgiveness? Did he want to make it up to her? Or was he simply annoyingly attracted to her, and for the first time in years he actually cared if someone liked him as a person or not? Ah, misery.

No. He would leave her in peace. The end.

He started to step away, to let it go, to drink his coffee and behave himself, but he stopped when he saw one of the other players, that doctor from Boston . . . Dustin? Yes, him. He walked up to Lucy and caught her by the arm.

Hugo went to the window and cracked it open. He told himself he wasn't eavesdropping, just letting in the breeze.

"Are you serious?" Dustin asked. His tone was demanding, intimidating. "Are you insane?" He put his fingers to his temples and lifted his hands as if she had just blown his mind.

"You heard the lawyers. We cheat, we get disqualified. I don't want to cheat, and I don't want to get disqualified. Do you?" Lucy sounded like a teacher trying to talk sense into a particularly dense child.

"I'm not talking about cheating. I'm talking about teamwork. Like we just did. Nothing else."

"That wasn't a real game, just one of Jack's challenges."

Dustin rolled his eyes to the sky. "Jesus, do you want the money or not?"

"I want to win the book, but I told you I'm not selling it to some collector who will never let it be published. Kids have been waiting forever for—"

"Who gives a shit? That lawyer said eight figures. That's ten million dollars bare minimum split between the two of us."

"I give a shit," Lucy said. Hugo wanted to applaud her backbone.

"I'm not buying the angel act, Lucy. Markham told me you were flat broke. Well, so am I."

"No."

"Then you're as stupid as you look."

That was enough for Hugo. He left through the studio door and headed straight to the beach.

"Lucy," Hugo called out. Lucy's mouth fell open. Dustin turned and stared daggers at him. "You all right?"

"She's fine, and we're talking," Dustin said. "Private conversation."

"No, Lucy was talking," Hugo said. "You were being an ass."

Dustin scoffed. "We're allowed to talk to each other."

"You weren't talking. You were trying to intimidate the one person in this game who has a chance of winning. Not that I blame you. Markham called me too. Tempting offer."

"See?" Dustin said to Lucy. "He's got a brain."

"I do have a brain. So does Lucy. A better one than yours, otherwise you wouldn't be trying to scare her into working with you."

"I'm a doctor. I was top of my class. I don't have to listen to this." Dustin raised his hands and stormed off, saying, "Bye. I'm out of here."

When he was gone, Hugo turned to Lucy. "What a prince."

She looked a little dazed. "He seemed nice yesterday, this morning. Wow."

"Some boys can't handle losing. What do you call them in the teachers' lounge? Poor sports? Sore losers?"

Lucy groaned and faced him. "I came to find you," she said. "I was going to tell you I was sorry for the whole, you know . . ."

"Calling a man who grew up with a single mum in a moldy council flat a 'spoiled brat'?"

"Yes, yes, that," she said sheepishly. "Exactly that. Got a little worked up last night."

"I deserved it."

"No, you didn't. I just . . . This game is my one chance to get ahead a little."

"Understood. Completely. Say no more."

"Thanks." She nodded, then looked around. It seemed she wanted to say something else but decided against it. He would have paid eight figures if he'd had it to know what she'd been about to say. "Well, I better get back to the house."

"Let me walk you," he said. "You need a bodyguard in case anyone else tries to force you to join a multimillion-dollar conspiracy."

"It's not as fun as it looks in the movies. Disappointing."

He led her along the shore toward the house. Sunlight broke apart the morning clouds and danced across the water. The ocean breeze was warm and gentle. Hugo felt a foreign sensation. Happiness? No. Hope? Not that, but something like it.

"I have to say," Hugo said, "I'm impressed that you would turn down a chance at ten million or more dollars."

She shook her head. "If he hadn't been such an asshole, I might have been tempted."

"Are kindergarten teacher's aides allowed to say 'asshole'?"

"I'm off duty. If I were on duty, he'd be a butthole."

"How's about a queen mum?"

"Queen mum?"

"Cockney rhyming slang," he explained. "Rhymes with *bum*."

"I'll remember that. The kids will love it."

"Just don't ask me what a Jack and Danny is." He gave her a wink.

"Now you have to tell me." She elbowed him gently, which he rather liked.

"I'll draw you a picture instead."

"Please do. Then I'll sell it for millions and buy some new shoes."

"You're vastly overestimating my popularity on the secondary market."

"I'll sell it for hundreds and buy some new shoes?"

"Now you're getting closer," he said and smiled at her. Smiling? Him? Oh, God, he was flirting.

Damn. So much for his vow to stay away from Lucy Hart.

YEARS AGO, ONE OF the Clock Island books had come with a poster folded up in the back. Carefully, Lucy had torn it out and unfolded it, pinned it over her bed. She stared for hours at that poster, the delicately painted girl sitting in the window of a strange stone tower overlooking Clock Island, a raven soaring toward her carrying a note clutched in its talons. *The Princess of Clock Island*, Book Thirty, cover artwork and illustrations by Hugo Reese.

Lucy loved that book, loved that poster, wanted to be that girl, the princess of Clock Island. She didn't tell Hugo that from age fourteen to sixteen, she'd slept under his artwork hanging over her bed. Now here she was, strolling on the beach of Clock Island with him like they were old friends. She liked the thought of being friends with Hugo Reese. If things were different—very different . . . except they weren't different. Christopher needed her. That was all that mattered.

"Thanks again for rescuing me," she said, trying to break the suddenly awkward silence.

"You two were arguing outside my studio, and I was attempting to paint. My motives were entirely selfish."

"Do you live in the cottage, or is that just your studio?"

"Live there. Work there. Hide from work there. Why?"

"Guess I assumed you lived in the house with—"

"No, no, no, no, no." He raised his hand. "I've heard all the rumors, heard all the stupid jokes. Yes, Jack is gay. No, I'm not. Even if I were, the man's like a father to me, nothing else."

She laughed. "I didn't say that. I didn't say anything about that. It's just, you know, a very big house."

"The Big House is a synonym for a prison."

"It can't be that bad. It's beautiful." They left the beach walkway and took the gravel path that led to the house.

Lucy hesitated before speaking again, not wanting to be rude, but curiosity overcame her.

"Can I ask . . . I mean, I assume it's not typical for a book illustrator to live with the author of the books he illustrates? I could be wrong."

He didn't seem offended. "Not typical, no, but nothing about Jack is typical. I told you how I won the contest my brother made me enter? Two years later, he died. When I was younger, I partied with the lads a bit harder than I should've, but after Davey was gone, I went off the rails. Booze, drugs, the works. Coke to get the work done. Whiskey to forget enough to sleep. Bad mix."

"Oh, Hugo . . ."

He wouldn't meet her eyes, though she sought them out. "I was flirting with death back then. Jack saw the signs, staged an intervention. Right up there in that room." He pointed to the house, to the window Lucy remembered that Jack called his writing factory.

"I'm sorry," Lucy said.

"Losing my brother was the worst thing that ever happened to me, but Jack was the best. He sat me down and told me people with my kind of talent weren't allowed to squander it. He said I was like a man burning money in front of a poorhouse, that not only was that cruel, but it stank. That got to me. My father walked after Davey was born, and Mum had to work night and day. The image of a man burning cash in front of our flat when we needed every penny . . ."

"Yeah, been there."

He stared at his feet as he shuffled along the path, kicking sand. "They wanted to fire me. Jack's editor, I mean. Here he was writing wholesome children's books, and his illustrator was in rehab? Not very good press."

"Wholesome? Those books are all about kids running away, trespassing, breaking the rules, hanging out with witches and fighting pirates, running away from home, stealing treasure, and then getting rewarded for it."

"See? You understand the books better than the critics." He lightly elbowed her. She tried not to enjoy that too much. "Jack refused to let them sack me. He said he'd quit writing Clock Island books if they tried it. Still can't believe the most famous writer alive stuck his neck out for me like that. It was humbling. He got me sorted, and I've stayed that way ever since."

"That must have been hard. You should be proud of yourself."

"I couldn't disappoint him, not after what he'd done for me. When I started working with Jack, I lived in the guest cottage for a few months while we worked on the new book covers."

"That's when I met you," she said.

"When Jack's rough patch started six years ago, I came back. Been here ever since. Couldn't bear the thought of him being here all alone. Now he swears up and down he's better, which I hope he is. Anyway, it's past time for me to go."

"You're moving?" Lucy couldn't believe it. Who would want to leave Clock Island? "Why?"

"I can't stay here forever, can I?"

"Why not?"

He ignored the question. "I admit I'm worried that my art will suffer if I leave. I've done my best work on the island. Probably because I've been absolutely miserable here."

"How can you be miserable on Clock Island?"

"I can be miserable anywhere. It comes with the job."

She elbowed him in the side. "I don't believe that for one second."

"Name me one happy artist. I dare you."

Lucy scrunched up her face, thinking deeply, trying to remember everything she'd ever learned about every artist she'd ever heard of. She held up one finger.

"Degas?" she said. "Didn't he do those gorgeous ballet dancer paintings?"

"He did. He also loathed ballet dancers and women in general. Notorious misogynist. Notorious misanthrope, really. Try again."

"Um . . . well, I know Van Gogh was miserable. What about Monet?"

"Two dead wives. Dead son. Lifelong financial struggles. Went blind. One more guess."

Lucy gave it more thought. Finally, she snapped her fingers.

"Got one—Bob Ross."

He looked at her through narrowed eyes. "Fine," he said. "I'll give you that one."

"I win. This game anyway."

"No points, sorry."

"It's all right. I'll just bask in the glory," she said as the sun rose higher in the sky, sending its warm rays to kiss every hour, every minute, and every second of Clock Island.

"You're smiling," he said.

"So are you."

"Am I?"

"You're a very talented painter, but you're not as good at being miserable as you think you are."

"Take that back."

"Methinks the artist protests too much," Lucy said.

"Well . . . even I have to admit things are starting to look up."

"Because Jack's writing again?"

He gave her that smile again, the smile that made the sun shine a little brighter.

"Right. That," he said, but a part of Lucy wished he wasn't just talking about Jack.

"Want to get some tea in the dining room?" Lucy asked as they entered the house.

"Raincheck. Gotta talk to Jack."

"Talk to me about what?"

They both turned to see Jack coming down the hall toward the dining room.

"Hello, Lucy," Jack said.

"We have a situation," Hugo said before Lucy could speak.

"I hate situations," he said. "Couldn't we go one day without a situation?"

"Hugo—" Lucy said. "It wasn't—"

"We need to call the ferry in," Hugo said, ignoring her protest. "The good Dr. Dustin disqualified himself."

"Jack, I—" Lucy began.

"Don't try to protect him," Hugo said. "He wouldn't do the same for you, and you know it. Jack, Dustin tried to get Lucy to cheat with him, and he wasn't very polite when she told him no."

Jack took a moment to absorb the information. Lucy could imagine his heart was a little broken by the news. She had the feeling that when he looked at them—Melanie, Andre, Dustin, and her—he saw them still as kids, as his kids.

"Call in the ferry," Jack said with a sigh. Hugo pulled his phone from his pocket and walked out the front door.

"Sorry," Lucy said.

"Don't be sorry, my dear. It's not your fault Dustin forgot the second rule of Clock Island. *Always trust the Mastermind. He's on your side, even when it seems he isn't.*"

CHAPTER EIGHTEEN

LUCY TOOK A LONG hot shower, trying to wash away the stress of last night and this morning. When she got out, she found a note under her door.

Scared it was some kind of cruel parting shot from Dustin, Lucy didn't open it at first. But the paper was sky blue, the color of Jack's stationery. She finally opened it. Someone had written, *Gift outside the door. Don't freak out. It doesn't bite.*

The note was signed *H.R. (Not Human Resources).*

Lucy opened her door and found a cardboard box. She picked it up and took it to the bed, closing the door behind her. What had Hugo given her? She opened the box.

Shoes. That was all. Just a pair of women's hiking boots, dark brown leather, L.L.Bean, of course, because this was Maine. Slightly worn but otherwise in excellent condition.

Lucy knew she should have felt grateful for the gift, but she didn't. She felt like crap.

She sat on the bed and stared down at the shoes. Stupidly, she'd almost convinced herself he'd been flirting with her today—rescuing her from Dustin's creepy scheming, offering to play bodyguard—and yes, she would absolutely let him guard her body. But the free shoes? That didn't feel like attraction. More like pity. More like charity. Those were the last things she wanted from him. He was a nice guy. That was all. He was nice to her because he was nice, not because he liked her. And even if he did like her, she had no business liking him back. The last thing she needed was a hopeless crush on a famous artist.

And, she reminded herself, he'd been flat broke before. He knew how it was—no money, single mother. Okay, so maybe giving her the shoes wasn't charity. Maybe it was solidarity. Still, it stung. But she was going to be a grown-up about it. Only an ingrate or fool wouldn't accept a pair of high-quality hiking boots that looked almost new, especially when her shoes were falling apart.

Lucy fished her phone out of her jeans pocket and sent Theresa a quick text.

Tell me to stop being an idiot.

She doubted she'd get a reply, but one came in fast. Lucy checked the time. Only 6:46 A.M. in Redwood. Theresa had probably just gotten out of bed fifteen minutes earlier.

We don't let the kids call people "idiots," so you can't either.

Lucy wrote back, *Just tell me "eyes on the prize" or something so I can stop thinking about this guy on the island.*

Theresa immediately called. Lucy laughed, answered her phone. Before she could even say hello, Theresa said, "Who's the guy?"

"Good morning," Lucy said.

"Forget morning. Who's the guy? Another player?"

"His name's Hugo Reese, and he illustrated the Clock Island books. And he is beautiful."

"I'll be the judge of that." There was a pause. Theresa was probably googling Hugo on her phone. A few seconds passed. Then, "He'll do. He'll do twice. He looks like a sexy college professor."

"He does now," Lucy said. "I met him when I was here the first time. Back then, he looked like a guitar player in a nineties punk band. Full-sleeve tattoos."

"I gotta see this." Theresa paused, and Lucy waited for her to find some older pictures of Hugo. "Oh my . . ." She must have found a good picture.

"English too."

"Like Prince William?"

Lucy thought about it. "More like a guy who would punch Prince William outside a pub."

"Even better."

Lucy laughed. She knew Theresa could cheer her up.

"He likes you?" Theresa asked.

"I don't think so," Lucy said. "But he gave me a pair of shoes."

"Um . . . shoes? What the hell?"

"Are you cooking while talking to me?" Lucy asked when she heard pots and pans rattling in the background.

"I'm a kindergarten teacher. I can multitask like an octopus. Tell me."

Lucy told her everything that had happened so far—the coat, the lawyer, the "spoiled brat" remark, Dustin, the rescue, the shoes.

"He likes you," Theresa finally said.

"You think the shoes were flirting, not pity?"

"Martin bought me a fish tank when he was trying to get with me. Men are crazy when they're crazy about a girl. He gave you his shoes. You give him your panties."

"You teach kindergarten, Theresa."

"I also have a husband. Get him."

"I'm not here to get a husband, remember? You're supposed to tell me to keep my eyes on the prize. I'm doing this for Christopher."

"Honey, if anybody deserves two prizes, it's you. Win your game. Get your boy, then get your man. The end."

Lucy rubbed her forehead. "Theresa. This is *not* helping."

"Call up someone stupid then. I'm too smart to tell you not to flirt back. Flirt back. Hard. Make him give you a fish tank, baby girl."

"I love you," Lucy said. "You're insane, but I love you. Thank you for making me feel slightly less like shit."

"You don't feel like shit. You are *the* shit, baby. Don't you forget it. And I love you too. Be good but not too good, okay?"

"You too." They hung up.

Talking to Theresa had helped. Lucy took off her old Converse sneakers and tossed them under the bed. She found her thickest pair of socks and put them on. The boots fit pretty well. Traipsing all over the island would be much easier now with a pair of almost-new hiking boots. She looked herself over in the mirror. They looked great with her red skinny jeans—a Goodwill find—and her favorite black crewneck sweater, an old gift from Sean.

After she brushed her teeth, it was almost two o'clock. She walked to the picnic tables at One O'Clock.

Andre and Melanie were there. No Dustin.

"Take a bow, Lucy," Andre said, giving her a golf clap. "You figured out the puzzle this morning, and you got rid of Dustin."

"I didn't mean to."

"Take it as a compliment," Melanie said. "He didn't try to cheat with us, just you."

"Yeah, lucky me." But it was, in a weird way, a compliment. Lucy had won the first game, and she did guess what the puzzle meant this morning too. If she won the next game, she'd be nearly halfway to victory and only on day two.

Jack came up the path and stood in front of the picnic table. Ms. Hyde stood at his side clutching a leather portfolio.

"Hello again, kids. As you've seen, we're down a player," Jack said. "Dustin left an hour ago. He told me to pass along his sincerest apologies to you, Lucy. Apparently, he's suffering from what he calls S.L.S.D.— Student Loan Stress Disorder."

"It's okay," Lucy said. "I forgive him."

"Let me remind everyone," Ms. Hyde said, "cheating—or attempting to cheat—in any form or fashion will have you disqualified immediately."

"Which is a shame," Jack said. His tone was melancholy. "Personally, I'm all for cheating, lying, and stealing. Where do you think I get all my book ideas?"

"That was a joke," Ms. Hyde said. "No credible accusations of plagiarism have ever been lodged against Mr. Masterson."

"I believe they knew I was joking," Jack said. Then he clapped and rubbed his hands together with fiendish glee. "Now that that unpleasantness is out of the way, let's play a new game."

Ms. Hyde opened her portfolio and passed them each a single sheet of paper.

"What's this list?" Andre asked. "*The Utterly Impossible Scavenger Hunt?* Seriously? We have to do a scavenger hunt that nobody can do? How's that supposed to work?"

Lucy took her sheet of paper and glanced at the items on the list.

A wheelbarrow for a fairy garden
The wind under a kite
A solid-black checkerboard

"A jar of nine-legged spiders?" Melanie said. "Are you kidding? Either I'm having a stroke, or this list is crazy."

"Both, possibly," Jack said. "I'd bet on both, myself. Two points if you can divine the secret of the hunt. No points for second place on this game."

"We gotta get a hint, Jack," Andre said. "I can't spend all day chasing down an origami salami or a damn fish with a secret!"

"Please," Melanie said, her eyes pleading. "I felt so stupid after the last game. I know it will be something totally obvious when we find out. Could you make it a little more obvious before we begin this time?"

She smiled, but it was a shy and nervous smile. Did Melanie need to win the book as much as Lucy did?

"Ah, but that's how life is," Jack said. "Hindsight is twenty-twenty, they say, and they aren't wrong. We only know the right thing to do after we've done the wrong one. To quote the supposedly great but mostly incomprehensible Søren Kierkegaard—'Life can only be understood backwards, but it must be lived forwards.' Or, as all writers know, you can't understand the beginning until you've read the end. And those are all the hints you get. Happy hunting, children."

THE THREE CONTESTANTS READ the list over and over again.

A crying wolf
An assortment of octopi
A ray of darkness

Lucy wanted to laugh, but the stakes were too high. The first two games had seemed so easy that a small part of her believed she had a shot at winning. Now her stomach sank. She had no idea what to do.

"There has to be a trick here," Melanie said. "Right?"

Ms. Hyde cleared her throat before turning on her heel and following Jack back to the house.

"Right," Melanie said. "No colluding. I'll go figure this out somewhere else."

Lucy watched her head off down a random path. Andre, looking too sure of himself for her liking, took a separate trail. Although the day was bright and breezy, the ocean gentle, and the sky filled with birds floating on the air currents, they had eyes only for the list.

Lucy stayed at the picnic table, re-reading the clues. Melanie was right, of course. There had to be a trick, a double meaning, something obvious she was missing. Her first instinct was to get on her phone and google some of these phrases, see if they meant anything. But that would be cheating.

Also, Lucy highly doubted the internet would be much help. This game seemed like something Jack had invented all on his own, like something from one of his books. And if it was like something from one of his books, it meant it was a game even a child could figure out.

So what was it? What was the secret of the list?

A scavenger hunt was like a treasure hunt, wasn't it? Lucy decided a visit to the City of Second Hand was in order. Redd Rover's Treasure Hunt Supply Store was housed in what looked like a cartoonish version of an old miner's shack from California's Gold Rush days, complete with a slanting roof, mismatched boards, and hand-painted signs. But when she peeked into the windows, she saw that all the shelves were empty. No help for her here.

She kept walking, following the train tracks to Samhain Station until they ended abruptly in the middle of a clearing in the woods. There was nothing there but an overgrown meadow of wildflowers. Pretty but not the Samhain Station from the books. No tower. No pumpkin thrones. No Lord and Lady of October. Just train tracks that went nowhere.

Lucy sat on the ground in the middle of the wildflowers, careful of the ants and the bees. She studied the list again, but nothing came to her.

A chicken-fried Kentuckian?
A slice of Pi?

"Jack, what are you doing to us?" Lucy whispered to herself.

The answer had to be staring her in the face. She wasn't going to be able to figure it out and someone else would win this round and put an end to her lucky streak. What if Hugo was wrong about her having a shot, and she lost—not just this round, but the game? Then it would be back to Redwood, back to knitting scarves to sell on Etsy until she gave herself arthritis, back to carbo-loading on cheap spaghetti so she could sell her plasma twice a week without fainting, back to waiting for her life to start and knowing it wouldn't until Christopher was her son.

And if he was never her son, did that mean her life would never start?

No, it meant his life would never start. The life they'd dreamed of together anyway, the life she'd promised him. Their stupid simple life. No castles. No towers. No magic islands. Just a two-bedroom apartment and a half-decent used car. And all that was keeping her from it was her brain, which couldn't seem to figure out what the hell a "doll condo" and a "loaf of cat" were supposed to mean.

The ground was cold and hard, and Lucy's feet started to go to sleep. She stood up and dusted off the seat of her pants. Fighting back tears, she trekked on through the woods, unsure of what she was looking for but unable to sit still. Nobody had ever won a scavenger hunt sitting in one place. Soon the forest thinned, and tall seagrasses took their place. The stone path ended at a wooden plank bridge. She crossed it and followed it around a bend, and there, about fifty yards ahead, stood the lighthouse.

It wasn't big, but it was charming. White, maybe twenty-five feet tall and with a bright red dome on top, jaunty as a red cap. Lucy stood in the bright sun with a brisk wind blowing her hair and chapping her face. She remembered the clock in Jack's living room with the lighthouse at the top.

The Noon & Midnight Lighthouse had an exterior ladder that led to a viewing platform. Lucy dried her hands on her jeans and gripped the rungs. She climbed to the top and found that it felt a lot higher than it looked from the ground. Her head swam at first, but she held tight to the railing and gazed out at the water.

It was dazzling, or it should have been—the blues and the grays and the golds and the silvers. The sun was playing hide-and-seek behind the silver clouds. But it might have been a blank brick wall in front of her for all the pleasure she could take in it. The minutes were ticking past—*tick-tock, tick-tock*—and her time was running out. She'd seen that look in Andre's eyes. He could be halfway through the list by now, while she was stuck at the starting line.

Jack had told them on their first night here that they would be playing the Clock Island game. If only. The kids in those books always got their wishes granted by the end. Except . . . not always, now that she thought of it. Often the kids wanted one thing and got something else, something better, by the end. Something they didn't even know they wanted. In the first book, *The House on Clock Island*, Astrid and her brother, Max, wanted their dad to move back home. In the end, that wasn't the wish that he granted.

Instead, Astrid and her brother went to live with their dad again in the city where he'd found work. By coming to Clock Island, they learned to face their fears. And once they'd found their courage, they were brave enough to finally tell their mother they would be willing to give up their friends and their school and their home by the ocean if it meant they could all be together again.

Of course the Mastermind had a secret going-away gift for them. As they were pulling away in the moving van after selling their house, Astrid opened an envelope that had just arrived for her to find a note inside and a key. The letter told her it was the Mastermind who had bought their little blue house by the ocean, and it would be waiting for Astrid when she was all grown up and ready to come home again.

It was a bittersweet ending but one full of hope and promise. Ironically, it wasn't Astrid's gift for solving riddles that helped her wish come true, but her courage and her honesty. Very sweet. Very touching. But it didn't help Lucy. Or did it?

What did the kids in the books have to do to get their wishes?

First, they had to make a wish. Then they had to get to Clock Island. After that, they answered riddles or played strange games. Then they had to face their fears. Was she afraid of anything? Anything other than failure?

Lucy took a deep breath of ocean air and started down the lighthouse ladder. She found the path again and started to make a circuit around the island. She walked past the picnic tables again, then reached the Tide Pool at Two.

She stood on the gray stones, worn smooth by the endless comings and goings of the water, and looked deep into the glassy water, hoping to see something in there. Fish or algae or starfish or sea urchins . . . but she saw nothing. The ocean kept its secrets.

Secrets. Secrets. *A fish with a secret.* What could that possibly mean?

As Lucy walked along the beach toward Puffin Rock at Three O'Clock, she re-read her list.

A crying wolf
An assortment of octopi
A humble actor
A jar of nine-legged spiders
A fish with a secret
A loaf of cat
A doll condo
A shelf on an elf
A slice of Pi
A wheelbarrow for a fairy garden
A solid-black checkerboard
The bang from a drum
The wind under a kite
A shadow's shadow
An origami salami
A chicken-fried Kentuckian
A ray of darkness

She wanted to scream but didn't. Jack's riddles were always obvious once you knew the answer. Hindsight was twenty-twenty. He did say that to them, right? So that had to mean something, didn't it?

She pulled a pen from her coat pocket, counted with her finger, and read out every twentieth letter. *M . . . A . . .* She counted them all several times, including the numbers and then excluding the numbers. Nothing.

What else had Jack said?

Life can only be understood backwards, but it must be lived forwards. A quote by Kierkegaard, the philosopher.

Understood backward?

All right, she tried reading the clues backward.

A crying wolf became *flow gniyrc A.*

That wasn't it either.

Jack had also said that all writers knew that you couldn't understand the beginning until you've read the end.

So she read the clues backward to front.

Darkness of ray a Kentuckian . . .

That wasn't it.

She was about to give up when she decided to look at the last letter of each phrase. With her pen, she circled all the final letters, and instantly, she knew she was onto something.

A crying wolf—F

An assortment of octopi—I

A humble actor—R

A jar of nine-legged spiders—S

A fish with a secret—T

FIRST

Heart racing, blood pounding, Lucy circled all the last letters until she had the answer.

FIRST TO FIND ME WINS.

CHAPTER NINETEEN

LUCY RAN HER GUTS out. While she walked everywhere and biked everywhere back home, she hadn't done much running since leaving school. Now she was furious at herself for quitting 5Ks. Her legs and lungs were screaming at her after only a couple of minutes of hard sprinting.

But she kept on running, wouldn't stop. She ran like kids run when the final bell rings on the last day of school before summer break. Jack was most likely in his writing room, so that's where she was headed. If he wasn't seated behind his desk . . . well, she'd worry about that once she got there.

She wasn't even halfway back to the house when she had to stop to catch her breath. Leaning over, panting, stupidly grateful for the hiking boots Hugo had given her—no way could she have run in her old Converse sneakers—Lucy's lungs burned as she gulped air. She could see the house in the distance.

She saw something else too. Someone was on the Five O'Clock Beach.

Andre. Andre was on the beach, unmistakable in his baseball cap and bright blue windbreaker.

And he was running.

Running toward the house.

Lucy took off as fast as she could, the soles of her new shoes echoing off the wooden boards of the walkway that ringed most of the island.

Andre was taller than her, bigger, faster, but she was closer. It was neck and neck as he ran up the beach, and she ran down it, the house just ahead five hundred yards, then four hundred . . . Lucy's heart felt like it could burst from her chest. Three hundred yards . . . she wanted to throw up. Two hundred yards. She slipped on a loose board but caught herself before hitting the ground. Had those two seconds of delay cost her the win? She kept running. Andre was close, but so was she. Lucy ran up the cobblestone walkway to the front door with a last explosion of adrenaline and burst into the house. Andre was only a few steps behind her. Now she had to find Jack. Her best guess was the library. But Andre was heading up the stairs, maybe seeking out Jack in his office. Had he seen Jack up there in the window? Was she going to win the race only to lose by picking the wrong room?

Lucy burst into the living room, and there was Jack standing at the fireplace, a cup of coffee in his hand.

And there was Melanie standing with him, also with a cup of coffee. She was smiling.

Lucy collapsed onto the sofa. Andre came in one second after her and stared at the scene in front of him.

"Damn," he said and kicked the door shut behind him. The sound made Lucy jump.

"Sorry, kids," Melanie said with a shrug. "Like Jack said, no points for second place."

Lucy didn't begrudge Melanie her moment of triumph. She wasn't going to be a sore loser like Dustin.

"I might as well go home," Andre said, though he didn't sound heartbroken, merely resigned. He sat on the sofa, shoulders slumped, looking defeated. "My wife was right when she told me girls were smarter than boys."

Good to see he still had a sense of humor about the whole thing. Lucy wanted to cry, but she would save that for later.

"Ah, don't give up, son," Jack said, patting Andre on the back and winked. Andre smiled. The tension lifted a little in the room.

Andre scoffed. "No offense, Jack, but maybe this would have been fun when I was eleven, but now? It's stressful as hell."

Jack didn't seem surprised or offended. "I'm only giving you what you kids wanted back then—to make a wish and play a game and win the prize."

That wasn't what Lucy wanted. She loved the books, and she daydreamed about being a character in one of them the same way her friends dreamed about going to Hogwarts or Narnia. But what she'd truly wanted was what Jack jokingly offered in his letter—to be his sidekick. She'd wanted to live here with him, help him, be a daughter to him, let him be a father to her. As much as she'd loved the books, she wanted the reality, not the fantasy.

"What's the next game then?" Andre asked Jack. "I'm not giving up yet."

"You'll find out tonight after dinner. But until then, have fun. This is Clock Island, not the gulag."

LUCY'S HOT STREAK WASN'T just over, it was dead and buried. That night they played "Clock Island-opoly," which was the Clock Island version of Monopoly. Andre, a corporate lawyer, won without breaking a sweat. Melanie came in second. No points for Lucy. She'd never played Monopoly before. She might have enjoyed learning how if it hadn't been such an important game. Instead of going straight to jail, they went into the Clock Tower, and they were not allowed to collect two hours. Time was money, said the box.

By the end of night two, the score stood at:

Lucy: 2

Melanie: 3

Andre: 2

On the third day, there were more games. A Clock Island trivia game. Lucy won easily. Melanie came in second. Then they played a variation on "Mother, May I?" called "Mastermind, May I?" out in the garden. Finally, after dinner, they played a Clock Island–themed game of Charades. It was incredibly embarrassing to act out scenes from the books while Hugo watched from the back of the library, trying not to laugh too loudly at them.

Lucy noticed a strange thing happening over the course of two days. They almost forgot why they were playing. Especially during Charades, when Andre had to act out the Lord of October fighting the Pumpkin Boys and their ghost army. How did one mime a ghost army, exactly? Surprisingly, he found a way. And then Lucy had to act out Astrid climbing up the side of the lighthouse to find her missing brother who'd been stolen by the infamous Clock Island bandit, Billy the Other Kid.

It was anarchy. And it was fun. So much fun she had to keep reminding herself to stay focused. Christopher needed her to win. She couldn't forget what was at stake.

By the end of the third day, the scores were too close for comfort.

Lucy: 5

Melanie: 6

Andre: 5

But they still had two more days of games. Anything could happen. Anyone could win.

After the Charades game ended, they all lingered in the library. Kitchen staff appeared and passed around hot chocolate with a mountain of whipped cream to everyone. They sipped their hot chocolate as a low fire simmered in the fireplace.

"Okay, Jack," Andre said after taking such a big swig of his hot chocolate he ended up with whipped cream on his nose. "I apologize for saying I wasn't having any fun."

"Don't be hasty with those apologies," Jack said. "Tomorrow won't be much fun at all."

Melanie and Andre looked at each other. Lucy glanced over her shoulder at Hugo. He gave her a wink that made her temperature shoot up a degree or two.

"What's tomorrow?" Andre asked.

"You don't know?" Jack asked, pointing his finger at Melanie, then Andre, then Lucy.

"I know," Lucy said, looking back at Jack. "I think I know. Maybe."

"What is it?" Melanie leaned forward. She looked nervous. They all did.

"We're in a book, right?" Lucy asked Jack. "You said we're playing like the kids in the Clock Island books."

"Indeed," Jack said.

"Well, it goes like this—first a kid comes to the island, then they answer riddles and play games, which we've been doing. Then they—"

"Face their fears," Andre said. "Right? That's what the Mastermind always says to the kids—'Time to face your fears, my dears.'"

"Very good," Jack said, nodding.

Andre said, "I always got nervous when the Mastermind said that. It meant it was about to get real on Clock Island. I had nightmares for months after reading *The Ghost Machine* when that boy was chased by that ghost that looked just like him? I mean, what the hell, Jack?"

"My editor tried to talk me out of that scene," Jack said.

"Why?" Melanie asked.

"Because she said it would give children nightmares for months. I said it wouldn't. I might owe her an apology." He tapped his chin. "She won't get it, but I do owe her one."

"You're really gonna make us face our fears?" Andre asked. He sounded skeptical, as if he were too old to be afraid of anything anymore.

"Ah, but that's the most important challenge of them all," Jack said as he set his mug aside on the fireplace mantel. "You can't win until you face your fears. Until you face your fears, your fears are winning."

"We're old now," Andre said. "I'm not scared of spiders and snakes and ghosts anymore. I'm scared of my dad dying because we can't find a matching kidney for him. That's my big fear, and I promise you, I am *never* not thinking about it. What can you do about that?"

It was a fair question. How could Jack make a group of adults face their fears? It wasn't like they were ten anymore, afraid of the dark, afraid of telling the truth to their parents about who broke the antique vase, afraid of telling their best friend they're sorry . . . How did you make adults face their fears when being an adult was nothing but waking up every morning with their fears already in their faces?

"I'm only afraid of losing my bookshop," Melanie said. "Ever tried to keep a children's bookshop in business in a small town? We can barely keep a grocery store. How do you make us face something we're already facing?"

Jack replied with an enigmatic, "You'll find out."

Lucy shivered. She believed him. If anyone could figure out a way to make them face their fears, it was the old Mastermind.

"And, fair warning," Jack said. "Facing your fears doesn't earn you any points. But if you won't do it, you don't get to play the final game."

Lucy took a deep breath. He'd warned them this was coming, but it had seemed so far away. She would do it, though, whatever it was. Kiss a snake. Walk a tightrope over the ocean. Anything to win.

"Now," Jack said, "on an even more serious note, the weather service has issued a storm warning for tonight. Gale force winds and rains. If you were planning on rowing out in a dinghy, I'd suggest rescheduling that trip. Good night, kids. Sweet dreams." Jack started to leave, but Andre stopped him with a question.

"Did you face your fears, Jack?" Andre said. His voice was polite, but there was a note of challenge in it that Lucy picked up. No fair making them face their fears if Jack had never faced his.

Jack was quiet a moment, though the house was not quiet. The wind was picking up. Tree branches knocked on windows. Wind buffeted the roof. The fire in the fireplace danced with every sudden gust.

"Here's a riddle for you all," Jack said. "*Two men on an island—*"

"Oh Lord," Hugo said with a groan.

The room was silent again but for the wind and the crackling of the fire. Jack began again:

Two men on an island and both blame the water
For the loss of a wife and the death of a daughter
But neither ever married, and neither's a father.
What is the secret of the girls and the water?

With one last look around, Jack said, "No points for unraveling this riddle, I'm afraid. But if you do, maybe you'll win a different sort of prize."

With that, Jack left them alone in the living room.

Lucy looked at Hugo. He met her eyes. "Sorry, but don't ask me. If you guess it, I'll tell you, but it's not just my story."

"But you know?" Andre asked him.

"Of course I know. I'm the other man on the island. Unfortunately."

"You got any ideas?" Andre looked at Melanie.

"Makes no sense to me. How can you lose a daughter if you never had a kid?"

Andre looked at Lucy. "What about you?"

Lucy met Hugo's eyes. "No idea," she said.

But she was lying.

She had a very good idea.

PART FOUR

Face Your Fears,
My Dears

"Astrid? Max? Where are you? Astrid!"

Astrid recognized her mother's voice. She'd know it anywhere, though it sounded strange. She realized she'd never heard her mother terrified before. Of course she was terrified. Astrid and Max had disappeared from the house last night. How did their mother know they were on Clock Island?

"What do we do?" Astrid asked the Mastermind. He stood in the shadow cast by a mighty suit of armor so that it looked like the shadow around him was his armor. She'd been on Clock Island all night, and she still hadn't seen his face. Maybe she never would.

"If you were her, what would you want your children to do?" The Mastermind's voice was gentle, gentler than she'd ever heard it before.

Max answered before Astrid could.

"She wants to find us," Max said. "Maybe we should tell her where we are."

He looked toward the shadow, but the shadow said nothing.

"We can't. She'll kill us," Astrid rasped to Max.

"We can't hide here forever," Max said. He met her eyes. "Right?"

"Max? Astrid? Where are you?" They could see their mother on the beach, her hair and coat being whipped madly by the wind and the rain. She must be cold out there, cold and scared. "Astrid!"

It hurt to hear her voice like that, hurt to see her so scared.

"I'm scared," Astrid said.

"Because you'll get into trouble?" the Mastermind asked.

"Because she'll ask us why we ran away," she said. "Then we'll have to tell her."

"Tell her what?" The Mastermind had a way of asking questions that made you think he already knew the answer, even before you knew.

"Tell her we want to have Dad back, even if it means moving away," Max said. "They decided Dad would leave for his new job, and we'd stay behind so we wouldn't have to change schools. But if we tell her we want to be with Dad more than we want to stay . . ."

"Then we'll move," Astrid said. And that was what she was most afraid of . . . leaving everything behind, starting over. A new life in a new town with new friends—or maybe no friends. What was scarier than that?

Staying, she realized. Staying here without their dad. That was the only thing scarier.

Astrid grabbed Max by the hand and said, "Let's go."

They ran together out the front door, forgetting even to tell the Mastermind goodbye.

"Mom!" she shouted. "Mom, we're here!"

—From *The House on Clock Island*, Clock Island
   Book One, by Jack Masterson, 1990

CHAPTER TWENTY

HUGO LEFT THE LIBRARY, following Jack. Lucy waited a while, but he never came back. Back to the guesthouse, she supposed. Could she follow him? Yes. But what would she say? *I forgot to tell you but thanks for the shoes. By the way, if I'm getting the riddle right, that means your wife dumped you for another man. Tell me all about it.*

That might not go over well.

Something knocked loudly against the house, kicked by the wind. All three of the contestants were jolted by the sudden noise. Jack hadn't been kidding about the coming storm.

"Maine is crazy," Andre said, his dark eyes trained on the window and the churning ocean in the distance. "Sounds like a hurricane."

"Just a bad storm," Lucy said, hoping it wouldn't turn into a nor'easter.

"I hate storms," Melanie said, shivering as she glanced at the window, then shook her head. She gave a little scoffing laugh. "Wonder if Jack arranged this to make me face my fear of storms."

Andre looked at her. "Thought you said you were only afraid of losing your bookstore."

"If you want to know the truth, I'm afraid of proving my ex-husband right by losing my bookstore. He told me during the divorce that I'd never make it work. I hate to think he was right, that I didn't know what I was doing."

Lucy's heart clenched at Melanie's confession. "When I met you," Lucy said, "I assumed you had this perfect life. You seem like you have everything together."

"I have nothing together except my outfit," Melanie said.

"Truth is," Andre said as he got up to stand in front of the dying fire, "the thing I'm most afraid of is telling the truth to my son. He knows his granddaddy is sick, but we haven't told him he's not going to make it if he doesn't get a kidney transplant soon. They're best friends."

"You're not a match?" Melanie asked.

Andre shook his head. "Dad's got a rare blood type. It's been a nightmare."

"Maybe you don't want to tell your son," Melanie said, "because you don't want to make it real yet for you either."

Andre nodded but said nothing.

"I'm sorry about your dad," Lucy said. "But pretty jealous you and your son have such a good relationship with him. I would have killed for that."

"I keep forgetting how lucky we are to have each other," he said. "Thank you for reminding me of that." He smiled. "God, I miss the things I was afraid of as a kid. I'd kill to be scared of ghosts and closet monsters again, and not my dad dying before he sees his grandson grow up."

"And spiders," Melanie said. "And rats. Real rats are so much less scary than the rat I married."

"Come on now. What about you, Lucy Lou?" Andre said. "We ponied up. What's your real fear?"

"I don't think I have just one," she admitted as she mindlessly spun the dregs of her hot chocolate in the bottom of her mug. "I mean, take your pick. Seeing my ex-boyfriend again. Or worse, letting him see how little I've done with my life. Never getting to do the one thing I really want to do with my life. Finding out the reason my parents and my sister didn't love me is that there's nothing to love about me. And trust me, I know how pathetic that sounds, but no matter how old you get, no matter how many times you tell yourself it was them and not you, you never really persuade yourself that it wasn't you."

Andre leaned in, met her eyes. "It wasn't you," he said. "Speaking as a father who'd move mountains for my son, it wasn't you. Any parent who makes their kid feel unwanted has something wrong with them." He pointed at Melanie. "And you, bad times come to every business. Man, even Apple was on the edge of bankruptcy in the nineties. I'm smart, okay? They don't let dummies into Harvard Law School, and you skunked me in the last game."

Melanie grinned broadly. "Thank you." Then she made a face of almost-comical disgust. "Dammit, now I want you all to win as much as I want to win."

"Jack's sneaky as hell," Andre said. "He probably planned this."

"I wouldn't put it past him," Melanie said.

"Definitely. See y'all at breakfast." Andre stood and went to the door. Then he turned around and faced them. "I hope I win, but if either of you wins, I'll be happy for you. I hope you both get your wish somehow. I hope we all do."

Melanie smiled at him, and Andre left.

"What is it you don't have the money for?" Melanie asked Lucy as she stood up from her armchair.

Lucy hesitated. She hated telling her sob story, but she also relished any chance she got to talk about Christopher.

"There's a little boy I want to foster. Actually, I want to adopt him, but I'd have to foster-to-adopt first. I don't meet the qualifications for foster parenting. He and I . . . we want to be a family, but we probably never will."

"Unless you win and sell the book."

"Right. Unless I win."

Melanie smiled and said, "That's a very good wish."

FROM THE WINDOW IN her bedroom, Lucy watched the storm rising. God, she'd missed the wild skies of Maine in springtime. Scary sometimes, but beautiful with the clouds racing toward some unseen finish line and the ocean churning as if the Kraken were about to rise. She imagined Christopher here with her, standing in front of her, face pressed to the glass. And when the storm passed, they'd run out to the beach to look for driftwood and throw stranded starfish back into the water.

Her phone buzzed on the nightstand. She picked it up and saw a long message from Theresa.

I don't know how to tell you this, but Christopher just came by the classroom. He said he's getting a new foster placement. In Preston with an older couple. They're letting him finish the last week out at school. I'm in a meeting right now, but I'll call you as soon as I can. He's really scared and upset, of course, but I don't think he realizes he'll be going to another school next year. Honey, I'm so sorry.

Lucy read the message over and over until the words sank in. She was in too much shock to cry. Denial was her first instinct, that there must be a mistake. Preston was almost twenty miles away from Redwood. Same county but . . .

She knew in theory that kids in foster care were moved around all the time, that they were forced to pack their bags at a moment's notice all the time, that they were transferred from school to school all the time no matter how much it traumatized them and made keeping up with their schoolwork nearly impossible.

Of course she knew all that, but she never thought it would happen to Christopher. Maybe he'd get moved, but not to another town, not to another school.

This was her worst nightmare.

Lucy took deep breaths, deep gulping breaths. She stared wildly around the Ocean Room as if somewhere in there, she'd find the answer. But there was nothing to help her. The bed. The dresser. The vanity. Hugo's shark painting over the fireplace. A few books on the mantel tucked between grandfather clock bookends.

She recognized those books. They were the first four Clock Island books in their original covers—*The House on Clock Island, A Shadow*

Falls on Clock Island, A Message from Clock Island, The Haunting of Clock Island.

Lucy laughed, groaned. She shook her head and wiped the tears from her cheeks with her hand.

Good job, Jack, she thought. She had to hand it to the man. He had found a way to scare the holy shit out of her. Face her fears? Well, he'd found her worst fear, hadn't he?

She stood up and went to the door, into the hall, and strode to the opposite end of the house to Jack's writing factory, as he called it.

Lucy knocked once and loudly on the door.

"Yes?" Jack said from inside. Lucy opened the door and entered, shutting the door behind her. Jack sat at his desk behind a pile of papers that looked like letters.

"Lucy," he said with a genuine smile. He always looked so happy to see them. It couldn't be real, could it?

"Nice try, Jack," she said. "How'd you do it?"

His head tilted slightly to the side. "Do what?"

"Make it look like my friend Theresa sent me a text message? I know she wouldn't do it herself, so you had to fake it. You went in and changed her contact number to yours. Face your fears?" she asked. "This is my fear, right? I told Hugo about Christopher and Hugo told you."

"Yes, I know about Christopher. But what happened?"

"You know what happened. You or one of your lawyers or somebody sent me a text message telling me he's being transferred to a new foster family twenty miles away."

He exhaled, then sat forward. "Oh, Lucy." He shook his head. "I might play some infuriating games, but I wouldn't torture you. Never, my dear. Never."

She didn't want to believe him, but she believed him, and now that she looked at his face and his eyes—that wise rumpled face, those gentle, tired eyes—she knew she'd been crazy to believe for one second that Jack had engineered that message.

"I have to go home," she said.

"What? Now? Tonight? There's a storm."

"I don't care. I have to get to the airport to catch the first flight back. He's moving the day after the last day of school. Friday is the last day of school. This Friday, Jack. He'll be gone Saturday, and if I don't get home right now, I won't get to spend time with him before he moves. I have to be there when they transfer him, or he'll . . . He won't be okay. He'll be terrified if I'm not there. He'll be—"

Alone. He'll be scared and alone. No, she couldn't let that happen. Not to him. Not to her Christopher. She had to be there when he left. She had to be there to tell him it would be all right, that she would see him as often as she could, that he was going to be okay, that it would be scary, but he wasn't alone. Lies, of course. She had to be there *now*.

"Lucy, I would put you on my private plane if I had one and fly you home right this second, but there is no pilot in the world who would take off in this weather."

As if on cue, something hit the side of the house. A broken branch from a tree limb, most likely. But she didn't care.

"Fine then," she said. "I'll find my own way to shore and then rent a car."

She turned to leave, and when Jack called her name, she looked back, desperate for help.

"Don't do this," he said. "Please? We can help you. And we will. But you must be patient."

"Patient?" She shook her head, laughed bitterly. "Since I was a little girl, you've been promising I'd be all right when I grew up. I am *not* all right. And now you bring us here to play this game for what? Because you think we're like kids in your stories who'll do anything you tell us to do? Even Clock Island is fake. There're no storms in the bottles, and the train tracks go nowhere. *Nowhere*. Christopher is real, though. He matters to me a billion times more than any book, any game. And I'm not going to tell him that he has to wait until he grows up to be happy. He's going to be happy now, even if it kills me to make him happy."

Lucy turned on her heel and left Jack alone in his office.

Forget him. Forget it all.

All she had to do was get to Portland. She'd rent a car and drive down to New Hampshire or Boston, wherever planes were still taking off. She had her debit card. Of course she'd blow half her savings on the rental car and the plane ticket, but it wasn't humanly possible for her to stay here on the other side of the country while Christopher was back in Redwood, scared and alone. The image of him in his bedroom at the Baileys' house packing his few clothes and books into garbage bags made her want to throw up.

Surely the rain wasn't so bad she couldn't at least get to Portland tonight. As she threw her things into her suitcase, she glanced out the window and saw a few boats out there on the water. It wasn't a hurricane, not even a squall. Just a storm. She'd run down to the dock and see if there was a boat she could borrow. Sean owned a speedboat, and she'd learned how to drive his. A speedboat would do, or a fishing boat. She'd even take a rowboat if that was her only choice. Borrow first, apologize later. Jack would understand.

With her things packed, she grabbed Hugo's coat and threw it on, went down the steps to the front door, and walked out into the rain. It was a cold rain, fast and driving, but it didn't matter to Lucy. Her mind was set. She was getting back to California by tomorrow morning, and nothing and no one could stop her.

Lucy put her head down and walked into the wind. No amount of tightening the cord on her hood would keep it from blowing back. Forget it. She'd just get wet.

The dock was ahead. She could see the two lights at the end of it, but the boats were gone. Of course. It was night. All the household staff had gone back to the mainland.

There had to be more boats somewhere. This was an island owned by a man worth millions of dollars. Where was the boathouse?

Lucy glanced up and down the beach, saw nothing, peered through the trees swaying wildly in the wind, and spotted a small stone building. Maybe that was it. She lugged her suitcase back up the path and took the fork into the woods that led toward the stone building.

When she got closer, she realized it wasn't a boathouse but a storage shed behind Hugo's cottage. But he could tell her where to find a boat.

She knocked on his door, pounded on it.

"Hugo?" she called out. "Hugo, it's Lucy!"

He opened the door, phone in his hand. He was talking to someone, but he didn't seem at all surprised to see her.

"Call you back," he said and shoved his phone into the pocket of his jeans. Hugo must have just gotten out of the shower. His hair was damp and his feet were bare.

"Hugo, please, I need to get to Portland."

"Not tonight, you don't." He reached out and took her by the arm, then pulled her inside his house. It must have been Jack on the phone.

"Let me go," she demanded and pulled her arm from his grasp.

She started to turn, to open the door, when Hugo said something that stopped her.

"This isn't what Christopher would want you to do, and you know it."

CHAPTER TWENTY-ONE

LUCY'S CHEST BURNED WITH white-hot rage. She shook her head at Hugo, not believing what she'd heard. "You have no idea what Christopher wants or doesn't want. You don't know him, and you don't know me."

Hugo didn't back down. "I know you want to adopt him. I know you need money. I know it will take a miracle for you to get it. You said so yourself. Well, here's your miracle." He held out his hands to indicate the entirety of Clock Island, that she was here, that she was standing in the middle of the miracle. "There are only two days left. The game isn't over. Why give up now?"

"The game? The game I'm losing?"

"You're one point behind."

"Who cares about points?" Lucy snapped. "I have to get back to Christopher. He's freaking out right now. I know he is. He needs me."

"He wants you now. He needs you forever. You can give him what he wants by leaving, or you can give him what he needs by staying and winning this stupid game. And you can win it. Any idiot can win Jack's games. Obviously." He pointed at his face.

She laughed a sharp, sudden laugh, then burst into tears.

"Lucy . . ." Gently, Hugo put his hands on her shoulders.

"I have to go," she said through tears. "I can't be here while he's there by himself. You don't know what it's like to be a child sitting alone in a room and knowing nobody is coming to help me."

"Help *me*?" Hugo said softly.

"I mean, help you. Help him. You know what I mean."

"No," he said. "Tell me what you mean. Who was supposed to come and help you?"

Lucy turned away from him, hands on her forehead. "I thought my sister was going to die," she said. "She spiked a fever, so they rushed her to the hospital. There was no time to get a babysitter, so they took me and dumped me in the waiting room at the hospital. Alone." She met his eyes. "I was only eight. They were gone for hours. Hours, Hugo. I could tell time. It was five hours I was alone in that room. Nobody came for me. Not even to check on me. Not even to tell me if Angie was dead or alive."

Hugo pulled her into his arms, but she couldn't accept the hug. She kept her arms crossed in front of her stomach.

"I thought they were going to leave me there forever. When you're eight and your parents don't love you very much, you think things like that."

She sniffed and gave a little laugh.

Hugo touched her chin, made her look at him. "What's funny?"

"That's the night I started reading the Clock Island books. There was one in a basket of coloring books. I think that book's the reason I didn't, you know, lose all hope that night. Because I had company finally. And you know what? They never did come and get me. My grandparents came to take me home with them. Mom and Dad didn't even come down to kiss me goodbye. I never lived with my parents or Angie again. Just visited sometimes, not that they ever really acted like they wanted to see me." She stepped out of the circle of Hugo's arms. "You have no idea what it's like to be alone and scared when you're that little, and you know nobody's coming to save you."

Hugo's eyes were imploring. "Call him, Lucy. Ask Christopher if he wants you to leave. I will bet you every penny I have that he'll want you to stay and keep playing."

"I can't call him. He's—" A fresh sob caught in her throat. "He's scared of phones."

His brow furrowed in confusion. "What do you mean?"

"His mother's phone wouldn't stop ringing and buzzing one morning. Ringing and buzzing over and over and over. Nobody answered it. Christopher went to answer it, and that's when he saw them—his mom and dad were dead in their bed, and the phone was ringing because her boss wanted to know if she was ever showing up for work."

"Shit." Hugo winced painfully.

"He's scared of phones now," Lucy said. "That's why I can't call him. I can't ask what he wants. I just have to go to him. I just have to."

She started to turn to the door, but Hugo moved to block her. He held up his hands in surrender.

"Listen to me," he said. "I will help you. But I'm serious—you can't go tonight. I wouldn't walk to Jack's house in this storm, much less go out on the water. You will drown, Lucy. What would that do to Christopher if he lost you too?"

She dropped her head. Hot tears ran down her face. She knew Hugo was right, and so was Jack. Tree branches were dancing against the side of Hugo's house, scratching at the windows, cracking, breaking, snapping. She heard the angry roar of the ocean.

"When is he moving?" Hugo's voice was calm, steadying, like a man talking to a spooked horse he didn't want to bolt.

"Soon as school's out," she said. "So Friday evening, Saturday morning."

"Tomorrow is only Wednesday, all right? You have time. When the storm is over in the morning, and we know for certain that we can get you a flight home"—Hugo pointed in the direction of the mainland—"I will take you to the airport myself. You can be back in Redwood by tomorrow night. Safely. If you try to leave now, you won't get home. Ever."

She pursed her lips at him. "You're being a little melodramatic."

"Pot, meet Kettle."

She snorted another laugh. "You're also being a little sarcastic."

"Sarcasm is my native tongue. Now, will you promise me you're done with this foolishness, or do I have to tie you to the dock with a boat rope? I know the clove knot and the pile hitch, and trust me, neither of them will feel very good around your waist."

"Fine," she said, waving her hand. "But only if you swear you really will take me to the airport when the storm is over."

He took a deep breath. "I promise that *if* you still want to leave when the storm is over, I will take you to any airport in a two-hundred-mile radius. Deal?"

Her urge to bolt was still so strong. She turned back, looked past him to the door. Could she trust him? He's given her no reason not to . . .

"Lucy," Hugo said softly. "Please. Jack's lost one of his kids already. Losing another would kill him. Believe me when I say yours would not be the first girl's body to wash up on Clock Island."

Two men on an island, and both blame the water . . .

Lucy turned around. He was giving her a tenuous smile.

"Fine," she said reluctantly. "I'll stay until morning."

Hugo put his hands together, said, "Thank you," with obvious relief. "I'd recommend waiting for a break in the storm before heading back to the house. Have a seat?" He took her—his—coat and hung it on the coatrack. She slipped off her shoes—which were the shoes he'd given her—and set them by the door. He invited her into the living room. He'd started a fire in the fireplace, and it danced red, orange, and blue and sent earthy warmth into her chilled skin. She stood with her back to it while Hugo disappeared through a door.

Alone, she got out her phone and sent Theresa a reply to her text.

Tell Christopher I'll be home as soon as I can. It's storming here, but I should be able to get on a plane tomorrow morning.

Theresa must have been waiting for her text because she replied immediately.

You don't have to come home. I'll make sure you get to see him this weekend. Stay and finish the game. That's what he would want.

Lucy stared at the screen, not knowing what to reply, so she just put her phone back in her pocket.

Hugo came back, carrying a pile of towels.

"Here." He handed her one. She rubbed it on her hair and her face. She didn't want to think about how she looked. Probably insane.

"Who was she?" Lucy asked. She wrapped a dry towel around her shoulders. "Or am I not supposed to know?"

He sat on the coffee table in front of her while she pressed close to the fireplace, trying to dry herself.

"You figured out the riddle?"

"It says the two men lost 'a' wife and 'a' daughter. Not 'his' wife or 'his' daughter. Could be anyone's wife, anyone's daughter they lost."

Hugo nodded. "You're clever."

"I'm a teacher. That's all. Who was the lost girl?"

"Her name was Autumn Hillard," Hugo said, saying the girl's name as if it were covered in dust, a hidden name no longer spoken. "NDAs were signed, and the family couldn't go to the media with their story, so there's nothing online about it."

Lucy's stomach clenched. A nondisclosure agreement.

"There was a lawsuit? Against Jack?"

He crossed his arms over his chest. "Jack is Jack, you know. It's why he's so easy to love. Also why he's so maddening."

She was almost afraid to ask, but she had to know. "What happened?"

"The day I met him, Jack told me the number one rule of Clock Island—*Never break the spell.*"

"The spell?"

He shrugged. "Kids believed Jack was the Mastermind. They thought Clock Island was real. They thought if they told him their wish, he'd grant it. Seven years ago, Autumn wrote Jack a fan letter. She told him her wish, that her father would stop coming into her bedroom at night."

"Oh my God." Lucy covered her mouth with her hand.

"You don't want to know how many letters he gets like that."

"No, I probably don't." She lowered her hand. "What happened?"

"She lived in Portland, so he thought he might be able to help her. Really help her. Not just do the usual—write back and encourage her to tell a trusted grown-up what was happening. All those letters were turned over to the authorities, but it's hard to get the police to investigate an accusation made in a piece of fan mail." Hugo rubbed the back of his neck. It was apparent this was a story he didn't want to tell. "He called her."

"He called her?"

"She put her number in the letter. Jack called her. And this is where it all went off the rails. He just can't help himself, you know. His own father was an absolute tyrant. Our Jack's a teddy bear until you show him a child in trouble, and then you'll see a teddy bear turn into a grizzly." Hugo smiled. Then the smile was gone. "At some point during their conversation, he told her something like, 'If I had one wish, it would be to bring you to Clock Island, where you'd be safe with me forever.'"

It all made sense now. "She believed him."

"She did. She thought if she could get to Clock Island, she could stay with him. She did what you did—hopped a ferry. But the ferry wasn't coming to Clock Island that day. When no one was looking, she jumped off and tried to swim for it." Hugo met Lucy's eyes. "Jack used to walk on the beach every morning before breakfast. That stopped the day he found her body washed up on the Five O'Clock Beach."

Lucy was too shocked to speak.

Hugo went on, fast, like ripping off a bandage. "The family threatened to sue, accused Jack of being a pedophile. Pretty rich of them, right? But like I said, the police can't do much with a single accusation made in a fan letter written by a dead girl. Jack's lawyers paid them off. I don't know the number, but I think it was several million dollars, and everyone signed NDAs. Jack was a zombie then. Otherwise, he would have fought it. After that, he stopped writing, stopped walking on the beach, stopped living. That's when I moved in."

The story was so much worse than she'd ever let herself imagine. She'd told herself Jack Masterson had had a stroke, and that's why he stopped writing. Or he decided to retire young and enjoy his money, or maybe he'd gotten tired of writing kids' books and started writing boring books for boring adults under a pen name or something. She never dreamed he'd inadvertently killed a child with his wishes, that he'd had to pay off a child molester.

"I can't believe he gave them millions," she said.

"If you were wondering why he has a mostly hate-hate relationship with lawyers . . ."

"If it got out in the news—"

Hugo nodded. "It would have ruined him."

The story would have been sordid, sick, sinister. A children's author accused of luring a girl to his private island. Jack's career might have never recovered.

"Poor Jack," Lucy said. She wished she could talk to him now, tell him she was sorry, and give him one long hug.

Hugo stood up. "Now you know why I've been living here for the past six years. Someone had to keep an eye on him, keep him from taking a long walk off a short pier. And there were a few days I literally had to keep him from walking off the dock."

Lucy gave him a small smile. "Thank you for doing that for him."

"He did the same for me." Hugo took the towel from around her shoulders and lightly smacked her in the arm with it. "Now, are you anywhere close to being warm and dry yet?"

"Warm, yes. Dry? Not even close. Guess men with short hair don't keep hair dryers around, do they?"

"Nope," he said. "But artists do."

HUGO FETCHED HIS HAIR dryer out of his studio for Lucy. She took one look at it, then at him.

"Wait. Do you paint with your hair dryer?" she asked. His hair dryer was covered in a hundred flecks of paint in every color of the rainbow.

"If I need to dry acrylic paint double-time, I can use a hair dryer. Little secret of the trade."

"When would you need to dry a painting that fast?"

"When I was supposed to have shipped it yesterday?" He tried to look guilty but knew he'd failed. "According to Jack, deadlines are like parties. One should always be fashionably late. Easy for him to say. He's rich as King Midas. We pitiful commoners show up five minutes early and pray nobody tosses us out."

Smiling—Hugo was relieved to see her smile again—Lucy took the hair dryer and her suitcase into the bathroom. While she was gone, Hugo slipped into the walk-in closet in his bedroom and called Jack.

"Is she there?" Jack asked as soon as he picked up.

"I've got her. Gave her an earful, and she calmed down. Not sure she'll stay put, though." He'd only talked her into staying until it was safe to get to Portland, not all week.

"Distract her with something. Make her help you with a project."

"Distract her with a project?"

"Works every time," Jack said.

"I'll do my best. You—" He hated that he was about to ask this, but he had to know. "You swear to me you didn't arrange this? Because you did tell them all you were going to make them face their—"

"I would not involve Christopher or any other child in this game."

"If it's not this, what are you going to do to Lucy?"

Jack's answer was as infuriating as Hugo expected. "Nothing too sinister."

"If you hurt her—"

"What? You'll punch me in the nose? Call me out for a duel?"

"Keep your hair on," Hugo said. "I'm only saying she's a little fragile right now."

"You like this girl, don't you?" Jack sounded annoyingly pleased with himself, as if he'd masterminded the whole thing. "You have my approval."

"I didn't ask for your approval."

"You have it anyway."

Hugo ignored that. "You should know, I told her about Autumn. Had to. She was distraught, Jack."

"It's all right. She needed to know." Jack was quiet a moment. Then, "Son, try to get her to stay another day at least, please. There's someone coming tomorrow I want her to meet."

"Who?"

"That is for me to know and for Lucy to find out."

CHAPTER TWENTY-TWO

WHEN LUCY CAME OUT of the bathroom, Hugo had disappeared. "Hugo?"

"Come hither!" he called back from the end of a short hallway.

Confused but intrigued, she followed his voice. "Come hither? Who says, 'Come hither'?" she replied.

"I do. Are you coming hither yet?"

She reached a half-open door to what should have been a bedroom, but when she pushed it open, she found herself in Hugo's studio.

"Fine, I'm hith—Wow," was about all she could say. Lucy stood in the doorway, staring before stepping carefully inside. It felt like that moment in *The Wizard of Oz* when Dorothy went from black-and-white Kansas to Technicolor Oz. Every single wall was covered, floor to ceiling, with paintings. The drop cloths covering the floor were stained every color of the rainbow. The few tables in the room were piled high with paints, brushes, water jars, and magic potions, for all she could tell. One ancient metal bookcase held what looked like a hundred well-worn sketchbooks. Even those were covered in paint.

Lucy had to ask, "Do you just stand in the middle of the room and throw paint over things when you get bored?"

"Yes." Hugo was kneeling on the floor by a stack of canvases.

"Is this all Clock Island stuff?"

"More or less. Besides what's gone to charities, I've kept every sketch, every photo, every cover painting, every single bloody note that Jack ever gave me about the paintings." He pulled a yellow Post-it off the back of one canvas and showed it to her.

Lucy took it and read it aloud. "*Spooky Ooooooooh not spooky AHH!*" it read. "That's not helpful."

"Tell me about it."

She handed the note back to Hugo, though she sort of wanted to keep it as a souvenir.

"Everything's here or in storage in Portland," Hugo continued. "Let's just say Jack's publisher impressed upon me years ago the historical and literary importance of . . . all *this*." He waved his hand around.

"You just have them here all stacked against the wall? Not in plastic? Or locked vaults?"

"Only blankets," he said, "and a very good dehumidifier." Hugo tossed a few of the blankets off the painting stacks. "Oh, tea and biscuits over there. Help yourself."

Lucy went to the one table that wasn't covered in paint. "Biscuits? These look like cookies."

"I'm going to teach you to speak proper English," he said. "Cookies are biscuits. Biscuits are scones, but we eat them with clotted cream and jam, not gravy. Gravy is for meat, not biscuits."

"That I can get behind." Lucy picked up the mug. It was warm in her cold hands. She carried it around the room, feeling as if she were at the world's smallest, strangest art gallery.

"I also have cheesecake, which in England we call . . . cheesecake."

"You bake?"

"Never. Stole it all from Jack's kitchen." He picked up his own mug off the floor and stood up. "I'm the world's worst houseguest. Hair dryer work?"

"All dry." She playfully flipped her hair. "Thank you for lending me your, um, paintings' hair dryer?"

"You can repay me by helping me here." He gestured at the stacks of canvases leaning against the wall and piled on a cart. "Long story short, my ex-girlfriend works at a gallery, and she wants some Clock Island covers. Help me pick. I need five."

"You want me to help you pick out paintings for an exhibit?"

"Nobody likes the ones I like, so I need a neutral opinion."

Flattered, Lucy set her mug down and walked over to Hugo. "I don't know how neutral I can be because I love all your work equally."

"Fine," he said. "I'll send her this one."

He held up a painting for the cover for *A Dark Night on Clock Island*.

"Not that one." She waved her hand at the black-and-white painting. "Too dark."

Hugo laughed and stepped back. "See what you can do then."

Lucy knelt on the drop cloth. Luckily the paint was long dry. Slowly she flipped through the paintings, every one of them a book, every one of them a memory.

> *The Pirates of Mars Versus Clock Island*
> *Goblin Night on Clock Island*
> *Skulls & Skullduggery*
> *The Clockwork Raven*
> *The Keeper of Clock Island*

She loved them all, and every kid who loved Clock Island would be thrilled to see the covers like these—painted on large canvases so you could see all the little details.

"Can I ask a personal question?" Lucy said while flipping through another stack of paintings.

"You can ask. No promise I'll answer."

"Is this ex-girlfriend who works at the gallery the original owner of the hiking boots you gave me?"

"Piper," he said. "Here she is."

He plucked a small portrait off the wall—a painting of a beautiful black-haired woman. She looked like a silver screen siren, like Elizabeth Taylor. Lucy wished she hadn't asked. She felt like a plain Jane in comparison.

"*Two men on an island*," she said, meeting his eyes. "I know about the death of a daughter. I guess she was the wife you lost? If she's someone else's wife, she must have gotten married."

Hugo hung the small canvas back on the wall. "I wanted her to be my wife. Back then. She works at one of my favorite galleries in New York. That's where we met. When I moved here to keep an eye on Jack, she came with me." He paused. "I don't think either of us realized how long it would take for Jack to come out of his depression. And island life isn't for everyone. She managed six whole months out here before she couldn't stomach it anymore. Hated being so isolated. Between her and Jack, I had to pick Jack." He took the painting off the wall again and put it on a floor stack, as if he were done with looking at it every day. "She's now happily married to a veterinary surgeon and has a gorgeous little girl. And I am very happy for her."

"More sarcasm?"

He didn't answer at first. Then, "No. I saw her not long ago, and it was gone. The anger. The love, the lust, all of it—gone. I was happy for her." He sighed. "It's too bad. I do much better work when I'm miserable. But I'm moving to New York. That should take care of that."

"And what's the rent here again?"

The smile on his face rendered him so painfully handsome that Lucy pretended to look through the stacks of paintings again, hoping he wouldn't see her red face.

"Find anything you like?" Hugo asked.

You, she thought but kept that to herself. "Um . . . I like all of them. Just trying to find *The Princess of Clock Island.* That one's my favorite."

"Donated to St. Jude's along with *The Prince of Clock Island.*"

"Ah. What about *The Secret of Clock Island?* That's Christopher's favorite."

"Donated to . . . somewhere."

Lucy looked at him, suspicious. "Somewhere?"

"Somewhere."

"Are you not allowed to tell me where?"

"I can tell you. I just don't want to tell you where."

"Hugo . . ."

"The Royal Family has this . . . you know, drawing-school charity and—"

"Stop right there. I already hate you enough," Lucy said.

"It's not that impressive. I mean, it's not like it's hanging in Buckingham Palace. Actually, it could be."

"You can stop talking now."

"I'll fetch more biscuits."

"I was told there might be cheesecake?"

Hugo rolled his eyes. "I'll fetch the cheesecake."

While he was out of the studio, Lucy stood up to stretch her back and noticed another painting half-hidden behind an industrial gray storage shelf. She went to it, pulled it out carefully, and saw it was another portrait. She knew that face, those eyes, that sweet nose.

"Ah, Davey," she said. Lucy heard her host returning, and glanced at him over her shoulder. Hugo wasn't smiling. "I'm sorry. I was being nosy."

"It's all right. It's a good painting. Just . . . some days I want to see him. Some days it's too hard."

"Can I ask what happened?"

"Sometimes kids with Down syndrome have heart trouble. He was one of the unlucky ones."

Hugo set the two plates of cheesecake onto the worktable, moving aside a half dozen paint-stained cups and glasses to make room. "When he was fifteen, they decided he wasn't going to make it much longer without an operation." He paused. Lucy wanted to reach out and take his hand but knew she shouldn't. "There were complications, blood clots. He died in the hospital. Mum was with him, but I was over here. Working."

"I'm so sorry, Hugo." She touched his arm lightly, but he didn't respond, just took the painting back out of its hiding spot again. He hung it on the hook that the portrait of Piper had been occupying. "It's a beautiful portrait."

"Easy to make something beautiful out of something beautiful." He was quiet a moment. Then, "Davey would tell strangers on the street that his big brother drew the Clock Island books. He'd go into a bookshop with Mum, and he'd grab the books off the shelves and walk around, telling everyone who'd listen that his brother drew the pictures. One woman asked him for his autograph. It made his year." He smiled, then the smile faded. "Jack was a prince when it happened. Absolute legend. He paid for the funeral, paid for me to fly over, paid off my mother's house because there was no chance in hell she'd be able to work for months, as hard as she took it. He saved us both."

Lucy knew she was treading close to dangerous waters. Open wounds needed careful handling. "Ah, no wonder you moved in when Jack was struggling," she said softly.

"I owed him so much. And I never thought it would . . ." He looked out the studio window toward the ocean that had killed Autumn and carried Piper away from him. "I thought he'd come through it faster than he did. I don't even know if he is through it yet or if he's putting on a show for my sake so I can leave without feeling like I'm abandoning him."

"He's the Mastermind, remember?" Lucy picked up her plate of cake and gave the other one to Hugo, trying to get a smile out of him again. It worked. "You can guess all you want, but you'll never know what he's really up to."

"I'll eat cheesecake to that." They clinked their forks and dove in.

AFTER ANOTHER FORTY MINUTES and a few thousand calories of cheesecake, Lucy had five paintings picked out from Hugo's archives. He flipped through her choices.

"Ah, *Goblin Night on Clock Island*," Hugo said, nodding his approval. "One of my favorites too."

"That book actually scared me when I was a kid. Most of his books are spooky, but he managed to make that one genuinely scary."

"You want to know the dark secret behind that book?" Hugo set the *Goblin Night* painting on an empty easel.

Lucy stood up, brushed the dust off her clothes, and stood by Hugo. "I don't know. Do I?"

"You remember what that book's about?"

"A boy comes to Clock Island to . . . I don't remember what exactly." She furrowed her brow. "Oh, he thinks his dad is a werewolf, and he wants to find the cure to save him. The Lord and Lady of October send him on a quest into a castle full of monsters. Right?"

"Close enough," Hugo said. "Jack's father was an alcoholic. He said it was like growing up with a werewolf. When he was a normal man, he was all right, he was . . . human. When he was drinking, he turned into a monster, just like that." He snapped his fingers. "Beat him. Beat his mother. Makes my father look like a saint. Mine just sodded off when he decided he didn't want to be a father anymore. He broke only Mum's heart, not her arm."

"My God." Lucy stared at the painting, at the boy in the corner of the canvas, working up the courage to enter the castle where he'll either find the cure for his father's illness or die trying. "I never knew that about him. Does he ever—"

"Talk about it? No. First rule of Clock Island—*Don't break the spell.* Kids need to believe in the Mastermind. They don't need to know who's behind the curtain."

She understood that and appreciated it, but it broke her heart that Jack had to keep so many secrets. What else was he hiding from the world?

Hugo went on. "Jack told me years ago how he invented Clock Island on those nights his father turned into a werewolf. He'd hide under the covers staring at the face of his glow-in-the-dark watch, waiting for the hours to pass. Clocks were magic to him—ten and eleven at night were dangerous hours, werewolf hours, but six and seven and eight in the morning were human times. If he were king of the clock, he could keep those werewolf hours from coming. Somehow the clock became an island, a place where scared kids could go to find their courage."

"That's what I always loved about the books," Lucy said, "even before I knew that's what I loved about them. I just knew that if I could get to Clock Island, I would be welcome there." No wonder Jack understood children so well, knew how to write them so well. Just like a part of Lucy was always going to be in that hospital waiting room, hoping her parents would come back and check on her but knowing they wouldn't, Jack was always going to be in that black castle fighting off monsters to save someone he loved.

She groaned and rubbed her forehead.

"I feel like absolute crap for telling Jack off earlier," she said.

"Don't. He needs to be reminded every now and then that people are not characters in his stories and he can't do whatever he wants with them. And trust me, love, he's taken much worse abuse from me." Hugo lightly elbowed her. She hated how much she liked standing close to him. And she really hated how nice it sounded when he called her "love." In his white T-shirt, the colorful tattoos on his arms were on full display. Every time one of his arm muscles moved, the colors fluttered and shifted. It was like standing next to a living, breathing painting.

"What other paintings did you decide on?"

Lucy showed him her stack. He flipped through them, nodding at her choices. "You picked *The Keeper of Clock Island*."

"Is that bad? I love it." Lucy picked up the canvas and set it on the easel. "The lighthouse and the guy standing on it looking at the night sky . . ." She gestured to the male figure on the walkway, illuminated by the full moon. "It's so striking, you know. So mysterious."

"Jack said it's his favorite. No idea why."

"I can guess."

Hugo looked at her, eyebrow raised.

Lucy gently elbowed him. "Look around," she said, waving her hand at the stacks of memorabilia in his studio. "All the Clock Island paintings, the sketches, the notes, the messages, the whole archives you have here . . ."

"And?"

"*You* are the keeper of Clock Island, Hugo," she said. "If he loves that cover, it's because he loves you."

Hugo looked away. "He'll need another keeper when I'm gone."

"Can I apply?"

He glared at her but with a twinkle in his eyes. "Vulture. The body's not even cold yet."

"Well, hurry up and get cold," she said. "I need a house."

He pointed a finger in her face, then flicked the tip of her nose.

Lucy gasped in feigned shock.

"You deserved that," he said.

"No regrets."

"Out," he said. "Or no more biscuits for you."

Reluctantly, Lucy left his beautiful paint-spattered studio. She returned to the living room and stood at the fireplace. She was warming her hands when her phone buzzed in the back pocket of her jeans. She took it out. Another message from Theresa.

Please stay and finish the game. I promise I'll watch over Christopher. He'll never forgive himself if you give up now because of him.

"Everything all right?"

Lucy looked up. Hugo was standing in the doorway to the living room. His brow was furrowed in concern.

"My friend Theresa just texted to beg me to stay and finish the game. I don't know. Jack said it's a long shot any of us would win. If it's that impossible—"

"It's not impossible. Jack would do a lot of bonkers things, but he wouldn't set you all up for failure. Look, I shouldn't have won my contest. I should be working at a dingy tattoo shop in Hackney, trying not to get knifed on my way home every night. Instead, I'm here." He waved his hand around. "This house, this place, my career . . ." He walked over to her, stood in front of her. "I can't make you stay all week and finish the game. But I can make you this promise—if you leave without seeing it through to the end, you'll wonder the rest of your life what could have been. And trust me, it could be something very beautiful."

"I thought you were miserable," she said.

"I thought I was too." He raised his eyebrows and lifted his hands. "A wise woman recently told me I'm full of shit."

Lucy sighed. "Maybe you are, but you're also right. I don't need any more regrets. I have enough for a lifetime."

Hugo gave her a smile before disappearing back into his studio.

Lucy wrote back to Theresa that she was going to stay and play.

Theresa replied, *And win!!*

And to that Lucy could only write back, *I wish.*

CHAPTER TWENTY-THREE

AFTER TALKING LUCY INTO staying, Hugo sneaked back into his studio and called Jack again. Although it was late, well after midnight now, Jack answered.

"Your evil plan to distract her worked. She's decided to stay," Hugo said. "She's going to finish the game."

Jack breathed a sigh of relief so loud it rattled Hugo's ear. "Good job, son."

"I'll walk her back over to the house now."

"It's still—"

Suddenly there was a shift in the room, a weird dull silence, then darkness.

"Or not," Hugo said. He heard Lucy let out a quick yelp of surprise as the lights went out.

"Batten down the hatches," Jack instructed. "We'll see you both in the morning. If we're still here."

"Do you think it's safe to let Lucy stay here? I don't want them accusing her of cheating because we're, you know—"

"Making gooey eyes at each other?"

"Friends."

"Hugo, my boy, you couldn't help her win the next two challenges if you tried." He hung up.

Hugo checked on Lucy. She agreed staying the night at his cottage was probably the safest bet in this storm. He left her safe in the living room by the fireplace while he gathered blankets and supplies. The softest pillow. The plushest blankets. Even a candle or two. How long had it been since he had a woman staying the night? Too long. He shouldn't be enjoying this as much as he was. He chalked it up to novelty and loneliness. And it didn't hurt that his toes curled in his shoes whenever Lucy smiled in his general direction.

When he returned to the living room, Lucy had built the fire high, hot, and bright. By the firelight, she sat on the floor pillow. He grabbed another pillow and sat by her to get warm.

"Pillows and blankets galore," he said. "You won't freeze to death tonight, at least."

Lucy was peering at him as if he had something on his face.

"What?" he demanded.

"Don't take this the wrong way," Lucy said, "but you look so bizarre without your glasses."

He'd forgotten he'd taken them off in the bathroom when he'd brushed his teeth by flashlight. "Sorry. I'll go and fetch them. I'm fully aware that my face looks best when covered."

She pursed her lips and glared at him. "I meant you look good bizarre. Like really young."

He lifted his eyebrows. "I knew I should have gone for the contact lenses instead."

She picked up the sketchbook he'd left on the floor by the fireplace.

"Were you working tonight when I interrupted you with my, you know, crazy?"

"You weren't crazy, you were upset. And no, just noodling," he said.

"Noodling?"

"That's a Davey word. Noodling instead of doodling. And my drawings were noodles. He was a funny kid." It felt good to talk about Davey, just talk about him with someone who didn't flinch or shy away when he mentioned him like so many other people did, as if grief were catching.

"He sounds like an amazing kid. Can I see your noodles?" she asked, grinning innocently.

He waved his hand to say *be my guest.*

Lucy brushed her hands off on her shirt, which he found painfully endearing because she didn't want to get so much as a smudge on his drawings. She opened the book to the first page. He'd drawn the full moon, craters and all. The circle of it took up the entire page. A pirate ship flying the Jolly Roger floated in the ocean in front of the moon, a corgi at the helm.

"Is there a pirate ship in Jack's new book?"

"No idea," Hugo said as he sat back on the pillow and propped his feet in front of the fire. "But I felt like drawing a pirate ship captained by a corgi floating in front of the full moon, so I did. And to think I once thought I was going to be a serious artist."

"Thank God you didn't," she said. "I don't know a single kid on the planet who has, I don't know, Rembrandts on their walls, but I know a whole lot of kids who have your art hanging in their bedrooms."

"Really?"

She pointed at herself without making eye contact. "*The Princess of Clock Island* poster that came with the book? It hung over my bed for years."

He groaned dramatically. "Thank you. Now I feel ancient."

"You should be flattered."

"Fine. Thank you. I'm very flattered." And he *was* flattered. Old, but flattered.

Lucy kept flipping through the book. "Very nice," she said, eyeing an old drawing of a charcoal raven wearing a watercolor red hat.

"That's Thurl, except with a hat."

"It suits him," she said. The next page was a pencil drawing of a clown holding his head on a balloon string. She turned another page, and her eyebrows shot straight up. She turned the sketchbook around and showed the drawing to Hugo. "Ahem."

"I told you I'd draw you a picture of a Jack and Danny," he said, grinning. Hugo knew he ought to be embarrassed, but sometimes an orchid was just an orchid. Then again, sometimes an orchid was—

"It looks like a vulva," Lucy said.

"That's an orchid from Jack's greenhouse. Second, blame Georgia O'Keeffe, not me. She started it."

She merely shook her head as she turned page after page. "These are amazing," she said. Hugo's chest tightened. Like any artist, he was a sucker for flattery, but it was more than that. Lucy seemed so happy losing herself in his sketchbook, smiling or laughing at every page. He'd forgotten how good it felt to be the reason behind the smile on a pretty girl's face.

"I wish I had any artistic talent whatsoever," she said. "I can knit scarves, but that's more of a craft than an art."

"*Craft* is what they call artwork that's useful to humanity," Hugo said. "And don't let anyone tell you otherwise. I've seen Amish quilts more impressive than a lot of Picassos."

She smiled but said nothing as she studied one particular page for a long time.

Though he knew he should be trotting off to bed, he didn't want the conversation to be over. He enjoyed spending time with Lucy more than he probably should.

"Did you ever want to be an artist?" he asked.

She closed the sketchbook and set it carefully onto the coffee table. "No, but I wanted to work in the arts. Closest I ever got was working as a semiprofessional muse."

He raised his eyebrows. "Semiprofessional muse? How did that work?"

"I dated a writer once," she said. "He called me his muse. I might have taken it as a compliment, except that he wrote books about miserable people."

Hugo laughed softly as she tucked her feet under her legs, making herself smaller.

"Anyone I've heard of?" he asked.

"Sean Parrish?"

Hugo sat up. The name not only rang bells, it rang alarm bells. "Sean Parrish? You're joking."

She winced. "Do you know him? I mean, personally?"

"He and Jack were at the same agency for years, but we never met. His reputation precedes him. Good and bad."

Lucy raised her hands like she was miming a scale. "On one hand, Pulitzer Prize winner," she said. "On the other . . ."

"Legendary arsehole," Hugo said. And not his favorite writer by any stretch. After reading the first fifty pages of one of his books, Hugo had wanted to give himself a paper cut and go swimming with the sharks.

"Right. So . . . yeah," she said with a sigh. "I was his girlfriend."

"Where on earth did you meet him?"

"He was my professor," she said. "Creative writing. Back when I thought I'd work for a publisher someday. I was pretty naive. I thought I could just show up in New York with a degree in English and get a corner office at a publisher's. Why not take a writing class with a famous writer? Maybe he could help me get a job."

"So Sean Parrish sleeps with his students? Not surprised." Hugo tried not to sound judgmental but knew he'd failed. Sean sounded like a lot of male artists he'd known, the sort with egos to match their talent but secretly so insecure they preyed on younger artists like vampires.

"In fairness to him—not that he deserves much fairness—nothing happened until after I was out of his class. Ran into him at a bar on New Year's Eve. I went home with him to his incredibly nice apartment and didn't leave for three years. Well, I mean, I left the apartment. I didn't leave *him* for three years."

"He's . . . Isn't he even older than I am?"

"He's in his early forties now. Forty-three, I think? He'd just won the National Book Award for *The Defectors* when I met him. He had two huge bestsellers and one movie adaptation while we were together. He told me I was his lucky charm, his muse. He thought taking in a stray nobody else wanted or loved had tilted the universe in his favor. I was his good deed."

Hugo's eyes widened. "He said that? He called you a 'stray'? Unbelievable."

"He liked that I was an 'emotional orphan.' That's what he called me. '*The only thing worse than having dead parents is having parents who might as well be dead.*' Or something like that. That's a line from *The Small Hours*. Or maybe it's from *Artifice*. I get those two mixed up." She looked away, stared at the fire a moment. Her voice was hollow when she spoke again. "He was an emotional orphan too, he said. Divorced parents, drugs, cheating, no stability at home, raising himself by age twelve. We were so screwed up we belonged together."

"Cite your source."

"What?" She laughed nervously.

"Jack says you must always cite your sources. Who said you were so screwed up you belonged together? Him? Or you?"

"Him. And I guess I believed him."

She smiled like she was joking, but he could see cracks in the façade. "Lucy . . . That's bloody awful."

"Don't get me wrong. It was fun sometimes. I went to house parties on Martha's Vineyard, ate at Michelin-starred restaurants. I went on his European tour with him. I," she said, pointing at herself, "have had sex in a castle."

"And here I thought you were just a kindergarten teacher's aide," Hugo said, stretching out on the floor. "Who knew I was with an actual muse? Every artist's dream come true. Lucky man."

"Want to see my ink?"

"More than life itself."

"Here, I'm not flashing you, I promise." She turned and lifted her shirt to show him her rib cage, which sported a tattoo about eight inches high of a beautiful Greek woman holding a scroll in her hands. He rolled over on his side, got in close, and studied the outlines in the firelight. He wanted to trace them with his fingertips, but if he started touching her, he wouldn't want to stop.

"Her name is Calliope," Lucy said. "She's the chief of the Greek muses. The muse of epic poetry."

"Please don't tell me Sean Parrish made you get that."

"Oh no, I did this to myself. Thought it would make him happy since I was his 'muse.'"

Hugo looked at it closely, not a man ogling a woman's body but an artist admiring a work of art.

"You know anyone looking for an unemployed muse?" she asked, lowering her shirt.

"I'm a modern artist." He put his hands behind his head. "My muse is the fear of poverty and obscurity."

She smiled, but her eyes looked far away, as if remembering something she wished she could forget. "I will say this for him. He was the first person who made me feel wanted in my entire life. Really wanted. And when you feel wanted for the first time in your life, you realize how much you've been starving for it."

Hugo heard something else in her voice, some old secret sadness creeping in. He sat up and softly asked, "What happened with you two?"

She let out a long breath before she began to speak.

"I should have known the first month we started sleeping together what kind of man he was," she said. "He asked me why I'd taken his writing class when I didn't want to be a writer. I told him I was thinking of working in publishing someday, getting a job in New York at a children's book publisher. I remember hoping he'd say something like, 'You'd be great at that.' Or, 'Sounds like a dream job for you.' Or even just a vague, stupid, 'You can do it. I believe in you.' But no, he rolled his eyes, said children's books weren't real literature, and I should find something to do that didn't involve—you know."

"Books with pictures," he said. He'd heard all the jokes before about his work.

"Right. That. Sorry."

"Don't be. I know you don't believe it."

"No, but I didn't have the guts to say that. I just nodded along and let him kill that dream. But he could be charming and funny and sexy, and we traveled, and his apartment was nice . . . so I stitched a sort of patchwork relationship out of all that. You don't have to be happy to convince yourself you're lucky. Lucky me, dating a famous writer. Then I got pregnant and it all fell apart."

"Oh, Lucy." *Poor mite*, he thought. He wanted to hug her but knew he shouldn't.

"Deep down, I always knew what I was to him—the younger woman he kept around to make people think he was younger. But kids were *not* in his plan. He wanted me to end it. He told me to do it a hundred times, even made an appointment for me."

She took a deep breath.

"And that's how I ended up in California," she said, continuing. "Every time I got out of the shower and looked in the mirror, I saw that stupid muse tattoo. It reminded me how much of myself I'd given up to make him happy. If I stayed, I knew he'd eventually wear me down. So . . . one evening we went to his launch party in Manhattan. I faked a headache and went back to the hotel, grabbed my bags, and ran for it. Put the whole trip out west on the one credit card I had. A friend from college let me stay with her while I figured things out. A couple of weeks later I started bleeding."

Hugo didn't say anything, too afraid of saying the wrong thing.

Lucy's hands clutched into fists. "And . . . I . . . I didn't tell Sean. Anything. At all. Didn't tell him where I was, even. I was still scared he'd talk me into coming back to him. I decided to stay, start over. That's what California's for, right? For people who are on the run, who need a fresh start. I got a job. Started over from scratch. And here I am, still scratching."

"I'm sorry," Hugo said. What else could he say?

"After my miscarriage, there was this little voice in my head that said maybe Sean was right that I shouldn't be a mother."

"No," Hugo said. "No, not a chance. You were ready to swim to California just to hold Christopher's hand. That's not something a bad mother would do. Sean Parrish didn't want a child because that would force him to think of someone other than himself, and don't you dare believe anything else."

She looked up at his ceiling, blinked as if trying to stop herself from crying.

"Listen to me," Hugo said. "If Davey were still alive, and I had to pick someone to take care of him, I would trust him with you before anyone else—Jack included." He was shocked to find as he said it that he meant it.

She smiled. Her eyes were bright with unshed tears. "That's very sweet of you to say, but I can't even take care of myself."

"Do what I did—sponge off your rich friends. That's your real problem—no rich friends."

He was trying to make her laugh. The ghost of a grin flitted across her lips.

"Anyway, that's the whole story. The end."

"The story isn't over yet."

She smiled tiredly. "Yeah, of course. Because I'm going to win this game, right?"

Hugo took her face in his hands and met her eyes. Although he wanted to kiss her, he didn't. That's not what she needed.

"You can do it," he said instead. "I believe in you."

CHAPTER TWENTY-FOUR

LUCY WOKE UP ON Hugo's couch to the sound of a gentle breeze, a tranquil ocean, and the delicious scents of coffee brewing and bread toasting. The sun was out. The power had come back on. No more excuses to run or hide. Lucy slowly sat up and ran her fingers through her hair.

"Hugo?" Lucy called out. He stuck his head out of the kitchen. Already up. Already dressed. Already cooking breakfast. And she was already remembering how nice his large warm hands felt on her face last night, the intensity in his eyes when he said he believed in her. She pushed the thought away before she started blushing.

"Morning," he said. "How do you take your coffee?"

"Injected directly into my bloodstream," she said.

"I'll get the IV drip. Shower's all yours if you want one. Towels in the cupboard in the hall."

Lucy followed his directions but stopped to examine a display box hanging on the wall. Inside was a large gold coin stamped with the image of a man riding a horse. She narrowed her eyes to read the printing on the coin. It was a Caldecott Medal. The highest award a children's book illustrator could receive. Hugo had won a Caldecott? He hadn't told her that. Sean told everyone he met he'd won the Pulitzer.

Quickly, before Hugo caught her in the act, she searched online for the book that had won him the prize—*Davey's Dreamworld*, a gorgeously illustrated picture book about a young boy with Down syndrome who stumbles into another world where all his dreams come true. Flying a plane, climbing a mountain, fighting a giant . . . but when he's offered the chance to stay, he goes back home because he misses his family. It was, of course, dedicated to the memory of David Reese.

The dedication page read, *To Davey, when you're done visiting the Dreamworld, don't forget to come home to us.*

If she wasn't careful, she was going to fall madly in love with Hugo. She already liked him. A lot. Too much. And it seemed he liked her too. Why even think about it? She'd be leaving in a couple of days, as soon as the game was over, and probably never see him again.

But if she won the book for Christopher, that would make it all okay. *Focus on the game,* she told herself. *This isn't about you. It's about Christopher.*

She showered, toweled off, and dug jeans and a light blue sweater out of her suitcase. Hugo rapped lightly on the bathroom door.

"You can come in," she said. "I'm decent."

"Shame," he said, opening the door. He looked so handsome in the doorway in his jeans and T-shirt with dead sexy bedhead. Her heart skipped. She didn't know hearts actually did that in real life.

"Jack called. He says he'd like to see you. Please. The 'please' is from him, not me. But also, please. That one was from me."

"Did he sound mad?"

"If by mad you mean angry, no. He always sounds a little insane, if you ask me."

She sighed and rubbed her temples. "Do I have to?"

"Go on," he finally said. "You know how it works. *The only wishes ever granted are the wishes of brave children who keep on wishing even when it seems no one is listening because someone always is'—*"

"Right, right."

"Hey, Hart Attack," he said with a smile. "Don't be afraid."

Scared but determined, Lucy returned to Jack's house. It was eerily quiet inside, like she was all alone. Then she heard the soft murmur of voices coming from the library. After yesterday, Lucy thought Jack might be angry at her for how she'd overreacted. Maybe he was planning to send her home like he had Dustin. She'd been so awful to him last night.

Still . . . she didn't think she'd been wrong. Overwrought, angry, unkind? Yes. But not wrong. They were real people, and they didn't deserve to have their lives, and their hearts, played with like toys.

Jack was waiting for her in the living room. The doors to the library were closed.

"Ah, Lucy," Jack said with a smile. "How are you?"

Jack had this way of saying *How are you?* like the answer mattered, like the answer was the only thing that mattered.

"Better," she said. "I wanted to say how sorry I am for getting so upset last night. I was a little—"

"Think nothing of it. Please. This has been a hard week for you. And I'm afraid it might get a little harder before it's over."

"Harder?" She glanced at the doors to the library again. Closed. As if someone was in there, hidden away. Someone Jack didn't want her to see just yet.

Someone she was afraid of.

"I hope you don't mind, but I invited a friend of mine here. Someone who would like to speak to you, and I think . . . has a right to speak to you."

"A friend?" Lucy looked at him. Then she knew who was behind those doors.

It was Sean. Of course it was. The man whose baby she'd wanted to have but lost. He and Jack were with the same agency. It wasn't difficult to draw a line between the two men.

Jack had promised to make them face their fears. But inviting her ex-boyfriend to the island? She couldn't believe he would do this to her, but maybe he understood something she didn't. All she had to do was talk to him, tell him what had happened after she left him. Then it would be over.

This was the game. Lucy had to play it to win.

She opened the door to the library.

A woman was seated on the sofa.

A woman? Not Sean?

When she saw Lucy, the woman stood up. At first Lucy didn't recognize her. Then the woman smiled a million-watt smile. Bright white perfect teeth. Just like in her picture on the real estate agency web page.

"Angie?"

CHAPTER TWENTY-FIVE

THE WOMAN RAISED HER hand in a little wave.

"Hi, Lucy. Long time no see."

A heavy silence descended onto the library like a fog. Lucy froze, unsure what to say, what to do, what to feel. At once, she knew. She turned and left without so much as a look back.

"Lucy?" Jack called after her as she brushed past him. "Lucy!"

She reached the stairs. Her gut told her to get away, get to her room, shut the door, and lock it.

She was halfway up the stairs when Jack caught up with her.

"Please, Lucy, I'm an old man. Don't make me run."

His hand clutched the railing. His eyes were wide and imploring.

"Why, Jack?" she hissed. What else could she ask? Why would he do this to her?

"Five minutes," he said. "All I ask. Five minutes to explain. Please?"

Still in shock, Lucy didn't know how to answer. Her sister was downstairs in the library, the last person on the planet she wanted to see—she would have served Sean Parrish wine from a golden goblet before sitting down for a cozy chat with her sister.

"You know how much she hurt me. You know." Lucy's eyes were filled with tears, but she refused to blink, refused to shed them. She'd shed enough tears in her life over her sister.

Jack put his hand over his heart and said, "My kingdom for five minutes. Please?"

Something in his voice, his eyes, gave her pause, made her think her pain was causing him pain. Even in her anger, her shock, her sadness, she remembered that his books had gotten her through the worst years of her life. She might not owe him much, but she could give him five minutes.

"Five minutes," she said.

"Thank you, dear girl. My office?"

On leaden feet, she walked down the hall to his writing factory. She felt like a kid again, scared and unsure. Jack opened the door for her and let her in. He pointed to the old sofa, the same one she'd sat on at thirteen, but she shook her head.

"I'll stand," she said.

He didn't argue, just sat behind his desk.

"It's fun, isn't it?" he said. "Reading all about people facing their fears. Not so much fun to do it yourself."

"I'm not afraid of Angie. I hate her. There's a difference."

"I know fear when I see it," he said. "Trust me. I see it in the mirror every morning."

Lucy glared at him. "What are you afraid of? You're rich. You can buy anything you need or want."

"I can't buy time. No one in the world can buy time. All those wasted years of my life . . . I can't buy them back. And if there was one thing I would buy if I could, it would be the time I wasted running from what I was afraid of instead of facing it."

His voice trembled with regret. Lucy sank slowly down onto the sofa.

"What do you regret?" she asked. He'd achieved so much—fame, wealth, the love and adoration of millions . . .

He sat back in his chair and gave a little whistle. Thurl Ravenscroft flew over from his perch and landed on Jack's wrist. He stroked the bird's graceful neck.

"I wanted to be a father," he said. He pointed at her. "Bet you didn't know that about me."

"No, I didn't know that about you. Why—"

"Oh, you know why. Even now, it's hard for a single man, especially a single gay man, to adopt children. Imagine how impossible it seemed thirty years ago when I was young enough to do something so brave and stupid as try to be a father on my own."

"It wouldn't have been stupid. Brave, maybe, but not stupid."

"My writing career was just getting started," he said. "I used that as an excuse to put it off. Then I was in love with someone who didn't love me back. That old song and dance. After that I was famous, and I used that as another excuse to put it off. Fact is, I was worried the truth about me would get out, and schools would ban my books. And if you think I'm being paranoid, let me remind you that a cute little book about two male penguins raising a chick is still one of the most banned books in America, Land of the Free."

"I'm sorry, Jack. You would have made an incredible father. Better than mine. Not that that's saying much, but I . . . God, I wanted you to be my father so bad when I was a kid. You know that."

He gave her a wan smile. "Hugo tells me you know about Autumn?"

She paused before replying. "He told me, but you could have told us. We would have understood."

"I've always believed that children should never have to worry about adults, that something's gone very wrong when they do."

"I believe that too," Lucy said. "But we're not kids anymore."

"You are to me." He smiled at her. "And Autumn . . . after that phone call with her, I contacted my attorney. I wanted a police investigation of her father. I would pay for it myself if I had to. Stupid old man . . . I thought I could save her, bring her here, adopt her. In my heart, she was already my daughter. And then she was dead all because of me and the promises I couldn't keep. What kind of father . . ."

"You aren't the one who made her want to run away in the first place. You just gave her somewhere to go, somewhere she knew she would be safe, if she could only get there. I mean, that's what Clock Island is to kids. Even the kids who'll never ever come here, they can go to Clock Island in their imaginations. When things got too bad in my real life, I came here in my dreams. It helped."

"That's sweet of you to say, but I admit that for years I've wished

Clock Island had never existed—on the pages of my books or under my own two feet. She might still be alive."

"Don't wish Clock Island away," she said. "Too many of us need it. I started reading the books to Christopher the first night he came to stay with me. He'd found his parents dead that morning, and he was . . . lost. In shock. A zombie. Then I got out the books and started reading. Got to the end of chapter one, and I asked him if he wanted me to stop. He shook his head, and I kept reading. The next day, he asked me to read him another Clock Island book. The stories brought him out of the bad place he was stuck in. And me. And Andre. And Melanie. And Dustin. And Hugo."

"Hugo," Jack repeated. "I'll tell you a secret, kiddo. I think I dallied so long pulling myself together after Autumn's death because I knew the minute I was back at work, Hugo would leave. I would lose the closest thing I ever had to a child of my own."

"You could still adopt," Lucy said. "It's never too late."

"Ah, but I'm too scared," he said with a smile. Then the smile was gone. "People think I put myself into my own books, that I'm the Mastermind. I'm not. Not really. I'm always the child, forever the child, scared but hopeful, dreaming someone will be able to grant my wish someday." He met her eyes. "Sometimes the thing we want most in the world is the thing we're most afraid of. And the thing we're most afraid of is often the thing we most want. What do you want most in the world?"

"Christopher, of course. You know that."

"And what are you most afraid of? I think we both know, don't we?"

Lucy looked away, blinked, and the tears fell.

"What if I can't do it on my own? I don't know how to be a mother," she finally said. "Christopher's already been through hell and back. I can't fail him. It'll kill me to fail him. Sometimes, deep down . . . I think maybe he would be better off with someone else."

She remembered what Mrs. Costa had said, that once Lucy told Christopher she would never be his mother . . . it would be a relief. What if she was right?

Jack looked at her. His eyes were gentle and kind.

"We tell people," he said, "to follow their dreams. We tell them that they won't be complete until they do, that they'll be miserable until they start reaching for that brass ring. They never tell you how good it feels to give up on a dream. That it's a . . ."

"Relief?" Lucy said.

"A relief, exactly," Jack said, nodding. "I decided one day that kids weren't ever going to happen for me, that I was going to be single and childless and that was that. And I awoke the next morning and the sun was dancing on the water and the coffee tasted better than it ever had. It tasted like one less thing to worry about. One less promise to keep. One less fight to fight. One less heart to break. And it was sweet. Almost as sweet as victory. The sweetness of giving up."

Lucy stared out at the sunlight dancing on the water for her. "Last night at Hugo's . . ." she began, not believing she was saying this but knowing Jack—if only Jack—would understand. "I had this thought. What if I gave up? On me and Christopher, I mean? What if I never did become his mother? Maybe I could be somebody's girlfriend instead, let someone else drive the car. Let someone else, you know, drive my life. Obviously, I shouldn't be at the wheel, right?" She gave a sad little laugh. Jack only looked at her with compassion. "Like you said—one less thing to worry about."

"He likes you. Our Hugo. I bet if you went down to the house right now and told him you wanted him to kiss you, he would. If you told him you had decided you didn't want to finish the game, didn't want to talk to your sister, he'd understand."

"Maybe so."

"So why don't you? It's either talk to Angie or quit the game."

Lucy pictured herself giving up, giving in—one less thing to worry about, as Jack said—and it was a nice picture. Walking down the stony path to Hugo's little house, knocking on the door, telling him what happened, that Jack had sprung her sister on her, the sister who'd hurt her unforgivably. Hugo would be sympathetic. He'd hold her. He'd kiss her if she told him to. She'd cry to him. He'd comfort her. They'd go for a walk on the beach . . . the first of many walks on the beach together. *I can't do it anymore,* she'd tell him. *How can I take care of Christopher when I can't take care of myself?*

And maybe he would say, *It's all right. I'll take care of you.*

And someone else out there could take care of Christopher. And he'd be fine. Eventually.

A nice dream.

Tempting.

Lucy stood up and went to the big picture window in Jack's office. She gazed down the path to Hugo's, then at the sunlight dancing on the water.

"I went to live with my grandparents when I was eight. I always wanted my parents to come for me at school," she said. "Just show up one day, pick me up and take me home. Never happened."

Jack went to the window, stood beside her. "I'm sorry. It should have happened. If you'd been mine, I would have gone into your classroom with balloons, an ice cream cone, and then put you on the back of a pony and thrown a parade to have you back."

"I can't give Christopher a parade," she said, "and I can't . . . I can't even pick him up and take him home. But I can show up. I can do that."

Jack turned and kissed her gently on the forehead—like she always wanted her father to do—and said softly, "See? I was right. I told you Astrid was still here."

Astrid. Her.

Lucy went downstairs to face her fears.

LUCY OPENED THE LIBRARY door and found Angie standing at one of the bookshelves holding a copy of *The House on Clock Island* in her hands. She closed it and held it against her chest like a shield.

"Hey," Angie said.

"Hey."

"Sorry to surprise you. I . . . Anyway, you look great." Angie smiled. "I can't believe how old you are. I barely recognized you. What were you, seventeen, eighteen maybe, the last time I—"

"Angie," Lucy said. "I'm here only because Jack asked me to talk to you."

Her sister didn't seem surprised by that. She looked at the floor, then said, "Sorry. Really." Angie sounded scared. Or was it ashamed? She finally looked up at Lucy. "But it is good to see you."

"Is it?"

"It is. Believe it or not." She crossed her arms over her chest, pressing the book to her heart.

Lucy sat on the sofa's arm where Hugo always perched when in the library. Angie gave her a wary smile and sat opposite her on the sofa.

"Before you say anything else," Angie said, "I wanted to tell you that I'm sorry for showing up here without warning you. I wanted to call you, but Jack asked me not to tell you. Plus, I thought if I tried calling you, you'd hang up on me."

"I would have."

"Yeah, which I understand."

"Do you?" Lucy leaned forward, studying this stranger who was supposedly her closest family. "Do you have any idea what it's like to grow up feeling unloved and unwanted by your entire family? And not just to feel like it but to know—*for a fact*—you weren't wanted? Didn't you say so yourself? Your exact words: 'Mom and Dad only had you because they thought I needed a bone marrow transplant. They didn't want you and neither do I.' You said that, right? And in front of literally twenty people at your sixteenth birthday party. Your birthday party I was so excited I was allowed to attend? You were like a celebrity to me, Angie. I used my own money to buy a new outfit. Grandma did my hair up perfect. Stupid me thinking maybe I could finally move back home? Oh, but you couldn't stand that idea. You couldn't share Mom and Dad for a single second. All I did was ask Mom if I could move home and you decided to tell everyone in the entire house that I was basically an expensive purchase you all couldn't return." All the anger and pain Lucy had bottled up for years poured out at once. "Do you remember that? Because I remember it almost every single day."

She could still hear those words ringing in her ears—*They didn't want you and neither do I . . .*

Lucy had been twelve years old.

"I . . ." Angie glanced away.

Coward, Lucy thought. Her own sister couldn't even look her in the eyes.

"I did say that, yes. I did say those awful words." Finally, Angie looked at her. "I would give anything to take them back. And I'm sorry. I'm very, very sorry. Sorry enough I won't ask you to forgive me or make excuses. I was only sixteen, but you know what? I knew I was being horrible, and I said it anyway. I'd take those words back if I could, but I can't. All I can do is tell you I'm sorry."

Lucy couldn't say anything. Words refused to form. She'd imagined this day a thousand times, when her mother or father or sister or all of them would come crawling to her, begging for forgiveness. Sometimes in her daydreams, she forgave them. In most of her dreams, she didn't. She told them it was too little too late, that Lucy had moved on, didn't need them anymore. Then she got up and walked away, never turning back no matter how loudly they called her name.

Finally, Angie broke the silence in the room. "Anyway," she said, "I'll go now. You deserve an apology, but you also deserve to be left alone if that's what you want."

Angie pushed herself slowly up off the sofa. Lucy noticed a grimace of pain and wondered if her sister had lingering complications from all her childhood illnesses. This wasn't part of her daydreams.

"You can stay," Lucy said.

Angie looked at her, suspicious, before slowly easing down onto the sofa again.

"Can I just ask," Lucy said, "is what you said true? Did Mom and Dad have me because the doctors said you might need bone marrow someday? And when you ended up not needing it, I was just taking up space?"

Angie sat back on the sofa, her eyes staring blankly at the cold and empty fireplace.

"Can I tell you something?" Angie asked. "Will you listen?"

"I'm here," Lucy said. "Go on."

"Did you know that the kids who grow up as the 'favorites' in families are usually more screwed up than the kids who aren't the favorites? The first lesson we learn is that our parents' love is conditional and that failure to perform means that they can take all that love away. We see it with our siblings, so we do everything we can to make sure that never happens to us. Fun, right? I learned that in therapy."

Lucy couldn't quite speak yet. She took a moment and then said, "You're in therapy?"

"I've been in therapy since I was seventeen," she said and gave a cold little laugh. "Mom and Dad's idea. Well, command."

"Because you were traumatized by being sick your entire childhood?"

"Because they weren't happy unless I was sick," she said. "They liked me when I was sick. They liked sending me to doctors and getting me treatment. Once I got better physically, I had to have other things wrong with me for Mom and Dad to fix. So first they said I had a learning disability, then an eating disorder, then they decided I was depressed and possibly bipolar. You name it, they tried to find a doctor to say I had it. They sent me to every psychiatrist and psychologist and psychotherapist they could find. If they weren't heroes, trying to do everything they could to save their precious baby, what else would they do with their lives, right?"

Lucy couldn't believe what she was hearing. It was like learning her sister was a spy, and now she was double-crossing their parents.

"They're not healthy people," Angie went on. "I don't know if they're both narcissists or it's just Mom, and Dad's so weak he can't help but follow her lead . . . Who knows? Not that it matters. Whatever's wrong with them . . ." She looked up at the ceiling as if trying not to cry. "Let's just say, looking back, I envy you for growing up with Grandma and Grandpa instead of at home. I know you're pissed at me for what I said at my birthday party, but I promise you this—you're the lucky one, Lucy. I wish you knew . . ."

Lucy simply stared at her while her brain tried to process what she was hearing. "I'm sorry. I can't wrap my mind around all this."

"Really? I thought you left because you'd figured it all out. Another thing I learned in therapy?" Angie said. "The kids in dysfunctional families who act out and rebel are the ones who are the healthiest mentally. They're the ones who see that something's wrong. That's why they act out—because they see the house is burning down, and they're screaming for help. That was you. The rest of us were just sitting at the kitchen table, eating dinner, while everything was burning down around us. I should have listened to you. I should have screamed for help too."

Warily, Lucy listened while Angie shared her side of the story, haltingly at first, but then it all seemed to come out in a rush, like a dam breaking at last ...

Angie spent half her childhood sitting at her window, watching other kids playing in the streets, going trick-or-treating, riding bikes, sitting in their backyards reading or running around or climbing trees. She hated other kids, but it was jealousy and nothing else. She knew that now. And yes, she'd really been sick. That had all been real, but there was no need to send Lucy away, except it made her parents seem like bigger heroes to the world, that their oldest child was so ill they had to focus 100 percent on getting her better. Oh, and what a sacrifice to give up their youngest daughter. What heartbreak! What heroism! It made Angie want to puke.

Then, finally, Angie was better. Stronger, healthier ... Angie figured out fast that when she wasn't sick, her parents lost all interest in her. She started to fake illness, to fake a fever, to pretend to be sick. It played right into her parents' hands. Then it started all over again. The therapist appointments. The martyrdom of Mom and Dad.

"Except it didn't work out how they wanted," Angie said, her face triumphant. "My therapist saw what was going on. I wasn't the screwed-up one in the family. Mom and Dad were. And I was done playing along."

"Done? What do you mean?" Lucy asked.

"I haven't seen Mom and Dad in years," Angie said with a note of pride in her voice, the satisfaction of a woman who'd escaped from prison. Lucy's mouth was too dry to speak. She had never been so stunned in her life.

"I can't stand being around them," Angie continued. "Now that I'm better, they don't have much use for me either. They've adopted two kids from Eastern Europe. Mom's got a blog about everything she does for them. Don't read it. The comments about what a hero Mom is will make you throw your phone out the window."

Lucy could only shake her head. Her parents? Heroes? They never even called her on her birthday.

"The thing is," Angie said into the silence, "of all the things I'm angriest at them about . . . it's you. It's losing my sister that hurts the worst. I remember . . ." She smiled, as if remembering something beautiful. "Mom and Dad lost their shit when you ran away to live here. They thought you would get them arrested for child neglect or something. That's all they cared about. Not you, just their reputations. But I thought you were amazing. Absolutely amazing. I'd never read the books, but I read a couple of them after that, even wrote Jack Masterson a letter, telling him I was your sister. He wrote me back and told me what an incredible girl you were, how lucky I was to have such a smart and brave sister. He tried to get me to apologize to you for what I said, but I just couldn't do it. Every time I wrote him, he'd write back and tell me to talk to you. Eventually I stopped writing him. I felt too guilty. Then he set up this contest, and you were part of it. And I got a phone call from Jack Masterson, and now I'm part of it too. So . . . here I am. And I'm sorry. Again. Always."

"I've been waiting my whole life for you to tell me you were sorry."

"You don't have to wait anymore. I'm sorry, Lucy. I was scared of losing Mom and Dad's love. I already felt myself losing it the healthier I got. And I was scared you would take the attention away from me. I was healthy then, and you were, too, and if we were playing by the same rules, you know . . ." Angie looked up, looked away, then finally looked at Lucy. ". . . you'd win."

Lucy laughed in shock. "Win? Win what?"

"Life." Angie shrugged. "You'd win life. Because of Mom and Dad treating me like a Fabergé egg . . . I didn't even know how to make tea. I . . . I didn't even know if I *liked* tea."

"I didn't know if I liked tea either," Lucy said, because she had to say something. "Jack made me tea with tons of sugar. It was pretty great."

"You call the most famous kids' writer in the world by his first name. He made you tea with sugar. The police hauled you off his private island." Angie held out her hands to Lucy. "You won life. And I didn't even come in second."

Something happened inside of Lucy's heart. The wall around it began to crumble and fall.

"They wouldn't even let me have a cat when I was little," Angie said. "And it was the only thing I wanted. One cat. I have two now," she said and smiled. "Vince Purraldi and Billie Pawliday."

"You stole those names from Jack's books."

"He said he approves of that sort of theft." She leaned forward. "Oh, Lucy, you have no idea how many times I wanted to call you over the years and tell you all of this, but I kept talking myself out of it. I was just a coward. I'm still a coward. Jack had to talk me into coming here to see you."

"I thought about calling you too. But only because I needed money."

"I would have given it to you. Still need it? I've got it."

"No. I mean, yes, I still need it, but I don't want you to give it to me."

"Well, if you change your mind." Angie gave her a fragile smile. "Is there anything else I could give you? I promise, if you want more horror stories about Mom and Dad, I've got them."

"Are you ever scared that if you have kids, you're going to screw them up like Mom and Dad screwed us up?"

"Oh yeah. All the time. I've only had two boyfriends, and one was a total narcissist—"

"Been there."

"But the other was so nice I didn't . . ." She shook her head. "He deserved better. But not you."

"Not me what?"

"I'm not worried about you having kids. You'd be a great mom. You know kids deserve to be loved. You knew *you* deserved to be loved, and you tried to tell us all that, and we just didn't listen."

Lucy wanted to say something. She wasn't sure what, but maybe something like, *Thank you for telling me all this.*

But then Jack rapped his knuckles gently on the library door and peeked his head in. "Sorry to interrupt, but the ferry's coming, Miss Angie. If you're ready."

Angie smiled at him, then at Lucy. "Don't want to overstay my welcome."

She stood and walked to the door. Lucy said, "I can walk you to the dock."

Her sister smiled. "Thanks. I'd like that."

On the way down the path to the dock, Angie looked around. "This place is incredible. You're so lucky."

At the dock, they waited as the skipper moored the ferry. The water was calm. Seagulls circled overhead, looking for lunch among the broken branches and other storm debris.

"Anyway," Angie said, the moment growing awkward between them again, "I hope I see—"

"Why now?" Lucy asked suddenly.

"What?"

"Why are you talking to me now? Why not a year ago, three years ago? It's not just a contest. Why did Jack have to talk you into—"

"I didn't want to waste any more time," Angie said. "That's all."

The skipper helped Angie onto the ferry.

"Talk to you soon?" Angie asked. "I'd love to hear from you when the game's over. Tell me if you win?"

Lucy hesitated before replying. "Maybe."

The boat engine revved, and they moved away from the dock. Jack came and stood by Lucy as the ferry churned its slow way through the shallows and into the deep waters.

"She thinks I'm lucky."

"Ah, well, you do have your health."

"Why did I always assume her life turned out perfect?" Lucy said.

"Because she had your parents' love. You thought she'd won the lottery. But you've heard about the lottery winner's curse, yes?"

She had. And it seemed Angie had been cursed. She'd won their love but lost it just as easily.

"I can't forgive her just yet," Lucy said as the boat disappeared from view.

"Of course not."

"But I don't hate her."

"Hate is a knife without a handle. You can't cut something with it without cutting yourself."

"Jack—"

"Lucy, please know that I'm sorry for hurting you today," Jack said. "I know that wasn't easy, and that I'm a meddling old fool, but if you take a little time—"

"Jack?"

He turned to face her. His expression was that of a condemned man waiting for the axe to fall.

"Thank you."

PART FIVE

One Last Little Question

"One last little question," the Mastermind said from inside the shadow that seemed to follow him wherever he went.

Astrid's blood went cold. One more question? Hadn't she passed all the tests? Answered all the riddles? What was left for her and Max to do? Her mom and Max were waiting for her at the dock. She wanted to be with them, wanted to get home, start packing. Oh, but first they were going to call Dad and tell him the big news, that they were going to move to be with him instead of sitting at home, wishing and hoping he'd magically get a new job in town. Time to go. Time to start a new life. Time to put their family back together. Tick-tock, the clock said. Tick-tock, time to leave the Clock.

"What's the question?" Astrid stood in the doorway, one foot in the house on Clock Island, one foot out, ready to sprint to the dock.

"You can tell me the truth," he said. "The whole truth. No . . . the deep truth. Is this what you want more than anything else?"

The truth. The whole truth. The deep truth.

"I love it here," she said and turned her head to look at the endless silver water, the forever blue-gray sky. "I want us all to be with Dad but also . . . I wish I could come back here someday."

"To your town?"

"No, here. Clock Island. Can I?"

"*Can you come back to Clock Island? If you're brave enough, perhaps you'll get that wish granted too.*"

"*Why do only brave kids get their wishes granted?*" she asked.

"*Because only brave children know that wishing is never enough. You have to try to make your own wishes come true. Like you and Max did.*" The shadow moved a little closer to her, and it seemed almost to smile. "*Run along. Your mother is waiting, and the fairy boat is on its way.*"

Astrid glanced over her shoulder. The boat, skippered by a fairy with dragonfly wings instead of sails, was almost at the dock.

"*One last little question from me,*" Astrid asked. "*What's your wish?*"

The shadow of the Mastermind smiled again, but then the smile was gone, and the shadow was just a shadow once more, and she knew he was gone too. Someday, when she got her wish and returned to Clock Island, she would ask him again.

Astrid turned and ran to the dock, to her mother, her brother, and the new life waiting for them on the other side of the water.

—From *The House on Clock Island*, Clock Island
  Book One, by Jack Masterson, 1990

CHAPTER TWENTY-SIX

TODAY WAS THE LAST day of the contest. Someone would win the game. Or no one would win. But whatever happened, by tomorrow the game would be over, and they would all go home.

Lucy was sitting on the front porch in a white rocking chair, watching the sun shimmer as it set across the water. Though all seemed peaceful, her heart raced. The stillness in the air wasn't the stillness after a storm, but the stillness in the eye of the storm. She tried to pace her breathing with the slow back-and-forth of the rockers. As she rocked back, she breathed cool salt air in through her nose. As she rocked forward, she exhaled the warm breath out through her lips. Back-and-forth, back-and-forth . . . The sound of the rhythmic roll of the rockers on the white wooden porch boards returned Lucy to the age of ten. She was sitting on her grandparents' porch in their double rocker—Grandma and Grandpa Hart in the porch swing swaying, the coils squeaking—the soundtrack of a quiet evening, peaceful and safe.

She had been loved. Not by her parents, no, but her grandparents had loved her even if they hadn't understood her loneliness. They would call her out to their porch on warm evenings, wanting her with them as they relived the day in soft conversation. No TV. No radio. Just them and the crickets.

Yes, she had been loved. Her grandparents, so different from the aloof and hard-hearted son they raised, must have wanted to travel and be free of toys on the floor and bake sales and parent-teacher conferences, but they had sacrificed for her, had taken her in—happily, without complaining—and given her love. She'd wanted her parents and her sister, wanted to have what other kids seemed to have. Still, she'd gotten something else instead, and now, after her talk with Angie yesterday, she wondered . . . had she gotten something better?

Maybe so. She knew what it was like to love a child well. She knew what love looked like, and she knew what sacrifice looked like. Her grandparents proved that you didn't have to be *the* parent to be a good parent. Whatever happened with Christopher, someday she would be a good mother to him. If she lost, she would go back to Redwood. On Friday, she would tell Christopher goodbye, tell him she loved him, and make him the same promise she'd made him two years before—*I will do everything I can for us to be together.*

Then she would do whatever it took to keep her promise.

The sky was pink and orange and blue and wild as the sun went down. A screen door opened, swung shut with a clatter. A hand gently touched her shoulder and squeezed it.

She looked up. Hugo, of course. He smiled at her.

"You ready?" he asked.

Lucy nodded her head. "As ready as I'll ever be."

The sky was red as fire as Lucy went into the house. Sailor's delight, Lucy remembered. She hoped it was a good sign.

The other contestants were in the library when they arrived, waiting. What fears had they faced down yesterday in order to be here? The three of them had kept their distance from one another the past twenty-four hours as they awaited the final game.

Andre stood with his back to one of the bookcases. His jaw was set, and his eyes were like two penetrating lasers. He lifted his chin, eyes narrowed, eyeing her like one gladiator greeting another. His expression said, *I like you and respect you, but I will try to beat you, and I expect you to do the same.*

Melanie sat on the sofa, hands clutched around her knees, rocking slightly as if to self-soothe. She gave Lucy a shaky smile that Lucy returned. All of them could have their lives changed by winning the game. As she walked past Melanie to the armchair where she always sat, Lucy put her hand on her shoulder. Melanie looked up at her.

"I wish we could all win," Lucy said. Melanie took her hand and squeezed it.

"Same."

Ms. Hyde was there, of course, watching but not speaking to anyone. She wore a smug look on her face as if she already knew she'd be walking out of this house with the book in her pocket for Lion House.

After a few minutes, Jack entered the library. He took his usual station in front of the fireplace and faced them all. The room was so quiet Lucy could hear the rush and roar of the ocean, even the cry of a gull or two in the twilight.

"Tick-tock," Jack said, "time's running out on the Clock." He smiled. "Before we begin, let me say how wonderful it's been for me to have you all here. You kids, I mean. Not the lawyer."

"I get that a lot," Ms. Hyde said.

Jack went on. "When you get to be my age, and there is more sand run out of your glass than in it, you have to choose whether you'll finish what you started or if you'll leave the world with . . ." He paused, met Lucy's eyes, "with a train track that leads to nowhere." He smiled again and looked at them all. "Years ago, I promised that when you were older, you could come back here someday. I'm glad I was able to keep that promise. Andre, Melanie, Lucy . . . I couldn't be prouder of you all than if you were my own kids. And I will confess there were times I wished you were my own kids."

"I wanted that too," Melanie said.

"All of us, Jack," Andre said. "No disrespect to my parents, but I wouldn't say no to an island of my own."

Lucy didn't say anything. She didn't have to. Jack knew how much she loved him, wished she could have grown up with him as her father instead of her useless parents. But as a kid, she wanted him to be her father. Now that she was an adult, she wanted to be his daughter.

"Alas, as they say, all good things must come to an end. And as you all know, in my Clock Island books, the story isn't over until the Mastermind asks one last little question. And now it's time for me to ask that last little question. And if you get it right, you'll be awarded five points. And since five points will take all of you up to or past ten to win, the game is up for grabs."

He looked at them all again. "Do we all have our phones with us?"

Lucy, Melanie, and Andre looked at one another. They all had them but only out of habit. They weren't allowed to use their phones during the games. What was going on?

"I'm a firm believer," Jack said, "in the power of love and friendship. So if you need to call a friend to help you answer our last question, then you may. None of us should have to make our wishes come true on our own."

The room was quiet. Everyone seemed to be holding their breath.

"Ms. Hyde?" Jack said. "Would you care to do the honors?"

The whip-slim lawyer stood up. She faced them with an icy smile. "One last little question . . . for five points and to win the game," Ms. Hyde said, "and as Jack said, you may phone a friend . . . What two words appear on page 129 of *The Secret of Clock Island* paperback edition, copyright 2005? You have five minutes to answer. Oh, and you cannot leave the room."

Lucy gasped. Melanie looked shell-shocked. Andre put his hand over his mouth. Was he smiling behind his hand, or had his jaw dropped?

At once, he and Melanie began scrolling through their phones. Lucy held her phone like a dead thing in her hand, hardly able to believe Jack would do this to her. The one person she could call wouldn't talk to her over the phone; Christopher wouldn't talk to anyone over the phone. She'd given him her entire Clock Island collection, though. He was still her best shot at winning this thing. She sucked in a deep breath and called Mrs. Bailey's cell, already dreading the extra time it would take using her as a go-between but having no choice. Only Christopher would know at a glance of the spines which book she was after.

Andre had already gotten someone to answer. "Baby, put Marcus on the phone right now." A pause. "Don't ask questions, Marcus. You run to your room right now and get a book off your shelves. It's a Clock Island book." Another pause. "What? Who'd you trade them to? You traded my

Clock Island books? We're going to talk about that when I get home. Right now, you get your mother's phone and call her."

Melanie was scrolling through her phone contacts. She stopped on one name, dialed. "Jen? I need you to run to the Clock Island books on the shelf, see if we have number thirty-two."

Lucy's call went to voice mail. It took all of her willpower not to bean Jack with her phone. She could feel Hugo's eyes on her. Lucy called again, betting that Mrs. Bailey was probably just in the next room with the twins. With every ring, precious seconds were draining away. When it went to voice mail again, she simply redialed. Someone had to hear her calling over and over in that house. Where was Mr. Bailey? Even though she knew Christopher wouldn't pick up, there was still a chance he would see she was calling if the phone was sitting out on the counter.

If you're there, Christopher, get Mrs. Bailey to answer her damn phone, she said in her mind like a prayer. *It's your mother calling.*

CHAPTER TWENTY-SEVEN

IN HIS BEDROOM, CHRISTOPHER was packing his clothes into his bag. It was a nice bag. Mrs. Bailey had gone to the Goodwill that day and bought him his own suitcase. He'd never had a suitcase of his own, and this was a really cool one. It was blue and red with a rocket ship with the words BLAST OFF! on it in big letters made of smoke. It had some scuffs and scrapes, but otherwise it was nice and looked almost new after Mrs. Bailey wiped it off with Windex and some paper towels. Better than the last time he moved when all his stuff had to go into a garbage bag. His books that Lucy had given him would go into a cardboard box Mrs. Bailey promised to find for him. Maybe he should ask her about that. He couldn't leave his books behind, but she had taken the babies for a walk around the block, and Mr. Bailey was asleep in their bedroom and wouldn't get up until it was time to start his night job.

Christopher remembered that sometimes there were cardboard boxes by the back door set aside for recycling. He'd feel better once his Clock Island books were packed up and ready to go with him. Mrs. Bailey had told him his new foster family, Jim and Susan Mattingly, were a really nice couple with two kids in college, and they'd decided they weren't ready for an "empty nest." He thought that meant they kept pet birds, but Mrs. Bailey explained that just meant their kids were growing up and leaving home.

He found the recycling area in the kitchen, but it looked like the boxes in it this week were all too small.

Maybe he'd better wait for Mrs. Bailey to come back inside to help him find a box. Until then, he'd open the fridge to look for a Capri Sun. They didn't have them all the time because Mrs. Bailey said they were expensive, but because he was leaving this week, she'd bought a bunch for him.

As he drank his fruit punch Capri Sun—his favorite because it was the sweetest one, and it always turned his tongue red—he thought about his plan. He was going to be really good at the Mattinglys' house and make them see how smart he was and how well he could read. After a day or two, he'd tell them about Lucy, and if they were as nice as he hoped, then they would let Lucy move in with them too. She could be his mom and they could be his grandparents, and everybody would be happy. He didn't remember much about his grandparents— they'd died even before his parents did—but he did remember his grandpa being funny and laughing loud and giving him great big hugs and throwing him in the air and catching him. Life would be great with a mom *and* a grandpa.

It would be really great. It would be the best. And Mrs. Bailey said the Mattinglys were "supernice." He liked the sound of "supernice." But if he liked the sound of "supernice" so much, why was he crying so hard?

The phone began buzzing in the hallway. Christopher sniffed and sat up. He got out of the chair and went to check it, since Mrs. Bailey was still out with the babies. She'd told him to let her know if the Mattinglys called.

He stood in front of the table where it was plugged into the charger. The screen flashed a name.

Lucy Hart.

Christopher wiped his face as if she could see through the phone that he'd been crying. Lucy was calling. If he answered the phone, he could talk to her. He wanted to talk to her so badly it hurt. Nobody was as nice as Lucy. She's the one he wanted to live with, not these other people. She was the one who read to him. She was the one who bought him all those cool sharks. She's the one who he wanted to tell his good news to—that he was so good at reading he was getting worksheets from a fourth-grade book, that he scored six points in basketball at recess yesterday, that Emma, the most popular girl in his class, had wanted to partner with him in the math quiz today because she wanted to know all about Lucy and how she'd gone to Clock Island.

Even if the Mattinglys were supernice, even if they lived in a castle, even if they lived on a boat or even Clock Island, he didn't want to live with them. He wanted to live with Lucy in their two-bedroom apartment with sharks painted on the walls.

Because he knew that if Lucy promised to paint sharks on his walls, she would paint sharks on his walls.

Christopher reached out to pick up the phone, but at the last second before he touched it, Lucy's name disappeared. The buzzing stopped.

He gave a little cry. Maybe Mrs. Bailey could call her back for him?

The phone lit up and started dancing on the table again.

Lucy Hart.

If he answered the call, he could hear her voice. He could tell her about his plan. He could ask to say hi to Master Mastermind. He could ask about the contest.

What if she won? Maybe that's why she was calling?

Christopher wished the phone wouldn't buzz like that—like a snake or a bee. Why hadn't Mrs. Bailey set it to ring like a song? But he wasn't going to be afraid.

"The only wishes ever granted," Christopher whispered to himself, "are the wishes of brave children . . ."

He knew how to be brave. He knew how to do it, but he didn't know if he could do it.

But the Mastermind had told him he could do it. And Christopher had promised he would try.

His hands were shaking. His heart was racing. The phone kept ringing.

But he was brave, he told himself.

The Mastermind himself said he was brave. Lucy said he was brave.

So he was going to be brave.

. . .

LUCY GASPED AT THE sound of Christopher's voice as he said hello. "Christopher? Is that you?" Tears streamed down her face. "I can't believe you answered the phone."

"I saw it was you, Lucy! I wanted to talk to you! That Mastermind taught me not to be afraid of the phone!"

"Sweetheart, I'm so proud of you. I've never been so proud—"

According to the timer Ms. Hyde was rapping her fingernails on, over three minutes had already slipped away. *Tick-tock.*

"Christopher, Christopher," Lucy said. Her hands were shaking. "Listen. Could you do me a huge, huge favor? If you're at home, could you run back to your room and get *The Secret of Clock Island* off your shelf, okay? We're playing a game, and I need to know what's written on page 129. Okay? Can you do that? Can you? Good. Just don't hang up."

"One minute," Ms. Hyde said.

The next few seconds of silence were agony. She was close to hyperventilating. She could hear Christopher knocking books off the shelves.

Christopher yelled into the phone. "Found it!"

"Page 129, Christopher. One-twenty-nine. Just get to that page and read me what it says. Got it?"

"Fifteen seconds," Ms. Hyde said. Then, "Ten seconds."

"Did you find it?" Lucy asked. She looked around. Andre was talking to someone, but he didn't look hopeful. Melanie was standing, pacing with her phone still plastered to her ear.

"Got it!"

Ms. Hyde counted down, "Five, four, three, two—"

Christopher gave Lucy the answer.

"I win!" Lucy shouted. "It says, 'I win!'"

CHAPTER TWENTY-EIGHT

I N *THE SECRET OF CLOCK ISLAND*, a girl named Molly runs away from an orphanage to Clock Island. When the Mastermind asks her what her wish is, she tells him she wants to stay there with him. That's her only wish. He tries to scare her away, but she says there's nothing he can do or say that's scarier than what went on at the orphanage. He gives her impossible riddles to answer, and instead of answering, she pelts him with a barrage of questions—

Why do you always stay in that shadow? How does that shadow follow you everywhere you go? Is it like a hat? Can I wear your shadow hat? Do you have a weird face? Is that why you always wear a shadow? Can I see your weird face? Is my face weird? What's so wrong with a weird face after all? Why is this place called Clock Island? Is the island a clock, or is the clock an island? Why is your house so big when you live alone? Is that a saber-toothed ferret? Do you have kids? Do you want kids? Do you want me to be your kid? Can I stay here with you and be your kid?

And he tries to make her face her fears, but she only laughs and tells him she already did that ages ago after her parents died and she was taken to that orphanage. If he really wants to scare her, he'll have to drive her back there, but unless he grabs her, throws her in a bag, and carries that bag over his shoulder all the way to the orphanage, there's no way she's going back. No sir. She'll just stay. She'll sleep in the ferret's room.

Finally, he says he'll let her stay if she plays a game with him—the hardest game for any child to win. She must play the staring contest game, and it isn't easy, she knows, to win a staring contest against a shadow.

But Molly knows how to stare. Her mom taught her how before she died in that accident.

Molly agrees though she's scared. If she wins, she gets to stay on Clock Island. If she loses, she has to go back to the orphanage. She has to win.

They play the game.

Molly tries not to cry as she thinks of her mother teaching her to stare. It's hard to play through her tears, but she does it because she likes this Mastermind guy. He seems sort of scary, but really, all he does is stand in shadows—weird—and grant wishes to kids. And it is a big house for one person. Well, one person and Jolene, the saber-toothed ferret. If the guy goes around granting kids' wishes, he must like kids. He's not going around locking them in the washing machine and turning it on the spin cycle, right?

She makes herself focus on the game and play even though it feels like her mom is standing right behind her, and if she looks over her shoulder, she'll see her mom. She wants to see her mom again, but if she looks back, she'll lose the game. She can't look back. She has to look forward. If she keeps her eyes on the Mastermind—well, on the shadow that's staring at her—she might get to have a family again. A new family. A different family. But a good family—just her and the Mastermind and Jolene.

Finally, the shadow blinks. She didn't know shadows could blink, but this one did.

On page 129, Molly shouts, "I win!"

On page 130, it says this and only this:

The Mastermind had let Molly win.

CHAPTER TWENTY-NINE

"DID WE WIN?" CHRISTOPHER asked.

No. They hadn't won.

Lucy's heart was on the floor. She didn't know what to say. Ms. Hyde's timer had stopped less than one second before Lucy had shouted the answer. They'd lost the chance to be together over one single second.

"Hold on, baby," Lucy told Christopher. "Just . . . need a minute here." She was trying to sound okay, put together, but she was falling apart trying to understand how she'd come so close and still lost.

"Thank you all for playing," Ms. Hyde said. She turned and gave Jack a pointed look. "It seems we do not have a winner."

"I'm so sorry, kids," Jack said. "I really hoped one of you would win."

He reached into the pocket of his rumpled navy-blue trousers and pulled out a key. "The book is in a bank safe-deposit box," Jack told Ms. Hyde, laying it in her hand. "I'll get you the information, but that is the key to the box."

She wrapped her fingers tight around the small silver key. "On behalf of the publisher, thank you, Jack." She looked at the contestants and was decent enough to look almost apologetic. "I know you all wanted to win this contest very much, so I'm certain you're all feeling some disappointment. Each of you will receive signed first edition copies of the book for your own collections. Thank you for being a part of one of the better accidental marketing campaigns in the history of children's literature."

"Again," Jack said, "I wish it could have been otherwise. I will do my best to make it up to you."

Andre was the first to smile. "No hard feelings, Jack." He walked over and held out his hand. "It was just so damn good to see you again. I'll be telling this story for years."

Jack hugged Andre, who had already ended his call.

"Lucy?" Christopher said. "What's going on?"

"Sorry, sweetheart," Lucy said, moving her hand away from the phone speaker. "They were talking to us about something."

"Did you win? Did you get the prize?"

"Um . . . well, it was—" Lucy began. She thought she might throw up she was shaking so hard.

Hugo held out his hand. "Let me talk to him."

"What?" Lucy said.

"Please?"

With a trembling voice, Lucy said, "Christopher, someone here wants to talk to you. His name is Hugo Reese, and he does all those cool paintings in the Clock Island books."

"Really?" Christopher said. "Like the map and the puzzle and the train?"

"He did all those. And he wants to say hi. So here he is. Hugo?"

She gave the phone to Hugo, who put it to his ear.

"Christopher? This is Hugo. I'm a friend of Lucy's."

She sat back in the chair, silent and in shock, half-listening as Hugo introduced himself to Christopher. What could he possibly say? They couldn't lie. You could keep things from children, but this wasn't a lie she could tell. The whole world would soon know that nobody had won the book and that it was going to Jack's publisher. She breathed through her hands, mind racing, as if she could think of a way to fix this, to turn the clock back, to have a second chance and answer the question one second quicker.

"No, no, Lucy didn't win the book, but she won second prize. It's a painting. One of mine. A big shark painting. She said you'll love it."

Hugo smiled, met her eyes. "What's your favorite shark? Hammerhead? Good choice. More animals should have heads shaped like that. Hammerhead cats. Hammerhead dogs. Hammerhead snakes. Wait. I think you gave me an idea for a new painting."

Lucy watched Ms. Hyde walk out of the library, triumphant.

"You should hold on to my painting that Lucy won. In about ten years you can sell it, and it'll pay for your college. Well, not a very good college, but still—"

Lucy laughed. A small laugh, so small Hugo didn't even hear it. Second place, he'd said? She had come in third, tied with Melanie's five points. Andre had finished with six. Not that it mattered. Not that any of it mattered. She reached out and rested her hand on Hugo's shoulder. He looked at her, and she mouthed a silent *Thank you.*

Then she laid her head back on the chair and cried.

CHAPTER THIRTY

UP IN THE OCEAN Room, Lucy packed her suitcase. She felt drained, exhausted, more zombie than person, but it helped to keep moving. Hugo offered to help, but there was nothing for him to do but keep her company, distract her from falling apart again.

"I'm taking you to the airport in the morning," he said when she zipped up her suitcase.

"I have to be on the ferry at five," she reminded him. Her voice sounded faraway and hollow to her own ears. "Five A.M."

"Don't care. I'm going with you, and you can't stop me."

"I won't stop you," she said.

It was half past nine already, and she needed to get into bed soon, but she wanted to spend more time with Hugo. It might be the last time they'd ever get to spend together. They didn't exactly run in the same circles. And when was the last time she'd been to New York? Never.

"If you want to take the shark painting back with you, I'll have to wrap it and crate it, which takes ages, or I can send it to you in the post or—"

She picked up a pillow, tossed it at him.

He caught the pillow, wincing like it had hurt.

"What was that for?" he asked.

"You didn't have to do that," she said. "You didn't have to give me a fake second prize."

"I want Christopher to have it," he said. "And yes, I had to do it. I had to or I would have hated myself. You know, more than I usually do."

She glanced up at the painting of the flying shark over the fireplace mantel, the one he called *Fly-Fishing*. At least that was something she had to show for her week here, an actual Hugo Reese painting. Her favorite painter. Christopher's too.

"That's a big gift, Hugo. I know your stuff sells for a lot of money."

"I'm not exactly Banksy, you know, but if you were to take that to a gallery and sell it, you—"

"Don't. Don't even think about it," she said. "I'm not about to sell the painting you gave to Christopher. That painting will pay for his college someday if that's what he wants to do with it, or he'll keep it and pass it on to his kids or grandkids, but I'm not going to pawn it. Ever."

"Lucy—"

She dropped the T-shirt she'd been folding, turned, and faced him.

"Come here," he said.

"No," she replied, but she went to him anyway, went to his arms and let him hold her. She cried again, big, hard sobs. The sort of sobs that come out of a heart broken cleanly in two. Hugo just held her, rubbed her back while she cried and said nothing.

Always be quiet when a heart is breaking.

Finally, her sobs settled, and she took a deep breath, followed by another.

"I'm going to be okay," she said softly.

"I know you will be."

"I'll do what every other single mom in the world does—work my ass off and take care of my kid. I've decided I'm going to get a second job, even if it means not seeing Christopher as much. But he can talk on the phone now, so we can Facetime or call each other even when I can't see him in person. When I take him home with me, it'll be worth it."

"I suppose you wouldn't let me lend you—"

"No, I wouldn't. If only because what happens in six months when I need more? When the car breaks down in two years? When my rent goes up, or I lose my job?" She took another deep steadying breath and dragged herself away from Hugo's arms. "I need to be able to take care of him myself. But thanks for the shoes."

"I only wish—" He looked at her.

"Yeah. Me too."

He stood up, looked at her. It seemed he wanted to say more but wouldn't or couldn't let himself.

"Can I ask a favor?" she said.

"Anything in the world." The way he said it, she thought he might mean it.

"Maybe you could draw a little shark sketch or something for Christopher that I could take to him tomorrow while we wait for the painting? Maybe something with his name on it? I'll let you keep the red scarf."

"Absolutely. I'll go and fetch my sketchbook. Besides, I was going to keep the red scarf anyway."

He started for the door, then stopped, turned around. "That kid loves the hell out of you, Lucy. He answered the phone because it was you calling him. Because it was his mum calling him."

She smiled. "As terrible as this day went . . . I'm still happy. Even after he moves into his new foster home, at least now we can talk to each other on the phone until I buy a car and visit him in person. It's so funny. He says the Mastermind helped him answer the phone? I guess reading books about kids being brave got to him?"

"He was incredibly brave," Hugo said.

She shrugged. "Too bad he didn't get his wish."

"He's got you in his life," Hugo said. "He's a lucky kid." She felt her face growing hot. Hugo smiled back. "Don't go anywhere. Back in a tick."

Lucy breathed deeply through her hands when he was gone. Okay, so she'd lost the game. It hurt. It sucked. She wanted to cry again, wanted to scream . . . but here she was—still standing, still breathing, and tomorrow she would see Christopher. That's all that mattered.

She got out her phone to check for messages. Nothing important. They hadn't released the news to the press yet about the contest. Jack had warned them that tomorrow they would be inundated. Lucy considered calling Angie. Jack had given her Angie's phone number. Even after all these years, all the neglect and loneliness and cruelty, she still wished she had one person in her family she could call when her heart was breaking.

She put her phone away. She just wasn't ready to get hurt again, not when she was already hurting so much.

"Knock, knock?"

Lucy composed her face. Jack stood in the open doorway to her bedroom. He was still wearing his usual uniform of rumpled trousers, a light blue button-down shirt with a coffee stain on it, and a baggy cardigan starting to unravel at the seams. He had a paperback stuffed in one of the cardigan pockets, and she wondered if that was why he wore such huge sweaters—book-sized pockets.

"Jack," she said. "You're not in bed?"

"No, no, finishing up some paperwork in my office. May I?"

"Sure, come in."

He shuffled into the room. "I hope you're not too upset about not winning."

"Hanging in there. I'm glad the book is going to be published. I'm kind of glad I got to see Angie. I'm very glad I got to see you again."

"And Hugo?"

She blushed bright red. "And Hugo. But not for the reasons you think. He's my favorite artist."

"I don't blush when I talk about Paul Klee."

"You should," she said. "I'm sure he was very handsome."

Jack laughed. It was good to see him laughing. He looked just like he did the day she met him when she was thirteen. The years melted away along with the pain.

"Where is our Hugo anyway? Wasn't he just here?"

"He's getting his sketchbook to draw something for Christopher."

"Ah, well, before he gets back, I wanted to give you a little something." He pulled the book from his cardigan pocket. "I'd like you to have *The House on Clock Island*."

She looked down. It was a well-worn copy of Book One in the Clock Island series.

"Ah, thank you," she said. "Is it signed, I hope? Can you make sure it's signed to Christopher?"

"The book isn't your gift. Or Christopher's."

She furrowed her brow. "What?"

"The book isn't your gift. I don't want you to have *The House on Clock Island*," he said. "I want you to have the *house* . . . on Clock Island."

He opened the book. A key was lying in the center of it. A house key.

A house key.

A key to a house.

A key to the house on Clock Island.

"Jack . . ." she breathed. "What—"

"You don't get the book, but you do get your wish. Lucy Hart—do you still want to be my sidekick?"

CHAPTER THIRTY-ONE

SHE SAT DOWN HARD on the bed. Her feet had failed her. Her vision was blurry. Then everything cleared. The fog lifted. Her heart lifted.

"You're giving me . . ."

"The house," Jack said. "If you'll have it—and me, because I don't plan on leaving until I'm carted off in a box. And if you can talk that Christopher of yours into moving to Maine, I'd love to have him here too."

"I'm not even fostering him yet. Even if I were, I can't take him out of the state. It'll take months—" She could hardly think, hardly breathe. Was this really happening?

"Oh, I can help with that. Luckily, I have more money than I know what to do with."

"You can't . . . This is too generous, Jack. I can't accept—"

"You can, Lucy. You can accept help. And if you can't, Christopher can." He took a bundle of papers out of the other pocket of his cardigan and handed it to her.

Lucy unfolded the papers. In Christopher's sweet, shaky, lopsided crayon-colored handwriting, he'd written, *My wish is Lucy can adop me.*

She flipped through the stack and found half a dozen letters from Christopher to Master Mastermind. Apparently, he and Jack had been writing to each other for several months. Christopher, with a thousand misspellings, had told Jack—in his guise of the Mastermind—his dreams of being Lucy's son, the death of his parents, his fear of phones. In the last letter, Christopher promised that the next time Lucy tried to call him on the phone, he would answer it.

"You helped Christopher get over his fear of phones," she said, looking up at him. "Not the books. You did."

"If anyone knows anything about fear, it's me."

"You . . ." She pressed the letters against her heart. Her throat had closed up. Jack had quietly and secretly and without fanfare helped a little boy on the other side of the country find his courage. "That stinker didn't tell me a thing."

"He wanted to surprise you. He did, didn't he?"

Tears fell from her eyes. Jack took her gently by the shoulders, looked intently at her face.

"Lucy Hart, thirteen years ago, you wished to be my sidekick. Wish granted," he said. "If you want it to be an honorary title, it can be. Or you really can move in and live with me and help me try to start living my life again. And Christopher's wish was that you could adopt him. Wish granted." He smiled fiendishly. "I've already asked my attorney to start the process for you. She thinks she can get all the ducks in a row in a few months' time."

"I know I can."

Lucy spun around. Ms. Hyde stood in the doorway.

"You?" She couldn't believe her eyes.

"When you have a moment, Lucy, I'll need you to sign some paperwork for me. I'll be in the library."

"Wait . . . Don't you work for Jack's publisher?"

She didn't smile, just raised her chin. "I take the Fifth."

When Ms. Hyde was gone, Lucy turned to Jack.

"I . . . I'm in shock."

"If you can't say yes for me, say yes for Christopher."

"But . . . Hugo? What about Hugo? Are you trying to replace him with me? He'll be—"

"Fine," Jack said. "He'll be more than fine when he knows someone is with me. Then he can stay of his own free will or move of his own free will. No more worry. No more guilt. And don't worry. I'm giving you the house on Clock Island when I pass. But he gets the island." He sat down in the chair by the bed, met her eyes. Lucy looked at him. He'd aged in the thirteen years since she'd seen him, faded. But he was still the Mastermind, still wrapped in shadows, still strange and mysterious and weird and good.

"I've waited long enough to be happy. Don't make me wait any longer." He reached out and took her hand in his. "What do you say?"

What could she say to that?

Lucy smiled and said, "I win."

CHAPTER THIRTY-TWO

OF COURSE, THE MASTERMIND had let Lucy win.*

* Jack Masterson, *The Secret of Clock Island*, 2005. Remember, always cite your sources.

CHAPTER THIRTY-THREE

Three Months Later

"NERVOUS?" JACK ASKED.

"Do I look nervous?" Hugo glanced around the airport baggage claim area, watching for double takes and knowing looks. So far, nobody had recognized Jack. One of the perks of being a writer: even the most famous ones could be anonymous in public. Although every now and then, a child or a teenager would give Jack a second or third look, as if they knew they'd seen him somewhere before and couldn't quite place him.

"You look excited. I look nervous," Jack said with a sigh.

"Don't blame you there, old man. Not every day you meet your grandson for the first time."

Jack looked at him, raised an eyebrow. "Grandson?"

"If Lucy's your honorary daughter now, doesn't that make Christopher your honorary grandson?"

Jack seemed to mull that over. "Did you know that in the state of Maine, you can legally adopt another adult?"

"Just don't adopt me and Lucy both, please."

"No kissing your sister."

"Exactly," Hugo said.

"After she sees Christopher's room, she'll probably marry you."

"Let me kiss her first before I marry her."

Jack scoffed. "If you want to be old-fashioned."

Hugo didn't know what he was more excited about—seeing Lucy again or seeing Lucy see Christopher's bedroom. He'd spent the entire month preparing Christopher's bedroom for him based on what Lucy had told him he liked. He'd painted the ceiling like a cloud-wild blue sky. The walls were ocean scenes—boats being skippered by sharks in captains' hats, octopi knitting fishing nets that caught letters, the letters spelling out Christopher's name. It was some of the best work he'd done. Who knew happiness was the best muse of all?

"Next time a child asks me if the Mastermind is real," Hugo said, "I'm telling them yes."

"I had no idea you would take to Lucy like you did," Jack said with a soft chuckle. "Don't lay that one at my feet. That was all you."

"For some reason, I don't believe you." Hugo glanced at the arrivals board. Soon. Very soon . . .

Jack smiled his Mona Lisa smile. He had the mind of an author, always seeing ten, twenty, a hundred pages ahead of the rest of the world. "I am sorry for keeping you in the dark about the contest. I really am. But I was afraid you'd talk me out of it, and it wasn't the time for second-guessing. I'd been a coward too long. It was time to take my own advice and be a little bit brave. Or stupid. Hard to tell the difference sometimes."

Jack checked his watch. They were both counting the seconds.

"While we're waiting, I meant to tell you," Hugo said. "Got a strange email from Dr. Dustin Gardner. He wanted me to make sure you saw his thank-you card."

"I did, yes."

"Thank you for what? Kicking him off the island?"

"No reason." Jack wore a look of purest innocence that Hugo didn't buy for one second.

Hugo stared at Jack, though Jack would not meet his eyes. "You paid off his student loans, didn't you?"

"No comment. But," he said, "if I did such a thing, the gift would come with the condition to get anger management therapy."

"What about Andre and Melanie?"

"They didn't win the game, but no one said I couldn't give them nice consolation prizes."

"I did notice that for some reason the book's release party is being held at something called the Little Red Lighthouse Bookshop in Saint John, New Brunswick. New Brunswick? We've never even been to Old Brunswick."

Jack put his hands in his pockets and shrugged. "I've always been a supporter of small independent bookstores."

Supporter? More like savior. Hugo could already see it. Reporters and fans would descend on Melanie's bookshop in droves the week the book came out. There'd be lines snaking around the block to meet Jack and get his autograph. The online orders alone for signed copies of his new book would keep a roof over Melanie's head for a decade.

"I'm afraid to ask about your kidneys," Hugo said. Andre's one wish was a kidney for his dying father. When Andre was on the island, they'd yet to find a match.

"I didn't give anyone either of my kidneys. Doubt anyone would want them after all I've put them through. But with the help of a detective in Atlanta, they were able to find a second cousin who was a match. Looks like the surgery is going to happen very soon."

"Jack, you can't save the world."

"And I would never try," Jack said. "All I did was keep my promise to those kids."

Hugo still wondered . . . why now? Why had Jack suddenly shrugged off his grief and started writing again? Opening his home again? Start living again? He'd been wondering this for a while, and Jack's mention of time opened a door that Hugo was afraid to step through. But he knew this might be his only chance for a while.

"Are you ever going to tell me why you started writing again? We're not going bankrupt, are we?"

Jack smiled. "I'll tell you but only in a riddle."

"Never mind."

"It comes after Q."

He almost said R, but Jack had his brain so well trained—or possibly damaged—that Hugo knew it wasn't R. It was U.

You.

"Me," Hugo said. "You did all this for me?" He could barely hear his own voice speaking. The words were like knives in his throat.

"You were going to leave, yes? And here you are. And you haven't packed a single bag yet."

He swallowed. "Jack."

"Can't see my own hand in front of my face sometimes. Kicked myself for years for not having children. Didn't realize until we started getting flyers in the mail from real estate agents in New York that I was about to lose my only son. And when I did, I would have no one to blame but myself. I knew you'd stick around long enough to see what happened with the contest. And depending on how the game went . . . well, maybe if I found a reason for you to stay, you would."

Too moved to speak, Hugo could only look at Jack for a moment.

He remembered the night Lucy had shown up at the guesthouse, ready to go home. What had Jack told him to do to make her stay?

Distract her with something. Make her help you with a project. Works every time.

He was right. It worked.

Finally, Hugo said, "This whole bloody game was a ploy to try to trick me into staying?"

Jack laughed his old laugh. The laugh he laughed when his cleverness astonished even him. He elbowed Hugo in the side and pointed to the escalator where Lucy and Christopher were slowly descending.

Jack said, "We win."

HERE WE GO, LUCY thought as she and Christopher reached the escalator. Their new life together in Maine would start the second they reached the bottom. Christopher paused at the top of the escalator and looked up at her.

"It's okay," she said. "I can carry you down, or you can try it. Just grab the railing and step onto the top step fast."

He reached out, touched the railing, snatched his hand back as if it had been burned. But then, instead of jumping into her arms in fear, he tried it again.

This time he did it. He grabbed the railing and stepped onto the escalator. Lucy held him by the back of his T-shirt just in case.

"Whoa," he said, then laughed at himself.

"Good job, kiddo," she said. Christopher grinned in triumph. He'd been doing that a lot lately. The dark circles under his eyes were long gone. The hundred-yard stare he sometimes wore on rough days rarely showed itself. And he smiled and laughed and did somersaults around their house for no reason except he could. Because he was safe now. Because he was loved. Because that safety and love weren't going anywhere ever again.

Lucy tugged gently on the back of his shirt. He looked up at her.

"Mama loves you," she said.

He rolled his eyes and said, "I know." But then he quickly leaned his head back against her, his way of saying he loved her too.

Lucy peered down the escalator and saw Hugo and Jack waiting for them. She smiled but didn't wave or say anything to Christopher. She didn't want him getting too excited and running down the moving stairs. Right now, he was chattering away about how crazy it was that he would be taking a boat to school every day when it started in a week. *A boat! To school! Every day!* He had never been on a boat in his life, and now he was taking *A boat! To school! Every day!*

Jack waved at her. Hugo was too busy messing around with a roll of what looked like white wrapping paper. She saw him slap Jack on the arm. What on earth were they doing? Then he and Hugo started walking apart from each other and unfurled a banner that was at least ten feet wide and three feet tall that read, WELCOME LUCY & CHRISTOPHER.

Obviously, Hugo had painted the banner. Their names were written inside the bellies of sharks. Hers was an elegant great white shark, and Christopher's was a hammerhead. When Christopher saw the sign, his mouth dropped open. No stopping him now. He ran down the last few steps and toward the sign.

First, there were hugs for Hugo. And then Lucy got to do something she'd been dreaming about for weeks.

"Christopher," she said as she took him by the shoulders and gently steered him forward. "This is Jack Masterson. Jack, this is Christopher." She smiled and, with the greatest pride she had ever felt in her life, added, "My son."

Christopher stared up at Jack, wide-eyed, silent with awe.

"Say hi," Lucy prompted.

"Are you really the Mastermind?" Christopher asked.

"What has two hands," Jack said, "but can't scratch itself?"

Slowly a smile spread across Christopher's face. "A clock!"

"Good job, my boy. You'll do just fine on Clock Island. Let's go, shall we? Mikey's waiting with the car."

When they reached the car, Christopher claimed the middle row with Jack while Lucy and Hugo sat in the back row all alone. As Jack got into the car, he gave them a wink.

For the drive to the dock, she and Hugo whispered to each other in the back while Christopher and Jack competed to see who could talk each other's ears off first.

"I've never seen him so happy," Hugo said. "Not in all the years . . . even before Autumn died."

"Christopher's on cloud nine, and we're never going to get him down."

"And you?" Hugo asked. "Happy?"

She rested her head on his shoulder. "He's mine. Enough said."

THE PAST THREE MONTHS had been wild, the best three months of Lucy's life. She'd arrived back in Redwood to a hero's welcome from the kids at school. While she was gone, Jack had sent three hundred complete sets of Clock Island books—one set for each child at Redwood Elementary. Lucy spent the weekend doing interviews with national and local TV. Then on Monday morning, because school was out, she met with a local family law attorney who worked in conjunction with Ms. Hyde. It took two weeks—renting a small house in a safe neighborhood, filling it with furniture, leasing a car—but then Christopher was hers. She'd finally been approved to foster him.

Every day this summer, they'd gone on bike rides or to the library or for walks. Even roller-skating. And all the while, she and Ms. Vargas, the family law attorney, were working on Lucy's adoption application. Every penny of it was bankrolled by Jack Masterson.

And Hugo thought money couldn't buy happiness.

But the best part, though it was hard, was the first time Christopher had a tantrum over something Lucy asked him to do. She'd been waiting for that moment, the moment Christopher misbehaved with her. It meant he knew he was really her son, that she was really his mother, that he knew Lucy wasn't going anywhere, even if he whined about putting his breakfast dishes in the dishwasher or refused to brush his teeth or pick up his LEGOs, which were literally strewn all over the entire house. Talk about a messy roommate.

"He's driving me nuts today," Lucy had told Theresa on a particularly rough evening.

"Congratulations," Theresa had said, laughing. "Now you're a *real* mama."

There were harder times, nights when Christopher woke up sweating from old nightmares and crying for his parents. And there was nothing she could do then but hold him tight and talk to him or read to him until he fell asleep. Strangely, it was those hard heartbreaking nights when she felt most like a mother.

When the time came for Lucy to adopt Christopher officially, not only did Ms. Theresa and her whole family come, but Christopher's teachers and his entire second-grade class attended. Even Mrs. Costa, the social worker, brought balloons for Lucy that said, *It's a boy.* Lucy was happy to see her there. She'd been right, after all. It did take a village to raise a child. And Lucy was getting a brand-new village. Because that evening, Hugo stood before them in their rented living room and announced that, as a duly appointed representative of the Enchanted Kingdom of Clock Island, he was inviting Lucy and Christopher to become official citizens.

"He's asking us if we want to move to Clock Island," Lucy whispered into Christopher's ear. "You think we should?"

He said yes. He said yes ten thousand times in a row.

The next day, feeling stronger than she'd ever felt in her life, Lucy called Sean and managed to have a short but civil conversation with him. She told him about her miscarriage, apologized for not telling him sooner, then politely said, "Never," when he asked her if she wanted to talk it over in person next time she was in Portland. And that was that. Sean. Her parents. Her failures. Lucy had put her past and all its ghosts, real and imagined, behind her.

Almost all of them.

"HERE WE ARE, LUCY," Jack said from the front seat.

"Thanks," Lucy said. "I promise I won't be long. Just a quick visit."

Jack reached over the seat to gently grip her arm. He met her eyes.

"Take all the time you need," Jack said.

"Can I go?" Christopher asked.

"Not yet. But soon, I promise," Lucy said. "Stay with Jack and Hugo."

"No," Hugo said. "I'm going too. I'll wait in the hall."

Lucy could tell from Hugo's tone there was no point arguing. She gave Christopher a reassuring smile, and she and Hugo got out of the car. They went through the revolving glass doors of the cancer care center.

"Where to?" Hugo asked as they reached the elevator.

"Third floor," she said, stomach tight, voice small. A sign by the elevator read, NO CHILDREN UNDER EIGHTEEN ARE ALLOWED TO VISIT PATIENTS.

Hugo hit the button. The elevator went up.

"You didn't have to come—"

"Yes, I did," he said. "Does she know you're coming?"

"I told her I'd see her this week, but she texted back that she'd been admitted for some tests today."

Hugo asked the question she'd been avoiding thinking about. "Do you know how bad it is?"

"Bad," Lucy said, shuddering. "She has maybe three months. Four months if she's lucky. God, we wasted so much time."

He said nothing, only took her hand and squeezed it.

The elevator stopped, the doors opened. Lucy found room 3010.

"I'll be right here," Hugo said. Lucy took a deep breath.

"It's so unfair," she whispered. "I just got her back. But you know that better than anyone."

"I know." Hugo kissed her forehead.

Lucy took another steadying breath and went into the room.

"Angie?" she said as she pushed aside the floral curtain that hung around the bed.

Angie was sitting up in a chair, a pretty paisley scarf on her head, a blue blanket on her lap, her iPad in hand.

"Lucy," Angie said with a tired, happy smile. She set the iPad on the side table. "When did you get in?"

She wanted to hug Angie, but she had an IV catheter or some sort of port in her arm and was afraid to touch her. But Angie held out her free arm and Lucy took her hand. Her skin was cool and her hand too thin, but she gave Lucy a strong squeeze.

"Twenty minutes ago."

Angie's eyes widened. She pointed at the door. "Go. Now. Go away and come back tomorrow. I'll still be here."

Lucy ignored the marching orders and instead sat down on a spare chair in the room. "You have to stay the night?"

"With my medical history, they're being overcautious," Angie said with a shrug. "It is what it is. Now you go away right *now* and come back *later*."

"I just wanted you to know we made it. You want me to give you a ride home tomorrow or feed the cats tonight or something?"

"The cats are with my neighbor. And I have a ride. What I want you to do is go out that door, get your son, and take him to Clock Island. And I want you to take videos and pictures and then send them all to me. And then I want to see you tomorrow and Christopher later this week when I'm home. Okay? Now go before I get really mad. You're interrupting my reading." She picked up her iPad again.

"I'm going." Lucy raised her hands in surrender. "If you're gonna be grumpy."

Angie laughed but the laugh didn't quite reach her eyes. "Thanks for coming, sis."

Lucy took her sister's hand again. "I used to get so mad when they wouldn't let me visit you in the hospital."

"Lucky you. Now you're old enough. It's fun, right?"

"The funnest." Lucy tried to smile, but couldn't quite pull it off. "You okay?"

"I'm at peace." She smiled tiredly. "So go. Shoo. I'll see you soon. Please hug my nephew for me."

"Will do." Lucy started for the door, then remembered something. "Oh, Christopher gave me something last night to give to you. It's weird, but he really wanted you to have it."

"Then I really want to have it."

Lucy opened her bag and pulled out a wad of blue tissue paper tied up with a shoelace. "As you can see, he also wrapped it himself."

Angie took the gift from her, grinning as she untied the shoelace and tore off the paper. Under all that wrapping was a hammerhead shark toy, the same one Lucy had given him.

"He loves sharks," Lucy said. "You should be honored. That hammerhead is his favorite."

Angie held the plastic shark in her hand as if it were a priceless antique. Then she wrapped her fingers around the sleek shark's small body and held it against her chest, at her heart. And right then and there, without any fanfare or ceremony or fireworks or tears, Lucy forgave Angie, and they were sisters, real sisters, for the first time in their lives.

Angie said, "Tell him I am honored."

When Lucy went into the hallway, Hugo was still waiting for her. He stood up out of the chair and held out his arms. She went to him, and he held her close and tight.

"Don't tell me it'll be all right," she said.

"Never," he said. "I know better."

He kissed the top of her head. "Come on," he said. "Let's go home."

By the time they got back to the car, Lucy had dried her tears. There would be plenty of time to cry, but not today. Today was Christopher's day, not hers. As a mother now, she had to put her own feelings aside.

Twenty minutes later, they were at the ferry terminal.

"Ready?" Jack asked Christopher.

Christopher replied in a voice about ten decibels louder than necessary, "Ready!"

The air was warm and the sun bright, and the sky bluer than Lucy had ever seen it as the ferry carried them toward the island. Christopher and Jack stood side by side in the bow. Jack would point out something. Then Christopher would. When Jack put his hand up to shield his eyes to see a bird flying overhead, so did Christopher.

Hanging back with Hugo, Lucy had to laugh. "They look like grandfather and grandson."

"They are." Hugo smiled at her. "Have you and Jack decided what you're going to do as his official sidekick?"

"We have big plans," she said. "First off, we're going to start a nonprofit to provide free books, backpacks, and school supplies to kids in foster care. Care packages postmarked from Clock Island. What do you think?"

"I think that's one of the best ideas I've ever heard."

"I think we're going to call it—"

Hugo suddenly looked toward the front of the boat and held up his hand.

Lucy froze, whispered, "What?"

"Christopher, come here," Hugo ordered. Christopher turned and ran to him. "Look."

Hugo pointed out at the water where a single gray triangle cut through a wave before it vanished under the water again.

"Shark?" Christopher breathed.

"We have lots of them around here," he said. "Never go swimming with a steak sandwich in your pocket."

The ferry made its slow, steady way around the southern edge of Clock Island. Six o'clock, five o'clock, four o'clock.

Lucy pulled out her phone and started recording. Angie wanted pictures and videos. She would get them.

Finally, there it was, shining in the sun. The house on Clock Island.

"Home sweet home," Jack said to Christopher.

"What? That's our house?" Christopher said. He looked at Hugo, at Lucy, awestruck.

"That's it," she said. "Like it?"

The ferry reached the dock. The captain cut the engine.

"Tick-tock," Jack said. "Welcome to the Clock."

Christopher's grin was wider than the sky.

Hugo got off the boat first and helped Lucy, who helped Christopher. All three of them helped Jack.

CHRISTOPHER WAS AMAZED AT the sight of the sharks painted on the walls and the ocean, of course, right outside his window. Then, while Jack was teaching Christopher how to type on a manual typewriter and feed walnuts to Thurl Ravenscroft, Hugo motioned Lucy out into the hallway.

"What?" she whispered.

He looked left. He looked right. He had one hand behind his back, which Lucy found highly suspicious. "Don't tell anyone I gave you this. Jack's publisher would drag me through the streets by my ear." Hugo brought his hand out from behind his back.

A book. Not just any book.

"*A Wish for Clock Island*," he said. "Hope you like the cover."

Tears sprang to her eyes as she studied Hugo's artwork. A boy who looked just like Christopher was sitting up in a twin bed while a woman who looked just like her was reading him a bedtime story. Outside the window, the Man in the Moon peered over her shoulder as if trying to listen to the story.

Lucy didn't know what to say, other than, "Hugo . . ."

"I read it," he said. "It's about Astrid, the girl from the very first book who comes back to Clock Island when she's older."

"Am I Astrid on the cover?"

"Of course you are. She and her son hear the Mastermind has gone missing, and they work together to find him."

"Do they find him?"

He grinned. "Suppose you'll have to read it to find out. And you should read it. It's the dog's bollocks."

"Is that British for 'it's good'?"

"Now you're learning."

She couldn't take her eyes off the cover. That was Christopher—big hazel eyes, dark hair gone all wild. And that was her—her brown hair, her profile, even one of her knitted scarves around her neck. "I wanted to be her when I was a kid, you know?"

"Now you are. If you don't sue me for using your face without permission."

She put her arms around him and kissed him so hard she almost dropped the book.

Christopher ran out into the hallway, calling her name. Lucy pulled away from Hugo and tucked the book into her bag.

"Mom! Mom! Mom! I fed a real raven!"

She would never get tired of hearing him call her Mom. Even when he said it a few hundred times in a row.

"I saw! Good job. Where to next?" Lucy asked Jack. "The wishing well? The lighthouse? The Storm Seller?"

"Oh, I have a much better idea." Jack took Christopher by the hand and led him out of the house to the backyard.

Hugo took Lucy by the hand, and they followed.

"Stay right here," Jack said to Christopher. They all stood behind the house while Jack walked off toward the City of Second Hand.

"What's he doing?" Lucy whispered to Hugo.

"He's been very busy while waiting for you two to finally show up. See?"

They heard a sound then, the turning of iron wheels, and the cry of a whistle. And then the *Clock Island Express* chugged into view, gleaming black and yellow with Jack in the driver's seat.

"Lucy!" Jack called to her. "I finally finished laying down the track! Want a ride to Samhain Station, Christopher? I hear it's Halloween every day there!"

Christopher was silent. His eyes were huge. Lucy knew what was coming next and got out her phone to record it for Angie.

He breathed in, filled his lungs, raised his hands, and screamed with purest joy.

And why not? Lucy thought. She did too. So did Hugo. So did Jack.

When you gotta scream, you gotta scream.

THE CLOCK ISLAND ADVENTURES.
COLLECT THEM ALL!

1. *The House on Clock Island*
2. *A Shadow Falls on Clock Island*
3. *A Message from Clock Island*
4. *The Haunting of Clock Island*
5. *The Prince of Clock Island*
6. *The Wizard of Winter*
7. *The Quest for Clock Island*
8. *Goblin Night on Clock Island*
9. *Skulls & Skullduggery* (A Clock Island Super Adventure)
10. *The Clockwork Raven*
11. *The Ghost Machine*
12. *A Dark Night on Clock Island*
13. *The Pirates of Mars Versus Clock Island*
14. *The Phantom of the Clock Island Opera*
15. *The Headless Horsemen*
16. *The Ballad of Bigfoot*
17. *Clock Island Is Under Attack!*
18. *The Lost King of Clock Island*
19. *A Witch in Time*
20. *The October Spell*
21. *Werewolves of Clock Island*

22. *The Ship of Nightmares*
23. *The Count of Clock Island*
24. *The Enchanted Hourglass*
25. *The Secret Staircase*
26. *Sea Monster Say Monster*
27. *The Cloud Catcher*
28. *The Mysterious Circus*
29. *The Starry Knight*
30. *The Princess of Clock Island*
31. *The Skeleton Door*
32. *Mystery on the Clock Island Express*
33. *The Forest of Lost Hours*
34. *Grandfather Clock, Grandmother Time*
35. *Trapped! On Clock Island*
36. *Masks & Masquerades*
37. *The Key to the Clocktower*
38. *The Moonlight Carnival*
39. *The Keeper of Clock Island*
40. *The Castaways of Clock Island*
41. *Clock Island in Space!*
42. *The Stained-Glass Unicorn*
43. *The Fall of the House of Clock Island*
44. *The Map of the Labyrinth*
45. *The Hound of Clock Island*
46. *The Bizarre Bazaar*
47. *Forgotten Tales from Clock Island*
48. *As the Scarecrow Flies*
49. *A Christmas Peril*
50. *The Thunder Thief*
51. *The Lost Time Traveler*
52. *The Secret of Clock Island*
53. *The Puzzle Paradox*
54. *Escape to Clock Island*
55. *The Library of Almost Everything*
56. *The Cursed Clock*

57. *The Dinosaur Device*
58. *A Box of Riddles*
59. *A Spy on Clock Island*
60. *The Foxfire Lantern*
61. *The Story Bandit*
62. *The Black Cat Caper*
63. *The Cauldron of Time*
64. *Creature from the Clock Island Lagoon*
65. *Once Upon a Timepiece*
66. *A Wish for Clock Island*

Also by Jack Masterson

NONFICTION

Co-writing with Ravens and Other True Tales from Clock Island

POETRY

I, Cyclops
A Songbook for Spiders

ACKNOWLEDGMENTS

Writing a book is a solitary pursuit in theory, but a thousand unseen hands are also at the keyboard whenever a writer writes. First, I have to thank Gene Wilder's Willy Wonka for taking over my brain in the third grade. Can you imagine getting the chance to play a game that could change your life? Oh, to be Charlie! Also, my deepest gratitude to the hundreds of foster parents and the former children who were once in foster care who have shared their experiences on social media, in books, and in news articles. There is no one single foster care or adoption story. Some are happy stories. Some are horror stories. But I know we all can agree that every child in foster care deserves a happy ending like Christopher's. I wish that joy and love for all those children and their caregivers. My apologies for any errors or omissions in the book's depiction of the legalities and realities of fostering. I chose to focus on the hopes and dreams and wishes of a child in foster care more than the intricacies of a very complicated system.

Thank you to my own wonderful parents and fabulous sister for all their love and support. Thank you to my genius husband for spotting the issues in the book no one else noticed. Thank you to my early readers who gave me invaluable help. Kira Gold, talented author and costumer who, like Hugo, has a much-adored brother with Down syndrome. Also, many thanks to Kevin Lee, my favorite British artist, and Karen Stivali, writer, mother, and former therapist (and very dear friend). Earl P. Dean, the first writer to read a few pages, told me if I finished this book, he would be excited to read it. Thanks, Earl, and I hope you enjoy it!

Thank you to my fabulous, world-class brilliant literary agent Amy Tannenbaum and all the wonderful staff at the Jane Rotrosen Agency. To all aspiring writers, there is life after the slush pile! Thank you to Shauna Summers, editor extraordinaire. Your ideas and enthusiasm were priceless to me.

And a very special thank you to Episode 470 of *This American Life*—"Just South of the Unicorns." It's the story of Andy, the boy who, in 1987, ran away from his home in New York to Florida, where he showed up on the doorstep of Piers Anthony, bestselling fantasy author and Andy's hero. Really, Andy, this book is for you and all the kids who, in dark times, find a light shining from the pages of books.

Thank you all so much.

P.S. Kids, don't run away from home, please.

The Wishing Game

A NOVEL

MEG SHAFFER

A Book Club Guide

Discussion Questions

1. *The Wishing Game* revolves around the Clock Island books that so many children loved when they were growing up. Did reading this book remind you of when you fell in love with reading? What was your favorite book (or book series!) as a child?

2. The themes of "family" and "parenthood" are woven throughout the novel. Discuss each character's experiences with family and how this impacts their decisions and motivations.

3. Lucy, Hugo, Christopher, and Jack all struggle with deeply rooted fears. How does each character face and overcome these?

4. Why do you think Jack Masterson re-created Clock Island in the real world? Why do you think it wasn't finished before the game?

5. The author sometimes pairs scenes from the Clock Island books with chapters of *The Wishing Game*. Discuss how these two stories connect and why the author decided to use this stylistic choice to help tell her story.

6. So much of the novel deals with family, especially the idea of "found family." What do you think of the idea of "found families?" What do you think defines what "family" really is? Who is in your family of choice?

7. Were you surprised by the outcome of the contest?

8. What do you make of Hugo's comment to Jack that he "can't save the world"? How does Jack try to save everyone around him?

9. If you could travel to any fictional world, what would it be?

10. Who would you cast as each character in a movie adaptation of *The Wishing Game*?

Keep reading for a sneak peek
at Meg Shaffer's
The Lost Story

The Lost Story
MEG SHAFFER
AUTHOR OF *THE WISHING GAME*
A Novel

A young woman's search for her birth mother
leads her on an unforgettable adventure of self-discovery
in this enchanted novel about the magic of found family
from the author of *The Wishing Game*.

CHAPTER ONE

Fifteen Years Ago

ONCE UPON A TIME in West Virginia, two boys went missing in the Red Crow Wilderness Area, a few miles outside of Morgantown. Maggie knew about the boys, of course. It was all over the national news that spring, the local news that summer, but by autumn, it was only coffee gossip. Did anyone find those boys yet? Any news about those kids? Those poor kids. Their poor mamas. Tragic, but it had happened before, kids getting lost in the woods. It would happen again.

Nobody had found them. Nobody had any new news. By November of that year, Maggie had mostly forgotten about the West Virginia Lost Boys, as the media liked to call them, because what else would they call two boys lost in West Virginia? She didn't even think about them when Tom asked if she wanted to go hiking with him up at the Crow, as the locals called it.

It was a Monday, and they both had the day off, which is why she wasn't surprised to find the parking lot almost empty.

At the entrance to the main trail stood a wooden bulletin board, the kind all parks have. Weathered sheets of copy paper listed the rules and cautions and fire-safety warnings. Next to the signs no one ever read hung a fading poster that said in large letters, MISSING CHILDREN.

While Tom tightened his bootlaces, Maggie studied the pictures on the poster.

Ralph Stanley Howell, d.o.b. 5/5/92, 5'4, 118 lbs. Caucasian. Blond hair. Blue eyes.

He looked awkward in the picture, a boy too embarrassed to smile but would probably be a heartbreaker if he did.

Jeremy Andrew Cox, d.o.b. 3/13/92, age fifteen. 5'6, 125 lbs. Caucasian. Red hair. Brown eyes.

Jeremy had freckles and a shit-eating grin. Class clown, no doubt. Cute kid but nothing special. Not yet, but he'd be handsome when he grew up and out of the freckles. If he grew up.

Tom peered over her shoulder.

"Damn," Tom said. "Six months. Poor kids. Hope they turn up."

He hoped they'd turn up? Well, it was a sweet thing to say, if a little naive. Maggie was a nurse, and because she'd seen the worst, she knew to assume the worst. If the boys were missing in The Red, they had probably died the first or second night. If they weren't missing but kidnapped . . . they probably wished they were dead.

But that's not the sort of thing you say on a date. Instead, Maggie turned to Tom, smiled, and said, "Ready to go?"

"After you," he said, and when she stared off into the woods, he pinched her on the ass, which she didn't mind. Her yelp sent a bird flying.

The main trail took them to a scenic overlook, a fenced-in slab of limestone that offered a view of the entire park. Below them lay the woods like autumn-colored ocean waves. Trees forever and ever and ever and ever and ever.

"How do you find two kids lost out here?" Tom asked. He waved his hand toward the . . . the everything. The forest. The hills. The coyotes and the rattlesnakes and the cliffs and the rocks and the fast-moving stream.

Maggie said, "You don't." But to soften the blow, she added, "Probably."

The one story she remembered from that May when the boys were first reported missing was how the famous Marshall University football team from Huntington had taken their green buses all the way across the state to help their rivals at WVU with the search. They hadn't found the boys, though. Not even the Mountaineers, the Thundering Herd, or the prayers of an entire state could bring Ralph Howell and Jeremy Cox home. Still, it was a nice story. People turned their noses up at West Virginia, but Maggie didn't mind. They took care of their own here, at least. You couldn't say that for places like New York City or L.A. There you'd see someone passed out on the sidewalk and just keep going. Not here.

Before leaving the scenic overlook, Tom took a few pictures with his digital camera. It was the last day he would have that camera, though he didn't know that at the time, that the police would take it from him and he'd never get it back.

Two hours and a bucket of sweat later, they reached their destination— a small ravine where a waterfall tumbled over black rocks deep in the woods where the air always smelled like moss and cold morning rain. It was called Goblin Falls because two of the rock formations looked like little men with strangely twisted faces. Maggie squatted next to one of the goblins and made the best worst face she could while Tom took her picture.

"Nice," he said, laughing.

"Was I hideous enough?" she asked as she stood up. Tom held out his hand to help her across the gap between the goblin and the bank. The rocks were damp and slippery, and the air by the falls was shockingly cold.

"Disgusting." As he pulled her across, rocks at the top of the ravine skittered over the edge, hitting the water behind her with a terrifying slap. She nearly fell as she gasped and grabbed at Tom.

"Damn," he said, holding her tightly as he looked up and around. "Rockslide." He met her eyes. "You all right?"

"Fine. Just took a year off my life." She laughed at herself. "Can I see the pictures?"

He gave her the camera, and she clicked through the photos. The first was a close-up of her and the rock goblin. The second was a wider shot of the falls. And the third was . . .

Maggie's breath caught. She looked up to the cliff edge.

"What?" Tom asked.

She raised her hand and shook her head. Then she showed him the picture on the camera's display screen.

The falls. The water. The rocks. Her. And something else.

A dark shadow in the shape of a man.

Tom looked up and around at once, scanning for danger.

"It's probably nothing," she said. The Goblin Falls were off-trail, but people knew about it, hiked here all the time. Still . . . her heart raced.

"We know where we are, right?" Maggie asked.

"Sort of."

"Tom, we aren't lost, are we?"

"Nah. You're not lost until you can't find your way back."

"Comforting." She wasn't comforted.

"It's fine. Let's just head back," Tom said. She nodded and grabbed her backpack, eager to return to the trail. Then Maggie saw them and froze.

"What's wrong?" Tom asked from behind her.

About fifty feet ahead of them on the game trail they'd followed to the falls stood two boys who looked very lost.

Tom said, "Oh my God," then nothing else.

One boy stood upright, mostly. The other boy was slung over his shoulders in a fireman's carry.

Rooted in place, Maggie and Tom watched, fascinated, as if they'd spotted a rare white deer or a mountain lion.

The standing boy struggled under the weight of the other boy. Sweat-damp red hair hung across his face. The boy on his shoulder had blond hair that hung loose and long. Six months without a haircut long.

Under her breath, Maggie said, "It's them."

"Them?"

"Them," she said again. "The lost boys."

Tom started forward, but Maggie grabbed his arm to stop him. Why? She didn't know. Instinct. Fear. The uncanny feeling that they'd crossed the boundary into a story that they didn't belong in.

The one with the red hair appeared calm, if exhausted. His expression was serious, almost somber. A soldier's eyes in a boy's face. Carefully he made his way down the narrow game trail, walking past them as if they weren't there, carrying the other boy to the bank of the falls. He went down on one knee and gently laid the other boy onto the soft earth in a lone patch of sunlight.

When Tom opened his mouth, Maggie shook her head. The boy with red hair had an animal's quiet readiness about him. One wrong word and he might bolt like a deer, take flight like an eagle, vanish like a ghost.

The eyes of the other boy were open, but he was clearly confused, out of his head. He breathed heavily, mumbled and blinked, trying to see through eyes that couldn't focus. A sheen of sweat covered his body, and his blond hair was damp. Fever? Infection?

Tom ignored her and rushed to them, knelt down, and reached out toward the boy on the ground.

It happened so fast Maggie literally jumped. Lightning fast. Cobra striking fast. The red-haired boy struck out with his arm and caught Tom by the wrist.

Tom froze. Maggie gasped. Her heart hammered in her chest so hard she thought she might faint. She ran to Tom's side.

Maggie said, "Jeremy." She said it sharply, trying to break the spell.

Because it was Jeremy, of course. Jeremy Cox, whose name or face she would never forget again. She would forget nothing about this day, the day her life divided neatly in half, into the Before and the After. Everything in the After would sit in the shadows of this singular moment in her life when the universe allowed her to brush her fingertips along the spider-lace edges of a true-blue fairy tale.

Boys disappearing into the woods, then reappearing after everyone thought they were dead . . . because if that's not a fairy-tale ending, what is?

Jeremy looked at her. He'd recognized his name. And that meant the other boy on the ground, the one with the golden hair glowing like a lion's mane in the sun . . . he was Ralph Howell.

"It's all right, Jeremy," she said softly. "I'm a nurse."

He still had Tom's wrist trapped like a vise.

"You," he said to her, stern as a four-star general. "Not him."

She nodded. The boy released Tom's wrist. It was red. In a day or two, it would turn purple and black, that's how hard Jeremy had held him.

"Run for help," she told Tom. "Right now. Go!"

He didn't argue. He almost seemed relieved to run off, to get away from this moment that asked more of him than he had to give.

In her backpack, Maggie kept a small first-aid kit, a flashlight, and her stethoscope. She checked Ralph's pupils, breathing, heart rate, and temperature.

"Help me roll him," she said. They rolled Ralph onto his side so she could check his back for injuries. Damp leaves stuck to his clammy skin. She peeled them off one by one, revealing long thin scars. Deep animal scratches? A run-in with barbed wire?

She touched the scars. They were older wounds, long healed. Carefully she eased him onto his back again.

"Where did you go?" she asked Jeremy.

He looked at the boy on the ground, then at her, and his one-word answer was frightening enough that she asked him nothing more.

"Far."

Ralph winced in pain. Maggie placed her hand on his damp forehead and said, "You'll be all right, baby." She always called her youngest patients "baby."

The boy mumbled, "Mom?"

Jeremy, who had been so eerily calm until that moment, began to silently weep. Relief? Happiness? No. Grief. For what? He and Ralph had just been found. Why did he cry like something unbearably precious had been lost?

Then EMTs arrived and pushed Maggie out of the story.

Standing under a tree, she took pictures of the scene with Tom's camera. Each photograph looked about the same—Jeremy sitting and Ralph lying on the ground, a couple EMTs in uniform, a park ranger, a cop. But there is one photo she took that every newspaper in the world reprinted . . . Jeremy sitting on the ground by Goblin Falls with Ralph Howell unconscious in his arms, like La Pietà, except both figures were boys.

She watched from a distance as the EMTs did their work. Jeremy, who had stopped crying by then, wouldn't agree to get on a stretcher, so he walked out of the forest at Ralph's side. Someone had given him a blanket, but he didn't put it on. He put it over Ralph instead. Maggie and Tom followed them out of the forest silently, like the final members of a religious procession.

By the time they reached the parking lot, the cavalry had arrived. A dozen cop cars. A dozen fire trucks. Four ambulances for two boys. This wasn't just an emergency. This was a show, and everyone wanted to be part of it.

Maggie watched silently, Tom at her side, as EMTs loaded Ralph Howell into the ambulance, Jeremy climbing in behind him.

Tom said, "Does that look like a kid who's been lost in the woods for six months? He almost snapped my wrist."

He eyed Jeremy, who should have been a skeleton, but instead, he and Ralph looked muscular and healthy, not like the boys in their missing photos but young men. Maybe they figured out how to catch rabbits in snares? Or birds or fish? Later she would read that Ralph Howell had been an Eagle Scout, and both boys knew how to bow hunt. When she caught herself thinking too hard about the weight and the muscle they gained, she would tell herself there had to be a rational explanation. Boys that age have growth spurts. They can shoot up half a foot and put on fifty pounds in a few months. She'd seen it happen.

Still, the boys should have been filthy, haggard, and gaunt. But no, they looked and smelled clean and healthy. Their hair had grown longer, but it wasn't matted or stringy. Ralph had scars, yes, but otherwise neither of them seemed to have any injuries.

"Where the hell were they all this time?" Tom muttered when Maggie didn't answer his first question.

"Far," Maggie said, not because Jeremy had said it but because it was what she believed. For years to come, she would tell the story of the day she found the West Virginia Lost Boys, as the news called them. The story would begin with "Once upon a time" and end with the moment the ambulance carrying the boys drove away.

But there was one part she would leave out of the story and never tell a soul.

In her last moments alone with the boys, before the EMTs and forest rangers arrived, Maggie sat in silence and listened to Jeremy as he spoke softly to Ralph in a language she had never heard before or since. His words were like the sound of dry leaves rustling and skittering on the breeze through an autumn wood. And whatever he said, she knew that if she understood the words, she would know one of the deep secrets of the world, a secret the world needed to keep.

Then the sirens screamed in the distance like banshees. He looked startled by the sound, wide- and wild-eyed. She took his hand and held it.

"Help is coming," she told Jeremy softly. "I'll stay with you both as long as I can."

After she said that, as if she'd passed a test and won a prize, she heard wings flapping. They looked up. On a tree branch above their heads perched a red crow.

She gasped and looked at Jeremy. He raised his finger to his lips, asking her to keep the secret. She nodded.

Later she would tell herself she'd imagined it. She'd been swept up in the moment, half-crazed with adrenaline. No red crows. No magic words. A good story, yes, but not a fairy tale. They didn't have fairy tales in West Virginia. They were lucky to have a Target.

Then again, why not here? Why did England and France and Germany and all those places get to have fairy tales but not West Virginia? All around her was beauty—incredible, impossible beauty—and danger—terrible, terrible danger. And isn't that what magic was, just beauty and danger dancing together in the shadows? Why didn't they get magic here, where the hills rolled like ocean waves and the morning mist was as thick as the silence of a family keeping secrets? If fairies were in the world, they couldn't find a better place than this forest to tell their tales.

No, no, it couldn't be true, could it?

Or could it?

Maggie wanted to believe. Of course, she did.

Everyone wants to believe in fairy tales, don't they?

MEG SHAFFER is a part-time creative writing instructor and the author of *The Wishing Game*. She lives in Louisville, Kentucky, with her husband, author Andrew Shaffer, and their two cats. The cats are not writers.

megshaffer.com
Instagram: @meg_shaffer

ABOUT THE TYPE

This book was set in Jenson, one of the earliest print typefaces. After hearing of the invention of printing in 1458, Charles VII of France sent coin engraver Nicolas Jenson (c. 1420–80) to study this new art. Not long afterward, Jenson started a new career in Venice in letter-founding and printing. In 1471, Jenson was the first to present the form and proportion of this roman font that bears his name.

More than five centuries later, Robert Slimbach, developing fonts for the Adobe Originals program, created Adobe Jenson based on Nicolas Jenson's Venetian Renaissance typeface. It is a dignified font with graceful and balanced strokes.

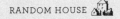